CIRC

BOOK ONE

Vitalia

ELIZA BENNER

Vitalia
Circus of Souls, Book One

ELIZA BENNER

Printed Worldwide
First Edition 2026

To everyone who is mystified by the circus,

Who want their fantasies deadly and their lovers dangerous,

This one's for you.

1

THE OFFER

Backbreaking.

The only word that even scratches the surface of what it feels like to work the mines.

Sort through the rock. Lift the shadowstone. Place it in the bucket. Repeat. When the bucket is full, haul it to the cart, which, mercifully, will be hauled away by a team of horses, and start all over again.

Shadowstone is dense, stubborn, and heavy as sin—how fortunate for those of us lucky enough to be here. The stones are small, though each handful can weigh as much as ten bricks, depending on the density of the pieces.

I hate it for its weight, but its beauty is unmatched. No diamond sparkles as brilliantly as shadowstone. No pitch is as dark. Yet, in the center of each piece, when caught at just the right angle, it's as if there's an internal, luminescent glow trapped inside.

I've always wanted to keep one. Just one tiny stone to have for myself. Something that could be my own personal "fuck you" to the powers that be. But after what happened to Alabris, I can't. I don't dare. Amputation of every finger for taking a stone the size of a pea? I want one, but not that badly. If I don't have fingers, then I can't work the mines. And if I can't work the mines, then I can't work. Living in the southern quarter means you're a miner. The lowest of the low, and the poorest of the poor. There's no way out without significant risk, and risk is something I can't afford. Not when I have Quinnic and Alabris to support.

"Quit dawdling!" a nearby guard shouts into my ear. I had been so lost in thought that I hadn't even heard him approach. One warning for moving slowly is a yell, though. Just a yell. Nothing physical. Not like the second offense in a week. And the third? I scarcely let myself think about the third. Down into the mines themselves, where death is a regular occurrence, and the only thing between you and a cave-in is luck. Down there, nearly every worker is a hardened man twice my age. Far fewer guards to make sure the work gets done, but also far fewer guards to make sure women are safe amongst all those hardened men. Yes, I should be grateful for my sorting position just outside the entrance to the mines.

I begin picking through the piles of rock again, motivated to move even faster than usual, loading stone after stone into the bucket. When it finally reaches its fill, I hoist it up onto the leather strap that protects my shoulder from the steel handle digging in, and begin walking.

When I started, I was unable to carry the bucket across the mine site without stopping to rest several times. Now I can do it without breaking a sweat, which at least earns me a sliver of respect from the other workers.

Though that doesn't mean that I don't hear the occasional crude remark when I bend to lift the bucket or dump the stones into the cart.

As I'm walking back to the pile, a bell rings out. Shift end, thank gods. I hadn't even noticed the sun nearing the horizon or the biting chill that had begun to permeate the air.

I join the line to receive rations and payment for the day—bread, rice, carrots, celery, and a glass bottle of milk. Not really enough to feed three people, but it would have to be. Soup with bread could make a nice dinner.

Along with the food, I receive a small payment for any other necessities. Or alcohol, which is arguably a necessity here.

I thank the man and turn away to head back through town to the house that Quinnic, Alabris, and I share. The familiar ache in my shoulders from the day's work is already setting in as I adjust the strap of my rations bag, trying to figure out how to stretch tonight's soup into tomorrow's breakfast, too.

That's when I see him—Blaine.

The son of the mine owner. He comes around every so often and is the only man here I've ever paid a lick of attention to. He's wealthy, but more importantly, he acknowledges me as a person. A 'hello' here and there, a brief glance that lingers just a touch too long, rather than the usual grunted invitation into some man's bed that I receive from others.

He's approaching. Oh Gods, what do I do? Do I turn to him and greet him first? No. Head down. Wait for him to say something to me if he deigns to do so.

"Naevyn," Blaine calls sooner than I expect. I pivot on one foot, hoping that my quick turn doesn't betray my excitement.

He's closer than I realized, which makes my heart drum faster. The green flecks in his eyes seem especially bright today, and I don't miss the smile playing on his lips. His golden locks are groomed to the side, looking orderly, as though he's here on some sort of business. He wears a shirt that's tight over his abdomen, but flowy in the arms. It's practical, considering the daytime heat of this place. He's taller than me, though that isn't an unusual occurrence, as I'm not as vertically blessed as some.

"Hi," I say dumbly, all too aware of the stench of sweat radiating from my clothes. I'm hopeful that he can't pick out my scent specifically with all of the other sweaty workers in the vicinity.

"You look well today," he starts. I want to interject and ask if he has eyes, because I'm absolutely positive that I'm covered with dust from head to toe, but I decide against it. "I have something for you."

"Oh?" I ask, eyeing him suspiciously. In all my days, not once has someone of an upper rank, someone like Blaine, given me anything.

"It's a good thing. Tickets to the king's Circus." He produces a yellow and red striped ticket from his pocket, dangling it in front of my face. "It's tomorrow night."

The king's Circus. An entertainment I'd only ever dreamed of going to. It only came around once per cycle and cropped up in places that seemed completely random. Often near the king's court, but it traveled to further territories sometimes, as well. Just… not here. Never here.

Surely, this is some sort of joke. Blaine couldn't possibly mean to invite someone like me.

"You're teasing," I accuse.

An easy smile spreads across his face, and he shifts his weight to his other foot.

"Not at all. I'd be honored to have your company. It'll be just inside the northern gate." He takes my hand and holds it open, using his other hand to drop the ticket into my palm.

And gods… my body is overreacting.

A single touch and suddenly my pulse is bouncing at an uneven pace, ricocheting around my ribs. His skin is warm, steady, unfairly gentle, and it sends this stupid little spark sliding up my arm. I have to pretend I didn't feel anything, even though my whole body is announcing otherwise.

I open my mouth to speak or protest or something, but before I can, a man calls to Blaine from across the mine. He gives me a quick nod before striding off, the sound of his heavy boots fading away as he goes.

Me. Invited to the circus with *him.* An evening out with a man. The first since, well, a very long time. Since before our parents passed. Back then, I actually had time for things like flirting and dates, when Dad's position as a high-ranking miner meant we lived off his provisions instead of scraping by on daily rations. He made more than enough to support us.

But his rat of a daughter? No. Not me. Six years since the plague took them both, and I'd foolishly thought Dad's reputation would count for something when I asked for a more advanced position. But apparently, being the daughter of a respected miner means jack shit when that miner is dead. I still remember the sticky saliva on my cheek as the guard spat on my face and threatened to send me down into the mines if I so much as breathed wrong again. I'd wanted to punch him square in the nose, but with Quinnic being only nine at the time and unable to support himself if something happened to me, I decided against it.

Gods, so much has changed, yet nothing at all. We still live in the same sandy hovel, still barely survive off of the crumbs that are rationed to us. But taking a chance on Blaine could be our way out. It may not be a very good plan, but I have to try. I saw the life my father was able to give my mother despite her unfortunate origins in this horrible district, and while marrying for money isn't something I'd be proud of, using my looks to improve my situation isn't something I'm above, either. Not if it means providing for Quinnic and Alabris.

With all my daydreaming, I hardly noticed how my feet carried me down the dirt road that led away from the mine and toward our house, if you could call it that. Yellow, patchy grass speckles the parched ground. The stucco of the building has cracked from baking so many years in the hot sun. Still, it provides shelter from the torrential rains that sometimes explode from the sky, and a safe haven from looters that can no longer work the mines and take to stealing from others in their same position. Yes, this house does the best that it can.

When I open the creaking front door, the first thing to hit me is the scent. Herbal tea wafts from the hearth to where I stand in the doorway.

"Naevyn!" Alabris calls from her position beside the fireplace. "Here." She crosses the small room and presses a cup of the sweet-smelling tea into my hands. She stares, eyes boring into me, urging me to take a sip. I do, and the flavor explodes on my tongue.

"Mmm." I let out a satisfied moan. "Lemongrass?" She nods. "And… where did you get honey?"

She smiles brightly, as if proud that my unrefined sense of taste could pick up on the flavor of honey.

"Quinnic found it. Harvested it from a beehive he found near the docks," she answers.

"He harvested it himself? Wait—did you say the docks?"

Alabris's smile falters a little, but she quickly pastes a forced one on in its place.

"Yes, Naevyn. He's fifteen, and it's legal for him to be there."

"It's disgusting, is what it is. He may as well be loitering around the mines for all the good it does him."

As if summoned, Quinnic swings around the wall from the hallway, hand grasping the corner, leaving dirty fingerprints on the wall.

"How many times have I told you not to touch the wall with those grimy hands?" I scold.

"Hello to you, too." He grins, showing me a full set of teeth. Quinnic looks less young these days. The baby fat of his pre-teen years has disappeared, and even his blue eyes look older now. He has the same waves in his hair as I do, though his is a brighter red, while mine is a soft auburn.

He reaches into the satchel I carry and tears off a piece of bread before I'm able to swat his hand away.

"Quinnic!" I scold for the second time.

"What? I'm hungry."

“We’re *all* hungry, but I think I speak for both of us when I say that you need to go and wash your hands in the basin out back before you put them all over our food,” I retort. I do my best to sound tough, but my voice carries no threat.

“Yeah, yeah,” he replies, heading for the door.

“And Quinnic?” I call.

He stops one step from the doorway.

“Yes?”

“Don’t go near the docks.”

He shoots me a sideways glance, but doesn’t protest as he exits the room.

“That boy is going to make my hair turn gray at the ripe age of twenty-five,” I say, turning to face Alabris. She’s managed to pour herself a cup of tea, with difficulty due to her lack of fingers, and now settles into a wooden rocker in the corner.

“Don’t be so hard on him. He’s only a boy,” she says, smiling.

“Yes, one who’s only weeks away from being a man in the eyes of the kingdom. I want his first experience with men to be hard-working ones by the mines, not the deadbeat drunks around the docks.”

“You can’t control him forever,” Alabris warns. I turn to face the hearth, bending down to exchange the hanging black tea kettle for a soup pot. “What is that?” she asks abruptly, sitting up a little straighter in her chair and craning her neck to see what’s fallen onto the ground.

“Nothing,” I mutter, uselessly trying to cram the ticket back into my satchel before she can get a proper look at it. “Absolutely nothing.”

Alabris’s eyes narrow into slits as she regards me. “It didn’t look like nothing.”

I continue preparing to make the soup, not saying a word. I don’t need anyone knowing my business and what I may or may not have going on tomorrow night. I haven’t even decided if I want to go yet. Sure, this could be a once-in-a-lifetime opportunity, but I also don't know Blaine well enough to know his motives. What if it's just his way to get me alone with him? A bribe of sorts to get in my pants. Not to mention, if Quinnic caught wind of it, he'd never let me live it down. A date with the boss's son? That's just *asking* for ridicule.

Not going to happen.

I walk to the counter and grab the knife to begin chopping carrots.

"Hello, Naevyn? Are you going to answer me?" Alabris asks.

My hand stops chopping to ensure she can hear my answer. "No."

I can already see her reproachful look, even without a glance in her direction.

"It looked like a circus ticket," she mumbles.

I whirl around, only to find her taking a long sip of tea with a knowing twinkle in her eye. Why is she so obnoxiously intuitive despite being three years my junior?

"Al-uh-bree!" I reprimand, drawing out each syllable of her name.

"I'm right, aren't I?" she asks, smiling, when she finally swallows the hot liquid.

"Fine. Yes, okay? You're right. But it doesn't matter because I'm not going," I answer, spinning around and continuing the rhythmic *chop, chop, chop*.

"We'll see about that," she mutters. My teeth grate together to keep from saying something I'll regret as I slam the knife back down on the counter and scoop up the carrots to deliver them to the pot.

"What the hell is that supposed to mean?" I ask finally.

Her voice softens when she speaks next. "It means we'll see. It means you work yourself to the bone for Quinnic and me day-in and day-out, never doing anything for yourself. Then you finally get the chance to do something fun, and you say no. I just think you should reconsider."

I stare at her, deliberating. "All I have are my mining clothes and a pair of tattered trousers. I can't show up to the king's circus with Blaine wearing—"

"Blaine?" she practically shouts. "The owner's son? Oh, you are *definitely* going!"

Alabris rises from the chair and crosses the room before I can blink. She drops down onto her knees in front of the storage trunk and lifts the lid, rifling through her garments. I feel a pang of annoyance that she's completely ignoring my wishes. Still, can I really be mad at her? She's right, after all. When was the last time I did something fun for myself? Before Mom and Dad died?

Alabris lifts a simple gown from the trunk. It's navy blue and long-sleeved with a ruched bodice and straight skirt. Simple and practical.

"I'll sweat like a pig if I wear something that covers my arms," I protest.

"The show's at night, right? After the sun goes down? You'll be *cold* if you don't cover up. Besides, the dress is cotton, not wool."

I pull a face at her but take the garment from her hands nonetheless.

I guess there's no harm in trying it on.

2

BLASPHEMY

The dress fit perfectly. Of course it had. I *did* have to inform Alabris that just because the dress fit me didn't mean I'd accept Blaine's invitation, but the smug look on her face told me all that I needed to know—she believed that I should go, and the dress fitting me well was a sign of that.

The soup in the hearth bubbles as it reheats. It served us well for dinner last night, and I hope that the remainder will be enough to satiate us all this morning. My serving last night was intentionally small to stretch the provisions out as long as I can, and judging by how little remained in the pot this morning, I'd be doing that again.

I kneel down, squinting at the broth in the pot. Had Quinnic snuck out and helped himself to another serving? He did have a bad habit of doing that after the rest of us went to bed.

"Have you seen Quinnic?" Alabris asks as she emerges from the back bedroom.

"Not yet today, no. Have you looked outside?" I ask her.

"I did. I checked the whole area, and even the tavern, but he's nowhere to be found."

Panic surges through my veins as I clamber back up to my feet, forgetting all about the soup and the mathematics of portioning what was left.

The sun outside is cresting just above the horizon now.

"Shit. I have to leave for the mines soon, but I can't go without knowing he's alright. Do you know if he came home last night?" I ask, searching her face.

"I never saw him," comes the reply.

I try to recount the events of the previous night. Quinnic left to wash his hands. He came back a while later and ate dinner, then announced that he was going out to meet up with his friend Thadic. Then… I went to bed. I had assumed he'd come back on his own.

"Watch the soup. I'll be back."

My mind races as I grab a cloak from the back of a chair and push through the front door into the still-frigid morning. A handful of men—mostly miners, based on their clothing—meander down the street. I pull my hood up and walk the other way to avoid notice.

Where would Quinnic go? Surely not back to the docks after I just berated him for doing so. But even as the thought crossed my mind, I knew that was exactly where he'd gone.

I imagined the kind of downtrodden people he could encounter there. Even if he had chosen to go back to the docks, he would have come home. Unless…

No. I couldn't think like that. He was fine.

Still, I found myself walking so quickly that I nearly broke into a run, but I didn't want to attract the attention of the wrong people here. My eyes dart across the road, searching for any sign of him, just in case he'd suddenly come to his senses and decided to drag himself home.

No sign of him.

But what I *do* see is Thadic.

I hurry over to him, catching him by the sleeve. "Where's Quinnic?"

"What?" His brows scrunch together, mouth hanging open like he's trying to catch flies. He's a good friend to Quinnic, but not the brightest. His face is round, and his rosy cheeks in the morning cold make him look even younger.

"He was with you last night," I say, my eyes searching his, looking from one to the other as if they alone can tell me Quinnic's whereabouts.

He starts to shake his head slowly, his black brows furrowed in confusion.

"No, he wasn't. I was at home last night with my family." He sidesteps, looking past me like he wants to get away. Do I look even more crazed with worry than I feel?

"Right, of course. Thank you," I say, though I feel anything but thankful. I feel frantic.

I carry on at a quick clip, headed directly for the docks. The smell of the salty water hits me even before it comes into view. A chilly breeze charges through the air, causing a shiver to run down my spine, and goosebumps begin forming on my arms, even under the cloak.

If he isn't here, I don't know where he'll be. It isn't like Quinnic to not come home. He has no girlfriend to speak of and, aside from Thadic, no close friends he might be with either. He *has* to be here.

I slow as I approach. A man sitting on a crate with a half-drunk bottle in his hand guards the end of the dock. Tall ships are being loaded just beyond him, and I strain to see if Quinnic might be on one of them.

"What brings ya' out here, little lady?" the man slurs, cracking a crooked smile in my direction that shows off his rotted, yellow teeth.

Don't show fear. Never show fear.

If there's one thing my mother taught me before she passed, it was that. If you show fear around men like this, they'll know that you're an easy target.

"I'm looking for my brother. He's fifteen, a little taller than me, with red hair and freckles. Have you seen him?" I ask, forcing a cold, hard edge into my voice.

The man eyes me up and down like a butcher surveying a cut of meat. He's heavyset, clearly not living on the same rations that I am. Hell, he probably steals from the same ships that he's paid to load.

"Aye, there was a boy 'round here matching that description." He takes a messy swig from the bottle and then wipes his mouth with the back of his sleeve. "Though, if you're looking for a good time, a man like myself is more likely to provide that for 'ya."

"Ew, he's my *brother*," I say, recoiling. "And I'm not looking for a 'good time', I just need to find him."

I push past the man blocking my path and duck as he reaches out to catch me with his free hand. My size comes in handy, though, because I'm easily able to slip under his outstretched arm and scurry away. I approach the ship, past its hull and over to where a makeshift ramp carries men from the dock to the boat, loading supplies.

A man wearing a flat, brown cap with a black bill stalks back and forth on the dock, eyeing the sailors as they do all of the heavy lifting.

The captain. It has to be.

If anyone has seen Quinnic, it would be him.

"Excuse me! Hey!" I call, a little winded from outrunning the overweight, drunken man on my heels.

The captain turns his attention to me, deep lines etched in his cheeks and wisps of wiry, gray hair escaping from the edges of his hat. He wears a blue jacket and brown pants that actually look like they've been laundered in the past month, unlike the rest of the sailors, who I wouldn't be surprised to learn haven't showered in over a decade.

A very out-of-breath voice slurs from behind me. "I'm… sorry, sir… I tried… to stop her."

The captain holds up a hand and tells him it's all right, dismissing the man back to his post. The drunkard snarls at me before turning around and hobbling back to the end of the dock.

I am *not* looking forward to passing him again.

"What do ya' need, girl?" the captain asks, keeping a careful step of space between us, his hands visible and nowhere near me. A blessed change from his drunken friend, whose eyes had practically crawled over my skin.

"It's my brother. He's been hanging around here, but now he's missing. Red hair, kind of obnoxious," I start, planning to continue with the description, but the knowing look in the captain's eye tells me that he knows Quinnic. Or, at least, knows *of* him.

"Aye, I've seen him. Boy was drunk as a sailor, muttering about immortal beings." The captain pulls off his hat, scratching at the back of his neck, then places it back atop his head. "Said something about the shadowstone, too. Kid was furious about the rations—kept saying how we're starving while shipping away the most valuable thing we produce. Seemed convinced there's some ancient creatures we're taking care of with our resources, and that the king's in on it."

Ancient… creatures? Of course Quinnic would be prone to getting caught up in fantasies like this. He's always wanted to believe that this isn't all there is for us.

"I just laughed it off and tried to recruit him for a trading voyage, said it might straighten out his thinking, but he wouldn't have a word of it. Stumbled back off the dock after that." The captain shakes his head, laughing to himself.

"Immortal beings?" I ask, still a little stunned.

"Aye," the captain says, stroking his gray beard with his left hand. Then his voice lowers. "There's talk of it, you know. Questions about how certain things came to be. Like how the guards and their families never seem to suffer the same hardships as the rest of us. Their children stay healthy even during the lean years, and their crops never fail. Almost like they're protected by something."

I consider his insinuation that legends of immortal beings have credibility to them. But then why are we on rations? Why are the guards so evil and unrelenting? If magical beings were real, wouldn't resources and food be plentiful?

It hits me suddenly—the sun's almost perfectly lined up with the ship's tallest mast from where I'm standing.

Shit. I don't even know how much time has passed, but the later I am to the mines, the more trouble I'll be in, and I haven't even found Quinnic yet.

This is a distraction. None of it matters.

"I have to go," I grunt, spinning on my heel and jogging back in the direction of the city. I keep as far to the edge of the dock as I can to stay out of reach of the heavyset man. His eyes are fixed on me as I cross, and I think I hear him mutter a crude remark under his breath, but there's no time to lay him flat right now. Now, I need to head further into the village.

I take the back paths, weaving through the tight alleyways to keep a low profile. The narrow passages between buildings are barely wide enough for two people to pass, red dust swirling up with each step and coating everything in a fine layer of grit. Sparse, gnarled trees struggle to grow between the cramped terra-cotta structures, their branches reaching desperately toward whatever sunlight manages to filter down between the rooflines. I make a left turn, and my breath hitches in my throat.

Red hair, medium build, and the same shirt that he had been wearing last night.

"Quinnic!" The sound of my voice bounces off the weathered stucco walls surrounding us.

I run to the side of his lifeless form. Rolling him onto his back, his head still hanging away from me, a sigh of relief escapes me as I notice the gentle rise and fall of Quinnic's chest.

"Wake up." I shake his arm, noting that every inch of clothing he's wearing is damp. "Wake *up*!"

His eyes roll around behind his eyelids for a moment before they begin to flutter open. He squints, blinking rapidly as if the early morning sun is a danger to his precious sight. The worry drains out of me in an instant, leaving a hollow space that is immediately filled with rage.

"What the *hell* did you think you were doing? You could have been seriously injured, or even killed! Do you even care that Alabris and I were sick with worry? Or that instead of going to the mines this morning, I had to go traipsing all over town looking for you?" Once I begin hurling accusations and insults, it's like the floodgates have opened and the words are rushing forth without an end in sight. "Now, when I go back to the mines, will they maim me like Alabris so *you'll* be the one forced to provide for us both? Maybe that would teach you a lesson about going off on your own, getting shit-faced, and spewing nonsense to anyone who'll listen!"

He turns his head fully toward me so I can finally see his entire face.

I recoil as I note his blooming black eye.

"Did you get that all out of your system, now, Nae?" Quinnic asks. Normally, a quip like that would make me angrier, but whatever he'd been through last night was probably significantly more intense than any berating I could do.

"What happened to you?" I ask.

"Rum," he replies with a smirk.

"Damn it, Quinnic, I'm talking about your eye," I say, my patience dissipating like water on hot stone.

"I know. Rum happened to it." His voice is raspy with sleep and a hangover. "Someone threw a bottle at me, and it clocked me right in the eye."

"Who?" I demand.

"I dunno. A sailor? Said I was 'encouraging blasphemy against the king', whatever that means." Quinnic presses his palm to his temple. "After that, it was all a blur."

"It serves you right," I tell him. "You're lucky there wasn't a guard around, or you'd be decorating the town square right now." I lower my voice. "People who speak out against the king don't just get *fines*, Quinnic."

"I *know*, Naevyn." I can tell he's mad because he isn't one to use my full name. Not ever. "I'm not a child."

Now it's my turn to blink rapidly. He's right, of course, but that doesn't mean I want to think about it.

"Right," I acknowledge quietly. "Care to explain why you're all wet?"

I stand, then grasp his hand and pull him up to his feet. Quinnic shuts his eyes before he speaks, like he's afraid of my reaction. "They threw me in the harbor."

I furrow my brows, looking him up and down for any other signs of injury, but there are none.

"The captain pulled me out and sent me off in this direction. I must've passed out at some point." Quinnic pauses, then looks at me with those bleary, hungover eyes. "But Nae, some of the things I heard last night… I think there might be truth to what I've said before about the immortal beings and… magic."

My jaw clenches. "Quinnic, no. We are not doing this right now."

"But listen," he says, looking like he's struggling to stay upright, "like Mom and Dad used to talk about—"

"Stop." My voice comes out sharper than I intend, and he flinches. I take a breath, reminding myself that he's hurt and hungover and probably still drunk. "Look, I get that you want there to be some grand explanation for why our lives are shit, but magic isn't real, Quinnic. There are no immortal beings pulling strings behind the scenes. There's just us, trying to survive in a world that doesn't give a damn about us."

His face falls, and I immediately feel guilty for crushing whatever hope he was clinging to.

"I know it sounds crazy," he says quietly, "but what if—"

"What if you focus on getting through today without getting yourself killed?" I interrupt, but my tone is gentler now. "What if we worry about real problems, like how you're going to explain that black eye to Alabris, or how I'm going to keep my job after missing half a day of work?"

Quinnic nods, but I can see he's not convinced. Just humoring his sister, who doesn't believe in anything beyond what she can touch and carry and sell.

The second he's done nodding, a guttural sound comes from Quinnic, and he staggers past me, leaning forward and emptying the contents of his stomach onto the red dirt. The smell is noxious, but I force myself to stay near him. I take off my cloak and wrap the fabric around his shoulders, pulling the hood up to obscure his face. It isn't that it's cold anymore—the sun is up, and sweltering heat has overtaken the town in full force—but rather, I don't have a clue who he got into a spat with last night, and if they're satisfied or still out for blood.

Leading him through the village, we make our way back home. As we move away from what passes for our commercial district—a handful of shops, inns, and a tavern at the center of the village—the buildings get progressively smaller and more run-down. The terra-cotta structures seem to shrink with each block, the alleyways becoming even tighter as we head toward the low-ranking residential area. Here, the red dirt isn't even packed down properly, just loose sand that gets into everything. The few trees that managed to take root look as tired as the people who live beneath them.

Thousands of questions swirl around in my mind as we walk, threatening to push their way out. That isn't what he needs, though. I know the sickly feeling of a hangover, and continuing this interrogation probably isn't the best idea.

The streets aren't too busy now. The main thoroughfares are just wide dirt paths, really, lined with those same cramped stucco buildings. Their open windows stare out like hollow eyes, some covered with faded cloth scraps for privacy. The red dust has settled into every crack and crevice, giving the whole place a rusty, worn-down look.

I open the door to our house, and immediately, Alabris is all over us.

"Gods, what happened to you? Here, sit, I'll get you a cup of tea." She hardly lets Quinnic find a seat before she shoves a steaming cup of tea into his hands. "Drink."

He complies.

"I'm fine," Quinnic insists, giving me a pleading look that says he really doesn't want to explain it all again right now.

Alabris watches our exchange. She's taken on a sort of motherly role for him since I'm gone so often at the mines. Normally, I let her handle him in whatever way she sees fit, but today, I pull her aside and ask her to let him rest.

Alabris purses her lips.

"Please?" I push.

She eyes me considerably. "Fine. But once he's better, I'm going to question him until the cows come home."

A smile crosses my face, but it doesn't touch my eyes. All of the possible scenarios waiting for me at the mines invade my thoughts, and none of them are pretty. Rule number one of the mines is that you don't miss work under any circumstances.

Alabris seems to sense what I'm thinking about.

"Everything is going to be okay." She gives my shoulder a reassuring squeeze. "And I'll talk with him later today. This won't happen again."

I want to believe her, I do, but something about all of this feels like it's just the beginning with him rather than the end.

Changing as quickly as I can into the mining clothes, I make my way down the paths, bracing myself for what's ahead.

When I come within range of the guards of the mine, one of them—a particularly burly man with a red face and red ears—catches sight of me and stomps over.

"You!" he barks into my ear, grabbing me by the collar and yanking me back and forth. "You're late."

I cast my eyes down at the ground and grit my teeth. He could shake me around, or beat me, whatever he needed to do, but he wouldn't see me flinch.

"Look at me when I'm talking to you!" His voice carries across the mine site, and I can feel the other workers' eyes on us. Some look away quickly, but I catch glimpses of sympathy in their faces. They know what's coming.

"I'm sorry," I manage, keeping my voice steady and bringing my gaze up just in time to see his bright face get redder. "My brother—"

"I don't want to hear your excuses!" His hand connects with my cheek just as he lets go of my collar, sending me stumbling backward onto the dirt. The taste of copper fills my mouth as I bite down hard to keep from crying out.

I don't fight back, but my eyes burn with defiance.

Around us, the other workers have stopped their sorting, watching with that horrible mixture of pity and relief that it's not them. A few shake their heads, their faces grim. Others look uncomfortable, but don't intervene—they can't afford to.

"Maybe a few days in the underground will teach you about punctuality," the guard snarls, raising his hand again.

"That's enough."

The voice cuts through the tension like a blade. I look up to see Blaine striding toward us, his jaw set in a hard line.

"Sir?" The guard's demeanor changes instantly, his hand dropping to his side.

"I said that's enough. She's needed in the sorting bay today." Blaine's tone leaves no room for argument. "Find someone else to make an example of."

The guard nods quickly, stepping back. "Of course, sir. As you wish."

But as Blaine helps me to my feet, I catch the shift in the other workers' expressions. The sympathy is gone, replaced by something colder. Resentment that I'm getting special treatment because the owner's son took pity on me.

Great. Now I'm not just the girl who was late and made them pick up the slack. I'm the girl who needs rescuing by the boss's son.

"You alright?" Blaine asks quietly, his hand still on my arm.

I pull away, brushing the red dust off my clothes, hating how his intervention makes me look weak in front of everyone. "I'm fine."

I glare at him, but there's no heat in it. Only humiliation.

"See you tonight?" Blaine asks, making lighter conversation. I wish he would stop talking. There's no reason for any of these people to know that I'm going anywhere at all with Blaine tonight. I feel their eyes on me, watching to see what I'll say.

I say nothing, only offering him the smallest of nods in response. He seems satisfied with that and turns away to do… whatever it is that Blaine does.

Slowly, I walk past the other workers and their scowls until I get to my usual station.

Sort through the rock. Lift the shadowstone. Place it in the bucket. Repeat.

3

STAY DOWN

The crystal lanterns dim as the show begins.

I'm watching the king's Circus alone, which is both humiliating and infuriating.

Unicyclists are spinning across the floor, clowns are squirting each other with water from flowers pinned to their vests, and somewhere in this crowd of hundreds, Blaine is blissfully unaware that he's a complete dickhead.

What an absolute fucking waste of my time.

The ringmaster's voice booms through the tent, welcoming us to "The king's Circus, where wonder and magic ignite," whatever that's supposed to mean. He stands on a circular center platform, seeming to direct all of the performers. Above me, a trapeze artist launches herself through the air with heart-stopping confidence. She swings back and forth until a man appears from the other side, dangling on a bar from the undersides of his knees. The woman lets go of her handhold, trusting the man completely. I notice that there's no net beneath to catch them if they fall. The move must be perfectly timed, even down to the millisecond, to prevent anyone from careening to their death.

The man's arms stretch out toward her, and he catches her with ease before throwing her across to the next bar. The trust involved is… unfathomable.

Especially after Blaine's betrayal. Like a fool, I'd assumed this was his way of asking me out. Even Alabris thought so.

When I arrived tonight, the place was already packed. Despite that, I spotted him immediately up in the seats. Unfortunately, he was wedged between some other men of stature like this was just another evening out with the boys. No seat saved for me.

And from the way they keep glancing in my direction and snickering, it's becoming painfully clear that this whole thing is some kind of joke between them.

So here I sit, stranded three rows back from them, seething at my own stupidity. When he saw me, he called out, "Glad you could make it!" with a grin that suddenly looked a lot less charming and a lot more smug. The bastard probably made some bet about whether the poor mining girl would actually show up. I should have left right then and there. Spun around and pushed my way through the door, though a dramatic exit through circus tent flaps might've been difficult to pull off. Instead, I figured that I traveled nearly an hour on foot to get here, so I may as well try to enjoy the show—even if I'm apparently the entertainment for a bunch of rich assholes.

The trapeze artist executes a perfect catch, and the audience erupts into applause. I clap along, but I'm mostly focused on how thoroughly I've been played. Twenty-five years old and apparently still falling for mixed signals from mediocre men.

Around me, couples lean into each other while families point excitedly at the performers. Everyone has someone. Everyone except me, apparently.

I force myself to sink back into my seat, determined to salvage something from this disaster of an evening. The worn velvet cushion beneath me smells faintly of sweat, but I settle in anyway. The least I can do is try to enjoy the show I'm apparently paying emotional dues for.

More performers flood the ring in cascading waves—acrobats in costumes that shimmer and shift a kaleidoscope of colors under the crystal lights, a fire breather exhaling plumes of flame in impossible shades of ruby, and a woman walking a tightrope forty feet above us like gravity is merely a suggestion she's chosen to ignore.

The crowd around me gasps and cheers at each death-defying stunt. A pair of contortionists twist their bodies into impossible shapes while maintaining serene smiles, and I find myself actually getting caught up in the spectacle despite my sour mood. Maybe this won't be a complete waste of an evening after all.

Then a man walks into the center ring with the kind of presence that commands attention, and even from here, I can tell he's absolutely stunning. Dark hair pulled back into a low bun, a sharp jawline, and broad shoulders that fill out his simple black shirt in all the right ways. He moves with the kind of confident stride that suggests he knows exactly how good he looks and has never doubted it for a second.

I lean forward slightly, almost instinctively, my irritation with Blaine temporarily forgotten. Now *this* is more like it.

At first, I assume he's just another performer preparing for some elaborate routine, but then something impossible begins to happen. His face starts to shift. I blink, thinking it's a trick of the light. But then his perfectly sculpted features begin to elongate, his skin taking on an otherworldly luminescence, becoming something decidedly not human. Iridescent scales appear along his neck, spreading downward in mesmerizing patterns that catch the light like liquid starfire.

All of the air leaves my lungs. What the hell is happening?

The entire audience falls silent, the air thick with tension and disbelief, but the other performers don't even flinch. The acrobats continue their routine, the fire breathers continue blowing plumes of light, the ringmaster continues directing, and the woman on the tightrope doesn't so much as glance down. It's as if watching a devastatingly handsome man transform into something mythical is just another night at work.

It has to be part of the act. Some incredible illusion I've never seen before. Maybe an extremely skilled magician or something equally mind-blowing. That's the only rational explanation.

But irrational explanations seep into my mind, as well. What was it Quinnic had been talking about? The shadowstone being some sort of product used by immortal beings?

No, it couldn't be.

Still, rational explanations become harder to maintain as the transition continues cascading down his body like a waterfall. His arms stretch and reshape into powerful wings that span at least twenty feet, his torso expanding and shifting into a midsection with obsidian scales that gleam like polished midnight, all while maintaining an otherworldly elegance. His legs lengthen and strengthen, ending in claws that look both deadly and magnificent.

What was once an admittedly gorgeous man is now something out of ancient legends—a dragon, honest to all the gods—standing in the middle of a circus ring. Even transformed, there's something unmistakably beautiful about him that sends a sudden, reckless punch of heat through my chest.

Then he takes flight.

The creature—because I can't think of him as a man anymore, not like this—spreads his wings and launches himself into the air. He soars through the tent with supernatural grace, spinning and swooping in aerial maneuvers that seem to mock the very concept of natural law. Now I understand why the tent is so extraordinarily large inside, though it didn't seem that way outside when I approached. I told myself it was just an illusion, but now I'm not so sure.

When I'm able to tear my eyes away from him, I see that the audience remains frozen, caught between terror and wonder, nobody quite sure if they should be screaming, running for the exits, or mesmerized at what has to be the most incredible performance in history. A few parents pull their children closer, whispering reassurances.

I'm definitely in the mesmerized camp, my anger at Blaine completely obliterated in the face of the most mind-bending performance I've ever witnessed. I guess he was right when he said that I might like the show. My hands grip the armrests of my seat, and I hold my breath as the dragon opens his maw and drives forth a plume of smoke that sets one of the performer's hoops alight, then zips through it with perfect precision.

What the hell kind of circus is this?

Next, one of the women who had previously been contorting her legs backward to rest her feet upon her own shoulders stands up with balletic grace. One of her toes is pointed forward, her foot turned out slightly like a dancer, then she begins shifting from head to toe into a dragon, just as her troupe-mate did.

The whole crowd seems to inhale at once, my own breath catching with theirs as she transforms. Her scales are rose-colored, and she is just slightly smaller in stature than her counterpart.

All around them, some of the other circus performers start to transform into dragons in a spectrum of colors that would make the royal palace's seasonal display seem muted by comparison. A panicky feeling rises in me, but I can't seem to tear my eyes away from the commotion in front of us.

My seat neighbor doesn't feel the same, though. When I glance in her direction, I see her try to rise, but she can't. It's like some invisible restraint is holding her there. I try to move now, too, but it feels like iron bands have materialized around my entire body. I struggle against them uselessly, desperate to get free from whatever magic is at work.

What *is* keeping us pinned here? There's nothing visible holding me down, no ropes or chains, but I might as well be carved from stone and fused to this seat. It's like the air itself has solidified around me, or like gravity has increased a hundred-fold. Is this more dragon magic? Some kind of enchantment that came with the transformations? The rational part of my brain that's still functioning is screaming that none of this makes sense, but apparently, sense checked out of this circus the moment the first transformation began.

Meanwhile, I count six dragons making larger and larger circles in the air, getting closer and closer to us.

As they near, the tension in the audience grows. Panicked screams fill the air, rising above the sounds of the cheerful music that continues to play from some unseen source as a handful of performers continue their tightrope routines and theatrics, creating a grotesque contrast that would almost be comical if it weren't so absolutely terrifying.

The dragons are above the audience now. I can't be sure if it's the predatory gleam in their eyes or the way their lips curl back to reveal rows of dagger-like teeth, but this feels less like a royal performance now and more like the opening scene of a nightmare. One dragon—a dark emerald one that I was too distracted by earlier transformations to track—descends toward the audience with deliberate precision, landing directly in front of a thin man in the first row.

Does he have something they want? Is he why they're here?

Then something happens that defies every remaining fragment of logic I'm clinging to. A wisp of light-colored smoke begins flowing from the man toward the dragon, drawn straight into its massive nostrils like some kind of supernatural inhalation. The man fights at first, his entire body straining against the same invisible restraints that hold the rest of us captive. He's clearly shouting at the looming green dragon, his face contorting with rage and terror, but then his flushed complexion begins to pale as more and more wisps flow out of him until, finally, his head falls back against his seat, completely lifeless.

When the man's life has been completely extinguished, the dragon appears satisfied and moves methodically to the next person.

That's when the full scope of what's happening hits me. I look around and realize that all of the dragons are now moving through the audience. One by one, they're creating those wisps. One by one, they're draining people of their lives.

This isn't a performance. This isn't entertainment or spectacle or even some twisted form of art. This is mass slaughter, carried out by creatures that shouldn't exist, using methods that belong in the darkest legends rather than reality.

I struggle harder against my invisible bonds now, all pretense of composure abandoned as I thrash wildly against whatever sorcery is keeping me trapped. Panic floods my system, feeling like ice water, and my chest constricts with such force it steals every breath I try to drag in.

The dragons seem to be moving faster now, more methodically. A royal blue dragon with scales that shimmer like sapphires seems especially efficient at the life-draining process, and—lucky me—it's making its way down my row with terrifying purpose.

My breath catches in my throat as my seat neighbor falls victim to the process, those silvery wisps flowing from her body into the dragon's waiting nostrils. She doesn't even struggle after the first few seconds, her resistance seeming to evaporate along with whatever essence is being stolen from her.

My heart feels like a boulder that's lodged solidly in my throat, blocking any oxygen from reaching my lungs. Acid surges up, burning the back of my throat. My hands go cold. My skin prickles. The world narrows to a thin, shaking tunnel, and every part of me screams to move, to do something, while my body stays frozen, useless, and trapped.

The royal blue dragon finishes with my neighbor and turns its attention to me. Up close, I can see that its pupils, blown wide, are the same deep blue as its scales, creating an almost hypnotic effect. The dragon is undeniably a beast, but those eyes look disturbingly… human. My gaze locks with the creature's, pleading silently for the mercy that my voice can't seem to articulate: *spare me. Please, spare me. I'll do anything.*

The dragon doesn't acknowledge my silent pleas. I want to scream then, but I've become mute with terror.

The dragon's scales are luminescent, catching and reflecting an entire spectrum of colors as it moves closer, floating just above us. That's all I can process before its massive head drops down toward me, close enough that I can feel the heat radiating from its skin.

Here it comes, my turn to become glassy-eyed and lifeless like the rest of the audience. Bled dry by whatever dark magic these creatures are employing.

Wisps begin to trail from my body toward the dragon's nostrils as it inhales deeply.

They rise off me in soft, silvery tendrils, drifting like smoke, but the pull behind them is anything but gentle. Each wisp tears loose something buried deep in my chest—a slow, deliberate extraction that sends cold needles racing through my nerves. My breath catches. My vision blurs at the edges. Fragments inside of me slip free and float toward those waiting, flaring nostrils.

My thoughts start to smear, losing their shape like wet ink. The world tilts. A heavy quiet blooms in my skull.

I claw for anything solid, anything real.

The coarse bite of the pilly armrests under my fingernails.

The hard brace of my boots against the footrest.

The scent of something wild and ancient hanging around this beast.

My final, defiant thought as the draining process begins rings loud and clear in my mind: *Blaine, you bastard. This is all your fault.*

The wisp makes contact with the dragon's nostril, but instead of breathing deeper, feeding harder, the dragon visibly recoils. Its massive head snaps back like it's been burned. Surprise flashes across its features—if dragons can even express surprise—followed by a look of disgust.

A sound like a hiss cuts through the air, but it's difficult to distinguish individual sounds over the symphony of screams still echoing through the tent.

The dragon's gaze darts left and right, furtive, as if checking whether anyone else witnessed its reaction.

Then its attention whips back to me, fast enough to punch a jolt of terror straight up my spine. I squeeze my eyes shut, bracing for whatever violent, hungry retaliation it's planning for my apparent inedibility. But instead of claws or teeth, warm scales press against my cheek.

My eyes fly open. Another spike of fear detonates in my chest. I thrash instinctively, stupidly, but the dragon pins my head with a gentleness so deliberate, so impossibly careful, it makes my breath stutter. It angles my head down and to the left, positioning me like a body that's already gone cold.

"Stay. Down."

The voice rasps into my ear. It's deep and male, and the heat of it scorches the side of my face.

My blood stops moving. Completely.

Wait.

What. The actual. Hell.

My brain tries to compute the impossibility of that voice coming from that dragon and just… fails. Dragons don't exist. Except the breath of one is hot on my cheek. Dragons don't talk. Except apparently this one does. And dragons absolutely do not give whispered commands to random, half-conscious circus victims… except that's exactly what's happening.

Shock fractures my thoughts, sending them scattering like broken glass.

Maybe I *am* losing it.

Maybe this is what dying feels like—hallucinating cryptic advice from mythical beasts while everyone else dies around me.

But his voice was so unmistakably real, so distinctly human despite emanating from something that absolutely isn't.

Fear roots me in place, locking every muscle so completely that obedience is the only option.

The pressure of his head releases, but mine stays lolled to the side exactly as he positioned it. By all appearances, playing dead seems like my best chance of survival.

The heat of his breath finally fades as he moves away, and without his form blocking my view, I see the full scope of the audience, which is now over half lifeless. The entire scene feels like watching a nightmare take shape in the waking world, something so horrific I can't bear to see, yet it's impossible to turn away from.

The screams that previously rang out so loudly have become quieter and more sporadic as fewer and fewer people remain conscious to produce them.

I dare to shift my head down just a fraction of an inch to bring Blaine into my line of vision. He's among those still alive, still struggling futilely against the invisible restraints. The rose-colored dragon I watched transform earlier is moving steadily in his direction.

She's three seats away from him now.

Blaine is hurling expletives in her direction, his face red with rage and terror.

Two seats away.

Now he's yelling that his father's ties to the royal court will have this whole circus gutted from the inside out.

One seat away.

Actually, scratch that—he's now vowing that blood will be shed by every performer and their families.

Zero.

She's directly in front of him now, beginning the same ritual of death that's claimed everyone else here.

I almost scream, but force the sound to die in my throat, knowing exactly what the consequences of drawing attention to myself would be.

A roiling, nauseous feeling wells up in my stomach as I watch. All these people… dead. My stomach has never been particularly strong, but if there was ever a day I wished it would toughen up, it's today.

It feels like an eternity that the rose-colored dragon spends draining Blaine's life away. Longer than all the others, I'm certain of it.

Maybe it's because he won't stop talking, still hurling threats and protests even as those silvery wisps flow from him toward her waiting nostrils. The dragon seems almost irritated by his resistance, having to work harder to extract the life from him. Where others succumbed quietly after the first few moments, Blaine keeps fighting, keeps protesting, his voice growing progressively weaker but never quite stopping. Part of me wants to shout at him to just give up, that his threats aren't going to save him now. But another part of me, the part that's still angry about being made into a joke, thinks he deserves every extra second of terror.

Or maybe I'm just starting to lose my mental grip, and that's what's making time feel like it's moving through molasses.

My eyes squeeze shut as I will her to just finish it already. Willing all of them to complete their grisly work so this nightmare can end.

When I force my eyes open again, the rose-colored dragon has moved on to her next victim. The sounds of circus-goers' screams have all but died out completely now. I let my gaze settle on Blaine one final time, and my stomach lurches violently. The man I had imagined sitting beside tonight, flawed as he was, is dead, and even assholes don't deserve to die like this.

The tent has fallen into an eerie silence, and I can't resist the urge to look around. Moving my head as slowly as humanly possible to avoid detection, I scan for any signs of life. Am I the only one left? I don't detect movement anywhere, and even the dragons are congregating back in the center ring.

The sight of so many lifeless bodies hits me all at once. Horror rises in a crushing wave, thick enough to strangle. The world around me muffles, sinking into that warped underwater sound I know far too well. My hearing is slipping. My vision collapses at the edges. I'm losing consciousness.

No, no, no. Not now. I cannot pass out now, not when I might be the only person left breathing in this place.

I try to force my focus to sharpen, but my body is done listening. It shuts down piece by piece, folding in on itself like a fortress falling under siege. Black spots swarm through my vision, swallowing the world.

My last coherent thought is painfully, unbelievably petty.

I will never get to tell Alabris I was right—I shouldn't have come.

Then everything goes black and silent.

4

KINDNESS

"Get up," a voice growls. "Now!"

A tight grip on my arm shakes me from slumber. If it weren't for the fingers digging into my flesh, I might think that I'm dead.

"Ow!" I complain, blinking rapidly to clear my vision, though it's a pointless endeavor because everything around me is black as pitch. My head throbs as I squint to see who's launching this assault on my ears.

Then it all comes flooding back. The circus, the dragons, and the mass murder of everyone else here.

I thrash around, realizing that I'm no longer glued to the seat. Instead, the stranger's hand is the only thing holding me in place.

"Let me go!" I scream, throwing as many punches and kicks as I can land at the figure that holds me hostage.

A low laugh rings out from my captor. "Cute," he says. "Now shut up and come with me if you don't want to die. Not that *I* really care, but Fenric might not forgive me if I don't bring you with us."

Who's Fenric? And holy hell, who is this mysterious stranger with a voice so devastatingly appealing that I'm actually tempted to go with him purely for the pleasure of hearing him speak?

No, Naevyn. Just because a man's voice is as sweet as honey doesn't mean he deserves your trust.

The rational part of my brain is waking up, screaming at me to run.

I manage to slam my knee into his groin, hard. He doesn't double over or anything, but he *does* loosen his grip just enough for me to slip my arm out and run the other way. I race across the bleachers, dodging the obstacles that I tell myself are very normal things and not at all the extremities of dead bodies.

My eyes adjust to the dark enough that I'm no longer entirely without sight, but to say that I can see *well* would be an overstatement.

"You're wasting your time and energy," the voice calls from behind me.

A whimper of doubt escapes me. I don't dare look back at him, but I can hear the smirk in his voice. He sounds like a smug prick if I've ever heard one.

I bank to my right, racing down the steps to the hard-packed ground beneath. Just as I reach the bottom, hands grasp both my shoulders, this time from behind.

"No more tricks," the voice commands, low and unamused.

Like hell.

I drive the heel of my sneaker backward, aiming for his ankle. Part of me knows it will do little more than irritate him, but instinct takes over. I have to try. Trying is the only thing left that's still mine.

He responds by shaking my entire body with a seemingly effortless movement of his hands, and I'm stricken by exactly how strong this man might be.

"Knock it off," he commands, more serious this time, "or I really will leave you here, and the next people who enter this tent won't be so kind."

"*This* is kindness? I'd hate to see what you call cruelty," I fire back.

"Look, if it were up to me, you'd be dead. So yes, I'd say that I'm doing you a kindness. Now walk, human." The tone of his voice suggests that he isn't joking, not in the slightest. He walks around the curve of the tent until we reach the exit. He pushes me through it, and we emerge outside. Except… not really.

"This isn't Xardon. Where are we?" I turn as best as I can while still being anchored in place by those impossibly strong hands. "The landscape is all wrong. The sky is wrong. The trees are all wrong. They're…"

"Glass, yes." The man finishes, spinning me around to face him. Well, to face his chest, at least. The man is built like he was carved from marble by someone with serious dedication. He's nearly seven feet of solid muscle that makes me crane my neck just to glare at him properly. His arms alone look like they could move mountains, and what I can see of his torso beneath that deceptively simple black t-shirt suggests the rest of him was designed with equal attention to devastating detail. His hair is darker up close, freed from the bun he had earlier. It hangs around his face in shaggy, chaotic strands, the sort of wild look that comes from either dragging your fingers through it or committing violence. It's hard to tell which.

My gaze drifts up to his face, tracing the lines of it before I can stop myself. My eyes start at the severe slant of his brow and travel down to his hardened, honey-colored eyes. His jaw looks carved from stone, and his lips… Gods, his lips. Full and unfair and so perfectly formed that it makes my fist twitch. I want to punch him almost as much as I want to—

No. Just punch him. Definitely just punch him.

A breeze stirs the air, carrying through the glass trees, making a sound like a million little windchimes playing at once, creating a musical piece that would be absolutely magical if I weren't currently being held captive by a homicidal dragon-man. The leaves are a warm amber color, like liquid sunlight at the golden hour. And glass trees? Since when do trees grow out of actual glass? And why are the leaves glowing like they have their own internal light source?

The forest stretches out in every direction around the circus tent in the clearing, each tree catching and fracturing light in ways that make the whole place shimmer like we're inside some kind of enchanted snow globe. It's the kind of breathtaking, impossible natural beauty that makes me question whether I'm actually awake or if I hit my head when I passed out. The ground beneath my feet is carpeted with fallen glass leaves that clink and crunch softly when I shift my weight, and the air smells like pine mixed with that crisp scent that comes right before it rains.

I'm about to press more about where we are when voices begin to carry over the wind-chime leaves.

"Shit. We have to go. Now," the man commands.

Then, surprisingly, he releases me. I nearly stumble, unaware of the extent that I had been relying on him to steady me. He turns his back and strides into the glass forest to our right without a second glance.

I shoot a look toward the left, to where the voices are rising. They sound close. Too close.

The man seems to think I'll follow him, but he's the one who just slaughtered an entire tent of people, not them.

I force a step toward the left, legs shaking with stubborn determination.

But what if he's right?

What if they *are* worse?

There are so many voices. Dozens, maybe more. And I know nothing about any of them. At least the dragon-man—monstrous as he is—dragged me out alive.

I hover in place, my body rocking in tiny, frantic shifts. Left or right. Known or unknown. It feels like choosing the manner of my own death.

The voices swell, almost upon the clearing now. My heart lodges in my throat, and survival wins out over pride.

I rush into the forest to the right.

“Hey! Wait up!” My voice cracks as I jog after him, more than mildly panicked, the glass leaves crunching sharply under my feet.

When I finally reach him, he glances over his shoulder. There’s the faintest curl at the edge of his mouth, subtle enough to deny, smug enough to infuriate. A ghost of a smirk, like he knew I would choose him all along.

“Good choice,” he lauds.

I want to wipe that stupid look off his face with another swift kick to the groin, but figure I shouldn’t push my luck. Again.

“So where are you taking me?”

“I’m not taking you anywhere. You’re following me,” he replies.

I’ve known this man for all of five minutes, and he's already going to drive me out of my mind. If everyone in this place is as impossible as he is, I might not survive the hour.

“Fine, don’t tell me where we’re going, but at least tell me your name,” I demand.

He gives me a sideways glance like he’s checking if I’m even worth the effort of uttering it. Then finally, “Cairos.”

Cairos. Damn it, I actually like it. It suits him—strong without being pretentious. Which is annoying, because I was hoping for something I could mock.

“Cairos. Got it.” The sun comes out from behind a cloud and nearly takes my breath away. Not the sun itself, that is, I see the sun all of the time living in Xardon. What I *don’t* see are the crystalline prisms being scattered around by the glass leaves that swivel and twist as they hang off of the branches. Tiny rainbows shine onto other rainbows, creating a cacophony of color.

But I can't let myself be distracted by shiny things. The last time that happened, the shiny things were the dragon's scales, and I had to watch them kill a horde of people around me. I can't let that happen again.

Besides, I need to get back to Quinnic and Alabris. They'll be wondering where I am by now, probably panicking when I don't come home from the circus. Alabris will worry herself sick. They need me. My wages keep us alive. If I'm gone too long…

No. I can't even think about that.

Better to focus on something simpler. Something I can control.

"So… aren't you going to ask *my* name?" I ask.

"No," Cairos replies with an air of finality.

Ouch.

"Well… why not?" I push, trying not to be offended by his lack of interest in me.

"Because you're irrelevant," he answers simply.

Double ouch.

"If I'm so irrelevant, why would you save me?" I ask.

The man stops so suddenly that I nearly run right into him. He twists, eyes boring down into me. His words are painfully slow.

"I didn't save you. Understood?"

Something about his manner of speaking sends ice into my veins.

"Yes," I breathe. "I understand."

"Good," he grunts, turning around and continuing to walk through the forest. I want to pester him with so many more questions like "where are we?" and "who *did* save me, then?", but something tells me he isn't in the mood for questions.

The glass forest becomes less dense, opening into an area with a cluster of small houses, though far different than anything I've ever seen. Instead of solid stucco, the structures match the trees. They're made entirely of glass, though these are opaque while the trees and leaves are crystal clear. The houses are arranged haphazardly in a sort of circle with one, slightly larger structure at the center.

I stick close to Cairos as he leads us past the central building and toward one on the far edge of the settlement. He knocks on the door three times, firm and loud.

A man opens the door immediately and ushers us inside. I check Cairos out of the corner of my eye, who strides in without a flicker of caution, so I take a breath and step after him.

The man is shorter than Cairos but still has an impressive stature. Where Cairos feels coiled, waiting for a target, this man radiates warmth. His bronze hair is neatly kept, his face approachable, and his eyes are the same impossible blue as the dragon that spared me.

The realization that this is the sapphire dragon in human form hits like a shove, and I instinctively take half a step back, though he doesn't seem offended.

The interior steals my breath. The walls glow with purples and midnight blues, bleeding into gold like carnival lights underwater. Jewel-toned furniture curves around the room, and silks drift from the high ceiling in impossible hues. The polished dark floor reflects everything, doubling the colors and shapes until it feels like the room is layered over itself.

It's like the circus, but refined.

And it smells warm and sweet and spiced, the kind of scent that wraps around you and tugs at your stomach.

Once the door shuts, the blue-eyed man steps closer, reclaiming the space I had backed away from. He takes my hand gently, lifts it, and presses a gentle kiss to the back.

A chill ripples through me. Not fear, though.

Just the unsettling awareness that nothing about this place is familiar.

"My lady," he says with reverence. "We're so happy you're here."

Cairos snorts, but doesn't explain himself.

"What is this place?" I ask, pulling my hand back to my side.

The man continues to hold his hands out in front of him as if he had never let go of mine at all. "This is my home. Welcome."

The way he looks at me like I'm one of the Gods themselves is completely unsettling. I look up at Cairos, hoping he'll say something, but his expression is annoyingly empty.

"Well, well, Fenric's pet has arrived," a woman's voice carries over to us as she glides into the room via a door to our right that I hadn't noticed before. Her sleek black hair falls in a perfect curtain to her waist, not a strand out of place. Like everyone else here, she's devastatingly beautiful with sharp cheekbones, full lips, and glowy skin, but there's something cold about her perfection.

For the first time, the man—Fenric, as the lady called him—looks perturbed instead of admiring. He crosses the room in a few quick steps and says in a whispered tone that I don't think I'm supposed to hear, but definitely can, "She is not a pet. She is the savior of our realm and to be treated as such."

"What savior?" the woman hisses. "The prophecy speaks of a warrior, not… whatever this is."

Fenric's anger flares. "She is *chosen*."

"And *you* are delusional." She eyes me up and down again, before turning her attention back to Fenric. "Which head were you thinking with, anyway?"

A dark smirk crosses Cairos's face while Fenric struggles to maintain composure.

"You don't have to like it. You just have to allow it," he says through gritted teeth.

"And you," the woman turns her attention to Cairos. "What were you thinking, bringing her here? You should have let the guards deal with her."

Cairos's expression goes flat, his jaw working like he's stressed. "An oath's an oath. I said I'd deliver her here, and I did." He turns and grabs the door handle, then stops, turns to Fenric, and says, "Have fun babysitting," before exiting, the slam echoing through the glass house so loudly that I fear it might shatter.

"Um, what's with him?" I ask. "And what prophecy?"

Fenric blinks, surprise flickering openly across his face. "You heard that?"

He brushes the thought aside with a quick shake of his head. "Never mind. You must be starving."

"No." The word comes out louder than I mean it to. "I don't have time to eat. I have to get home. My brother—"

"Selenia, get the girl a plate," he says, completely ignoring me.

The woman shoots him a cutting glare before disappearing back through the door into what I'm assuming is the kitchen. As soon as she's gone, the scent finally registers. Warm. Savory. Rich. Meat.

Real meat.

My stomach betrays me by growling so loudly that Fenric can definitely hear it.

Once Selenia is out of earshot, Fenric steps closer, lowering his voice. "She will come around. As for your situation, you'll be staying here until further notice."

Further notice. The phrase lands wrong. Either he's being deliberately vague, or he thinks that counts as helpful.

"The fuck I will," I snap, heat flaring up my neck.

Fenric flinches, genuinely wounded, and for half a second, I almost feel bad. The feeling dies instantly when I remind myself who he is—who all of them are. They butchered a tent full of people. I'm fresh out of sympathy.

"I understand you're confused," Fenric says, gentler than I want him to be. "We'll explain soon. But first, eat. You need to keep your strength up."

Strength up for what? I don't ask. And I don't argue again when he motions for me to follow, because hunger is making my decisions now.

He leads me into the next room, which has a table so lengthy, it's dizzying. Four plates are set out along with serving trays of what I suspect is some kind of fowl, fruits I've heard of but never had the pleasure of tasting, as well as breads and cheeses. So much food that all I want is to gorge myself.

But then I think of Alabris and Quinnic and can't bear the thought of eating while they starve. Had they figured out that I was gone yet? Were they looking for me? And more importantly, would they find provisions while I'm gone?

"Don't be rude, eat something," Selenia pushes.

I claim the chair closest to the door, and my knee bounces under the table as I try to act like I'm not one second away from inhaling everything in front of me. I weigh the options quickly—eat until I can stand again and maybe find a way home, or starve myself into weakness and lose whatever chance I have to fight back.

The choice isn't noble. It isn't even hard.

And if I'm being honest, I'm entirely too happy to make it.

The first bite of meat practically melts on my tongue, warm and rich and soft enough to swallow without chewing. It's so tender it almost doesn't feel real. I chase it with bread still hot from an oven, cheeses so creamy they coat my throat, and a handful of grapes that burst sweetly between my teeth. The flavors are overwhelming after years of thin soup and stale crusts. My stomach fills steadily, and for a moment, the sheer pleasure of it makes my eyes sting.

"A warrior, indeed," Fenric says. "Or at least she eats like one."

He sounds proud, but embarrassment crawls up my spine anyway. I must look feral beside these polished, impossibly graceful people who probably can't fathom what real hunger feels like.

Still… I can't bring myself to feel ashamed. Not really.

I'm too warm, too full, too deeply satisfied to care.

"It's late. Let me show you to your room," Fenric offers when I've finally gotten my fill. I consider protesting again, but he leaves no room for opposition. Maybe if I pretend to be complacent, I can let my stomach settle, then sneak out in the night, back home to Xardon, wherever it may be.

The hallways he leads me through make no sense to me. They seem longer than the house is wide, and there are so many rooms off of them that there's no possible way I'm inside the same glass structure that we originally entered.

When he finally stops at a door on the right, exhaustion hits me. From start to end, this entire day has been nothing but madness, and I have to admit, a good slumber does sound inviting.

What's also inviting is the luxurious bed perched atop a circular platform at the center of the room. A blood-red canopy flows over the six posters of the bed and cascades down to the ground. The red is accented with silky white cords at each of the corners, as well as white sheets, blankets, and pillowcases with gold edging.

The floor is the same mahogany wood, though this room has flowing patterns engraved into it every so often that break up the monotony. The walls are a deep plum, almost black in the shadows, but every time the light shifts, they bloom with flashes of violet and gold. It's dramatic, bordering on ridiculous, but the effect is so strangely cohesive with the rest of the house, I can't even complain.

A large, round window of transparent glass complements the platform on the floor. It's twilight now, though I imagine this room is a beacon in the daytime.

"Thank you," I reply as earnestly as I can muster.

"There are clothes in the armoire." Fenric gestures to the tall, wooden cabinet against the back wall. "Get some rest, er… I've just realized you never mentioned your name."

"Naevyn," I reply. At least someone here doesn't find me irrelevant.

"Naevy, of course. Get some rest, Naevyn. In the morning, we'll have… tasks for you."

Tasks. Great. If they're going to put me to work during the day, then all the more reason to get the hell out of here tonight, because if I'm going to be breaking my back for anyone, I'd rather do it in Xardon, where the effort actually means something for me and my family.

Once he exits, I cross over to the armoire to see the clothes he mentioned. Opening the door, I see… a nightgown.

Not great.

What a spectacular day to be wearing a dress. My options for tonight's daring escape are either my current dirty dress or a silk nightgown that would rip the moment I try to sprint.

Dress it is.

I remove my boots and slide into the bed, sinking beneath the covers, and whispering a silent apology to whatever poor soul is responsible for laundering these pristine sheets.

Now I wait.

And hope this insane plan doesn't get me killed before sunrise.

5

TRAITOR

I startle awake.

Fuck. Fuck, fuck, fuck.

So much for waiting until everyone falls asleep. There aren't any clocks in this place, and the window only tells me that it's still dark outside. Whether it's been five minutes or five hours, I couldn't say.

I curse the cloudlike mattress for being irresistibly comfortable as I slip my boots back on and head out the door. Every minute I waste in this fever dream is another minute that Quinnic and Alabris are wondering if I'm dead. Another minute they're splitting smaller and smaller rations, trying to make the food last. Quinnic will do something stupid trying to find me, I know it. And Alabris will worry herself into an early grave.

Getting back to them is the only thing that matters. The only thing that keeps my feet moving.

The hallway stretches ahead, silent as a held breath, and I creep through it, straining to catch even the faintest sound. The route through the house comes back to me easily. Left at the fork. Right at the painting of the castle. Straight on until freedom.

My boots squeak quietly against the floor as I make my way down the hall, but it may as well be claps of thunder for how loudly the sound rings out in my ears. I say a silent prayer that no one is awake to hear me.

At last, the front room comes into view. A fire crackles in the hearth, painting the place in warm gold. I hold my breath, tiptoeing in as I scan the room, but there's not a soul in sight.

I wrap my hand around the brass knob, take one steadying breath, and slip out into the night.

Outside, the reality of what I'm doing hits hard. Strange animal noises ripple through the dark—low, hungry sounds that don't belong to anything I grew up fearing. A knot tightens in my throat. Predators out here with growls like that might make the drunk sailors back home look like toddlers.

But turning back isn't an option. Quinnic and Alabris need me. I walked here from the circus tent. Walking back is the same thing in reverse. So what if it's dark now and predators are about? So what if I don't have a knight in shining armor of sorts to lead me through the forest as I did last time?

I'm perfectly capable.

The settlement is quiet now. No one lingers outside, and most of the glass houses have gone dark except for a few with fading hearth fires. I slip past the center house, through the break in the ring of buildings, and into the open night.

The night looks different here. The glass leaves scatter moonlight, flickering it across the ground in shifting patterns. It's disorienting… but helpful. Better than the pitch-black nights in Xardon where you can't tell your own feet from the void.

Reaching the edge of the forest, I feel ridiculous for abandoning a warm bed and more food than I've had in years, but comfort won't keep my family alive. Getting back to that tent will. If it hauled me across kingdoms once, then it must be able to haul me back.

Hopefully.

A scream tears through the forest, followed by a chorus of yips and snarls that don't sound even remotely friendly. My blood goes cold. The animals' calls are like the rallying cries of coyotes after they make a kill. Judging by their voices, these animals aren't coyotes, but they definitely made a kill.

Instinct begs me to turn around, to climb back into that bed before anyone notices I've been gone. But cowardice won't get me home. And if those creatures already have a kill, logic says they're not hunting for another. Unfortunately, logic doesn't stop my palms from sweating or my stomach from flipping at every rustle.

Somehow, I make it back to the tent. When its silhouette breaks through the trees, relief slams into me so hard my knees almost give out.

I'm close. So close. Back to Xardon, back to Quinnic and Alabris, back to thin soup and hunger pangs, but at least I'll be with them again.

The tent's flaps flutter in the wind. I brace myself for the macabre sight of the bodies, but when my eyes finally adjust, I see that they're just… gone.

My boots scrape across the dirt floor, making a gritty sound as I step inside. The emptiness is somehow more unsettling than the carnage would've been. Where did they all go?

What now? I could curl up in a seat and see if passing out triggers whatever transported me last time, but no. That feels too simple. Too convenient.

Maybe the ringmaster's platform has something to do with it. During the show, he directed everything from there—maybe that's where the magic is. I make my way toward the center arena, nerves prickling along my spine. The place feels wrong at night. Too open. Too quiet.

Nothing is in the dark that isn't in the light. Mother's old words echo through my mind, even though this entire ordeal has proven that everything I thought I understood about the world was laughably naïve.

The circular platform rises in front of me, taller than it had seemed before. I plant a foot on it, haul myself up, and stand there like an idiot. How does magic even work? Do I speak to it? Think really hard? Do… feelings matter?

I wave my hands around.

Nothing.

I jump.

Still nothing.

"Take me back to Xardon!" I shout into the empty tent, my voice cracking with desperation.

A single, slow clap slices through the silence, and I nearly leap out of my own boots.

"Holy fucking gods!" I exclaim. "Who are you? *Where* are you?"

I spin in a circle, following the sound of the clapping, but I can't see anyone at all. My heart pounds so hard I can feel it in my throat.

Boots ring out on the bleachers.

Stomp… stomp… stomp…

Finally, a figure descends from up in the back row.

"Quite the performance," he says, his voice dripping with amusement. "And to think I believed humans were useless. You do make excellent entertainment, I'll give you that."

I think I see him shrug, but I can't be sure. As he nears, he flicks one hand off to the side, and lanterns light up to my right.

My mind barely has time to panic before my body reacts. I try to leap off the platform, but my limbs lock mid-motion.

Frozen.

Shit.

Why did I come here? I could be safe in bed. Now I have two choices—beg or fight. Only one has ever worked for me.

"Who the hell do you think you are?" I snarl.

Laughter bounces off the canvas walls. Wild, untamed laughter that makes my skin crawl.

When it finally subsides, the man speaks again. There's a faint hiss threaded through every "s" he speaks, barely there, but impossible to ignore. "I promise, this will be quick. And it will be so much more merciful than living with the trauma of watching all your friends die." The words slide off his tongue with mock concern that doesn't fool me for a second.

He's close now, in the center ring and approaching my platform. Or rather, his platform. I recognize the ringmaster from the show immediately. Up close, he's even more intimidating—tall and menacing, like Cairos but without any hint of restraint. His slick, blonde hair looks too perfect for someone who's capable of murder, but looks can be deceiving.

"Fenric might have been too weak to drain you, but I assure you, I am not," he announces with terrifying confidence.

Each step tightens something in my chest. Panic swells again, sharp and familiar, making it hard to think. This is it. This is how I die. Quinnic and Alabris will never know what happened. They'll wake up tomorrow and think I abandoned them.

Now he circles the platform, eyeing me up and down.

"Pretty thing, aren't you? Such a shame. What a waste." His nose crinkles as he speaks, like he's really, truly disgusted by my humanity.

"Enough with the theatrics, just fucking kill me or let me go," I say through gritted teeth.

His eyes rake over me. "Now I see why you were so difficult to drain," he muses quietly. "Your defiance does make the process rather… challenging."

Suddenly, a hissing sound echoes from the far side of the tent. The ringmaster hisses back, his lips parting to reveal sharpened teeth that gleam in the lantern light.

Holy shit. Two supernatural creatures are about to clash right in front of me as I'm frozen in place. Saying I'm an easy target is the understatement of the century.

The hisses and snarls intensify. A breeze blows through the tent as if Mother Nature herself can feel the tension cracking in the air, and she's trying her absolute hardest to blow it out.

"Grendor," the voice from the shadows grounds out. "What are you doing?"

The ringmaster straightens, eyes widening just enough to look taken aback, but then they shrink back to evil-looking slits.

"What am *I* doing? I'm finishing the job we started. It seems that we had a little stowaway, hidden somewhere in the tent. How you and your companions couldn't smell her during the clean-up is beyond me. She's as ripe as a rotting harvest." His nose crinkles up as the words drip with disdain.

"There she is, the little rat." Cairos steps out of the shadows, fangs still bared slightly. His midnight hair hangs loose around his face.

Instead of panic, something else flickers through me—sharp, bright, embarrassingly warm. His size alone should be enough to make me crumble, but all I can focus on are his eyes. That impossible amber. Deep and liquid and… steady. Too steady for someone with fangs still visible.

Nothing about him makes sense to me. The teeth, the voice, and the lethal posture are all reasons to keep my distance. Yet the longer I look, the more the fear slips, replaced by something heavier, something that pulls low in my stomach.

Maybe it's stupidity. Maybe it's shock. Maybe something worse.

But whatever the reason, fear isn't what rises in me when he steps closer.

Not even close.

Or maybe I've been touched with lunacy, and I really *should* be afraid. But should or should not is irrelevant. I can't bring myself to feel any sort of fear of him.

He approaches with unhurried steps, a steadiness in the face of danger that sends a jolt down my spine. Three tattooed black bands circle his left wrist, stark and deliberate. A dagger hangs at his hip, half-hidden, and I can't tell if the ringmaster has noticed it or is too busy seething to care.

Cairos's jaw is working as he takes a wide and ready stance ten feet from the ringmaster.

"I've been looking for her all night. Escaped us during the cleanup. The guards thought she'd be dead within the hour from the stalkers in the forest, but it would seem that's not the case. Seeing as how they know about her, you can't have the soul for yourself, Grendor." He tilts his head at me menacingly, but again, I feel no fear. "I brought a vessel. Leave us, so I can finish her off."

The ringmaster hisses again, clearly displeased with how this turned out. "See to it that you do," he snaps, those razor teeth still pushing past his gums. Then he stalks toward the exit, fury rolling off him so thick it makes the air taste sour.

The moment he's gone, I shift my gaze to Cairos, suddenly very aware that I'm still frozen like a statue.

He frees me instantly, like he heard the thought forming in my skull.

"Who the fuck do you think you are?" he berates me in a hushed tone. His hand clamps around my arm and he yanks me off the platform, hauling me down to the dirt. He's towering over me now, full of fury. The fangs have vanished, but the anger in his face looks a lot more real without them.

"What?" I snap back, something flaring hot behind my sternum.

"Fenric gives you clothes, food, a warm bed to sleep in, and this is how you thank him?" He holds up his fingers, counting each offense like I'm a child. "Humans. Always so damn ungrateful."

My jaw drops. Is he serious? They kidnapped me. They slaughtered hundreds of people. And somehow I'm the inconsiderate one?

“Tell me how you really feel,” I fire back. “For your information, I have a family and a life I need to return to. But if it helps your fragile ego, then thank you *so* much for making everything a million times harder.”

He looked irritated before. Now he looks murderous. His fangs extend again, sharp enough to tear through bone, and for a second, I actually believe he might tear me apart. Not with magic, not by taking my soul, but in a very literal, blood-soaked way.

A chill races up my arms, and I almost regret not biting my tongue.

When he speaks again, his voice is deadly. “That smart mouth might have kept you alive back home, but where I’m from, someone will rip you to pieces for speaking like that. You’re lucky I swore an oath to Fenric. Otherwise, you’d already be in the ground. Now move.”

Hatred is not something I hand out freely, but I’m fairly certain I’ve never hated someone so quickly in my entire life.

Cairos turns and strides toward the tent’s exit. I follow, because apparently he can’t kill me, which is… not comforting, exactly, but still better than the alternative.

Outside, the air feels colder. Cairos doesn’t react. The moon hangs low, and a thin line of warm light is beginning to stain the horizon.

Morning is coming.

“I knew it! Six hundred years, Cairos, I’ve been waiting for you to slip up.” Did he just say six… *hundred?* Grendor emerges from around the side of the tent. “Your commitment to the king has been flimsy at best, but this is undeniable proof. The punishment for traitorous activities is death, and I would say that harboring a human in the glass village of Daersbane is traitorous, indeed.”

The smile that upturns Grendor’s lips is wicked and cruel and leaves no room for questioning if he will be the one delivering Cairos’s punishment. His sharp teeth are bared, and a sword materializes in his hands. He lunges at Cairos before my brain can catch up. Cairos reacts instantly. He draws his dagger in one clean, practiced motion. A dagger against a full sword feels like a terrible idea, but he makes it look almost possible. Steel flashes. Cairos slashes at Grendor's arm. Grendor pivots, sliding the sword sideways in a smooth, terrifying swing.

Blood beads along Grendor's arm from the dagger's cut, but Cairos pays for it.

The sword bites into his abdomen, deep enough that the sound he makes rips straight through me. He howls, raw and animal, while Grendor snarls in reply, the two of them locked in some hellish rhythm of violence.

I tear myself from the battle long enough to realize that neither of them remembered to freeze me into place. Their attention is fully on each other, and this may be my only chance of escape.

I don't think twice. My legs are already carrying me into the glass forest. The crunching of glass is loud beneath my feet. I have no idea if I'm running toward safety or straight into disaster. Instinct only gives me one command: run.

My feet carry me quickly across the leaf-littered ground, my ribs starting to ache as I break out into a sprint.

I don't get far, though.

A ruby red dragon crashes down through the trees in front of me, letting out a thunderous roar. The moment its feet touch down, it shifts into his human-like form, and Grendor slinks toward me with a dangerous, predatory look in his eye.

"Nice try, child," Grendor spits. His sword is sheathed at his back now as he's clearly confident that he can take me down without it.

But where's Cairos?

My heart pounds, realizing I'm alone with this creature. Alone, and very likely dying tonight.

"This will only hurt a lot," he says with derision.

Pain detonates in my arm as his jagged teeth tear through my skin. By the time my brain catches up, he's already several feet away, his movements bright and sharp like flashes of lightning.

My scream bursts out of me, raw and terrified, echoing that awful sound I heard earlier in the forest. Blood spills down my arm in thick, hot streams. The burn he leaves behind crawls up my skin like fire trying to claim me from the inside. And I know he's not finished.

But then something changes.

Grendor coughs.

Once, then violently again. A choking, hacking sound, like his throat is closing up. He stumbles and falls to his knees. His hands claw at his throat as he rasps for air.

His skin begins to take on a grayish pallor, veins darkening beneath the surface. The confident sneer melts from his face, replaced by confusion and then genuine fear. He tries to speak, but only a strangled whisper emerges.

Then, a heavy thud shakes the forest.

An onyx dragon lands just ahead of us in the clearing created by Grendor. Cairos.

He shifts to his other form and steps toward us, his expression blank as he watches the final moments of Grendor's life.

His black shirt is stained darker where Grendor's sword made contact, along with a variety of other wounds and gashes along his arms. His body is bent forward slightly to stem the abdominal bleeding.

Grendor's gasps turn to wheezes until he falls flat onto his stomach, his breathing stopped completely.

Grendor is dead.

6

CENTURIES

"You say she killed Grendor?" Fenric asks. His voice is low, solemn enough to make the obsidian walls around us feel even heavier. There are deep lines etched into his forehead that don't match the smoothness of the rest of him. He doesn't look older than thirty, but after hearing Grendor rant about centuries, who knows? He could be six hundred years old or more, for all I know.

"She did. Well, her blood did." Cairos corrects, lifting a glass of amber liquid to his lips. Whiskey, of course. He winces slightly as he drinks, a tight pull at the corner of his mouth that betrays the pain he's so desperately pretending not to feel. His hand drifts toward the bandage wrapped around his abdomen, pressing in just enough that I can tell the wound hasn't stopped bleeding entirely. He doesn't acknowledge it, but Fenric's eyes flick toward him with a flash of worry before smoothing back into neutrality.

Naturally, Cairos won't give me an ounce of credit for killing a murderous carnival overlord. Not that I did much. My forearm was torn open, and Selenia only patched me up because Fenric ordered her to. She muttered something about "weak mortals" while doing it, then stormed off.

The room we're in now is nothing like Fenric's whimsical home. This place belongs to Cairos, which means shadows and sharp corners. From the outside, his house looks like all the others, but inside, everything is obsidian. The walls. The ceiling. The doorframes. Even the air feels darker somehow. A single crystal chandelier hangs over a carved wooden table, throwing cold reflections across marble floors. Brass sconces line the walls, and an oil painting of a man I don't recognize watches us like he disapproves of the company.

Cairos told me I'm only here because his home is closest to the forest, which I understood to mean I would never be allowed within ten feet of this place if he had any say in the matter.

"Can I ask one question?" I cut in.

"No. Question answered. Now be quiet." Cairos's eyes stay locked on me, hard and unblinking. Heat crawls up my neck and settles in my cheeks. Irritatingly, he notices. A tiny curl lifts at the corner of his mouth, smug and knowing, as if my blush is for him rather than because he's the most aggravating male in existence.

"What are you?" I ask, ignoring the way my pulse jumps under his stare. "My brother ranted about immortal beings and magic, and I thought it was drunken sailor nonsense. But now…" My words fade as I wait for someone to confirm the thing I already know but don't want to believe.

"But now you know we're real." Fenric's tone softens, like he's speaking to a wild creature trying not to bolt. "*Fae* are real."

Fae. Folklore. Creatures from fairy tales that are supposed to put children's minds at ease as they drift to sleep, not grow fangs and shift into dragons to become nightmares.

"Fae?" I arch a brow. My voice comes out more level than I expect.

"Yes. Fae," Cairos answers. "Immortals with a strength five thousand times that of a human." There's a cold precision to the way he says it, like he wants the weight of the words to crush me.

"Is that a threat?" I hold his stare, refusing to blink first.

"If that's how you interpret it."

His gaze drags over my face, deliberate enough to make my pulse trip. He knows exactly what he's doing.

We glare at each other, locked in some silent battle I'm pretty sure I'm losing. His hand slips back toward his abdomen again, fingers pressing into the bandage as if he can will the wound closed. He doesn't flinch, but the tightness in his jaw gives him away.

Fenric finally sighs. "We need to focus. A fae has died. Our ringleader, Grendor. The guards will discover it soon enough and then…" His throat works around a swallow. "Then the king."

"Fuck the king," Cairos spits.

"You're drunk," Fenric replies. "You don't know what you're saying."

"I know exactly what I'm saying. I'm saying it's been hundreds of years since we were cursed by him to be this." He takes another large swig of his whiskey before slamming the glass down hard on the table.

"To be fae?" I ask, curiosity getting the best of me.

Cairos scowls, a flame dancing behind his eyes.

"No. *Fae* is what we are. *Dragons* are what we are cursed to be. And according to prophecy, our only salvation is a warrior who will upset the balance, and lucky for you, Fenric believes that warrior is you, otherwise, you wouldn't have breath in your lungs to be pestering us like this."

His words hit like a slap, but what pisses me off more is that I actually care what he thinks. I should be focused on getting back home, not on the way this asshole's jaw clenches when he's angry or how his shoulders fill out the sleeves of his shirt. There's something seriously wrong with me. Maybe all the magical air in this place is messing with my head.

"Go easy on her, Cairos. She's been through a great deal," Fenric says.

Cairos lets out a snort. "Like what? Being brought somewhere she's completely provided for? Poor human. What a terrible existence."

The way he says 'human' makes my skin crawl. Like it's a dirty word. Like I'm beneath him in every possible way.

"Cairos," Fenric scolds.

"I want her out of here," Cairos snaps, shoving his chair back so hard it clatters to the floor. He grips his own side like he had forgotten about his injuries, but turns away before his expression can betray him.

The sting hits deeper than it should. I barely know him. Hell, I don't *want* to know him. He's rude and arrogant and dismissive on a profound level. But something ugly and unwelcome still twists in my heart. Maybe because he dragged me out of that tent before the guards came. Maybe because he chased me when I ran. Maybe because some idiotic part of me thought all of that meant something.

Clearly, I'm delusional.

"You can't be serious," Fenric pleads. "If the guards see her —"

"If the guards see her, then she'll either prove herself as a warrior, or she won't." He heads for the doorway, then stops. For a heartbeat, I think he might actually look at me. My pulse kicks up like an idiot, but he doesn't turn around. "You have until midday to figure out where to bring her. Until then, I'll be at the practice hall being healed by Hessa."

He's gone before I can tell him exactly what I think of his ultimatum, leaving behind only the scent of vetiver and spice. I hate that I notice. Hate that the room feels smaller without him in it, and that part of me feels like I'm drawn to him just so I can keep fighting with him.

I blink a few times to get my bearings as I try to resist inhaling whatever is left of his scent in this room.

“Don’t give him another thought. He’s just stressed,” Fenric reassures, though I get the feeling that he’s covering for Cairos because he always acts like this.

“Why is he so upset?” My voice wobbles only a little, which I consider a remarkable victory considering the day I’ve had. Maybe Fenric will actually give me a straight answer instead of Cairos’s usual brand of cryptic riddles.

“There’s… a lot you should know.” He rubs the back of his neck, like he’s deciding where to start. “As you might have realized, the fae who died—the one your blood killed—was nearly a thousand years old. Fae aren’t supposed to die like that. Ever. And he wasn’t just any fae. He was blessed by the king himself. The ringleader of our troupe since the very beginning.”

“And the beginning was…?”

He hesitates long enough that I start counting heartbeats to keep from combusting. “Six hundred and twenty-seven years ago,” he finally says.

My jaw drops so fast I hear it click.

Six hundred. And twenty-seven. Years.

Holy stars above. That’s a centuries-long massacre. Generations of people erased. Parents. Lovers. Children. All of them walking into a tent the same way I did and never walking back out.

“How often do you hold the circus?” The words come out a whisper, like speaking louder might make the answer worse.

Fenric looks like I just stabbed him. The warm, bright man from earlier folds in on himself. His shoulders slump, and he can’t even meet my eyes. “Once per cycle. The trees shift through their colors—sapphire, emerald, then amber, where we are now. One rotation through all three is a cycle.”

He says it so casually, like he’s telling me about the phases of the moon instead of the timetable of ritual slaughter.

“How many days per cycle?”

“Twenty-four.”

The number hits me like a blow. My stomach twists hard enough to make me lightheaded.

Twenty-four days.

For six centuries.

My mind tries to do the math and immediately taps out, horrified. Thousands of shows. Hundreds of thousands of people, maybe more. All gone to feed some curse.

Faces flash in my mind—Blaine shouting threats he couldn't back up, families pointing at the performers, children tugging at their parents' sleeves, and couples leaning into each other with wide-eyed excitement.

All of them dead.

The grief slams into me, pressing against my ribs like it wants to claw its way inside my heart. But grief never stays long with me. I've learnt to sharpen it until it calcifies and morphs into something molten and dangerous.

By the time I open my eyes again, I'm burning.

"You kill people that often?" My voice is low, quiet.

Fenric flinches. He just nods once, tiny and miserable, his eyes glossy with whatever guilt he's been carrying for centuries.

"Only because we have to," he says.

"Why would you have to?" The fury in me thins just enough to make room for confusion.

"Because the king—the curse—requires us to."

"Oh."

It's all I can manage. One useless syllable for something too big to wrap my mind around.

Fenric seems to have recovered a little as he gets up and walks to a sideboard at the right wall of the dining room. He pours not one, but two crystal glasses of whiskey.

"Drink this," he says, placing one of the glasses in front of me. "You'll need it."

"Are you sure Cairos would allow a mere human to drink his whiskey?" That comment wins a ghost of a smile from Fenric, but it fades as quickly as it appeared.

"His bark is worse than his bite." Fenric sits down and takes a long drink of whiskey. I do too, and it burns my throat all the way down into my stomach, scorching my insides. We don't have drinks like this back in Xardon. Whiskey, yes, but it's cheap, sour stuff that makes your toes curl. Nothing like this that actually tastes good enough to savor, instead of just choke down to get the job done.

"Mmm." I let out a satisfied sound, and Fenric seems pleased.

"So," he says, staring down into his glass. "Here's what you need to know. The fae are not all the same. We worship the same gods, and bow to the same king, but we're not the same. There are factions that were formed by a war of long ago. Seven factions, to be exact. The first, and the largest, shares beliefs with the king. They support him fully. They're known as the Solmeren and primarily live in the city that surrounds the castle."

"I get the idea you don't share beliefs with the king," I say.

"We, the troupe and the fae in the surrounding towns, are called the Nytherian. We oppose many of the king's goals. It's what got us into this situation in the first place." Fenric takes another somber sip of his whiskey, and I nearly think I can see a tear forming in his eye.

"What happened?" I ask, then berate myself for prying into something that's evidently a sore subject.

Fenric doesn't bite my head off for it like I imagine Cairos would, though. He scrubs a hand through his hair, fingers catching in the strands like he's untangling more than just knots.

"It's too much detail for a night like this," he says finally. "Just know we dared to care about the rights of humans, and the king cursed us for it. Bound us to dragon form. Bound us to the circus. If we don't collect souls every cycle, we die."

My jaw goes slack. There's a lot to unpack, but all that comes out is a very eloquent, "Wow."

I drag in a breath, try to make my voice work again. "Did Grendor ever collect souls, too?"

His mouth twists. "Aye. Grendor was one of us… but not really. We were cursed. He volunteered. He is—was—the king's right hand man."

Volunteered.

I stare at him, stomach curling. It's one thing to be forced into damnation. It's another to sign up for it.

"I'm glad he's dead," I whisper before I can talk myself out of it.

Fenric's eyes snap up to mine, damp and sharp all at once. "Careful who you say that around, girl." He glances toward the door, then leans in, lowering his voice. "But I don't disagree."

Something in my chest loosens at that. For the first time, I see him as more than just the dragon who spared me. He's stuck under the same boot as me, just higher up the heel.

He straightens and keeps going like he has to get it all out before his courage runs dry. "The other factions don't concern themselves with the king's business. They see Valtheron as just another ruler. We're the ones bound to his curse, so—"

"Wait." My mind trips over the name. "Did you say Valtheron?"

He blinks. "Yes."

My pulse spikes. "That's *our* king. The king in Xardon. All this time…" My thoughts race, trying to make sense of it all. "He's fae, then?"

"Yes."

Of course he is. Of course the bastard sitting on top of our starving kingdom, forcing the weakest of us to mine shadowstone, is an immortal nightmare.

Another thought claws its way to the front of my mind. "Do you know what shadowstone is?"

Fenric goes still. "Of course. The most valuable mineral we have. It's rare, and not found in our realm."

Just the thought of it makes my shoulders ache like I've still got a full bucket strapped there. Then the ache slides lower, turns into something sharp in my chest when I remember Quinnic and Alabris. The mines. The rations. Me not being there.

How long has it been? A day and a half? Two? Long enough that they've noticed I'm gone, for sure.

"Naevyn?" Fenric's voice nudges me back. "Are you alright?"

"Define 'alright'," I mutter, then sigh. "Back in Xardon, I work mining shadowstone. I knew it went to the king, but I didn't know the king was… you know. Immortal."

"You mined shadowstone?" His brows climb like I've just told him I swallowed a mountain. "You don't look like you could carry the stuff. No offense meant."

"Buckets of it," I say, reaching for my whiskey and taking a long swallow. "Every day. If I don't get back, my brother will have to take my place, and he's only fifteen."

The stories about my situation and my family spill out before I can stop them. I don't know why I'm telling a fae stranger all of this, curse or not. But sitting here with him, with the burn of liquor in my veins and the memory of Grendor's death still fresh, he feels… weirdly safe. Safer than most people I know, which is saying something.

"I wish I could help you," Fenric says quietly. And I believe him. "But we can't let you go back. Not just because we think you might be the one to tip the scales, but because of what you've seen. It's forbidden."

A bitter laugh punches out of me. "Pretty sure I'm not exactly on the approved list in Daersbane either, but here we are."

Something shifts in his expression, like I've reminded him of a ticking clock he's been trying to ignore. He pushes his chair back and finishes his drink in one swallow.

"Speaking of where you're allowed to be," he says, glancing over his shoulder like Cairos might materialize out of the shadows. "We'd better move."

I knock back the rest of my whiskey, the heat searing a path down my throat, and stand to follow. I don't know where he's taking me, or what "move" actually means in a place like this, but Fenric hasn't lied to me yet, and in a realm like this, that passes for trust.

We step out into the blazing heat, and it feels thick in my lungs. I thought Xardon was brutal in the daytime, but this? This is some kind of sadistic torture. Sweat prickles at the back of my neck instantly, my hair sticking to my forehead like it's trying to fuse with my skin.

The sun is already high—too high. Mid-sky.

Did the day sprint past without me? Do days move faster here, too?

I can't tell. Maybe it's the lingering alcohol fogging up the inside of my skull, or maybe this place really is chewing through time the way it chews through everything else. Either way, hours feel like sand slipping through my fingers, and I need to figure out how the hell to get home before too many of them pass.

Fenric scans the area, his eyes flicking from shadow to shadow like he expects guards to burst out of the ground. Then he makes a straight line for the large glass house at the center of the circle.

I follow him in.

And walk straight into a room full of dragons.

7

STAY

Each of the dragons looks like it's about two seconds away from ripping me in half, fangs bared in a way that makes my stomach twist. Two slam into the ground at the same time and shift mid-impact, bodies snapping into fae forms before they hiss and hit a full run straight at me.

I squeeze my eyes shut and brace for the pain of a disastrous finale.

It never comes.

A violent blast of wind slams into me instead, stealing the breath from my lungs, and a heavy thud shakes the floor as something enormous lands inches from my toes.

"No."

One word, low and lethal. It rolls through the hall, filling every corner.

The hissing dies instantly.

I crack my eyes open. Slowly. Cautiously.

A dragon—onyx black, massive, and impossible—is crouched over me like a shield.

Cairos.

His scales fade in ribbons, dissolving from the ground up until the dragon is gone and he's standing there in his fae form.

Broad shoulders. Dark hair falling wild. Jaw set like he's one twitch away from killing someone.

"No one touches the girl," he snarls, and the sound vibrates right through me. My pulse skips. Like it actually skips.

Gods help me.

The way he says it, like he's ending the conversation and murder is on the table if anyone argues, sends stupid heat crawling through my whole body. His shoulders are still bunched tight with leftover violence. His fists flex. Any other sane person would be terrified right now.

Me?

I'm wondering what those coiled muscles look like under the fabric of his shirt.

This is the same asshole who called me irrelevant—who would happily toss me off a cliff if it meant less work for him. And yet here he is, all protective dark fury, and my body is reacting like he just whispered something filthy in my ear.

I don't know what to do with that.

With *him*.

One minute, he's ready to strangle me for breathing too loudly, the next, he's shielding me like it's his sole mission in life. My brain can't catch up. My body isn't even trying. It's like I'm stuck on some unstable internal tightrope, and he's shaking the line just to see me teeter.

And I'm still not sure if he hates me, wants me dead, or is going to tear someone else apart for looking at me wrong.

Probably all three.

"But she's human!" one of the men shouts. His voice has a strange accent, cutting as the glare he throws my way.

"We smelled her from outside—yesterday, even!" another man adds, his voice mirroring the first.

Past Cairos, I spot them. They're both blonde, green-eyed, and sharp-featured. Twins. Of course the universe gave them matching disdain.

"The girl is off-limits. Anyone who even thinks about touching her answers to me."

Cairos doesn't raise his voice. He doesn't have to. All of the fight in the room just… fades.

The twins drop their aggressive stances. The dragons shift back into fae form.

With violence no longer imminent, I finally take in the hall around us. It's huge, impossibly bigger than it looked from outside. Glass walls curve high overhead into a shimmering dome, making the whole place look dreamlike. Red silks hang from the ceiling like bleeding ribbons. Trapeze bars sway gently as if someone just jumped off them. The floor is dark and glossy, but soft beneath my feet, some kind of cushioned mat meant to catch falling bodies.

Rings float without chains. Beams hover in thin air. A tightrope stretches from nothing to nothing at all. And large, multicolored lights reflect off of the glass walls, making the place feel dream-like.

"Does Grendor know?" one of the twins asks. His tone is a challenge.

Cairos inhales once, slow and steady. "Grendor is dead."

The entire room gasps as one.

"You're lying!" One twin shrieks, pointing at him like Cairos broke his favorite toy. But Cairos doesn't even blink.

"He isn't, Kyreth."

A voice floats from behind the twins, and they part as a young woman flips cleanly between them, landing in a crouch. She rises with a practiced grace, curtsies, and her brunette hair —studded with gemstones—catches the light.

She looks like she stepped out of an enchanted ballet: forest-green tutu, sheer green tights to her ankles, bare feet. The tightrope walker, obviously.

"I felt it when he died," she says. "It felt like a shadow lifting from all of us at once."

Then she peers around Cairos and takes me in. Her eyes brighten. She drops to one knee.

"You have our thanks."

"Oh—uh—you're welcome?" Gods. Smooth.

"Hessa, the girl can't even form sentences," the twin whose name I haven't learned scoffs. "You can't believe she's the warrior. She's…" He tastes the air, searching for the word. "… frail."

My jaw nearly hits the floor. Frail? FRAIL?

"She killed the oppressor, Jexen" Hessa fires back calmly. "She arrived in our moment of need."

"She—"

"Enough," Cairos snaps.

The twin named Jexen steps forward, stupidly challenging Cairos, who's got at least a foot on him.

"And we should listen to you because?"

Cairos mirrors the movement exactly by taking one slow step until he's standing inches from the man. It would be comical, the height difference, if the temperature in the room didn't drop ten degrees.

"Because I'm second-in-command, and you forget your place," Cairos says, cracking his knuckles. "Though I'm happy to remind you."

The man's mouth shuts with an audible click.

Look who can't form sentences now, I almost blurt out, but I choke the words down. Survival first, petty revenge later.

Hessa slips past Cairos, who bristles, and takes my hands in hers.

"We're so relieved you're here. What can we do for you?"

The kindness catches me completely off guard. No one ever asks what they can do for me. Not in Xardon. Not anywhere.

"I want to go home to my family," I say, and her face falls like I slapped her.

"Have we done something wrong?"

"No. No, not at all. I just… need to know they're okay."

"You can't return," she says gently. "But I can check on them for you."

"Yes," I breathe, the word bursting out of me. "Please. Gods, yes."

Relief pours through me so suddenly I sway. For the first time since arriving in this realm, I can actually breathe. Someone is going to check on them. Someone is going to make sure Quinnic isn't doing something reckless, and Alabris isn't worrying herself sick.

For the first time since waking in this nightmare, I feel… steady.

Alive.

I don't realize I'm crying until Hessa squeezes my hands tighter, her expression soft in a way that almost undoes me completely. "They mean everything to you."

"They're all I have," I choke out, my voice thick and embarrassing. "They're the reason I do everything. If something happened to them because I'm here…" I can't finish. The thought is a cliff I refuse to step off.

Hessa pulls me into her arms before I can fall apart any further. She's deceptively strong, but the way she hugs is incredibly gentle. Certain. Like she knows exactly how long I've been holding myself together with grit and stubbornness and wants to give me permission to just… stop. Just for a breath.

It hits me how long it's been since anyone has held me like this. Quinnic's far too grown and prickly for that kind of affection now, and Alabris tries, but it's hard when your fingers are gone, and you've learned to keep distance so you don't look weak. And Mother and Father's arms were warm and safe, but gone too soon, like everything else that ever mattered.

But this feels like someone gathering all my shattered pieces and is holding them steady. Like safety. Gods, I'd forgotten what that felt like.

A hideous sob claws its way out of me, unrestrained and ugly, echoing through the hall full of fae who could crush me with one hand. Mortifying. Absolutely mortifying. But Hessa only tightens her grip, like she's absorbing every fear I've been carrying since the moment I woke up in this godsdamned place.

"It's going to be alright," she whispers against my hair, soft as a promise. "We're going to take care of everything."

When she pulls back, her own eyes shimmer, and somehow that makes the whole ordeal feel less pathetic. And when I look up, for just a second, I catch Cairos watching.

He's not glaring or sneering. Just… watching.

His jaw is tight, eyes darker than usual, like something in him doesn't quite know what to do with the sight of me falling apart. There's no softness, not exactly, but there's a flicker of something like discomfort, or restraint, or maybe even guilt. Something that betrays the wall of arrogance he hides behind.

He notices me noticing, and the flicker is gone in an instant.

Replaced by his usual brand of irritated disdain.

But the echo of it lingers in my chest.

"Good," Hessa says, squeezing my shoulders and bringing me back to the present before stepping back. "I'll check on them and report back as soon as an opportunity arises."

A dozen questions flicker through my mind, like how she plans to check on them, with what magic, with whose permission, but compared to everything else I've seen in the last two days, this feels almost… normal. Like okay, sure, check on my family with whatever magical circus-fae nonsense you want. Just tell me they're alive.

The others drift away, one by one, until only Cairos, Fenric, and I stand at the entrance.

"When I said she needed to find somewhere else, I didn't mean here," Cairos grumbles, spinning on his heel like I personally offended him by breathing in his vicinity.

"We wouldn't be able to hide her for long," Fenric reasons, rubbing his hands together. "Better she meet them while we're present to explain, rather than get spotted alone and killed."

"Right. What a tragedy that would be," Cairos mutters, flat and unbothered. I glare daggers into the back of his stupid, broad shoulders. "Bring the human back to your quarters."

"Cairos," Fenric says gently, "there are things we need to discuss."

Cairos's expression shutters, irritation fluttering underneath. "Such as?"

Gods above, he's a prick. One actual friend in the entire realm, and he treats him like a bothersome insect. If he ever smiled, I'm convinced his face would crack in half.

"The plan going forward, sir," Fenric says, voice careful. "The delivery of souls from this cycle is scheduled for two weeks from today. The king expects his performance, as well."

"As he always does. What's the issue?"

"The issue is that of the mortal, of course. We cannot leave her here on her own with the stalkers and guards around. For any chance of breaking this curse, we need the human to come with us. The prophecy says—"

"I know what the prophecy says, damn it!" Cairos thunders.

His amber eyes go storm-dark, and my heart slams hard against my ribs. His temper is a living thing, and for one long second, I think he might actually break something just to bleed the rage out of him. He paces once, twice, jaw shadowed with conflict. When he speaks again, his voice is rougher.

"Leave her here, then."

My stomach drops. Leave me… with him? This man who hates the air I breathe? Absolutely not.

"No. I'm not staying here with you." I turn to Fenric, eyes pleading. "Fenric, you'll stay, right?"

"I'm afraid not, my lady. Cairos has authority now, and the rest of the troupe must obey him, myself included."

Well, that's just great.

My pulse kicks up, and Cairos's eyes flick toward me at the sound. It's just a twitch, barely there, like he's trying very hard not to react, but he does. There's a flash of something unguarded in his face, a tightening in his throat like the sound of me panicking hits him somewhere he doesn't want it to.

I pretend I didn't see it. He definitely pretends he didn't feel it.

"Well, I don't. I'm not part of any troupe, and I don't want to stay here with you," I say, praying he can't hear the tiny shake in my voice.

He takes a step toward me.

"Where will you go?" he asks, soft in the way a blade is soft. "Fenric won't take you in—none of them will if I command it. You'll go into the forest with the wolves and shade stalkers? Risk being spotted by the castle guards that patrol the outer factions? If so, then I say good luck to you; it's been a pleasure. Though if you'll consider coming to your senses, you'll recognize that between a wolf and myself, the choice is obvious."

A spark of fury flares so hot I almost sway.

Between a wolf and myself?

Gods, what an insufferable menace.

"You arrogant bastard," I spit. "You think you're better than wolves? At least wolves are honest about wanting to tear me apart. They don't pretend to save me just so they can hold it over my head later."

Fenric cringes, like he's watching a shipwreck happen in slow motion.

"Fenric, leave us," Cairos orders, never taking his eyes off of me.

Fenric hesitates, which tells me even he doesn't think this is a great idea. He throws me one last apologetic look and slips out. The door closes behind him with the faintest thud.

Silence falls between us.

I dare to lock onto Cairos's gaze and find that his eyes are nearly black, a deep, fathomless shadow that snatches the breath right out of my lungs.

He takes another step closer.

I should step back, but I don't.

"You act like you can't stand me," he murmurs, "but your body tells a very different story." He leans in just enough that I feel his breath on my cheek. "I can smell it on you."

Mortification barrels through me so fast, I swear my soul tries to escape my body.

He can *smell* it on me?

Gods, kill me now. Smite me right here. Let a dragon drop from the ceiling and end my life. I'd prefer it. I'd *welcome* it, actually. My entire body burns so hot I'm convinced the air around me is shimmering. I want to deny it—scream it and claw it out of existence—but my throat won't cooperate.

How dare he say that?

How dare he *notice*?

How dare my traitorous body react in the first place?

I fold my arms so I don't have to figure out what the hell else to do with them. My knees feel unstable. My thoughts scatter like startled birds. And the worst part is the horrifying, bone-deep awareness that he's not wrong.

The internal war raging in my chest is almost as infuriating as he is. Part of me wants to storm out just to spite him, to prove I don't need him and I'm not some helpless thing unravelling whenever he so much as exhales. But walking blindly into danger is exactly the kind of idiotic choice that gets people killed. And if I die here, they'll never know why. Quinnic and Alabris will think I abandoned them, and that thought alone is enough to keep my feet rooted to the floor.

Gods, I hate this. And more than anything, I hate that some part of me is even considering staying with a man who would humiliate me like that.

“Fine,” I grind out. “But don’t mistake my staying for gratitude or a desire to be around you. I’m only here because you’ve made it impossible for me to leave.”

His lips curve into something dark that settles under my skin.

A silent acknowledgement that I’m right where he wants me.

8

CAIROS

"I wouldn't dream of it," was Cairos's reply when I told him exactly why I was staying, and it was said with a smirk so smug I briefly considered discovering whether fae could be throttled.

I thought *that* would be the most infuriating thing he'd do today.

I was wrong.

Apparently, if I want to go with them to the king's circus, which I *absolutely do not*, I need to "be useful."

His words, not mine.

When I demanded clarification, he pointed toward the silken aerial ropes.

"No. No fucking way. Back in Xardon, I work around the mines. You know, things *below* the ground? I don't do heights," I say, crossing my arms.

Cairos lets out a laugh as if I've just told a joke, his head cocked back slightly, throat exposed just enough that throttling him climbs to the forefront of my mind again.

"You do now, Little Wren."

"Wren?" I repeat, confused.

"Yes. You know, a small, agile bird? They're known for their reluctance to fly as fledglings, but once they're pushed out of the nest, they thrive."

"Ugh." I make a noise that is one part groan, one part murderous intent. "Did you not hear the part where I said I don't do heights? Or jump or flip or fling myself through the air? I don't do any of that. And for your information, I have a name. And seeing as I'm apparently some vital piece of your future, I'd like you to learn it."

A look of smug amusement dances in his eyes. "Alright then, what's your name?"

"Naevyn," I say, "My name is Naevyn."

"Nae-vyn?" He sounds out the syllables separately, testing out how they feel on his tongue, slow and insulting. Then he wrinkles his nose. "I don't like it. I'll stick with Wren."

"Excuse me? You don't *like* it? Remind me what your name is again. Oh yeah, Cairos? What the hell kind of name is that? You're like a thousand years old, shouldn't your name be more regal, like Edward or something?"

He lets out a laugh. A deep one that fills the entire space. "Edward?" He wipes at his eyes, still chuckling. "Edward. That's rich, coming from someone named after… what exactly? A sneeze?" His amusement fades back into that familiar smirk. "At least my name has history behind it. Yours sounds like something a child would name a pet."

He crosses his arms, looking entirely too pleased with himself. "Besides, I'm not a thousand years old. I'm barely nine hundred. And Cairos is a perfectly respectable fae name with ancient roots, unlike whatever backwater human tradition produced 'Naevyn.'"

He says my name with exaggerated pronunciation, making it sound ridiculous. "No, Wren suits you much better. Small, stubborn, makes a lot of noise when agitated." His eyes glint with satisfaction. "The name stays."

I'm going to kill him. That's all there is to it. If I have to spend one more second with him, I'm going to rip his head off, and then *I'll* be the one sporting a smirk.

The audacity of this man.

"Fine," I say. "Let's just get whatever I need to do over with."

"Good plan, Little Wren," he says, and I grind my teeth so hard I feel it in my temples. The smugness in his voice makes me want to kick him in the shins.

Cairos leads me to the aerial silks that dangle from the ceiling. Up close, they're more intimidating than they looked from across the room. The fabric looks slippery, like it's just waiting for me to humiliate myself, and I genuinely don't understand how anyone manages to hold onto it without falling.

"Show me what you got," he instructs.

"What do you mean? I 'got' nothing," I say, throwing my hands in the air. Did he even listen to a word I was saying?

"Well, if you plan to come with us to the castle, then you need to learn something. I don't really care what it is, though, seeing you in a costume like Hessa's…" His eyes drag over me in a slow sweep that makes my entire soul want to recoil.

"Ew. No. Absolutely not. You cannot be thinking about me like that." My voice goes shrill at the end, which only makes it worse.

A laugh rumbles out of him that's low, rough, and meant to mock. It grates against every last one of my nerves, and something hot twists tight in my chest. Great. He's out of his shell now. I liked him better when he was silent, glaring, and pretending he didn't know how to form complete sentences.

"I don't plan to go to the castle anyway," I snap. "Your little prophecy? Not my problem."

He tilts his head, tasting my words like they're bitter. I think maybe they'll be enough to finally shut him up. But no, I wouldn't be that lucky, would I?

"Well then, your little desire to get back to… Vardon? Not my problem."

"It's *Xardon.* And you're an ass."

"Not an ass. It's just fair. You scratch my back, I scratch yours." The way he says it makes it sound vaguely dirty, which I'm sure is intentional. Everything with this man seems calculated to get under my skin.

I glower at him for the second time in a short while. But I refuse to give him the satisfaction of my agreement. Instead, I step forward and place the ball of my foot into the bottom loop of the silk.

Before I can hoist myself up, his voice bellows behind me. "Hey!"

I nearly fall backwards, catching myself with the silk at the last possible second. I whirl around, casting an astonished look in Cairos's direction.

"Respect the silk. Shoes off," he says, as if I'm the unreasonable one.

"You couldn't have said that in a normal voice?"

"Maybe. But watching you fall on your ass would be an entertaining side effect, so a chance like that? Couldn't pass it up." There's that smirk again, the one that makes me want to wipe it off his face with my fist.

I mutter curses at him under my breath as I sit on the ground and remove my boots. The floor beneath my bare feet is surprisingly warm, like it's heated by some unseen source. When I stand again, I make an exaggerated gesture toward my bare feet, earning me a nod of approval from Cairos.

I place my foot back into the loop and this time succeed at pulling myself up. The red silk starts spinning from my disruption to its equilibrium, and my stomach lurches with the movement.

"No laughing," I warn, already knowing he will.

A low sound vibrates in his chest that's half-laugh, half-growl. "No promises, Wren."

Gods, I miss him being silent.

An invisible breeze carries through the practice hall, sending the fabric twisting again.

“What now?” I ask, trying to keep the panic out of my voice.

Instead of answering my question with words, the silk suddenly lifts up, up toward the ceiling.

I shriek, scrambling to wedge my other foot into the loop, my fingers searching for purchase in the slick fabric. My heart bounces around in my chest, wild and furious, as the ground drops away beneath me.

“You bastard! What are you doing?” I scream down at him. Though I’m not exactly sure how far down is because my eyes have glued themselves shut from sheer terror.

“Providing motivation,” he calls back. And yes, the bastard is laughing. I can hear it dripping off every syllable. Which would already be infuriating, but is made infinitely worse by the fact that I’m still wearing the stupid navy dress Alabris dug out of that trunk, and the angle up here is… compromising.

“Not to mention, this view is—”

“Don’t you dare finish that sentence, Cairos. Don’t you *fucking* dare.” My eyes fly open just so I can glare daggers down at him, but the effect is probably ruined by how frantically I’m trying to cover myself. He’s definitely enjoying this. I can practically taste the smugness rising off him.

“Oh, fine,” he says with mock disappointment. “Here.”

A shimmery black cloud pours from his hand and drifts upward, swirling around me like a ghostly cocoon.

“What are you doing? What is that? Cairos, I swear if this is some kind of—”

He doesn’t answer.

The cloud wraps closer around my body, tingling over my skin, somehow warm and cool at the same time. When it pulls away, retreating back down to his palm, I realize my clothes have changed.

Gone is the dress.

In its place is a deep burgundy, full-body leotard dusted in rhinestones that glint like stars. The skirt fades into black, shimmering, the tights match perfectly, leaving only my bare feet to grip the silk. It hugs my skin like it was sculpted for me.

It's… beautiful.

Infuriatingly beautiful.

"Thank you," I mutter.

He still doesn't lower me. Fine. If he wants a performance, I'll give him something, though it's probably going to be a concussion when I inevitably fall and crush him.

I hook a knee over the silk the way I saw Hessa do in the circus the other day, but it goes about as well as expected for someone who has never done anything remotely graceful. The silk twists me sideways. My leg goes the wrong way. My hair gets caught. I look like a drunk monkey trying to fight a curtain.

"This is harder than it looks," I call down, trying to untangle myself without plummeting to my death.

"Most things are," he replies. It's shockingly sincere. Easily the least sarcastic thing he's said all day.

Every movement feels clumsy and awkward, like my body doesn't understand what I'm asking of it.

My arms are starting to burn from holding my weight, and sweat is beading on my forehead despite the magical outfit.

"Can't I just, I don't know, work backstage or something?" I finally gasp.

"No," Cairos yells back, as if it's obvious. "Everything backstage happens by magic."

Of course it does. Because nothing in this realm can be simple.

"Fine. Then can't you use magic to make me do this gracefully?"

"I can use magic to make you do it, but gracefully, I cannot." There's something almost apologetic in his tone, which surprises me. "Grace comes from practice, Little Wren, and even magic has its limits."

I huff at his comment.

By now, I've learned to wrap my foot into the fabric to hold me in place, but as I strain to attempt another move, my foot gets wrapped too tightly, cutting off my circulation. Using every ounce of strength from years of hauling shadowstone, I pull myself upward while trying to hook my left leg over the silk. The fabric sways wildly under my jerky movements, and I'm pretty sure I look more like I'm wrestling with a giant red snake than performing graceful aerial art.

Somehow, miraculously, I manage to lean back into something that might generously be called a backbend if you squint and lie. My free leg flails around trying to find the right position instead of extending gracefully, and I can feel the silk digging into my wrapped foot as it takes all my weight. But for just one perfect, impossible moment, I'm actually suspended in the air like I'm supposed to be.

"Holy shit, I'm doing it," I breathe, hardly believing it myself.

The silk immediately disagrees.

It unravels from around my foot like it's sick of my bullshit. Slow at first… then faster and faster. Gravity yanks me down, my arms giving out with the force of it.

"Oh, fuck—"

The floor rushes up toward me. Air punches past my ears. My stomach lurches.

I clamp my eyes shut.

But instead of slamming into the ground and breaking bones, I collide with something solid. Warm. Alive. Arms lock tight around me.

Then I hear that familiar, infuriating voice right next to my ear.

"I didn't think you'd be throwing yourself into my arms so soon, Little Wren."

My eyes snap open to find myself staring directly into Cairos's smug face, his honey-colored eyes glinting with amusement. He's holding me like I weigh nothing, one arm under my knees, the other supporting my back, his stupidly strong chest pressed to mine

"Though I do typically have that effect on women," he finishes.

"You absolute—" I start to say, but the words die in my throat because everywhere his skin touches mine feels like it's been struck by lightning. Heat shoots through my entire body, starting from where his hands rest and spreading outward.

What the hell is wrong with me? This is the same arrogant bastard who's been nothing but condescending since I met him, and my body is reacting like he just whispered something tantalizing directly into my bloodstream.

"Let me go," I manage to get out, though my voice sounds breathier than I intended.

"Gladly," he says, but he doesn't move to put me down. "Though you might want to work on your landing technique. Falling isn't usually part of aerial silk routines."

I try to squirm out of his arms, but that just makes it worse because now I'm even more aware of how strong he is, how easily he's supporting my weight. "I said *let me go!*"

"If you insist." His grip loosens like he's about to drop me flat on the floor, and I instinctively grab onto his shoulders to steady myself.

Big mistake. Now I'm touching him too, and the lightning bolt sensation gets about ten times worse.

I let out a frustrated groan. "Put me down. Feet first. Now," I say through gritted teeth, cursing that these fae are tricksters just like in the faery tales.

"As you wish." He sets me on my feet with infuriating gentleness, but doesn't step back. We're standing way too close, close enough that I can smell that vetiver and mineral scent that seems to follow him everywhere.

I take the lead and stumble back a full step, desperate to reclaim even an inch of sanity between us. My skin is still buzzing from where he touched me, and I have to physically stop myself from scrubbing at my arms, because gods forbid he see me reacting in any way to his touch.

"Again," he says.

"Again? I *nearly died.*"

"But you didn't." He says with a casual shrug. "And you won't, so long as I'm here."

For a split second, it almost sounds comforting, like reassurance.

Then he ruins it.

"Can't have the prophesied warrior dying from a training accident. That would be inconvenient."

There it is.

"Right," I mutter, stalking back toward the silk.

Cairos makes me climb, twist, wrap, spin, and do all number of things my body wasn't designed for. I fall repeatedly, which would be humiliating enough, but every single time, he catches me and smirks like he's laughing at how rubbish I am at this.

By the time he announces we're finished, I'm drenched, trembling, and pretty sure I've torn some muscles I didn't even know existed. My palms burn. My ankles burn. My everything burns.

But I pulled off three separate moves without plummeting, which feels like cause for celebration.

He lowers the silk until I'm able to step down. "You're not completely hopeless."

"Wow." I flop onto the cushioned floor, long past caring what I look like in front of him. "Please try to contain your praise, I'm blushing."

He stands over me, staring down like he's deciding whether to insult me again or let me suffer in peace. "Tomorrow," he says, "we'll work on not looking like you're being attacked by fabric."

"Can't wait," I deadpan.

He turns to leave, pausing at the doorway.

"You're stronger than you look."

And then he's gone, leaving me alone on the practice room floor, wondering why those five words affect me more than all of his thinly-veiled insults combined.

9

RUN

"How was your sleep?" Fenric asks from an armchair in the corner as I shuffle into the sitting room.

The fireplace crackles softly, filling the space with warm pine and woodsmoke that reminds me so much of home it makes my heart ache.

"It was fine," I say. A lie. It was terrible. Every muscle in my body feels like it's been ground down and pieced back together. Apparently, nearly dying, being dragged into the fae realm, and then being forced to perform acrobatics by someone bordering on deranged will do that to a person.

"Good." Fenric lifts his tea and gestures toward the tray on the table. I give him a tired little smile and pour myself a cup. The tea tastes like honey. That alone nearly undoes me. Quinnic risking a broken neck climbing trees for honeycomb feels like a memory from another lifetime. My chest aches. I don't know if he's safe. I don't know if he's angry. I don't know anything except that I'm here, and he's not, and it feels wrong in ways I can't put into words.

"You'll need to have rested well for today's outing," Fenric says.

My head snaps up. "Today's… outing?"

Hope flickers in my chest. He couldn't mean Xardon, could he?

He studies me a moment before answering. "Word of Grendor's death has spread. It is customary for those in direct servitude to the king to be honored at the castle, at Shillhain. A death like this is rare. If you remain here, the guards will smell you as soon as they arrive. You wouldn't survive the encounter. So one of us will take you to the sea for a few days until they have made their sweep. The salt air should mask your scent, and the Tidetreaders may be able to help. Just until we've had time to learn what the king plans to do about it all."

Whatever hope I had collapses. Of course they aren't taking me home.

"Then take me back to Xardon," I say. "If I can't stay here, take me to my family." This is my chance. My only chance. I latch onto it with everything I have.

"It isn't that simple," a feminine voice answers.

Selenia steps through the hall in a teal dress that laces up the bodice. Her sleeves become wide and flowing just below the elbow, edged with white silk. Her hair falls in perfect coils that look impossibly effortless. She is, in short, incredibly beautiful. I feel small, even in the simple, forest green dress Hessa lent to me, like the only imperfection in an otherwise pristine painting.

"Why isn't it simple?" I ask.

She glides across the parlor, pours herself tea as if she has infinite time to waste, and only when she's finished does she bother looking at me.

Her face is calm. Too calm.

"You're not an ordinary mortal," she says. "Not anymore. The guards aren't the only threat. If the king realizes you killed his right hand, we have reason to believe he'll tear through every faction until he finds you. Not to mention some of the factions aren't exactly… friendly."

My stomach sinks. "So you're hiding me."

"For now."

"And dragging me off to the sea fixes things?"

"It buys us time," Selenia replies. "The Tidetreaders owe the Nytherian a favor. They can hide you until the danger subsides."

"We also must be sure you are the one the prophecy speaks of. Renetta is a seer, and she is one of the Tidetreaders. She will be able to read you, and tell us if you are the one. Only then, will it make sense for you to come with us to the castle—to Shillhain," Fenric speaks solemnly, yet tentatively.

My head is spinning, as I struggle to come up with a response. What could I say? That I'm not the one they're looking for? None of them will believe me, unless this "seer" confirms it.

Fenric sets his cup down and stands, hands gentle even as his voice turns firm. "We leave within the hour. Gather whatever you need. I'll prepare transport."

"Why can't I just go back to Xardon instead?" I ask. "I can hide out there with the rest of the humans where my scent will blend in."

"Because Xardon is a death trap for you right now," Selenia says, voice as flat as a cutting board. "And frankly, I don't particularly care if you walk back into it, but your death would complicate things for the rest of us."

"I don't care." I set my cup down hard enough that tea sloshes over the rim and bleeds across the glass table. "I have my family to think about. I've gone along with whatever nonsense you've thrown my way so far. Now I'd like a say in my own life. Please."

"Your family will be fine as long as you don't lead the king's guard straight to them. You killed Grendor. You think Valtheron will just… let that go? You think he won't tear Xardon apart looking for you if he catches so much as a whisper of what happened?"

The words land like a slap. Heat crawls up my neck.

"I didn't try to kill him," I snap. "I didn't choose any of this."

"Choice is irrelevant now. What matters is that you're here, our ringleader is dead because of you, and now you're our problem to deal with. The moment Grendor's death was confirmed, guards were sent here. They know of the prophecy —*everyone* knows of the prophecy. A human that comes along and kills Grendor in the amber cycle, then—"

"Enough, Selenia," Fenric cuts in. "That's enough for today."

"No, wait." My fingernails dig into my palms, hard. "Finish your sentence."

Selenia looks to Fenric like she's asking permission, which is shocking. So she *can* listen to other people. Noted.

Fenric stares down into his tea like it's suddenly become fascinating. His silence stretches. Selenia takes it for what it is —surrender.

"Then Valthaeron," she says quietly. "Then the human either kills Valtheron, or gives him ultimate power. Though, we believe you will kill him."

My stomach drops like a stone down a mine shaft.

"I don't want to do that." My voice sounds thin, even to my own ears. "I don't want anything to do with any of this." I back up on instinct until the backs of my knees hit a side table and nearly knock a vase to the floor.

"They know a human survived." Fenric leans forward, hands on his knees, his expression grave where Selenia's is just cold. "They know Grendor didn't just die. He was killed. With his own life on the line, the king will want answers, and we expect he'll call for the one who did it to be brought to him. He'll tear apart every settlement in this realm and the mortal realm to get it."

His words knock the wind right out of my lungs. Just a few days ago, my biggest problem was Quinnic getting drunk at the docks and mouthing off to sailors. That kind of chaos I can handle. This feels… insurmountable.

"So what," I say, my voice thin, "I hide here forever while you all decide what to do with me?"

"Half of a cycle," Fenric replies, and there's already regret in his eyes. "Long enough for the king's initial fury to burn itself out and for us to deal with Valthaeron during the next delivery of souls. After that, you go back."

I let out a short, humorless breath. "Back to my life?"

"Yes," he says, meeting my gaze. "As much of it as can still be waiting for you."

I don't like that answer. I like even less that it's the only honest one anyone's given me.

"Half of a cycle…" My mind stutters. "How long is half a cycle, again?"

"Just shy of two weeks," Fenric replies.

Two gods-damned weeks, hiding in a realm that isn't mine, helping people I barely understand to stop a man I never meant to get involved with from becoming something worse.

"I don't know how to be what you need," I say, because it's the closest I can get to the truth.

Fenric's expression softens, just slightly. "We don't need a savior," he says. "We need the person who already changed the course of things once, whether she meant to or not."

The room falls quiet again, the decision settling in slowly, not with resolve or courage, but with the dull certainty that there's nothing else for me to do except comply.

The front door explodes inward, interrupting my thoughts, and slamming into the wall so hard the glass around us rattles.

Hessa stumbles in, looking a mess. Her face is flushed, braids half undone, chest heaving like she sprinted the whole way here. Cairos is right behind her, jaw clenched, eyes bright with something that looks uncomfortably like urgency.

Or maybe panic. With him, it's hard to tell because everything looks like anger on that face.

"They're here," Hessa gasps, pressing a hand to her chest. "Not tonight. Now."

Oh, fuck.

The room snaps into motion. Fenric is on his feet so fast he bumps the table and his teacup tips, spilling onto the floor.

"How many?" he demands.

"At least a dozen," Cairos says. He moves to the window, pulling the curtain back just enough to look out, every line of him going taut. "They're going door to door, starting on the east side. We have ten minutes, maybe less, before they reach this house."

My heart slams against my ribs. "But you said the funeral isn't until—"

"They sent an advance guard," Hessa cuts in. Her complexion has gone a shade too pale for a fae. "To make sure nothing interferes with the ceremony."

"We need to get her out." Fenric straightens, scanning the room like he's trying to pick who'll babysit me. "Now. Who can take her?"

"Not me." Selenia's replies. "I'm performing the death rites. If I'm missing, they'll know something's wrong."

"The twins are leading the chorus," Hessa adds, twisting her hair around her fingers. The motion makes her look younger. Fragile. "And I'm supposed to sing the lament. If any of us are gone, they'll know."

"I'll go," Fenric says, already stepping toward the door.

"No." Cairos cuts across him, voice flat as stone. "Valthaeron knows your loyalty. If you're missing, it's a dead giveaway, and they'll tear this place apart looking for you."

The truth of that settles over the room like a suffocating blanket. Every gaze swings to Cairos.

My stomach knots.

No. Absolutely not.

"No," I blurt, my inner voice giving up on staying internal. "There has to be someone else."

Cairos's eyes find mine. Something flickers there—annoyance, probably, but there's a glint of something harder to name buried under it.

"There isn't," he says.

"What about the others?" I ask. "The fae from the circus I haven't met yet? There were eleven dragons, but I've only met six of you."

"Naevyn." Fenric steps in front of me, hands finding my shoulders. His fingers squeeze just enough to ground me, to make sure I'm listening. "None of them know the Tidetreaders like Cairos does. I know this isn't ideal, but Cairos knows these woods better than anyone. He can get you to the coast safely."

"I don't need—" I start, but the words die as a sound from outside cuts straight through our conversation.

Voices.

Not the easy murmur of neighbors, but clipped, cold commands. Boots crunching on the glass. Metal scraping metal as they move in their armor.

Guards. And they're close.

"There's no time to argue," Fenric says, and the urgency in his eyes makes it impossible to look away. "Listen to me. Hessa will still check on your family. I promise. As soon as the guards leave, she'll send word to Xardon, and make sure Quinnic and Alabris know you're safe."

"But—"

"Go." It's not a request. It's a command, spoken in a voice that makes me understand why he has everyone's respect. "Out the back window. Stay low. Cairos will get you to safety."

Cairos moves, crossing to the back of the house with quick, silent steps that shouldn't be possible for someone his size. I want to demand another option, but the voices outside are getting louder now. So close I can almost make out words.

Boots land on the path leading to the house. It's now or never. My choice is certain death or possible death. I consider that certain death might actually be the better option, but I can't seem to actually choose that. My feet move before my brain catches up, following Cairos across the room.

Selenia's hand snags my arm. She holds me there, close enough that I can smell jasmine in her hair and see something fierce and unsettling in her eyes.

"Trust him," she whispers. "He's kinder than you think."

I open my mouth to demand when, exactly, he's ever shown a shred of kindness, but then Cairos's fingers clamp around my wrist.

Firm. Unyielding. Hot.

"Move," he growls. "Now."

And just like that, I'm being dragged down the narrow corridor, my pulse thrashing in my throat.

He yanks open the small bedroom door at the back of the house. One quick motion and he's crossing the room and throwing open the window like he's done it a hundred times. Silent hinges, fresh air, and a clear path into the forest.

Then he turns toward me, unbuttoning his shirt.

I freeze.

He shrugs the fabric off his shoulders and the world briefly… stops. It just stops.

Holy. Shit.

Clothes lie about the shape of a person. His lied *spectacularly*. I noticed his muscles, of course, but bare, he's iron and intention, scarred muscle with ink wrapping his shoulder and running down his arm in lethal lines. More tattoos slice across his ribs, disappearing beneath the band of his pants like they're daring me to imagine the rest. A fresh looking gouge where Grendor's sword sliced him is still angry and red. There's a wide scar cutting across his abdomen, pale against his skin, and I have the insane urge to trace it with my fingers.

"Normally I'd find your interest amusing, Little Wren," Cairos says, voice low and gravelly, "but we don't have time for you to stand there gawking."

My mouth goes dry. "I wasn't—I'm not—"

"The shirt." He thrusts it toward me, impatience rolling off him in waves. "My scent will mask yours and make it harder for them to track you."

That's… very practical.

"Put it on." There's urgency now, real urgency, and it cuts through the fog in my skull. "Now."

I reach for the shirt, fingers shaking. When mine brush his, a jolt shoots up my arm, and I gasp.

His eyes flick up. They darken just slightly, just enough to notice.

The shirt is still warm from his body. And when I pull it on, drowned in fabric and scent and heat, I nearly sway. It smells like him, and I strain to resist the urge to breathe in deeply.

Focus, Naevyn. You're being hunted.

I try to button it, but my hands are trembling too much, the fabric slipping between my fingers.

"Gods, you're useless," Cairos mutters as he steps in. "Let me."

"I can—"

"Clearly you can't." His fingers brush mine away like I'm a distraction he doesn't have time for, then find the bottom button.

I go still.

This is somehow so much worse than him being shirtless.

His hands are big, steady, and gentle as he fastens each button. One by one. Moving upward. Each one he fastens feels impossibly intimate, like he's undressing me instead of the opposite. He moves slowly enough that my heartbeat has time to misbehave between every touch. The heat rolling off his bare chest might as well be touching me directly.

If I leaned forward, he's close enough that I could press my forehead against him. The image blindsides me. Mortifies me.

He reaches my throat, knuckles grazing the hollow there, and I feel the touch all the way to the soles of my feet.

“There.” His voice has gone rougher, threaded with something that tightens everything inside me. He meets my eyes. For one suspended moment, something flickers—want? No. It couldn’t be.

Then it’s gone, swallowed by the hard lines of his face.

“You first,” he says, nodding at the window.

He’s still shirtless, muscles on display like he’s carved from the night itself. My eyes betray me again, sliding down his chest before I snap them back up.

“Stop looking at me like that and move,” he says, a ghost of a smirk tugging at his mouth. “We can continue this later if you survive.”

“There’s nothing to continue,” I sputter. My face burns as I turn toward the window, not daring to give him even a moment's glance.

Cairos crouches and laces his fingers together to give me a boost.

I hesitate for a second, looking back toward the front of the house where Fenric and the others are probably arranging themselves like this is an ordinary morning and not one where armed fae are about to tear the place apart.

The sound of a sturdy fist rapping on the front door echoes through the house.

My heart seems to stop.

Cairos’s eyes lock onto mine.

“Now, Naevyn.”

Hearing my name from him, not Little Wren or some other insult, jolts me into action. I step into his hands and he lifts me effortlessly. I scramble through the window and land on a bed of cool moss. The morning air hits my face, sharp with pine and something wild underneath it.

A moment later, Cairos lands beside me in a soft crouch, barely disturbing the ground.

"Stay low. Follow me. And for Gods' sakes, don't talk."

I make a face at his back, which does absolutely nothing to help our situation but somehow makes me feel better for half a heartbeat.

We move through Fenric's back garden, staying behind the tall hedges. I hear the front door open and Fenric greeting the guards in a steady, calm voice. My heart is pounding so loud I swear they'll hear it from inside.

Can they smell me from here? Even with Cairos's scent soaked into the shirt he gave me, will they catch mine underneath it?

Cairos leads us along a narrow path behind the house, keeping to the shadows like he was made from them. The settlement is too quiet. Everyone is inside, hiding, even though I'm the one they're really looking for.

We're almost to the trees when a shout rings out behind us through the open window.

"Search the house. Every room."

"Run," Cairos says.

Then we're sprinting.

The forest swallows us whole, the glass trunks flashing and the amber leaves tinkling above us like a thousand tiny chimes. This is where Grendor died. Where everything I knew came apart.

We run deeper, the leaves crunching under our feet. I pray the sound is lost in the noise of the leaves that still cling to the trees and chime overhead. I don't know if fae hearing is as strong as their scent, but if it is, I pray the forest will work in our favor.

More shouts. Closer now.

Cairos takes a sharp right turn, pulling me away from the path we used before. Away from the circus tent. Away from anything familiar. Deeper into the glass forest.

"Where are we going?" I gasp.

He doesn't answer.

He moves through the forest like he was born inside it. Every step is exact. Every shift of his weight is balanced. I, on the other hand, slip on moss and stumble over roots, but he reaches back without looking, and his hand finds mine.

The jolt hits me again, unwelcome and unmistakably strong, but there's no time to think about it. This time, I just hold on and run.

An ache pulses and burns deep in my sides, a brutal stitch that feels like it's trying to carve its way further and further inside. My muscles were already a wreck from yesterday, and now the pain has decided to evolve. Every step sends a flare through my ribs, sharp and insistent, as if my body is galled that I'm asking it to do anything besides lie down.

"This way," he hisses, yanking me left.

We crash through a cluster of branches that ring like wind chimes when we brush past them. It feels loud enough to wake the dead.

We run for what feels like hours, until there's no noise but our rough breathing and the twinkling of the leaves. No voices, no shouting, and no other life. Just Cairos and me.

He must sense the same, because he slows his pace to a quickened walk.

"Are we almost to the coast?" I ask, when my breathing slows back to normal.

"No. Two or three days on foot, and that's if we move fast and don't get caught." He looks around the forest, and I can see him mapping out the paths in his mind. "There's a fishing village of the Tidetreader faction at the coast that's small and isolated. We can stay there until it's time to come back."

Two or three days alone with Cairos. The thought hits hard enough that I can't decide if I want to run faster or lie face-down on the moss and die.

"Can't we just hide here?" I ask. "In the forest?"

“No.” There’s no cruelty in his tone now, only grim certainty. “They’ll return with wolves. To lose them, we need distance and salty air.” His eyes meet mine. Something like an apology flickers there, then it hardens again. “I know this isn’t what you wanted.” He glances down at me, and I’m truly shocked to find that this man has the capacity for empathy. “Although being here and cleaning up your mess isn’t what I want, either.”

There it is, that's more like what I’ve come to expect from Cairos.

“My mess? You and the troupe are the ones who brought me here.” I defend, my voice rising unintentionally.

“Quiet.” He snaps. “Unless you want them to find us.”

I grit my teeth. Anger, fear, and exhaustion coil inside me, too tangled to separate. I reach for sarcasm because it’s all I have left. “Right, because being here with you is my lifelong dream.”

His brows pinch together for a fraction of a second, one tiny microexpression that speaks volumes of emotion and I almost feel sorry for the dig, but then I remember the ways he’s treated me, and my conscience is clean once again.

“We need to go,” he gruffs. “They won’t be fooled long.” Cairos starts walking without looking behind him.

I follow him deeper into the glass forest, where the morning light burnishes everything ember-orange and the trees twinkle their eerie song.

“You know,” Cairos says after a while, his tone casual in that dangerous way he uses when he’s about to irritate me, “most people say thank you when someone saves their life.”

I laugh. “Most people don’t get dragged into life-threatening situations by the person supposedly saving them.”

“I didn’t drag you into anything. That was Fenric.” His voice tightens in a way that makes me wonder if the reminder bothers him.

"And yet here we are—together again." I gesture at the forest around us.

He glances back at me. There is the faintest curl at the corner of his mouth. "Try to contain your enthusiasm, Little Wren."

"Back to that nickname? And here I thought we were having a moment of mutual respect." I say dryly.

"Mutual respect?" He laughs, one dry, humorless laugh. "You just called spending time with me a nightmare."

"I didn't say nightmare. I said lifelong dream."

He stops walking. "The sarcasm was heavily implied."

"Good. At least you're not completely dense."

Even from behind, I can see his jaw working, then he continues on. Satisfaction warms me in a smug way I can't help but to acknowledge.

The forest thickens. The trees get taller and any hint of civilization disappears. The air feels heavier out here, even though I know we're safer the further away we get from the Nytherian faction. Cairos moves with the alert focus of someone expecting danger at every turn.

We walk. And walk. Each step hurts, my muscles screaming, my breath coming shallow and tight. But I keep going.

Somewhere behind us, Fenric is lying to the guards, Selenia is preparing a funeral for a monster, and my family is sitting in Xardon with no idea that I'm alive. Two or three days alone with Cairos. Two or three days of survival and pretending that the way he looks at me sometimes doesn't twist something low in my stomach.

We keep moving through the trees, and a quiet truth settles in my bones. The guards don't frighten me the way they should. But being alone with Cairos, trapped between his moods and my reactions to him… that scares me more than anything.

10

SURROUNDED

When night finally settles and my legs feel like they're going to give in, Cairos graces me with the sweetest words I have ever heard.

"We'll rest here."

I collapse immediately and without dignity. Just a full-body surrender to gravity as I hit the ground.

"Thank Gods."

Cairos lets out a low chuckle that confirms, once again, he is a menace. "Who knew a little walking was all it would take to take you out."

"A little? Are you kidding me? We walked for… for…" I try to guess based on the sun, but Cairos's convoluted route has me turned around. "All day. We walked all day."

He quirks an eyebrow like he wants to keep poking at me but decides not to, which is shocking.

Instead, he pulls a dagger from his waistband. Then he slashes one of his palms with a precise movement, and blood beads up immediately, dark against his skin.

"What the hell are you doing?" I scramble backward, my exhaustion temporarily eclipsed by horror.

Cairos doesn't bother answering me. He walks a wide circle around where I sit, letting drops of his blood fall onto the glass leaves. Each drop hits with a hiss, releasing small curls of steam that smell like iron.

"Cairos, what are you—"

"Shade stalkers," he says finally, closing the circle and returning to me. "They hunt at night, and can smell humans from miles away." He wipes the blade on his pants, unbothered by the blood still dripping from his hand. "Fae blood marks territory and keeps them away. They won't cross it."

My heartbeat spikes so hard I might pass out. "Shade stalkers? What the fuck are shade stalkers?"

"Something you do not want to meet." He studies his own hand like he's annoyed it hasn't stopped bleeding yet. He releases a smoky black cloud from his other palm and the wound begins to knit itself back together. My jaw falls open watching it, but Cairos continues on as if this is the most normal thing in the world. "They're drawn to fear. The more you panic, the more appealing you become."

"Well, that's great," I say, voice embarrassingly high. "Because I'm definitely not panicking now. Not at all."

"Good. Because if they come, I need you to stay absolutely still and silent. Don't run, don't scream, don't even breathe." His eyes meet mine, and there's something deadly serious in them. "I can fight four or five, but they travel in packs of eight or more. If the circle fails and you make one wrong sound—"

"Don't. Don't say it, please. I understand." I squeeze my eyes, trying to push away a scene of these nightmares tearing us apart. "How long until we know if it worked?" I demand, already regretting the question.

"Within the hour. They're most active after sunset." He finds a tree within the circle, sliding down to sit at the base of it, leaning back like he's perfectly relaxed with the whole situation. "Rest while you can."

"Rest? Did you not just tell me we could be attacked at any moment?"

"Yes. The forest can be dangerous, which is why you sleep now. You'll need your strength tomorrow."

Sleeping does not sound like a safe idea right now, but I can already feel myself fraying at the edges.

I judge him for a long moment, trying desperately to decide whether I can trust him on this.

He must be able to read the suspicion in my features.

"Do you really think I brought you all the way out here just to let you die? I promised Fenric I'd get you to the coast. I intend to keep my word."

For Fenric. Of course.

"Right." I curl onto the unforgiving ground, feeling exposed in every direction. I let the dark take me. The last thing I see is Cairos watching me with an expression I can't even begin to decipher.

~

"Quiet, Little Wren."

His voice cuts through the haze of sleep, low and gravelly. Close.

Too close.

I force my eyes open and inhale sharply. Cairos is inches from my face, body hovering over mine. His arms are braced on either side of my head, caging me in. His shadow blocks out the twilight sky.

"Shhh," he murmurs, then lowers himself over me completely. His weight settles across me, solid and warm and terrifying. I try to move, but I can't. Something unseen holds me down, some fae magic locking me flat against the ground.

"What are you—"

His hand flies up to cover my mouth before I can finish. His palm is huge and rough, and still smells faintly of blood and the forest floor and something that's painfully him.

"Shade stalkers," he breathes into my ear. "I'm blocking your scent."

His eyes flick toward the trees. The amber has darkened into something almost black.

"Don't move."

My pulse trips. I draw in thin, shaky breaths through my nose.

Then I hear them.

Heavy footsteps crushing the glass leaves. Several sets.

Gone is the gentle chiming sound of the leaves, and in its place, heavy, menacing footsteps crunching them on the ground.

My eyes shift to Cairos, then follow his line of sight toward where he's looking, and I see them.

Creatures as black as midnight, enormous and feline, but cold and violent in every way. Each the size of a horse, their glowing green eyes sweep across the forest floor with a fearsome intelligence that makes my stomach twist.

I count nine.

Nine monsters circling the blood barrier.

One steps close. Very close. Steam rises where its paw meets the blood-marked ground. It pulls back with a yelp that sounds disturbingly human.

Cairos lowers himself more fully onto me, pressing every part of his body into mine. His face buries into the hollow of my neck, breath hot against my skin, sending a poorly timed shiver down my spine. If I didn't know him better, I would almost wonder if Cairos is genuinely afraid for us. His muscles feel coiled tight, and he's still. Too still.

The same stalker tests the edge of the circle again. It's so close, it could reach out and tear us in half. I don't know if it can see us.

I don't want to know.

My pulse rolls so loudly I'm sure the creatures can hear it. Cairos's hand stays over my mouth, his thumb brushing my cheek in a gesture that feels too intimate for the situation. His body is a wall of tense muscle, every line taut.

The largest stalker lowers its head, and its eyes lock on the spot where we lie hidden.

Cairos's breathing stops. I hold mine too.

The creature closest to us bares its teeth. There are too many of them. If they decide to storm the line all at once, there'd be nothing we could do.

I squeeze my eyes shut. This is it. This is where I meet my fate. Pinned beneath an ancient fae dragon-shifter, surrounded by nightmares, with my family never knowing what happened. Tears start to prick at the corners of my eyes.

As if he can sense my panic, Cairos's forehead presses against my temple. His lips brush my ear in a whisper so faint it might be a hallucination.

"I've got you."

Three words. Impossible words. From him.

My heart flips in my chest like it wants out.

The stalker snarls, then pulls back. The others retreat with it, dissolving into the forest shadows. But I can still hear them moving. Waiting. Watching.

I finally let out the monumental breath I've been holding. A feeling like pressure releasing inside my skull overtakes me.

But Cairos doesn't move. He remains draped over me, heat and strength and danger pressed tight against my body. His hand slips from my mouth, but he stays close. His breath ghosts over my neck.

"How long?" I whisper.

"Until dawn." His lips graze my skin as he speaks. "They hunt all night. Sunlight keeps them away."

"All night?" My voice cracks. "You're staying like this all night?"

"Unless you want me to move and let them catch your scent."

There's no mockery in his voice now, just fact.

A stalker pads closer, circling again. Cairos tightens his arms around me, pulling me closer, shielding me fully. Every part of him touches me. I should be terrified. I am. But there's something else under it. Something that feels warm and alive.

"What *are* they?" I whisper against his shoulder, grasping for anything to focus on besides the feel of his body over mine.

"Most of them are fae souls that died angry," he murmurs. "The rage binds them here. They kill because fury is all they have left."

"Most of them?"

"Some are lost. But these are hunters."

The largest one returns and sits at the edge of the circle. Watching us. Waiting for the barrier to weaken.

"Shit," Cairos breathes.

"What does that mean?"

"It means they're not leaving. We're trapped here until dawn. If the circle weakens, they'll tear us apart."

I suddenly feel every point of contact between us. His hips aligned with mine. His hand supporting himself just beside my ribs now. His breath on my neck. His lips too close. His bare chest pressed tightly against mine, the fabric of my shirts the only separation between us..

This night's going to be unbearable and so impossibly long.

And it's only just begun.

11

OUTSIDERS

Morning comes, bringing with it the mercy of the Gods. The blood circle held, and the shade stalkers retreated back into the depths of the forest just before the sun rose.

Cairos did exactly what he said—he remained stationary, covering me all through the night until dawn, then he removed himself to the other side of the circle, leaning against his tree again. The absence of his body on mine left me feeling cold and exposed, but I couldn't just ask him to come back, not when even the thought that I wanted to scares me.

"Morning, sleepyhead." I startle at the sound of his voice, and push myself up into a sitting position.

"I wasn't sleeping," I retort.

"Could've fooled me. You seemed quite… comfortable with the arrangement." That infuriating smirk I've come to know all too well in the past few days plays at his lips.

Heat rushes to my face so fast it makes me dizzy. "Comfortable? There were literal death panthers circling us all night. Comfortable wasn't even a whisper of a feeling."

"Shade stalkers," he corrects mildly. "And yet, for someone so terrified, you seemed remarkably content to have me pinning you down."

"Content?" I hiss. "You were crushing me. I could barely breathe."

"Strange." He inspects a nonexistent speck of dirt under his nail. "Your breathing sounded perfectly steady. Deep, even. Especially around the third hour, when you tucked your head into the crook of my neck."

My jaw drops. "That was fear."

"Mmm." His head tilts, eyes gleaming, as one side of his lips quirks upwards. "If you say so."

"You're forgetting that I was frozen in place," I snap, crossing my arms. "I *literally* couldn't move because of your magic."

"Nice try, but I released the binding once the first stalker retreated. When I thought I could trust you to not get us killed." His gaze drags over me slowly. "And you didn't struggle. Not even a little. In fact, at one point, you shifted closer when I tried to pull away."

Oh Gods. Did I? My brain supplies a vague, horrifying memory of pressing into the warmth of his chest, of my body seeking him out in the darkness. I did move. I wasn't frozen in place.

"I was cold," I mutter, the defense sounding weak, even to me.

"It's adorable that you think that's convincing." He stands and pushes off the tree, then steps toward me with a smooth saunter that should be illegal. "Keep going. I'm enjoying the creativity."

"Stop." My voice comes out too quiet, heat crawling all the way up my neck as I scramble to my feet. "Please stop talking."

"Why?" His tone drops to something low and dangerous as he closes in on me. "Because I noticed? Or because you liked it?"

I swallow hard. "I didn't like it."

He's standing right in front of me now, looking down at me, amusement dancing in his features.

He leans just slightly toward me. "Liar." he purrs. "And for the record, your body fits against me perfectly."

My mouth falls open. "You unbelievable—"

"Relax." He steps past me, brushing against my shoulder. "Your secret's safe with me. I won't tell anyone how tightly you held on."

"I was trying to survive. That's all it was," I manage.

"Of course." He turns away, but not before I catch the satisfied gleam in his eyes. "Whatever helps you sleep at night. Or should I say, whatever helps you sleep with me."

I grab a handful of glass leaves from the ground and throw them at his back. They tinkle harmlessly off his shoulders, and his low chuckle echoes through the trees.

"I hate you," I call after him.

"I know," he replies lazily without looking back.

I stare after him, outrage simmering in my chest.

I'm going to kill him. I swear I am.

Right after I stop blushing.

Fuck.

I follow him, but leave ten paces between us as a statement that I absolutely, positively don't want anything more from him than his keeping me alive until this is all over. Then I can go back to my life, and Cairos can go back to his circus, and everything will be normal once again. I trail along in silence, my legs still aching from the previous day's trek, and feeling significantly weaker.

"There's a stream up ahead," Cairos calls back. "We can get you something to eat."

Normally, seafood repulses me, but right now? I'd eat an entire trout raw if it could get rid of the gnawing feeling inside.

My feet carry me a little faster knowing that food is on the horizon. The sound of rushing water is music to my ears as we advance closer and closer to the source.

When we break through the tree line, I stop short. The stream is gorgeous with teal, crystal clear water tumbling over smooth stones, the sunlight catching on the surface. Small silver fish dart through the shallows, quick as lightning.

"How are we supposed to catch those?" I ask, eyeing the fish skeptically. "They're too fast. We need a net or something."

Cairos doesn't answer. He just walks to the edge of the stream, crouches down, and extends his hand over the water.

The fish stop moving.

Not gradually. They just… freeze mid-swim. The water keeps flowing around them, but the fish are completely motionless, suspended in place like they've been encased in invisible glass.

"What the—" I start, but Cairos is already reaching into the water, plucking out three of the larger fish with easy precision. They don't thrash or fight. They just hang limp in his grip, still frozen.

He tosses them onto the bank, and the moment they leave his hand, they start flopping around again. Alive. Just… temporarily stopped.

"How did you do that?" I move closer, staring at the fish. "Is that… is that a fae thing? Can all of you do that?"

"No." He starts gutting the first fish with a dagger he slides from the scabbard at his hip, movements efficient and unbothered. "Just me and Grendor. Well, now, just me."

"Just you?" I sink down beside him, fascinated despite myself. "What do you mean just you?"

He doesn't look up from his work. "Every fae has an affinity. A particular type of magic that comes naturally to them. Most of the troupe lost their original magic when the curse happened. Now, we're left with performance magic like illusions, physical ability—things that make the circus work. Fenric can project glamours. Hessa can heal." He pauses, wiping the blade on his pants. "I can stop things."

"Stop things," I repeat. "Like… freeze them?"

"Temporarily suspend their movement, yes. Living things only." He starts on the second fish. "It's useful for hunting. Less useful for most other things."

I watch him work. "That's how you caught me every time I fell from the silks. You froze me mid-air."

"Not quite, I just slowed you down, made you easier to catch." There's the ghost of a smirk on his lips. "Though you still hit like a sack of bricks."

"I did not—" I stop, because he's clearly trying to bait me, and I'm not taking it. I shake my head and take a deep breath, much to Cairos's displeasure. "Can you do it to anything? *Any* living thing?"

"Anything with a heartbeat." He finishes with the second fish and moves to the third. "So long as they don't shield against it, which most fae would. But humans and animals? Yes. Bigger things take more effort. A fish is easy. A person takes concentration."

The casual way he says it makes my stomach twist. It's a power I've seen him use for good, to keep me safe, and for evil, to kill, which is a dichotomy I'm unsure how to reconcile.

"That's how everyone stays still in the circus," I say slowly. "When everyone was stuck in their seats. That was you?"

Part of me doesn't want him to answer. My stomach churns at the thought of it, at the fact that I'm alone in the woods with someone who'd do that. But for some reason, I need him to confirm it. I need closure.

His hands stay on the fish. For a long moment, he doesn't answer, just stares down at the scaled flesh with an expression I can't read.

"Yes." The word falls out, flat and emotionless between us.

"But you said you could only freeze one person. Maybe two."

"I said bigger things take more effort. Freezing an entire tent full of people for hours…" His jaw works. "Let's just say the curse made sure I had the capacity for it."

The answer drops into the pit of my stomach like a stone, heavy and sickening, and I have no idea what to do with it. I wanted this answer, I'd asked for it, after all, but now that he's said it, I feel worse.

I'd half-hoped he'd tell me that no, it wasn't him, even if that was a lie. Or even that yes, it was, and he *wanted* to do it so I could hate him properly. But hearing this, the anguish in his voice… sympathy wells up in me that almost makes me want to reach out and comfort him.

"For six hundred years, you froze them?" My voice is faint when I ask.

"Yes." He says, voice biting. "I'm the one who froze them. The only one. Held them in place while the others drained the life from them. Every single time." His knife slices through the fish cleanly, almost violently. "Does that satisfy your curiosity?"

The coldness in his voice is back, the tone I haven't heard since we were in Fenric's house. That distant, unreachable tone that shuts doors.

But I know there's more buried under it than simple anger. There's guilt, and regret, and accountability. I see it in the rigid line of his spine, in the way his shoulders lock tight, in his knuckles gone white around the handle of his blade. And on top of all of that, he won't look at me, which is the biggest tell of all.

"Why you specifically?" The words leave me before I can stop them. "Why make freezing the audience your job?"

"Drop it, Naevyn."

"But—"

"I said drop it." The words are pernicious, eyes cold and unforgiving.

"Cairos…" I plead.

"Go wash up." He stands abruptly, gathering the fish. "Food will be ready in twenty minutes."

It's both a dismissal and a warning.

I watch him head toward the trees, wishing he'd let me in. But why should he? I'm just an irrelevant human. Someone who'll never know what it's like to face the horrors that he has.

For a beat, I just stand there watching him disappear into the tree line, my mind spinning. He froze them all. Every single person. Made them helpless while the others drained their lives away. For six hundred years.

And something about that specific punishment feels personal, like the king chose deliberately to hurt him.

The sound of the stream draws me in, and I cast a glance at my reflection rippling in the current, then back toward where Cairos disappeared, wondering how someone carries that much weight without breaking.

I spend way too long washing up. The fresh water feels too good on my arms and face, removing the dirt that's caked up from days without a proper bath.

Boots unlaced and set aside, my feet slip into the stream next, sending every tiny fish darting for cover. At first, the goal is simply to clean them, but after a minute, I lean back on my hands, letting my body lean into the support of the bank behind me. The currents running around my feet and through my toes feel like heaven. It reminds me of being a child, when Mother and Father would take Quinnic and me to the shore. Commoners weren't supposed to be at the shore, but Father had found a path leading to a small, secluded cove. When the guards were few—when they were needed at the king's castle—Father would rustle us out of bed as the sun set and we'd walk silently to that cove. The sea's waves created the same little currents that are swishing around my feet now, only stronger.

Gods, to have one more night like that. One more carefree night with them. The thought brings wet, stinging tears to my eyes that I struggle to fight off.

"Food's ready," Cairos's gruff voice calls from behind me.

"Be there in a minute!" I answer, hoping Cairos doesn't hear the heartbreak in my voice.

I swipe at my tears with the back of my sleeve as discreetly as I can manage, then pull my wet feet out of the stream. Standing, I pick up my boots and take a step, but yelp when I do. The foreign glass leaves slice at my foot, creating tiny pinpricks of blood on the soles of my feet.

"You might not want to do that," Cairos says, approaching.

"Yeah, I figured that much out, but thanks for the concern," I answer curtly, setting my boots down on the ground and pressing my wet, freshly injured feet into them. The sensation is more than uncomfortable, but I keep my face neutral so Cairos will keep his mouth shut about it.

It takes everything in me not to whimper as we walk over to the fire Cairos started.

"Won't this fire attract things? Like shade stalkers, or the guards?" I glance up at the dark plume of smoke escaping from the dense trees above us.

"No. It's daytime, which means no shade stalkers, and we've crossed onto one of the outer factions. The guards wouldn't look for us here because the fae in this faction don't take kindly to outsiders, and they wouldn't think us stupid enough to come here."

"What?" I ask, feeling tension in my forehead. "So your idea of keeping me safe is bringing me somewhere the locals might actually try to kill us?"

"That about sums it up." He sets a filet of fish onto a broad glass leaf and nudges it toward me. "Sit. Eat."

I open my mouth to dismantle whatever backwards logic he thinks he's operating under, but the smell hits me first. Warm, savory, and absolutely unreal after a day of surviving on almost nothing. My stomach clenches hard enough to answer for me.

We sit on the ground next to the fire, and I use my fingers to pick at the fish and place bits of it on my tongue. It's warm and moist and absolutely delicious. Honestly, maybe the best thing I've ever tasted. I start eating faster, desperate to fill up my stomach quickly.

I chance a look up at Cairos and find that he's watching me curiously. Embarrassment floods through me. What did I look like right now, hunched over and shovelling fish into my mouth? Probably more than a little insane. I sit up straighter, slowing down to chew at a normal pace.

"It's okay. You're starving." I search for any hint of mockery in his eyes, but I find none. "You can eat."

His hot-and-cold attitude is going to drive me insane, but for once, I bite back the commentary. He's actually showing a sliver of kindness and I'm too tired—and too grateful—to question it. I finish the fish on my leaf, and before I can even lower my hands, Cairos swaps it out with another filet. I don't give it a second thought, and I eat that one just as fast.

By the time I'm done, I'm uncomfortably full and somehow energized at the same time. Only then do I notice he hasn't taken a single bite yet. He eats only once I've finished, quick and efficient, then rises to his feet.

"We should go. If we leave now, we might make it there by nightfall."

Cairos stands and brushes off his hands, then lifts one palm over the flames, fingers spreading as if he's reaching for something I can't see. Tenebrous smoke gathers in his hand, swirling with what looks like intelligence.

With a flick of his wrist, that smoke spills downward in a soft rush, smothering the fire completely. The glow fades, and the coals hiss, then nothing.

He does it again, slower this time, coaxing out the last stubborn wisps until the pit looks like it's been cold for hours.

I stare, because I can't not stare. No matter how many times I've seen magic in this realm, it still snags wonder and disbelief in me. I grew up thinking magic was nothing more than bedtime stories and drunken sailor tales. Watching him bend smoke like it's an extension of his will… it never stops feeling unreal.

"I thought you weren't worried about fire drawing attention," I say, not sure if I'm poking him or asking an honest question.

"That doesn't mean we can be careless."

I nod. He's right. Any tiny sliver of a chance more we can give ourselves to make it through this is a tiny sliver of a chance more that I'll see Quinnic and Alabris again.

The day is uneventful. The forest that once intrigued me so much has become monotonous. Part of me wonders if Cairos even knows where we're going. We could be walking in circles for all I know, but trusting him is really the only option right now.

As the light is just beginning to die out, an unmistakable scent hits my nostrils.

Saltwater.

We made it to the sea. Cairos's walking speeds up and mine does too. Relief washes over me. We don't have to spend another night surrounded by shade stalkers.

Up ahead, the trees finally begin to thin out and I can see a rocky cliff-edge.

The sea air fills my lungs, crisp and clean and so achingly familiar it makes my chest hurt. I quicken my pace, nearly stumbling over glass roots in my desperation to reach the clearing, and see the water. To smell the salt and feel the spray and remember what home feels like.

Cairos reaches the edge of the forest first, stopping abruptly.

Too abruptly.

I crash into his back, about to make some smart remark about giving a girl some warning, but the words die in my throat when I see what he's looking at.

Five figures stand between us and the cliff edge. Or maybe six. It's hard to tell because they're arranged in a semicircle, blocking our path, and how close they're standing in the dying light makes it difficult to delineate where one ends and another begins.

They stand even taller than Cairos, which I didn't think was possible. Their skin has a strange, pearlescent quality like the inside of an oyster shell, all iridescent blues and greens. Their hair is long and white, almost translucent, and it moves even though there's no wind. Like it's floating underwater.

But it's their eyes that freeze me in place.

Black. Completely black. No iris, no white, just solid black.

And they're all staring directly at us.

"Cairos," I breathe, my hand instinctively reaching for his arm.

"Don't move," he says quietly. "Don't speak."

The tallest of them standing at the center takes a step forward. The movements are fluid, and they wear seafoam green robes, reminiscent of the ocean.

The tall one tilts their head at an unnatural angle, studying us with those bottomless black eyes. When they speak, their voice sounds like waves crashing on rocks.

"Outsiders." The word is marked by a hiss. "On Tidetreader lands."

My heart wants to explode out of my chest. My hands go clammy and I can feel panic rising in my throat like bile, but Cairos beside me is perfectly still. Perfectly calm.

"We seek the coast," he says evenly. "We mean no disrespect."

"The coast." The tall one's mouth curves into something that might be a smile but looks decidedly menacing as he cocks his head at us at the same time. "As if our lands are merely a place for you to travel to whenever you desire."

The others move closer, tightening the circle around us.

"We'll be gone within the cycle."

"You assume you'll leave at all." Another voice cuts through, keen and cutting.

The hairs on my arms raise. These are the people who are supposed to hide us away for safety?

The tall one glides closer, near enough that I can see water droplets beading on their skin. They lean down, eyes boring into mine.

"A human." Disgust drips from the word. "You bring pollution to our sacred lands!"

"She's with me," Cairos says, and there's an edge to his voice now.

The tall one straightens, turns those terrible eyes back to Cairos. Then slowly, deliberately, they lean forward and *sniff*.

Their expression shifts, and the contempt melts into something worse.

Recognition.

"You." His tone is deadly. "One of the king's pets."

The other Tidetreaders hiss. They surge closer, threatening to overtake us.

Oh Gods. Oh Gods, we're going to die here. All of that running and hiding, and for what? To die at the hands of beings in the place we travelled to for salvation?

"We don't serve him willingly," Cairos says, his hand moving to his dagger. "We're cursed."

"Cursed or not, you feast while we starve." The tall one raises their hand and water begins to rise from their palm, forming a weapon. "You parade before audiences while we hide in shadows."

My throat closes up. There's nowhere to run. I had barely taken notice that their semicircle shifted around, placing the Tidetreaders between us and the forest, leaving only the cliff edge open. We could jump if we had to, but who's to say if there are rocks at the bottom that would kill us instantly? We would have no way of knowing that until…

"Tell me, mortal." The tall one's eyes fix on me again. "Do you know what happens to outsiders here?"

I can't speak. Can't breathe.

"They become offerings. To the sea."

Oh Gods. Until that.

"And you," they turn back to Cairos, "will watch her die. As you've watched thousands die."

Everything happens at once.

The Tidetreaders surge forward, and the tall one lunges, the water-blade aimed at my throat.

I stumble forward to dodge the attack, and for one horrible moment, I think I'm going to fall.

Cairos moves fast, catching me, his body between me and the blade, but there are too many of them.

Everything narrows to a single certainty as they advance: we're going to die here.

I survived the circus and the shade stalkers. But I won't survive this—the fury of these fae who see us as nothing but the enemy.

They're going to end us.

And despite Cairos's unnatural calm, there's absolutely nothing we can do to stop it.

12

TIDETREADERS

"Enough!" a voice thunders from behind the angry fae.

They snap back into their more formal stances as if his words were a spell. The others parting, the figure whose voice rang through steps forward.

"No one shall perish here today. We shall welcome our guests for as long as they need."

The other Tidetreaders hiss, but they back away and disband, walking toward a nearby settlement I'd been too distracted by the mortal danger to notice.

"Harmond, it's good to see you again," Cairos says, approaching the Tidetreader and moving into a deep bow. Harmond bows his head slightly in response.

"How long has it been?" Harmond asks.

"Nearly seven hundred years."

"Seven *hundred*?" the man sputters. "Far too long, far too long." Harmond looks over Cairos, stretching his neck to see me, and sniffing, "And who's this? A human?"

"Not *a* human—*the* human," Cairos answers. "She comes, finally, to conquer the king."

"Excuse me? I'm not here to kill a king. I just want to go home. I'm only in this realm because I don't know the way back, not because I'm trying to fulfill whatever prophecy you all expect me to," I blurt out, adrenaline fueling my antagonistic rant.

Cairos's eyes are wide, reprimanding me with a look, but Harmond's brows are raised, amused. "She's a feisty one, no?"

I watch Cairos calm a little at Harmond's words, but I can tell from the tension in his jaw that I might still be in trouble.

"Yes, she is. She's also *very tired*." The emphasis placed on his words threaten that I'd better play along. "Perhaps, you have somewhere she could eat and sleep?"

"Of course, of course. Anything for you, our liberator."

Liberator? Cairos? Is he implying that Cairos has an ounce of concern for other people? Unbelievable.

"That was nothing," Cairos says, casting a glance down at the dirt. "Ancient history."

But Harmond shakes his head, his black eyes somehow softening in a way that makes them look almost human. "You saved my daughter's life. That is not nothing."

Cairos shifts uncomfortably, and I realize with a jolt that he's actually embarrassed. Like he can't stand the thought of everyone knowing that he did something kind when he paints himself as hardened and unfeeling. "She was young. Anyone would have—"

"But *you* did." Harmond's voice is firm. "When no one else would risk the king's punishment." He turns to me. "This one may seem like he cares for nothing, but his actions speak louder than his words."

I stare at Cairos, trying to reconcile this new information with everything I know about him. Or *think* I know. He saved a child? Risked the king's wrath to do it?

My eyes trace over him almost involuntarily, searching for clues I might have missed. His jaw is tense. His amber eyes that usually gleam with mocking amusement have gone carefully blank and shuttered. His dark hair falls messily around his face, and for once, he's not smirking or looking down at me with that insufferable superiority. He just looks… uncomfortable. Vulnerable even, though he's trying hard to hide it behind a wall of indifference.

He's still shirtless from earlier, and the tension in his shoulders is clearly visible, the way his muscles are coiled like he's just waiting for a chance to escape the situation. The tattoos on his left arm seem darker in the fading light, those three bands around his wrist that I still don't understand the meaning of. The scar on his abdomen pales against his skin. How many more scars does he have that I can't see? How many more stories is he hiding?

It doesn't make sense. None of it makes sense. This beautiful, exasperating man with his sharp tongue and sharper edges, who catches me when I fall but won't admit it means anything, who freezes people in place for six hundred years but also saves children at great personal cost. Who is he really?

I want to ask what exactly happened, to understand why this terrifying creature is looking at him with something like reverence, but Cairos changes the subject with the skill of someone who's had centuries of practice avoiding uncomfortable topics.

"She needs food. Rest. We've been walking for two days."

"Of course, of course." Harmond claps his hands together and two younger Tidetreaders appear from the settlement. A male and female with the same pearlescent skin and floating white hair. "Lynessa will take you to the baths first," he says to me. "Then we'll have a proper meal prepared."

"I don't need—" I start, but Cairos cuts me off.

"Go. You're covered in dirt and you smell like it."

Heat floods my face. "Well, excuse me for not having access to a bathtub while running for my life," I mutter.

The corner of his mouth twitches. It's almost a smile. "Go, Little Wren. I'll still be here when you're done."

The female Tidetreader, Lynessa, gestures for me to follow. I glance back at Cairos one more time, suddenly reluctant to leave him alone with these creatures who were just ready to kill us moments ago. But then he nods once, reassuring, and I force myself to turn away.

Lynessa leads me down a winding path toward the settlement. Up close, the structures are stunning. Built from what looks like coral and sea glass, the homes glow just like the glass houses in Daersbane. Water flows through channels carved into the pathways, and the sound of it is everywhere. A constant rushing that's nearly overwhelming, but somehow feels calming at the same time.

"Here," Lynessa says, her voice softer than Harmond's but still carrying a quality like none I've ever heard. She opens a door into a small building where steam rises from a natural pool carved into the rock. "Take as long as you need. I'll bring fresh clothing for you."

She disappears before I can thank her, leaving me alone in the warm, humid space. I don't waste time. I strip off Cairos's shirt and the rest of my filthy clothes, then sink into the water with a groan that borders on obscene.

It's perfect. Hot but not scalding. Something in the water makes my skin tingle in a relaxing way. I scrub at days of accumulated grime, watching the water turn cloudy around me. My feet sting where the glass leaves cut them, but the heat helps.

The warmth reminds me of something else. Something I absolutely should not be thinking about right now. The weight of Cairos on top of me last night, solid and real and warm just like this water. The steam rising around me feels uncomfortably similar to his breath on my neck, hot and uneven as the shade stalkers prowled closer. The way every point of contact between us had burned, like my body was hyperaware of exactly where he touched me and where he didn't.

Stop it, Naevyn.

But even as I wash, my mind keeps circling back to Cairos. What kind of person does something that heroic and then spends the next seven hundred years pretending to be heartless?

Maybe I don't know him at all. Maybe everything I *think* I know is just a wall.

I catch myself wondering about him for the millionth time today and tear my mind away from the subject. Who am I to spend this much energy thinking about someone who's made it abundantly clear he doesn't want to be thought about? Who deflects every genuine moment with sarcasm or cruelty? I should be thinking about Quinnic and Alabris. About how to survive here until I can get back to them. About how to possibly kill a king without getting myself killed in the process.

Not about the way Cairos's warm eyes soften when he thinks I'm not looking. Not about the scar on his ribs or the tattoos on his wrist or the way his voice changes when he says my actual name instead of "Little Wren."

Definitely not about how right it felt to have his body pressed against mine, even with death circling us in the dark.

I sink deeper into the water, letting it cover my burning face, and try very hard to think about literally anything else.

By the time I emerge, my body feels clean, but my mind is still a mess.

There's a set of clothes waiting. A simple tunic and pants in shades of sea-foam green, softer than anything I've worn in years. I dress quickly, my damp hair hanging loose past my shoulders, and find Lynessa waiting outside.

"Better?" she asks, and I think I detect the hint of a smile.

"Much. Thank you."

"Renetta wants to see you, right away. She's been waiting a very long time for this," she tells me with a soft smile.

My stomach growls a complaint about waiting even a minute longer for food, but I comply.

I follow Lynessa outside as she makes her way over to the rocky cliffside, and a set of natural stairs formed from the rocks.

“This better not be a trap,” I say, watching as small pebbles skitter down and splash into the water below.

From behind her, I can see her cheeks well up in a smile. “It's not,” she reassures me.

We carry on down the rocks until the mouth of a cave comes into view. The elder lives in a cave?

Lynessa leads me inside, and the beauty takes my breath away. The cave walls are iridescent, like the inside of an oyster shell, and small pools of water on the cave floor house bits of marine life like sea anemones and starfish.

What's missing, though, is Renetta.

Then, Lynessa makes a high-pitched squealing sound, like what I’ve heard dolphins communicate with at the seaside, and a woman swims up from one of the tide pools that I thought was shallow. She pulls herself up, sitting on the edge, and turns to see me. Her skin is the same aqua blue as the other and her hair it white. I can see what they meant by elder, as her hair looks less silky than the others, and age has touched the skin around her eyes.

Renetta stares at me for a long moment, water dripping from her stringy hair and pooling around her. Then her eyes widen, and her hand flies to her mouth.

“Six centuries,” she whispers, her voice cracking. “Six centuries I've waited to see this face.”

I glance at Lynessa, but she just nods encouragingly.

I take a step forward.

Renetta slides fully out of the pool now, moving closer so fervently that I have to fight the urge to step back. Her eyes scan my face with an intensity that makes my skin prickle.

“The eyes,” she breathes. “Blue as the sea, just as the vision showed me.”

Her gaze drops to my hands. Renetta reaches out, hesitating just before touching me, as if asking permission. When I don't pull away, her cool fingers make contact with my palm.

The moment our skin touches, her eyes shift from black to pale sea foam, swirling like storm clouds over water. She sucks in a sharp breath, her whole body going rigid.

I try to pull back, but her grip tightens. “I—”

“Shadowstone,” she whispers, her voice distant, as if she's speaking from somewhere far away. Her fingers trace the gray-black stains embedded in my skin. “The devil’s mineral. You know it better than you believe. You can shape it.”

The sea foam in her eyes churns faster now, and when she looks up at me, it's like she's seeing through me, past me, into something I can't comprehend.

“I see you.” Her words tumble out now, urgent and breathless. "Standing at Shillhain. Blood on your hands. Fire in your veins. A golden thread wrapped around your heart.” She blinks rapidly, tears gathering at the corners of her eyes. “I see the king fall.”

My heart pounds so hard I can hear it echoing off the cave walls.

Renetta takes a shuddering breath, her eyes slowly fading back to their natural black. "You are the forge-born child. The one the prophecy speaks of.”

I open my mouth, but no words come out.

“You killed Grendor,” she continues, her voice gentler now as she releases my hand. “The king's right hand, a thousand years old, and your blood alone brought him down." She studies my face like she's memorizing it. “That is not the power of a simple human, child.”

How did she know about that? The cave feels too small suddenly. I take a step back, wrapping my arms around myself. “I don't know what you want me to say.”

Renetta's expression softens with understanding. "You don't need to say anything. Whatever you believe yourself to be, the truth remains—you are so much more. The prophecy chose you before you were even born." She glances at Lynessa, then back to me. "And now that you're here, everything changes. The king's reign ends with you."

Renetta spins, turning to her cave walls and begins plucking small shells and bits of coral from crevices, muttering under her breath in a melodic language. She arranges them in a spiral pattern on the cave floor between us, her movements quick and precise. "An offering," she explains breathlessly. "To thank the currents for bringing you to us. To ask forgiveness for doubting." She places the final shell and bows her head. "The God of the tides has spoken."

"Thank you," Lynessa speaks for me. "For confirming what we believed."

Renetta nods, and dives back into her pool, looking more spry and gleeful than someone her age should.

I wish I could muster the same.

13

A WEAPON

I try not to think too hard about what Renetta said as Lynessa leads me into what must be their dining hall. It's a large open space with a table made from smooth driftwood. Cairos is there, along with Harmond and three other Tidetreaders I don't recognize. None of the people who tried to kill us earlier are present, though it seems that Harmond is the leading voice around here, so even if they were, they wouldn't attempt to harm us again.

I think.

They've laid out food. Fish, obviously, but also seaweed prepared in ways I've never seen, bread that smells like it was baked with salt water, and foreign fruits that I've never encountered, though they make my mouth water nonetheless.

I sink into the seat beside Cairos, suddenly ravenous. He doesn't look at me, but I can't stop myself from stealing a glance.

"Eat, eat," Harmond urges, pushing a plate toward me. "You must be starving."

I don't need to be told twice. The food is incredible. Nothing like the bland rations back in Xardon or even the fish Cairos caught earlier. Everything tastes fresh, vibrant, and alive. Like the ocean itself has been condensed into flavor. Spices explode in my mouth, setting my tongue alight with excitement. I've never had to try so hard to hold myself back from stuffing myself.

"So," Harmond says once we've all settled in and begun eating, "What has Renetta told you? Come, come. Tell us now."

I swallow too quickly, nearly choking, as I cast around at all of the eyes that are fixed intently on me.

When I don't speak, Lynessa steps in. "Renetta saw her," she supplies. "She *is* the one from the prophecy."

"Oh, how wonderful!" Harmond exclaims. "Wonderful, wonderful."

"It isn't wonderful," I retort. "I just want to go home."

"Home." One of the other Tidetreaders lets out a bitter laugh. He's an older male with scars running down his bluish, pearlescent arms and a he has a scrutinizing expression. "We all want to go home. But the king made sure that wasn't possible."

"Vezerain," Harmond says quietly. A warning.

But the being called Vezerain continues. "Seven hundred years ago, we lived in the deep waters, among the islands that float there. The sacred places where our ancestors are buried, where our children learned to swim, and where we were free." His knuckles turn whiter as he grips his fork. "Then the king decided he needed those waters, and the magic that flows through them. He drove us out, exiled us to these shores, and told us we should be grateful he let us live at all."

The table goes quiet. Centuries of anger are built up in these beings, and every ounce of it can be felt, thick in the air around us.

"The guards aren't supposed to cross into our territory," a female adds. "That was the agreement. We stay here, they stay away, and everyone pretends we don't exist."

"But they do cross," Lynessa says softly from where she's standing near the doorway. "All the time. Looking for dissidents or anyone who might be planning a rebellion. They take our young sometimes, just to remind us who's really in control."

My stomach turns. The fish I just ate sits heavy and uncomfortable. "That's awful."

"That's the king," Harmond says simply. "He rules through fear and through cruelty. And those of us who oppose him…" He gestures around the table. "We hide, we survive, and we wait."

"Wait for what?" I ask, though I'm starting to suspect I know the answer.

"For someone brave enough to challenge him." Harmond's black eyes lock onto mine. "Someone the prophecy speaks of, who can get close enough to strike."

Everyone is staring at me now, waiting. I glance at Cairos, searching his face for something—guidance, maybe, or reassurance. But he just continues eating, his expression unreadable.

"You killed Grendor," Cairos says quietly, setting down his fork. Of course, now, he speaks, and it's definitely not in my favor. "The king's right hand. A thousand years old, and your blood alone brought him down."

"That was an accident! My blood just—" I stop, realizing how ridiculous that sounds. My blood just happened to be poisonous to ancient fae? Right.

"Nothing about you is an accident," Harmond says, leaning back and sipping some sort of greenish-blue liquid from a cup made of seaglass. "The prophecy doesn't choose randomly. If you're here, it's because you're meant to be."

"Renetta saw you, Naevyn." Lynessa adds softly. "You heard her. She had a vision, and she's been waiting for you ever since."

She's right, but that still doesn't mean that this isn't putting a wrench into everything I thought I knew. The air feels too thick suddenly. I can't get a full breath.

"The king's Circus is coming up at the castle," Harmond continues, turning to Cairos. "The troupe is expected to perform, yes?"

Cairos nods slowly. "Yes. And she's coming with us."

"Excellent. Then she goes in with you and takes out the king, restoring freedom to all fae lands once again."

"That's never going to work." The words come out flat, resigned. I've already accepted this is happening, but that doesn't mean I have to like it. "There will be guards everywhere. And what am I supposed to do, stab him with a kitchen knife?"

"The prophecy says so," Harmond replies simply, ignoring my jab. "It says the human will be the one to kill the king. So it shall be, so it shall be."

Gods, that repetition is getting on my already frayed nerves.

"Does the prophecy say whether the human lives or dies after that?" I snap. "Because that feels like an important detail."

Cairos kicks me under the table. I kick him back, harder.

Harmond waves a dismissive hand. "Trust the prophecy, trust the prophecy."

"We've been planning this for seven hundred years," Vezerain says, his scarred fingers drumming on the table. "We're not suggesting you walk up and stab him. We need strategy."

"Great. What's the strategy then?" I lean back, crossing my arms.

"The king is obsessed with power," Vezerain continues. "Why do you think he forces us to perform every cycle?"

"And why does he make your people mine shadowstone?" Harmond adds, watching my face carefully.

I blink. "What does shadowstone have to do with anything?"

"What doesn't shadowstone have to do with everything?" Harmond counters.

"I don't know… It's just a rock. We mine it and ship it to the king. I always assumed it was for building materials, maybe, or decoration?"

The table goes silent. Everyone stares at me.

"You don't know," Harmond says slowly. "You've been mining it and you don't know what it actually is."

"Should I?" My voice comes out defensive. "We're not exactly given detailed explanations in the mines. We're just told to dig, sort, and load."

Cairos leans back in his chair, and when he speaks, his voice is matter-of-fact, almost casual. "Shadowstone isn't just a mineral, Naevyn. It's one of the most magically potent substances in existence." He says it like he's commenting on the weather, and somehow that makes it worse.

My stomach drops. "Magically potent? What does it do?"

"It absorbs souls," the female with silver markings says quietly. "The king collects souls and embeds them into shadowstone, fortifying his weapons and defenses."

I feel the blood drain from my face.

"So the king forces humans to mine it," Vezerain continues. "Then fae workers refine it and forge it into weapons and armor."

"I've been mining the very thing the king uses to protect himself." The words come out hollow. "All those years, I've been giving him the tools to oppress us."

"You didn't know," Harmond says gently. "How could you? How *could* you?"

But the guilt settles in my stomach anyway. Six years of carrying buckets of shadowstone. Six years of helping the king grow stronger while my people grew weaker.

"How powerful is he?" I ask, looking at Cairos.

"More powerful than any fae has a right to be." Cairos's lips are set in a grim line. "He wears shadowstone armor infused with centuries of harvested souls. It doesn't only protect him from magic, it amplifies his own power to levels that should be impossible."

Vezerain pushes his plate away, appetite gone. "If there's a weakness, we haven't found it in all our years of trying."

Silence falls over the table. The weight of it is crushing.

"What if we don't try to kill him immediately?" Cairos asks finally, breaking the quiet. "What if we get someone close to him first? Someone he'd welcome into his inner circle."

Harmond's eyes narrow. "Who? He doesn't trust anyone. Certainly not anyone from the factions."

"No," Cairos agrees, and his gaze slides to me. Something predatory flickers in those amber eyes. "But he might trust someone from the outside. Someone who could make him more powerful."

My stomach drops. "No. Whatever you're thinking, no."

Cairos continues, ignoring my protest. "Your blood killed a powerful fae. He'd see you as a weapon. A tool."

"Absolutely not," I say, my voice rising despite my best efforts to stay calm. "You want me to just walk up to the king and offer to help him?"

"I want you to make yourself valuable to him," Cairos says, and his voice is so fucking calm it makes me want to scream. "If you present yourself as someone who can help him become stronger—"

"He'd never trust me," I interrupt. "He'd see right through it and I'd be dead before I could take another breath."

"Not if you offer him something he wants." Cairos takes a slow sip of his drink, watching me over the rim. "The king is paranoid, yes. But he's also greedy. If he believes you can help him become more powerful, he'd want to keep you close."

"This is crazy," I say, looking around the table for support I know I won't find. "You're suggesting I become his… what? His consultant? His pet?"

"I'm suggesting you become his weapon." The way Cairos says it makes my skin crawl. "Someone he could use against his enemies."

"I'm not going to be his weapon."

"You'd only be pretending," Harmond interjects smoothly. "Working against him from the inside. Besides, if you show up at his circus, he'll be curious about you. Endlessly curious. Curious enough to let you in, let you in."

I look to the female Tidetreader, pleading with my eyes for even a shred of sympathy.

"It could work," she says slowly. "If she presented herself not as a threat, but as an asset. He's greedy enough that he might actually believe it."

Fuck.

"No," I say firmly. "This is a terrible plan, and he'll see through it immediately."

"You could appeal to his hatred of the Aelthren faction," Cairos continues, as if I haven't spoken. There's a glint in his eye now, like he's enjoying this. Like he knows exactly how this is going to end. "There's no one he hates quite as much as them. The only faction that isn't under his thumb."

"I said no!" My voice cracks. "I'm not walking into his castle and pretending to serve him."

"Then you'll die anyway." Cairos's voice goes flat, all trace of amusement gone. "I've watched Valtheron destroy anyone who opposes him. He doesn't forgive. He doesn't forget. You killed Grendor, one of his blessed. If you don't turn that into something that benefits him, he will come for you, Naevyn. And when he does, everyone you care about dies with you." He leans forward, his amber eyes boring into mine. "Your brother. Your friends. Everyone in Xardon who might have helped you. This way, at least you have a chance."

The truth of it sits like a stone in my stomach.

"Even if I get close," I say, grasping for any argument, "we still don't know how to kill him."

"You'll figure it out once you're inside," Harmond says. "You'll have access to information we've never had. Information we need."

"And if there's no weakness to find? Then I've handed myself over for nothing."

"Then at least you died fighting instead of waiting." Cairos takes another drink, and I catch the slight wince as it goes down his throat.

I want to hit him, and wipe that unyielding expression off his face.

"I don't want to fight!" My voice rises, breaking on the last word. "I want to go home! I want to check on Quinnic and Alabris and go back to my normal life where the worst thing I have to worry about is carrying heavy buckets, not assassinating kings!"

"That life is gone." Cairos slams his glass down, and for the first time tonight, I see real anger flash in his eyes. Flames behind amber. "The moment you killed Grendor, that life ended, and you can't go back to it. The only choice you have now is to move forward."

I've never seen him like this—so raw. And I hate that he's right. Hate that every logical argument I can think of crumbles against the simple truth that I'm being hunted and there's nowhere safe to hide.

The silence stretches. My mind races, searching desperately for an alternative. But there's nothing. Just empty air where hope should be.

"What does the prophecy actually say?" I ask desperately. "Word for word. If I'm supposed to do this, don't I deserve to know?"

A look passes between the Tidetreaders. Something significant.

"The prophecy is… complex," Harmond says carefully. "And often misunderstood. Sometimes the meaning only becomes clear when the moment arrives."

"That's not helpful," I snap.

"It's the only answer I can give, the only answer." Harmond's voice is gentle but firm.

I look around the table. At their desperate faces. At Cairos's hard expression that offers no sympathy, no comfort. At seven centuries of oppression being loaded onto my shoulders like another bucket of shadowstone.

"I need air," I say abruptly, pushing back from the table.

"Naevyn—" Cairos starts.

"I just need a minute." I'm already standing, already moving toward the door. "Please."

I don't wait for an answer. I stumble out of the dining hall, gulping in the salty air like it's the only thing keeping me tethered to reality. My head is spinning. The prophecy. The king. The shadowstone. And Cairos, without a shred of doubt, calmly suggesting I walk into the lion's den like it's the most reasonable fucking thing in the world.

"You're not alone in this."

I spin to find Cairos standing behind me. Of course he followed.

"No?" I seethe. "You just volunteered me for a solo suicide mission in there without even asking if I wanted to do it."

"I gave you an option," he corrects, and there's something almost defensive in his tone.

"You backed me into a corner with no escape!" My voice rises. "I'm one person. One human against a king who's been collecting power for centuries. How is that supposed to work?"

"I don't know," he admits, and the honesty surprises me. "But I do know that doing nothing guarantees you die. And probably your family with you. This plan is a chance. It's not a great one, but it's what we have."

"Why?" The question bursts out of me. "Why do you even care? You've made it very clear since I got here that I'm an inconvenience. That you'd rather I didn't exist. So why are you standing here trying to convince me to do this?"

Pain flickers in his eyes, just long enough for me to notice, but it's gone before I know it. He runs a hand through his hair, mussing it. "Because I've watched thousands of people die over the years. And I'm tired of it. I'm tired of the circus and the killing and the king's cruelty. If there's even a chance you could end it…" He stops. Swallows. "I'd rather take that chance than watch it continue for another six hundred years."

The rawness in his voice catches me off guard. This isn't the same man I'm used to. He's actually… vulnerable.

"That's not fair of you," I whisper. "Putting that on me. You can't use your guilt to manipulate me into this."

"I'm not trying to manipulate you." He steps closer, and I can smell salt and smoke from the cooking fire on his skin. "I'm trying to show you that you're not alone in this. That if you walk into that castle, you won't be doing it just for yourself or for the Tidetreaders or even for your family. You'll be doing it for everyone who's suffered under him. Everyone who's died in those mines or in the circus or in the factions. You'll be doing it because someone has to, and Renetta's vision says that someone is you."

"I don't know how," I whisper.

"You're not doing this alone, Little Wren. Like it or not, you're stuck with me."

"Lucky me," I mutter, and that easy smirk slides back onto his face.

"Indeed." He gestures back toward the hall. "Come on, you need sleep. Harmond mentioned something about setting up a practice arena tomorrow. Apparently, he thinks you'll need training to satisfy Valtheron."

"I definitely need training," I mutter. "Unless the plan is for me to kill the king by falling on him from the silks. That I might actually be able to pull off."

His quiet chuckle makes something warm bloom in my chest, which I immediately try to squash down. Not the time, Naevyn. Definitely not the time.

Lynessa is waiting back in the hall to show us to our rooms.

"Here," she gestures to a door in front of us.

She smiles softly, kindly, and I wonder if she knows how badly I want to run. How badly I want to be anywhere but here.

"Thank you," I manage.

The rooms are two small spaces connected by a thin wall. Mine has a bed covered in soft fabrics that smell like the sea, and a window overlooking the cliffs where waves crash white against black rocks.

Lynessa leaves, and I'm alone with Cairos in the doorway. He's about to turn away when I hear myself say, "Wait."

He pauses, one eyebrow raised. "Yes?"

"You're not going to stay?" I blurt out.

His smirk widens into something dangerous that makes heat flood my cheeks and spread down my neck and to other places I can't even acknowledge. "Eager to get me in your bed, Little Wren? I'm flattered, truly. Though I should warn you that if I stay, I won't be sleeping on the floor like some gentleman." His eyes rake over me deliberately. "And judging by the way you're looking at me, I don't think you want me to. We both know you've been thinking about what it would be like for me to fuck you since I had you pinned beneath me last night. I felt exactly how your body responded to me. Your heart rate quickened. Your breathing was shallow. And I swear I felt your hips grind against my—"

"Fuck, no!" I cut him off. "Out. Get out!"

The next thing I know, my hands are against his chest, pushing him backwards out the doorway. Or rather, trying to.

His body is so solid, my shove is less like pushing a person and more like trying to move a stone wall. He doesn't budge an inch, just stands there looking down at me with that infuriating smirk.

"Out!" I say again, pushing harder.

"You're the one who asked me to stay," he points out, raising his hands in an innocent stance.

"I meant for you to protect me, not—not whatever filthy thing you were about to say!"

"Ah." His expression shifts, the teasing fading into something more serious. He steps back on his own, giving me space. "They won't hurt you now, Naevyn. You're under Harmond's protection. You're safer here than you've been since you arrived in this realm." He nods toward the wall separating our rooms. "And I'll be right next door. If anything happens, I'll hear it."

"Promise?" I ask, hating myself for needing him, even for protection.

"Promise." He turns to take a step, then pauses with one hand still on my doorway. "Though, if you change your mind about wanting company…" He lets the sentence hang, suggestive and provoking. "I'm just one door away. I promise I'll make it worth the trip."

Before I can respond and tell him exactly where he can shove his promises, he turns and disappears into the adjacent room, and I pull my door shut behind him as quickly as I can.

What the hell was that?

I stand there for a moment, staring at the closed door, my heart still racing. My face is burning. My entire body is burning, actually, as I'm left in disbelief that he can make me feel—

No. I'm not thinking about what he makes me feel. I'm not thinking about the way his words sent heat pooling low in my stomach. I'm not thinking about the fact that when he mentioned having me pinned beneath him, my treacherous brain immediately supplied vivid detail of exactly what that felt like. The weight of him. The heat. The way every point of contact between us had felt electric.

And I'm definitely not thinking about the fact that he was right. That my body did respond to him, even with death circling us in the dark. That some part of me wanted him to stay.

"Fuck," I mutter, pressing my palms against my burning cheeks.

This is bad. This is very bad. I *cannot* be attracted to Cairos. He's infuriating and cruel and smug, and apparently, he noticed every single physiological response my body had to him last night and has been storing that information away to use against me.

The absolute bastard.

I change into the sleeping clothes Lynessa must have left out for me on the bed with frustrated, irrational movements that make changing ten times harder than it needs to be. When the wrestling match is over and I've finally won out against the fabric, I climb into the most comfortable bed I've ever slept on, but my mind won't settle.

Too much has happened. The revelation about what shadowstone truly is, the plan to infiltrate the king's castle, and the weight of everything now resting on my shoulders. And through it all, Cairos. Always Cairos. Him standing in my doorway, saying absolutely filthy things, his eyes dancing like he couldn't be more pleased with himself. Making me feel things I can't feel for someone like him.

Except he also said I fit against him perfectly, and he said it like it wasn't just teasing.

I turn and punch my pillow, trying to get comfortable, and trying to force my brain to shut up and let me sleep.

It doesn't work. My mind keeps replaying his words. *I felt exactly how your body responded to me.* The confidence in his voice and the heat in his eyes were enough to keep me restless and shifting under the sheets for hours.

This is a problem. A big problem. Because in just a few days, I'm supposed to walk into the king's castle and somehow find his weakness and kill him. I cannot afford to be distracted by Cairos.

I squeeze my eyes shut and try very hard to think about literally anything else.

It doesn't work.

I'm still thinking about him when I hear something outside. A sound that makes every hair on my body stand up straight.

A low, keening howl that sounds almost human but not quite.

My heart kicks into a gallop. I know that sound. I've heard it before, pressed beneath Cairos while creatures prowled around us in the dark.

I cross to the window, my bare feet silent on the cool floor, and look out over the cliffs. The moon hangs high, casting everything in silver light that makes the sea look like molten metal.

And there, standing at the edge of the tree line where forest meets shore, is a shade stalker.

It's bigger than the ones from before, but I can't tell if that's the truth or if my fear is amplifying its size. Its fur ripples in the breeze off the ocean. And its eyes are fixed directly on my window as if it knows I'm here.

As I watch, frozen in terror, it takes one step forward.

Then another.

Coming closer.

Coming for me.

14

THREE BANDS

My lungs seize. Every nerve in my body is screaming at me to move or scream or do literally anything except stand here like prey caught in a trap. But I can't. My feet might as well be rooted to the floor.

Something about the way it's moving is different from the creatures we encountered in the forest. They were hunting. This one is just… observing.

It stops maybe twenty feet from the building. Close enough that I can see things I didn't catch before, details that make my skin crawl and my heart stutter. Its eyes aren't just glowing green. There are flecks of warm gold in them. And its front right paw has three distinct bands of lighter fur circling it.

Three bands.

Like the tattoos wrapped around Cairos's wrist.

The thought slithers into my mind unbidden, and I shove it away violently.

That's insane.

It's just a pattern.

A coincidence.

My brain is making connections that aren't there because I'm terrified and exhausted, and nothing in this realm makes sense anymore.

The shade stalker tilts its head and studies me through the glass like I'm a puzzle it's trying to solve. Like *I'm* the predator, and it's trying to figure out if I'm a threat instead of the other way around.

I should be scrambling out of this bedroom, pounding on Cairos's door, and dragging him in here to see this. But underneath the cold terror flooding my veins, there's something else. Something that shouldn't be there.

Curiosity.

The creature isn't snarling. It isn't trying to break through the window. It's not circling or pacing or displaying any of the hunting behaviors I saw in the forest. It's just… watching me. The way you'd watch something familiar.

I watch it, too. We stare at each other. My heart thumps in my chest. My hands have found their way to the glass without me telling them to, palms pressed flat against the cool surface. I'm leaning toward it instead of away, and that should terrify me more than the creature itself.

What the hell am I doing?

The shade stalker takes another step forward. Stops. Its head tilts the other way, and there's something in the movement that feels almost… questioning. Like it's waiting for me to do something. To give some signal I don't understand.

"What do you want?" The whisper falls from my lips before I can stop it. Ridiculous. It can't hear me through the glass. Can't understand even if it could.

Nothing happens for a long moment. Just the two of us, locked in this strange standoff that makes no sense. Predator and prey, but I can't tell which of us is which anymore.

Then, slowly, the shade stalker sits, and its sitting is familiar. Like the first one that watched Cairos and me from the outskirts of the circle of protection.

Right there in the open, it sits. Its tail curls around its massive body like a house cat's.

Watching.

Waiting.

My mind fractures trying to process what I'm seeing. Shade stalkers don't do this. They're rage given form, anger and violence and death all wrapped up in deadly skin. They hunt, and they kill, and they don't stop until they're destroyed or their prey is dead.

They don't sit calmly outside windows.

But this one is.

Time becomes meaningless. Could be minutes. Could be hours. I lose myself in those eyes, in the impossible stillness of a creature that should be anything but still.

Finally, the shade stalker stands. It takes one last, long look at me, and I'd swear on everything I have left that there's recognition in its gaze. Like it knows me. Like we've met before in some life I can't remember.

Then it turns and lopes back toward the tree line with a measured gait, disappearing into the forest like it was never there at all.

I don't move away, though. My hands are still pressed against the glass, my reflection staring back at me with wide eyes and pale cheeks. I look like I've seen a ghost.

And maybe I have.

The cold finally registers, seeping through the thin fabric of my sleeping gown and into my bones, making me shiver. I force myself to step back from the window. To cross to the bed. To climb under the covers even though every instinct is screaming at me to keep watch, stay alert, and try to understand what just happened.

But as I lie there, staring at the ceiling, all I can think about is the intelligence in its eyes and those three bands.

And the strangest part is that I don't think I was ever actually in danger.

Sleep doesn't come easily. When it finally drags me under, I dream of smoke and shadows and three bands of light circling endlessly in the dark.

~

Morning arrives in shades of gold and amber, sunlight pouring through the window like liquid fire seeping through my eyelids. For one perfect, blissful moment, I don't remember. I don't know where I am or how I got here, only the warmth and comfort of the billowy blanket on top of me.

Then it crashes back. These people, the stakes, and the shadestalker.

I bolt upright, my heart already racing. The window shows nothing but morning light and the distant shimmer of the sea to the left and the treeline to the right. No creature made of the deepest black fur. No glowing eyes watching from the shadows.

Did I imagine it? Some stress-induced hallucination brought on by exhaustion and fear?

But no. I know what I saw. I know it was real the same way I know the sun is rising and my hands are shaking.

I dress in the same tunic as yesterday, using the simple movements of pulling a shirt over my head or my legs into the pants as meditation. My mind is trying to make sense of the impossible.

I need answers.

I need to understand what I saw, why it didn't try to kill me, and what those three bands mean.

I need Cairos.

The thought comes unsolicited and I immediately hate myself for it. I don't need him. I don't need anyone. I've been taking care of myself and my family for six years without help from arrogant fae who think they can just volunteer me for suicide missions.

But I move toward his room anyway and knock softly on the door. "Cairos?"

Only silence answers.

I knock again, harder. My pulse kicks up for reasons I don't want to examine. "Cairos, are you there?"

I don't wait for an answer again. The door swings open under my hand, revealing an empty room. The bed hasn't been touched. His things are here but he's not.

Something cold settles in my stomach. He said he'd be next door. Promised he'd hear if anything happened. Where the hell is he?

"He left."

I spin so fast I nearly lose my balance. Lynessa stands in the hallway, holding a tray laden with fruit and bread that smells like it was just baked.

"He left." My repetitious words come out flat. Disappointed, even.

She nods, offering no further explanation. She offers me the tray like it's normal for Cairos to just disappear without a word. "You should eat. It might be a while."

"Where?" I take the tray on autopilot, my hands moving without my brain's permission. "Why didn't anyone tell me?"

"It's none of our concern." When she sees the frustration in my eyes, something like sympathy flickers across her strange features. "Cairos is not well known to us, nor to you. We do not question his ways. We only thank him for the life he saved, and press on."

"That's insane. You let a near stranger just come and go as he pleases here?"

"We know his heart, and that is enough," she says gently.

"When will he be back?" I ask in disbelief.

"He left instructions for your training," she says, ignoring my question completely. "There are practice silks set up in the forest to the east. You'll train solo today."

Training. Right. To learn to lie with my whole body, and fool a king who's had centuries to perfect reading people.

"The forest?" The question comes out harsher than I intend. "The forest where shade stalkers hunt?"

"They don't come out during the day. Cairos thought you'd prefer privacy while you learn," Lynessa says, misreading my hesitation. "The silks are red. You can't miss them."

She leaves before I can ask any of the thousand questions burning through my mind.

I eat without tasting anything. The food turns to ash in my mouth. My thoughts won't stop circling back to the shade stalker and the three bands and Cairos's empty room. I'm supposed to go practice in the forest. Alone. Where that thing prowls.

But what choice do I have? Sit here and do nothing? Wait for Cairos to come back and tell me what to do like I'm helpless?

No.

I finish eating and head out, following Lynessa's directions toward the tree line. The morning is more beautiful than I want it to be. The world shouldn't be this pretty when everything in my life is falling apart. The glass trees catch the sunrise and scatter its rainbow colors in a thousand directions, making everything shimmer.

I find the silks exactly where Lynessa said they'd be. Red strands tied to branches, lengths of crimson fabric hanging from a sturdy bough. Someone's laid crash mats on the ground below. At least they're not actively trying to kill me with the training.

I approach slowly, my eyes scanning the tree line, casting around for any movement. For glowing eyes.

Nothing.

Just trees and shadows and the distant sound of waves.

I sit, always watching my back as I slide my boots off.

I'm being paranoid. It's daylight. Shade stalkers hunt at night—Cairos said so himself.

But I still can't shake the nerves I feel as I reach for the silk.

The fabric is cool under my palms. I place my foot in the bottom loop like Cairos showed me and pull myself up. The silk immediately starts spinning and my stomach lurches violently. I close my eyes, grit my teeth, and hold on, waiting for the world to stop tilting.

When it finally slows, I try to remember what comes next. Something about wrapping my other foot. Creating tension. Using my core instead of just my arms.

I attempt it.

My foot slides right out.

I'm hanging by just my hands now, the silk burning my palms, my arms screaming. For a horrible moment, I think I'm going to fall, hit the mats, and knock all the air from my lungs.

Then I do.

The impact drives the breath from my body. I lie there gasping at the canopy above, at the glass leaves tinkling softly in the breeze.

"Graceful," I wheeze, if only to speak to make myself feel less alone.

A sound in the trees makes me freeze.

Just the wind. It has to be the wind.

But my heart is hammering now, my eyes searching the shadows between the trees.

Nothing.

I'm still alone.

I force myself up to grab the silk again. If I let fear control me, I'll never learn this, and I'll certainly never be ready for what's coming.

I spend the next hour falling. My arms turn molten. My hands blister and bleed. Bruises bloom across my shoulders, my hips, and anywhere else that hits the mats wrong. But slowly, painfully, the muscle memory kicks in. How to wrap my foot so it actually holds. How to use the silk to support my weight instead of fighting it. How to hang upside down without immediately panicking.

Every sound in the forest makes me flinch. Every shadow could be a shade stalker. Every rustle of leaves or snap of twigs could be those glowing green eyes watching from the darkness. But nothing emerges or attacks. I'm alone with the silks, and my inadequacy, and the growing certainty that I'm going to die trying to do this.

The sun climbs higher. My body screams for rest but I push through it. Keep climbing, keep falling, keep trying until my hands are so raw I leave barely-noticeable blood smears on the crimson fabric.

By the time the sun starts its descent toward the horizon, I've managed what might generously be called progress. I can climb without immediately falling. Can hold a basic seated position for more than three seconds. Can wrap my foot in a way that actually supports my weight.

It's not graceful or beautiful like when Hessa performs, but it's something.

The walk back to the settlement feels longer than it did this morning. Every step is an effort. Gods, I wish I were back in Xardon. The long walk invites me to remember life there. If only I hadn't been so shallow, maybe I would never have come here. If I didn't want safety and security that I foolishly thought Blaine could give, I never would have gone to the circus. I wouldn't know that fae even exist, not to mention walk among them. Talk with them. Put my life on the line for them.

It was all so backwards. None of this was supposed to happen.

When I arrive back at the settlement of cool-tone seaglass houses, I feel like I could collapse. My hands are raw and bleeding, my arms trembling with exhaustion, and every muscle in my body is screaming. But when I open the door to the building I'd stayed in last night, a Tidetreader stands directly in front of me, blocking my path.

"Oh, uh, hello," I stutter out, giving a slight bow like I'd seen Cairos do before.

The male fae betrays no emotion and my stupid mouth carries on as if filling the silence with utter nonsense is better than silence alone.

"I'm just back from practicing with the silks. Cairos set them up for me before he… before his meeting. I was just going to get some food."

"We don't *all* believe in you," he says, his voice crashing like waves over rocks, harsh and unforgiving.

I blink in rapid succession and take a step back.

"What?"

"You heard me, human." His solid black eyes bore into mine with an intensity that makes my skin crawl. "Not all of us think you're the savior from some ancient prophecy. Not all of us believe you're worth the risk of all of this. Some of us are content to live here by the sea, shielded by the agreement that the king's guard let us be."

"I never said I thought I was some kind of savior. I don't even—"

"Harmond does. He believes Cairos when he says you're special." The tidetreader's lips curl up into a snarl. "That you'll be the one to finally end the king's reign." He takes a step forward and I instinctively take another step back. "But some of us remember what happened the last time someone claimed to be chosen by prophecy. We remember the executions and the purges, and the way the king made examples of entire families."

My mouth has gone dry. “He did what?” I whisper, feeling like all of the air has been sucked out of my lungs.

“He tore apart families. Killed mercilessly until our homes and our spirits were broken enough that we vowed we would never challenge him again. That was when Cairos…” he trails off, looking past me, and his voice is low when he speaks again. “You’re a liability. It’s like Harmond has forgotten what put Lynessa in danger in the first place.”

I can’t breathe. That can’t be me. I can’t be responsible for the deaths of all of those people if this goes wrong.

And Lynessa… *she’s* Harmond’s daughter?

“Tell them this is a terrible plan. Tell them to let me go home,” I plead.

He tilts his head, looking at me, confusion painting his features.

“You don’t want this.” It isn’t a question, but an acknowledgement.

I shake my head.

“Please. Please tell them,” I continue.

His expression goes from one of accusatory anger to one of understanding. But understanding doesn’t always mean helping.

“Now, I see,” he states, stepping aside and allowing my passage. He brushes past me and disappears into the hallway, leaving me in the doorway, still trying to catch my breath.

I stay paralyzed there, his words echoing in my mind. *The executions. The purges.*

He’s right. I’m going to fail and get everyone killed in the process.

And Cairos, wherever he is, is unable or unwilling to be here while I’m drowning in all of this.

I force myself inside, my legs feeling like they might give out at any moment. Lynessa appears from one of the side rooms, carrying a tray of food.

"You're back," she says, then sees my face. "What happened? Did you see something in the forest?"

For a wild moment, I almost tell her about the shade stalker the night before and my fear today, but something in me wants to keep that for myself.

"Nothing," I manage. "Just tired. Training was… hard."

She studies me for a moment, her black eyes seeing more than I'd like. "You're bleeding."

I look down at my hands. The blisters have opened, leaving smears of blood on my palms. "It's fine. Just part of learning, I guess."

"Let me get you something for that." She sets the tray down and disappears, returning moments later with a small jar of something that smells like herbs and sea salt, as well as a few pieces of seaweed. "Here. It will help them heal faster. Apply the salve, and then wrap them with the seaweed."

I take it numbly. "Thank you."

"Eat," she says gently, gesturing to the tray. "You need your strength. Tomorrow will be harder."

Tomorrow. And the day after. And the day after that. Until Cairos comes back, or until the king's guards find me.

Lynessa turns to leave, bare feet quietly padding across the tile floor.

"Lynessa?" I blurt out.

She pauses in the doorway, looking back at me.

"You're Harmond's daughter."

A small, sad smile crosses her face. "Guilty as charged."

"You were the child that Cairos saved."

"Yes." She doesn't elaborate, doesn't move closer or further away. Just stands there, caught between staying and leaving.

"Do you think I can do this?" I ask. "Really?"

Her fingers grip the doorframe, knuckles white as she mulls over the question. "You're still here when most would have run."

"But do you think I can actually kill a king?" I press.

"You don't have to have all the answers now, Naevyn. You just have to keep moving forward."

It's not exactly a ringing endorsement, but could I really expect anything more than a diplomatic response from the faction leader's daughter?

"A Tidetreader stopped me when I came in," I say.

Lynessa straightens at this. She's interested.

"Who?" she asks.

"He didn't say, but he was bitter. He said something about the last time someone claimed to be from the prophecy. About executions and purges. What happened?"

"Damn it, Feirzic," Lynessa mutters. Her expression shutters, and her hand tightens on the doorframe. "You don't need to know about that."

"Yes, I do." I stand, ignoring the protest of my exhausted muscles. "If I'm walking into this, I deserve to know what happened the last time someone tried."

She's silent for so long, I start to think she isn't going to answer at all. Then she lets out a breath and steps back into the room, closing the door behind her.

"It was about four hundred years ago." Her voice is hollow, distant. "A human woman named Osaja claimed she'd been visited by visions. That the prophecy spoke to her directly, and told her she was meant to kill the king."

My stomach twists. "What happened to her?"

"She believed it with her whole heart. She weaseled her way into Herethia, the fae realm. Convinced a small faction of Tidetreaders and Nytherian to help her, even though Renetta told her she wasn't the one. But the factions that believed in her got her into the castle, not unlike what we're planning now." Lynessa won't meet my eyes. "She wasn't ready. The king saw through the deception immediately. And when she tried to strike…" She trails off.

"She died," I supply.

"She died," Lynessa agrees. "But that wasn't the worst part. The king didn't just kill her—he made an example. Every fae who'd helped her, their families, and anyone who'd ever been seen speaking to them were all executed. Publicly."

The room feels colder suddenly. "How many?"

"Eighty-three." The number falls like a stone. "Eighty-three fae died because one human thought she was special."

I sink down onto a nearby chair. "And you were there?"

"I was young. I was supposed to be among them, because I befriended Osaja." Her voice cracks slightly. "Cairos saved me, though the guards made me watch the slaughter. Made all of us watch. They said we needed to remember our place."

"Gods, Lynessa—"

"So yes," she cuts me off, her black eyes finally meeting mine. "I have reservations about this plan. About you. About whether you're actually the one from the prophecy or if you're just another Osaja who's going to get good people killed." Her voice is quivering now. "But my father believes in you. And Renetta. And Cairos, who saved my life, believes in you. So I'm choosing to trust them even though every instinct I have is screaming that this is going to end the same way."

I know I've pressed her enough. That I should leave well enough alone now, but I just… can't.

"How did he save you? Cairos, I mean."

She looks at me earnestly, her hands wringing in front of her stomach.

"You need to ask him," she says finally. "I—I can't."

She moves toward the door again, her movements jerky. Unsteady.

"I'm sorry," I say. "For making you relive that."

"Don't apologize," she says without turning back. "Just… don't fail."

She leaves, and I'm alone with the food and the healing salve and the crushing weight of eighty-three deaths that happened because someone like me thought they could change things.

I eat mechanically, then spread the salve and seaweed on my ruined hands, each movement automatic while my mind spins. Osaja. The executions. Lynessa, only a child, forced to watch people die because they'd believed in a prophecy.

And now they're going to risk it all again.

When I'm finished, I pad to the door and open it, just a crack. The coast is clear, so I step into the hall and look at the door closest to mine, at Cairos's room. The lights are off and the door is open. I squint into the dark, trying to see. When my eyes adjust, I see that his bed is still empty. He hasn't come back.

When I return to my room and close the door behind me, the window draws me before I even decide to go to it. I press my wrapped hands against the glass and stare out at the darkening tree line, searching for movement.

For any sign that I'm not completely alone in this.

Nothing.

Just shadows deepening and the sound of waves against the cliffside.

I climb into bed, every muscle protesting. My mind won't quiet. It keeps relaying the bitter fae's words.

You're a liability.

Maybe. But I'm also the only option they have.

As I drift into a fitful sleep, I wonder if I'm any different than Osaja, or if believing I can survive this is just another form of the same delusion that killed them all.

15

FLEDGLING

Three days.

Three fucking days of waking up and checking the room next door. Three days of finding it empty, the bed still untouched. Three days of training alone in the forest, my eyes constantly scanning the shadows, waiting for either glowing green eyes or piercing amber ones. Neither appears.

The shade stalker doesn't return, and nor does Cairos.

I should be relieved. Should be glad that the creature with three bands on its paw has left me alone. That I don't have to deal with Cairos's smirks and cutting comments while I'm struggling to master the silks.

But relief isn't what I feel.

The forest feels emptier somehow, like something is missing that should be there. And the room next door mocks me every time I pass it, a constant reminder that he made a promise and then broke it.

On the fourth day, I stopped checking his room.

By the fifth day, the worry has hardened into anger, or maybe betrayal. He volunteered me for this suicide mission, mapped out my training, and then disappeared without a word and left me here to figure it out alone.

Fine. I've been alone before. I can be alone again.

The silks become my outlet. Every time I think about Cairos—about where he is, what he's doing, whether he's even coming back—I channel it into training. Climb higher. Push harder. Hold positions until my muscles scream.

It works. By the sixth day, I can execute transitions that would have seemed impossible a week ago, and I can climb to the top of the silk without my arms giving out. Can hold a split in the air for a full minute without falling.

Lynessa brings me food each evening, always with the same gentle reassurance. "He'll be back soon."

I stop asking when. Stop caring.

On the seventh day, I'm hanging upside down, my legs wrapped in the silk, when I realize I've stopped thinking about him at all. I haven't wondered if he's okay or if he's ever coming back.

I've gone from desperately wanting him here to feeling stupid for ever caring in the first place.

Good. This is better. Safer.

By the eighth day, I'm working on a drop sequence I saw someone perform in the circus, where I let myself fall and catch myself at the last second. It's terrifying and exhilarating and requires absolute trust in my own reflexes.

I'm mid-drop when I hear footsteps.

My concentration breaks. I grab for the silk too early, my hands sliding, and for one horrible moment, I think I'm going to hit the ground.

Then I catch. My palms burn, but I hold, dangling just above the mats.

"Sloppy."

The voice sends ice and fire through my veins in equal measure.

I drop the rest of the way to the ground and spin. Cairos stands there, leaning against a tree like he's been there the whole time, and everything is perfectly normal.

He looks tired. There are shadows under his eyes I don't remember seeing before, and his hair is messier than usual. But his expression is as unreadable as ever, giving nothing away.

"You're back," I say, and I try my best to keep my voice icy, detached.

"Clearly." He pushes off the tree, moving closer. "Your form is better. Still not perfect, but better."

That's what he leads with? A critique of my form?

"Where the hell have you been?"

"Away." He stops a few feet away, his amber eyes assessing. Taking in the blood on my hands, the bruises visible on my arms, the way I'm standing like I'm ready for a fight.

"Wow, okay, so fucking helpful." I can't help the sarcasm that drips from my tongue as I speak. "You've been away—I never would have guessed."

"I had business to attend to," he says, and there's an edge to his voice now, too. "I didn't realize I needed to report my movements to you."

"Business that lasted eight days?"

"Yes." I can see his jaw working like he's struggling with something.

"You could have let me know yourself that you were going to be gone."

"I didn't realize you cared." The words come out mocking, but there's something underneath them. Something that sounds almost like anger.

"I… I don't," I stutter out. "I don't care at all. You're the one who volunteered me for this insane plan, who told me to trust you and promised you'd be there, and then you disappeared!"

"I left you with training," he says, his voice hard. "With shelter and food and people to help you. What more do you want from me?"

"I want you to keep your promises. I'm a human in a land of all-powerful fae, some of whom want to kill me, and what do you do? Leave me by myself. Do you have any idea how asinine that is?" He looks surprised by my tirade, but I've started this and can't seem to get my mouth to stop moving now. "I want you to stop treating me like I'm a burden you're forced to tolerate. I want you to stop keeping me in the dark about whatever plans you have. I just want you to—"

"What?" He steps closer, his eyes blazing. "Say it. What do you want?"

I want you to let me know you're safe. I want to know I'm not doing this alone. I want to understand why I spent eight days being angry instead of relieved that you were gone.

But I don't say any of that.

"I want to know where you went," I say instead, my voice dropping as I take a step closer to him, trying not to get lost in his eyes. Those warm, amber eyes. "Wait… do you have a black eye?"

The proximity allowed me to finally notice hues of purple and blue blooming on his eyelid and under his right eye.

Cairos moves his fingertips to touch the puffy skin above his cheekbone as if this were news to him.

"I haven't been sleeping well, that's all." He drops his hand back to his side.

"Bullshit. I know a black eye when I see one."

It was true. I easily recognized a black eye because the guards at the mines wouldn't hesitate to give me or anyone else one if they felt we were out of line.

"You're wrong." The words are final.

"Excuse me?"

"I think you might be getting a little too comfortable, Naevyn. Where I go and what I do is *my* business, not yours." His expression has gone cold now, shuttered. "You're not my keeper."

Embarrassment floods my cheeks. "I never said I was."

"Then stop acting like it." He turns away, pressing his palms to his eyes. "Prepare yourself. We leave for the castle in the morning."

Disbelief floods through me. "What?"

"The king's Circus. It's been moved up to tomorrow. You'll need to be ready to leave first thing."

"Tomorrow?" My mind reels. "We can't even make it back by then! It took two days just to get here."

"Dragonback," Cairos answers. "Time to fly, Little Wren."

"Dragonback?" The word comes out strangled. "Fly as in... in the sky?"

"That's generally what dragons do, yes." He's already turning away, dismissing me. "Be ready at dawn."

"Wait—no. Absolutely not." I step forward, my heart already starting to pound. "I don't do heights. I told you that."

"You're training on aerial silks."

"That's entirely different and you know it. Those are maybe ten feet off the ground. You're talking about..." I can't even finish the sentence. The thought of being hundreds of feet in the air with nothing but Cairos's word that he won't drop me like an anchor makes my stomach turn.

"You'll be fine." He says it like it's a fact, not a reassurance.

His blank expression is inciting. Even if I *did* plan to allow him to carry me on his back to Shillhain—which I don't—I would require training first so I don't lose my balance and fall off.

A thought crashes over me.

"Wait... why couldn't we have flown here?" My voice is low, accusatory. I jab an angry finger in his direction. "Why make me walk for two days and put us in danger of the shade stalkers if you could have just flown us here in a few short hours?"

“Maybe because that amount of magic would have alerted the guards to where we were.” He waves off my hand. “Besides, the fledgling wasn’t ready to fly. But now you are.”

“I’m not riding you.”

The words hang in the air for a beat before I realize how they sound. Cairos’s eyebrow lifts, something dangerous flickering in his expression.

“As a dragon,” I add quickly. “ I am not riding a dragon to get to the castle. Not yours, not anyone else’s.”

I’m making it worse. I can tell by the way his smirk threatens to break through, but to my surprise, he keeps whatever dirty, vile comment he was planning to himself.

“Yes, you are.”

“No, I’m not.”

“Would you prefer I force you?” Cairos’s question comes out dangerous, laced with challenge. “Because I will. I’ll throw you over my shoulder like a sack of rice if that’s what it takes.”

I can see in his eyes that he means it. That he’ll physically force me onto his back if I refuse. The absolute bastard.

“I hate you,” I spit.

“I’m aware,” he says, walking away. “First light, Naevyn. Don’t make me come find you.”

He disappears into the trees, leaving me standing alone in the clearing with my heart racing.

“Argh!” I let out a frustrated sound that bounces off the leaves around me. Leaves that I hadn’t even realized until now had begun to take on a slight bluish tone.

I’m going to die. Not from the king or his guards or some elaborate execution. I’m going to die because I’ll panic mid-flight and fall off and splatter across the forest below like a dropped melon.

As I make my way back to the settlement, my mind is already spinning through every possible way this could go wrong. Heights. I don’t do heights. Never have. Even climbing the silks makes my stomach flip all around, and that's with solid ground right beneath me.

But what choice do I have? Stay here and wait for the guards to find me? Put Quinnic and Alabris at risk?

No. As terrifying as flying sounds, it's still better than the alternative.

The sun sets, painting everything in shades of orange and gold that would be beautiful if I weren't so busy trying not to throw up.

Lynessa meets me at the door with food I can't imagine eating.

"You're leaving tomorrow," she says.

"Apparently." I take the tray anyway, more to have something to do with my hands than because I'm hungry. "Did you know? About the circus being moved up?"

"We got word yesterday." She watches me carefully as I take a nibble off of a piece of bread. "Cairos will get you there safely."

"On dragonback." The words taste bitter.

"Ah." Understanding flickers across her face. "You're afraid."

"No more afraid than any normal person would be of being carried above the treetops on a near-stranger's back with nothing to hold me there but Cairos's promise that he won't let me fall, which doesn't exactly inspire confidence."

"He *won't* let you fall," Lynessa says, and there's certainty in her voice that I wish I could borrow. "Whatever else Cairos is, he keeps his word when it matters."

"Does he?" I can't keep the bitterness out of my voice as I mutter, "Because he promised he'd be in the next room and then disappeared for over a week."

"But he came back, Naevyn. He always comes back."

I want to believe her. I want with every piece of my soul to trust that Cairos won't drop me mid-flight just to prove a point or teach me some lesson about self-reliance.

But trust isn't something that comes easy to me. Not anymore.

"I should sleep," I say, standing abruptly. "First light comes early."

Lynessa nods, letting me escape. I make my way to my room and stare at the few belongings I have. The seafoam clothes the Tidetreaders gifted me, and the healing salve for my hands. Nothing else is really mine.

I change into the sleeping clothes and climb into bed, but sleep feels impossible with the window drawing me in like it always does. I allow myself to sneak out of bed and press my hands against the glass, staring out at the darkness, and searching for movement again.

Nothing.

The shade stalker hasn't returned since that first night. Whatever it wanted, whatever reason it had for watching me, it's gone now.

I lie back down and close my eyes. I drift in and out through the night, caught between exhaustion and anxiety, until the first hints of dawn start creeping through the window.

First light.

Time to fly.

Gods help me.

16

VALTHAERON

"Up," the low voice rumbles.

"I can't," I squeak.

Staring up at the massive, scaly form in front of me is more daunting than I even imagined it to be. His iridescent black scales are enormous up close. His giant nostrils flare with each breath that he takes.

Many Tidetreader fae stand watching, waiting for me to climb aboard and fly off into the sunrise, but that's not at all what's happening. Even if I wanted to, getting up onto the beast's back would be an endeavor all on its own.

"You can," Cairos booms back. His voice becomes a deep growl when he's in his dragon form, a tone that sends shivers down my spine.

Glancing around at the faces of the fae surrounding me with the black eyes I've grown accustomed to, I see an array of expressions from disbelief to anger, to encouragement.

Lynessa's is one of encouragement, of course. She had been a warm light in the darkness during our time here and I had thanked her profusely for her kindness before leaving, even though I may not have shown it while I was here. She had bowed her head and given me one of the many necklaces she wore, made of tiny seashells in vibrant colours.

“For courage,” she said as she looped the string over my head and around my neck. I touched the shell at the end, feeling its shiny surface that had been scrubbed clean by the sea. The hug she gave was tight, all-encompassing, as if she was trying to say all of the words she wanted to but couldn’t. *Good luck. I’ll be thinking of you. Please don’t die.*

Harmond, too, was there. He was thankful as well, but his regards were directed at Cairos.

“You are forever welcome here,” Harmond told him, though several other Tidetreaders let out tsks of disapproval.

Cairos took Harmond’s hands in his own and gave a slight nod before turning and walking to the clearing between the forest and the trees. He straightened, then began the transformation to his dragon form, wowing the Tidetreaders with the brilliant display of his scales appearing little by little, his size increasing until he became the vast creature that stands in front of me now.

We look like we should be at the circus, with Cairos in this form and me wearing the burgundy performance leotard Cairos conjured for me, but I feel anything but performance-ready right now. I feel… small.

I try to climb his side, gripping onto the scales, but they’re more slippery than I expected. Not only that, but touching him, knowing that Cairos is in there, feels… intimate. Wrong.

I don’t need to try anything else, though. Cairos sees my failure and lets out what sounds like an exasperated breath, swinging his tail around behind me and lifting me up with the large, flattened tip of it, dropping me unceremoniously down onto his back.

Holy shit.

His back may be only the height of a house, but it may as well be a mountain. For a moment, I feel myself begin to hyperventilate. We haven't even taken flight yet, and already, I'm panicking about the height.

"Breathe," Cairos commands. "Feel my breath."

I can. When I focus on the sensation of him beneath me, I can feel his breath. I take a moment to let my own breathing synchronize with his.

In, out. In, out. In, out.

It feels natural to do that. Before I know it, I'm not even trying anymore, and the two of us are completely in sync.

In, out. In, out. In—up?

Holy fucking Gods. We're flying. His wings beat around me, sending avalanches of air tumbling away from us, pressing us further and further into the sky.

I fall forward onto him, each of my arms spreading as wide as they can, looking for purchase. The slick scales made it difficult to grasp, but I dig my nails in as far as I can, trying to hold on.

I didn't even realize I had my eyes closed until the air passing by them pushed its way under my sealed eyelids. In a moment of bravery, I open them. First one, then the other, and…

It's beautiful. Breathtaking. To my left, the sun is barely past the horizon, a giant, yellow-orange fireball casting the most incredible glow across the ripples of the water. I can see shadows of sea creatures just beneath the surface. Tidetreaders wading into the shallows of the water, waving up at us. To my right, I see the forest with its sapphire blue leaves gleaming green in the sunlight.

The wind continues to rush past my ears. I realize that the longer we fly, the more comfortable I become. Suddenly, I'm not gripping on for dear life, belly flat against Cairos's back. Instead, I'm sitting up little by little, trying to take in every ounce of this impossible view. I want to ask Cairos about the different things I'm seeing—about small settlements scattered throughout clearings in the trees, and the things moving in the rivers below, too large and serpentine to be fish—but I know the rushing wind wouldn't allow for conversation.

I'm pulled back to the feel of him beneath my seat, breathing in and out, in and out, providing a comfort that I didn't realize I needed.

Minutes pass, or maybe hours. It's hard to tell. My only chance at timekeeping is watching the sun as it rises and moves higher into the sky, but the longer we fly, the more turned around I get and the more unsure I am of which direction the sun rose from in the first place.

The air up here smells crisp and clean—not salty like the ocean, and not filled with dust and dying hope like Xardon either.

Balancing is easier than I expected, too. Cairos shifts and maneuvers like he's carried people on his back before during flight, banking a little further to the left or right when he turns, so I keep my seat.

We've ridden in silence thus far, but I can't help the questions that bubble up and come tumbling out of me.

"You said the prophecy calls for the king's death in the emerald season, but it's sapphire now. What are we supposed to do if Valthaeron does let us into the castle? Just wait and twiddle our thumbs?"

"Yes," his low voice grumbles. I'm not sure if he gives me short answers when in his dragon form because he can't do anything else, or doesn't want to. Still, it's better than no answer at all.

"What if he kills me first?" I ask.

Silence.

Then, "I won't let him."

That's it. That's all Cairos has to say—that he will single-handedly prevent a thousand-year-old fae king from killing me.

I hate to admit it, but somehow that does do a little to settle the acid that's burning at my insides. I've hardly seen Cairos fight, but if there were anyone I would trust to protect me here, it would be him.

When the sun is just beginning to tilt a little past halfway in the sky, I finally see it. A settlement larger than any I've seen yet in this realm. Houses are lined up in organized rows with what looks like markets in between them. We fly lower as the castle in the center of the town grows closer.

When we finally fly near enough to the castle that it comes into clear view, the air leaves my lungs in a rush. Not because of its size—though Gods, it's grand—but because of what it's made from. Shadowstone. The same mineral I've hauled bucket after bucket of for six years, now transformed into something I can barely comprehend. Stones that must weigh thousands of pounds each are stacked impossibly high, forming walls and towers and spires. The architecture is second to none with smooth curves and sharp angles that work together to form a structure unlike anything I've ever seen or thought possible.

This level of wealth is completely unfathomable to me. My family's home in Xardon could fit inside one of those towers a hundred times over. We had cracks in the walls that let the rain in, holes in the roof we stuffed with rags, two rooms for three people, and all our worldly possessions. But this? This castle looks impenetrable. Seamless. Not a crack, not a gap, not a single weakness. No army would breach these walls to challenge them. No rain would seep through to make them wet. No cold would find its way inside.

And I helped build it. Every bucket of shadowstone I carried, every stone I sorted all came here to this.

A tangle of nerves sets up camp in the pit of my stomach as I think about what we need to do. Somehow, I'm supposed to make my way inside this impenetrable fortress. But how? My inferiority slams into me. I'm not a guard or a warrior or anything. I'm not even fae. I'm… nothing.

As if Cairos can read my thoughts, the dragon beneath me lets out a reassuring hum, one that vibrates through my legs and up to my core, untangling the knot just a little. He doesn't say anything. He doesn't have to. He knows that everything in my life has been a culmination up to this. All of the shadowstone I've lifted, all of the care and effort I've put into Quinnic and Alabris—it's what's going to drive me forward and give me strength, both physically and emotionally, to do what needs to be done.

Cairos starts to lower to the ground, preparing to land.

I say a small prayer to the Gods I'm not sure I believe in anymore that I won't be discovered by these cruel fae. It doesn't bring me the peace or reassurance that I had hoped.

As he flies around the side of the castle, the circus tent comes into view. It's already set up, just waiting for the performers to come inside.

Cairos lands just outside the tent. I swing one leg over and slide down with my belly to his scales until my feet hit the ground. The moment they do, he transforms, the scales disappearing into the air, leaving behind his fae form.

"See? That wasn't so bad," Cairos says as he straightens himself, preparing for what's about to come.

What *is* about to come? I don't really know. A circus, yes, but what else? What comes after that? Surely the king will notice my presence. What do I say when he asks who I am? How I'm here? All of the questions I don't have answers to make my head ache.

"You'll stay with me, won't you?" I look up at Cairos, begging him with my eyes. Pleading with him not to leave me alone. "I don't think I can do this."

"You can. You're the one the prophecy speaks of. I can feel it now."

Feel it? I know that was supposed to be reassuring, but somehow I still feel small and inadequate. Every nerve in my body is screaming at me to run. My legs want to carry me far, far away from this place. Back to Xardon. Back to my home.

But I don't let my nerves decide. I follow Cairos as he strides into the tent.

I remember the sheer size of the tent from that first night, the inside far larger than it should be, but from down here on the ground, it feels even bigger. The seats are filled, which I didn't expect. I knew this was the king's Circus, that he would be in attendance along with some of the guards, but I didn't realize that there would be so many other spectators. It seems that another faction—probably the Solmeren, if I remember correctly from what Harmond told me about the faithful fae that reside around the castle—is in attendance too.

Shit.

I feel like I'm going to vomit. I feel like my insides are going to snake their way up my throat. I feel…

"It's time," Cairos instructs.

I see the red silks that I've become so familiar with dangling ominously from one side of the tent.

"Deep breaths," he reminds me, then strides toward the center of the tent.

I had been waiting for someone else to come and announce, for a ringmaster, but then it hits me. Grendor did the announcing.

And Grendor is dead.

Oh my Gods. Cairos is going to announce.

Before I can fully process what that means, he's already climbing onto the platform—the same platform where I stood frozen just days ago, frozen in place by Grendor, waiting for death that never came. How merciful that death would have been compared to this. To standing here now, about to perform for a king who wants me dead, in a plan that has more holes than a fishing net.

"Ladies and gentlemen, welcome to the greatest show on earth!"

The audience cheers as if this circus is of the utmost importance. I scan their faces and can't find a hint of sadness or remorse—only amusement. Do they know what the circus is? What it *really* is?

Finally, I see the king. He's hard to miss once I spot all of those guards in their blood-red uniforms surrounding him.

Everything about Valtheron screams danger. His eyes are hard and dark, nearly black, empty of warmth or mercy. He's older than I expected, his beard heavily peppered with gray, silver threading through the dark hair at his temples and crown. But the age doesn't diminish him. It makes him more terrifying somehow, like a wolf that's survived countless hunts and learned every trick. The power radiating off him is palpable even from here, a pressure in the air that makes my skin prickle and my instincts scream to run.

I force myself to look away and stop cataloging all the ways he could kill me and start thinking about the one thing that might keep me alive—the performance. I need to be perfect up there. Light on my feet, strong with my hands, graceful in every movement. If I falter, if fear makes me sloppy, it's over. The fall will kill me, or the king's suspicion will. Either way, I'll be dead before the night is through. So I take a breath, then another, and prepare to put on the show of a lifetime.

The troupe is all here, along with some other performers I recognize from the first circus. I only now realize that the performers I don't know wear blood-red gorgets to cover their necks that match those of the kings guard. Are they guards disguised as performers, perhaps, who ensure everything goes as planned? That surely doesn't do anything to calm my nerves.

One by one, Cairos announces them with the practiced showmanship of someone who's performed for centuries. Selenia, with her pink dragon form. The twins, inseparable even in their introductions. Fenric and his acts of strength. Hessa, the trapeze artist who makes flying look effortless. Each name is met with applause from the audience, the sound washing over me like waves I could drown in. A few others are announced. Presumably, the guards.

And then he comes to me.

"And finally," Cairos's voice rings out across the tent, clear and confident, "making her debut performance with us tonight—Naevyn, expert on the aerial silks!"

My name. He used my real name. In front of the king. In front of everyone.

My eyes snap to Valthaeron before I can stop them, panic overriding every instinct that tells me not to draw his attention. He's already watching me, his black eyes fixed on my face with an intensity that makes my skin crawl. He's not applauding like the rest of the audience. He's studying me like I'm something that doesn't quite fit.

Then he leans toward one of the blood-red guards standing at his side. His lips move, words I can't hear from this distance. The guard nods once, his hand moving to rest on the hilt of his sword.

My blood turns to ice.

Expert. The word echoes in my head, mocking me. Expert? Is he completely insane? I've been training for barely over a week. I can hold positions without falling, yes, but expert? I'm one wrong move away from plummeting to my death in front of the king and his entire court. And now Valtheron is whispering to his guards, probably ordering them to investigate me the moment this performance ends.

But it doesn't matter what's true. This is the king's Circus, the highest stakes performance of my life. If I don't sell this, if I show even a flicker of doubt, the entire plan crumbles. Everything we've risked, everything we've planned, gone because I couldn't pretend to be confident.

So I force my teeth together and walk. Each step toward the center of the tent feels like walking toward an execution, but I keep my chin up, my shoulders back, and my expression serene. The audience watches with curious eyes. I can feel

Valtheron's gaze burning into me like a brand, tracking my every movement, but I don't look at him again. If I do, I'll lose my nerve completely.

When I reach the silks, they hang there like twin ribbons of blood, swaying slightly in the air currents created by the other performers' movements. My hands itch to grab them, to feel that familiar texture that's become almost comforting over the past few weeks. But I resist the urge to glance at Cairos, to look for reassurance or instruction. I can't afford to look uncertain.

I'm alone up there. Just me and the silk.

And the king's black eyes, watching.

My foot loops into the fabric automatically, the movement I've practiced thousands of times in the forest. The silk is warm from the lights above. Gripping it with both hands, I pull myself up. Hand over hand, wrapping and climbing, letting muscle memory take over where conscious thought would only make me fumble. Up and up and up until I'm halfway to the ceiling, where the ground below looks impossibly far away and my heart is hammering so hard I'm surprised the entire tent can't hear it. And then I spin. Slowly at first, methodically, letting the momentum build. The underside of my knee twists around the silk, creating the friction I need to stay suspended. My other foot leaves the loop, toes pointed out into the open air. The world blurs as I spin, faster now, the tent becoming streaks of color and light.

Then, keeping that same controlled pace, I lean my body outward. The silk slides against my palms, warm and secure. I take one breath. Then another. And then I let go.

For a heartbeat, I'm falling backwards, my arms stretching out into empty air, my body trusting the silk wrapped around my leg to hold me. The wind rushes past, created by my own movement, and somewhere below me, I hear the audience gasp. Other performers fly past on the trapeze—Hessa's laugh rings out as she swoops by, close enough that I feel the air displacement, but I keep my focus inward. On my core. On my balance. On not dying.

Now that I'm here, suspended and spinning with nothing but silk and air, I let myself cast one tiny glance down.

Cairos stands at the edge of the ring, his face tilted up toward me. Our eyes meet across the distance, and he gives me a small smile, reassuring and steady, like he's saying *I knew you could do this*.

The fear doesn't disappear, but it becomes manageable. Contained. I can work with this. I *can* do this.

I reach back to the silks, grasping them with both hands. Cairos's look gives me enough confidence to finish this routine. I spread my legs, doing a split—something I never would've thought I could do, nor imagined I ever *would* do. It's so freeing, so incredible to be this high in the air, feeling like a leaf in the breeze. Spinning when I want to spin, stopping when I want to stop, twisting in ways I would've thought unimaginable.

Cairos isn't the only thing that keeps me going. The audience applauds whenever I perform a complicated maneuver. They applaud for the other performers too, but I pretend it's all for me as encouragement to keep going.

Sweat beads on my forehead as I work under the bright, multicolored lights. The music is thunderous in my ears, my heart beating along to the pounding of the song. It feels like I've done this for a lifetime, my shimmery skirts with gemstones catching the light.

Suddenly, the urge to look at Valthaeron becomes overwhelming. Is he still studying me? Still whispering to his guards? Can he smell that I'm human? I'm an unfamiliar face in his troupe, which must have caught his attention immediately. But what kind of attention? Suspicion? Anger?

I steal a glance mid-spin, my eyes finding him in the sea of spectators.

He's leaning forward slightly in his seat, watching me with an intensity that makes my stomach drop. But it's not the murderous fury I expected. His black eyes are sharp with curiosity, tracking my every movement like I'm a riddle he's trying to solve. Even from this distance, suspended in the air, I can see the way his head tilts slightly, considering. Analyzing. Just like Harmond said he would.

I was terrified he'd be angry. His rage would come in the form of a hundred blood-red guards barreling toward me, swords drawn, ready to cut me down before I could draw another breath. Anger would mean death, swift and certain.

But curiosity?

Curiosity, I can work with.

I've been handling curiosity my whole life. Quinnic's been curious since he was three years old—getting into trouble I had to talk him out of, asking questions that could get us all killed if the wrong person heard. I learned early how to redirect it, how to satisfy it just enough to keep him safe. How to turn questions into opportunities instead of threats.

Valthaeron's curiosity isn't so different. He wants to know who I am, where I came from, and why he's never seen me before. And as long as he's asking questions instead of giving orders, I have time. Time to perform. Time to prove I belong here. Time to make him believe I'm just another fae in his circus, nothing worth worrying about.

I let myself smile then—the grand, wide smile of a performer doing exactly what they're supposed to do. Making the audience feel exactly what they're supposed to feel. Wonder. Awe. Entertainment. The sensation is strange, foreign, but somehow grounding. A reminder that right now, in this moment, I'm not me.

I'm not Naevyn from Xardon, the girl who hauls buckets until her hands bleed. I'm not starving or desperate or terrified. I'm well-fed and strong. I'm graceful in the air. I'm brave enough to perform in front of a king who wants me dead.

And I know somehow, impossibly, that I can do this. That I can fool him. That I can get close enough to end him.

I just have to keep smiling.

Song after song pounds through the tent, and I perform the routines as if I've been doing this all my life. Climb, wrap, spin, drop, catch. Over and over until the movements blur together into one continuous flow.

Finally, a slower song begins. Still in the same haunting tone as the rest of the circus, but the tempo drops, becoming more deliberate.

And then, one by one, the performers begin to shift into dragons.

Below me, Selenia transforms first. Her human form ripples and expands, replaced by her beautiful pink-scaled dragon in a shimmer of magic that makes the air itself seem to bend. She takes flight immediately, powerful wings carrying her up to the top of the tent, where she begins slow, elegant circles.

The twins are next. They transform in perfect synchronization, their bodies shifting simultaneously into two dragons—one silver, one gold—that fly side by side as if they couldn't exist without one another. Their wings beat in the same rhythm, their movements mirror images of each other.

Fenric goes next, the blue scales of his dragon reminding me of the night that changed everything. When he tried to extract my soul, but just… couldn't. I hope he knows how grateful I am to him for that moment, for passing me by and instructing me how to stay alive through the madness.

Then Hessa, her scales a deep emerald that catches the light. Then the man who'd been juggling fiery pins, his dragon a burnt orange. Then the clown, surprisingly graceful as a pale blue dragon. A few other performers I've yet to meet. And finally… Cairos.

His transformation is slower than the others' and more deliberate. The air around him seems to darken as his body shifts and grows, scales the color of storm clouds rippling across his skin. When his wings unfurl, they're larger than any of the others, and the sound they make as they beat is a rumble like thunder.

Six distinct dragons now circle the roof of the tent in a carefully choreographed pattern. The sight is ethereal. Impossible. Even though I'd seen it before at the circus I attended, seeing it from this vantage point, suspended in the air among them, makes it feel entirely new.

The wind from the beating of their wings sends the silks swaying to and fro.

My left hand loses its grip. For one horrible moment, I'm falling, truly falling, my body weight pulling me down. But my right leg is still twisted into the fabric, and the silk catches me with a jerk that sends pain shooting through my knee. I've practiced falling gracefully over the past week and, miraculously, I manage to turn the slip into a controlled drop. My arms sweep out as I descend, making it look like part of the routine instead of a panic-induced disaster.

The question is… what now? I'm fully aware that it's my job to get close to the king. What I'm not aware of is how to actually do that.

I continue to spin on the silks, pretending that I'm perfectly comfortable here. I briefly consider climbing down to the floor, but somehow I feel safer up here, unreachable by the king's guards.

Below me, the six dragons make impressive loops in the air. Their bodies twist in circles, sometimes in figure-eights, as they lower down from the top of the tent just as they had done in the circus I observed weeks ago.

They circle out toward the audience, slowing as they reach Valthaeron, who looks utterly pleased with the circus. One by one, with Cairos in the lead, they slow as if suspended by lack of gravity alone, their wings barely beating. And then they breathe out.

White wisps leave their nostrils, flowing through the air like smoke. And Valthaeron breathes in.

Souls, I realize with horror. Hundreds of souls flowing from them to him, out there in the open. He absorbs their power while the guards make a semicircle around him, protecting him from the rest of the fae in the off chance that any of them are crazy or stupid enough to get in the way. They wouldn't, though. They seem… ecstatic. Cheers and yells and applause rise from the audience members. They seem thrilled that their king is becoming even more powerful.

First Cairos, Fenric, then the twins, then Hessa and the rest of them, all handing over the power of the souls they collected during this cycle. When it's done, they fly back to the center of the tent to continue their performance as dragons.

I carry on as if nothing is happening, continuing my routine on the silks. But inside, I'm panicking. Blaine's soul is in there. Perhaps other people I knew from the mines or from Xardon. All handed over to the king.

Finally, after what feels like far too long and yet not long enough all at once, the dragons each make their landing.

As the circus comes to an end, each of the performers shifts back into their fae forms. I lock eyes with Cairos as he stands on the center platform just before his bow. The slight nod he gives me says it all. *You did it. It's time.*

The king doesn't waste time finding out who I am. As soon as the crowd filters out, he glides down the stairs as if by magic toward the troupe. Hessa takes my hand and gives it a tight squeeze. "You're doing amazing," she whispers.

"Who is the girl?" the king bellows.

The guards sense his anger immediately. Two of them draw their swords with a metallic hiss that makes my stomach drop. The rest maintain a defensive stance, hands on their hilts, ready.

"She is with us," Cairos states, his voice brave but careful.

The king steps closer, walking around me like a predator circling prey. His eyes move up and down my body slowly, deliberately, and a disgusting squirming feeling crawls across my skin. I want to put distance between us, but my feet won't move.

"What faction?" the king asks, his voice sharp.

Cairos thinks on his feet. "No faction, sir. She was a wanderer. We took her in."

Valthaeron seems to be digesting this information, his black eyes never leaving me. "No faction? Not at all?"

He's looking at me now. Waiting. I'm the one who's expected to answer. Surely, I smell human, so why is Cairos suddenly acting like I'm fae? My heart is hammering so hard I'm sure Valthaeron can hear it. It feels like the sound is echoing through the entire tent.

I don't have a choice. I have to answer.

"No, sir. I was alone." My voice comes out steadier than I expected, but I can hear the slight tremor at the end.

The king seems suspicious. He looks from me to Cairos and back to me again, his expression darkening. "And who gave permission for an outsider to join the king's Royal Circus, the most blessed circus in all of the realm? *I* don't recall giving permission."

His voice is deadly now. Pointed. Not curious. Dangerous.

I have to do something. Have to say something—anything—to bring that curiosity back. I think of Quinnic, how he would shut down when his curiosity was rejected, so I, as his big sister, would try my absolute hardest to satisfy it, to engage him without breaking his spirit. I channel that now, searching for the right words.

"No one gave permission, sir. It was I who approached them. I didn't ask—I told them I'd be performing with them." I force myself to meet his eyes, even though everything in me wants to look away. "Anything to meet the king I so fervently worship." I highlight my words but giving a long, deep curtsy, bowing my head as I do, partially to convince him, and partially to have a moment with my expression obscured so that I can let my fear be free to paint my expression for just a moment.

Valthaeron's eyes narrow to slits. He's considering. Weighing whether to let me go, kill me, or take me in. I can see the calculation happening behind those black eyes, and my stomach twists into knots.

One guard, as if assuming his answer, lifts his sword and rests it on my shoulder. The sharp edge of the blade presses cold against my neck. I feel the exact moment it breaks skin—a thin, burning line of pain. Warm blood trickles down, tracing a path along my collarbone. One small press. One command from the king, and this is all over.

I hold my breath. It's not intentional. My body is seizing up, trying to end itself before Valthaeron can do it for me. I can't even bring myself to look at Hessa or Cairos. Can't look at anything except the king's face, inches from mine.

Fenric is the first one to call out in my defense.

"You can't, sir. She's useful. She'll prove it to you."

The king's head snaps to the right toward Fenric. "You deign to tell me what I find useful?"

With that, the guard to his right draws back and drives his knee up into Fenric's stomach. The sound Fenric makes is a ghastly, wet, choking gasp as he crumples forward.

Cairos moves to aid his friend, but suddenly, he's frozen in place. Completely still, like a statue.

Valthaeron. Of course. That's where the power comes from. Why wouldn't he hold the same powers he's given to the troupe?

The guard whose sword is at my neck shifts just slightly. Intentionally or unintentionally, I can't tell, but the blade drives a touch deeper into my skin. The pain is sharp and bright, and my breath hitches. My entire body begins to shake with nerves, trembling so hard I'm sure the blade will cut deeper just from the movement. I do my best to hold still and stop the shaking, but I can't. Fear has taken over completely.

Valthaeron returns his full attention to me, stepping even closer. He's just inches from my face now, so close I can smell him. The scent is something metallic and cold, like old blood. "Let's see what the girl can do. Join me, will you, in the castle?" It's not a question. The alternative is death, and everyone here knows it. Then he turns to Cairos, and something in his expression shifts. Something that makes the hair on the back of my neck stand up. "You too."

Why would he invite Cairos? Why both of us?

The guard removes the sword from my neck, but I can still feel the blood dripping slowly down my skin. My legs are shaking so badly I'm not sure I can walk, but I force myself to stay upright. Force myself not to collapse right here in front of the king and prove that I'm exactly as weak as he might suspect.

Valthaeron starts to turn away, then pauses. His head tilts slightly, like he's heard something only he can detect. When he looks back at me, his eyes aren't curious anymore.

They're knowing.

"How strange," he says softly, dangerously. "I can't sense your magic at all."

17

SEPARATED

Being led into the castle is surreal. It's the first structure I've encountered in the fae realm that isn't made of some sort of glass. But what kind of stronghold would it be if it were made out of such a fragile material?

Valtheron leads us over the stone paths that wind around Shillhain. Cairos walks beside me, and we're flanked by guards on either side as if they want to make absolutely sure we don't run. Not that we would. How many guards are there in Shillhain? Hundreds? Thousands? Too many to count.

Bystanders look in our direction and scowl. Whether it's because I'm an outsider or because they recognize Cairos and dislike him, I'm unsure. From what Fenric told me about the settlement, the people living around the castle are the Solmeren fae—a faction who fully worship and believe in the king.

I can see why.

The houses around here are stately, palatial even. All of them are made entirely of beautiful white stone with stained glass accents that catch the light and throw a plethora of colors across perfectly manicured lawns. Lush green grass grows in sprawling yards, surrounded by shimmering glass trees. It's a kind of wealth I've never even imagined.

The castle sits elevated above where most fae live in this realm, which means the temperature here is more moderate. Perfect, even. Cool enough to be comfortable but warm enough that the breeze feels pleasant against my skin. The Solmeren have luxurious weather, beautiful homes, and, by the looks of it, all of their needs are met. Who wouldn't worship the king under these circumstances?

The front doors to the castle are thrown open as we approach, held by guards whose entire job must be to ensure the king never has to lift a finger. Inside, glass chandeliers hang from the ceiling, glass vines that hold glowing crystals extend outward from a central fount. Glass statues, one I recognize as Valthaeron himself, sit on either side of a grand staircase at the center of the foyer. The ceilings are towering, arched like a cathedral. Doorways branch off in every direction, and I imagine the castle is designed to be a maze to newcomers like myself. If anyone unwelcome were to break in here, they'd have no idea which path to take to reach their destination.

I glance at Cairos as we walk further into the foyer. His jaw is tighter than I've ever seen it, muscles bunched in his shoulders and neck. His hands move constantly, clenching and unclenching, clenching and unclenching, as if he stops, he'll explode. I desperately want to ask him what's wrong, but I don't dare make a sound in front of Valthaeron.

"Welcome home, Cairos." Valthaeron's voice echoes through the cavernous space. "Six hundred years, hasn't it been?"

Home?

My head snaps to Cairos, but his expression betrays nothing. It's carefully composed and neutral. But the tension is still there. His throat works like he's swallowing words. He won't give anything away, though. Not here. Not to Valthaeron.

Valthaeron grins, a slow, eerie smile that makes my skin crawl. Now that I'm up close, I can see the deep lines in his skin, the way age has marked him despite his power. His eyebrows are overgrown and gray. His salt-and-pepper beard matches his hair, just as I thought I saw from inside the circus tent. He wears fine clothing made of thick material in a deep red that matches the guards' uniforms. Gold buttons line the left side of his shirt to keep it closed, each one embossed with a crest. The collar is regal, something I've never seen in real life before, standing stiffly against his neck.

His eyes are a dark mahogany, almost black. I have to wonder if they've gone dark with his soul, or if he was born that way. Those eyes are fixed on Cairos now, scrutinizing and unrelenting. He's hit a nerve and he knows it. He meant to, I just don't know why.

Valthaeron moves to the left of the grand staircase, the guards surrounding us shifting to open a second set of doors as he walks through.

"So kind of you to be my guests," he says over his shoulder. "All this space does get rather lonely after a while."

I follow Valthaeron, waiting for him to get to the point. All this talk of loneliness and how long it's been, but really, it's just a mask for the cruelty he's somehow inflicting on Cairos.

The room we step into is wealth embodied.

The air is laced with the scent of old leather and something metallic I can't quite place. I wouldn't know the smell of gold, though, and looking around, I realize that may be the scent that's overtaking my senses. The floor is gold, shimmering and polished to such a shine that I can see a distorted reflection of myself in it. The walls are lined with glass shelving, but each shelf is decorated with flourishes of gold that catch the light from the chandeliers above. Books fill them—ancient texts that probably speak of war and manipulation, if I know anything at all about Valthaeron. More glass chandeliers hang from the ceiling, each one larger than the last, dripping with lavish crystals.

I think of our cracked terra-cotta walls, the holes in the roof we stuffed with rags. The way rain would drip through during the torrents, forcing us to scramble for buckets. This one chandelier could have paid to fix our roof. Could have bought us a year of food. Could have saved us entirely.

The injustice of it makes my stomach churn.

I stare up at one chandelier in particular that's directly above Valthaeron's head. I wonder for just a moment what it would take to make it crash down on him. A rope cut? A well-aimed throw of any number of objects that are right here in this room? How satisfying would it be to watch all that glass shatter against his skull? To watch him bleed out on his precious golden floor.

I wonder a little too long.

When I glance back down, he's studying me. His shadowy eyes are fixed on my face. My skin prickles under his attention, heat crawling up my neck. Can he read minds? Did he see what I was thinking? I struggle to compose my thoughts enough to defend myself, to say that I wasn't thinking about how to make that chandelier fall on his head and, of course, I wasn't hoping it would happen. My mouth opens slightly, an excuse forming on my tongue.

Thankfully, my brain has the wherewithal to prevent the words from leaving my mouth. I press my lips together and drop my gaze, hoping I look appropriately humble and not like someone who was just imagining his death. It's a skill I learned in the mines—keeping my face blank, and my thoughts hidden, while foremen barked orders. Look too defiant, and you'd be punished. Look too weak, and you'd be targeted.

Find the space in between. Survive another day.

Just like now.

Cairos, on the other hand, doesn't seem to notice anything at all. A faraway look makes his eyes look glassy and unfocused. Like he's looking but not seeing. His hands hang at his sides, but he isn't as at ease as he's trying to look. A tension in his shoulders gives his arms an unnatural posture, like he's holding himself back from committing violence.

I've seen him shift into a dragon and battle Grendor for me. Seen him smirk and joke and deflect with that insufferable confidence. But being in this place has broken something in him that I didn't even know could break.

What keeps him so caught up in his own mind here? What happened in this place that could shake someone who's lived nine hundred years?

"Care to try out your old seat, friend?" Valthaeron asks, his voice dripping with false warmth. He gestures to one of two glass thrones along the right side of the room—massive things, carved from what looks like a single piece of glass each, with cushions of deep red velvet. They look uncomfortable. Cold. Like sitting on ice.

Cairos responds for the first time since we entered this room, his voice rough. "I never belonged here."

"Nonsense." Valthaeron's brow presses down over his eyes with a look of feigned concern that doesn't reach the rest of his face. His mouth curves in what might be a smile but looks more like a threat. "You always belonged here. With Bellamie."

The name hangs in the air.

Bellamie. Who is that? The name means nothing to me, but the way Cairos's entire body goes rigid, the way his breathing stops, I know that whoever Bellamie is, she matters. Or mattered.

Everything happens at once.

Cairos closes the gap between them so fast I barely register the movement, his hands circling Valthaeron's neck. His fingers dig into the king's throat, knuckles white with pressure. "Don't you fucking talk about—"

The sound comes first—a sickening slash, fabric tearing, then the wet sound of steel meeting flesh.

A guard's sword cuts across Cairos's upper back in one brutal stroke, tearing through the fabric of his simple black shirt and leaving behind a river of blood that immediately begins soaking through the black material, spreading like dark wings across his shoulders.

The sound makes me flinch. It's too familiar. Too many times, I've borne witness to violence at the mines. Too many cuts and jabs from a sword or cruel punishments like the desecration of extremities.

Cairos grunts in pain, a sound that seems ripped from deep in his chest, but doesn't give Valthaeron the satisfaction of crying out. He releases the king's throat and straightens, breathing in and out through his nostrils heavily, gritting his teeth so hard I can hear them grinding together.

The salty copper smell of blood reaches me and a queasy flutter turns my insides. It smells like the mines.

Seeing Cairos so downtrodden against the cruelty of the king, hurt and bleeding, and still refusing to show weakness, makes me want to reach out and comfort him.

But the guards are all too close now. Two of them flank Cairos, gripping his upper arms hard enough that I see their fingernails dig into his flesh. He doesn't resist.

My hands shake at my sides. I ball them into fists, nails biting hard into my palms to keep myself still. The same hands that carried shadowstone, raised up my brother, and cared for my parents at their bedside aren't strong enough to help Cairos now.

Valthaeron adjusts his collar, smoothing down the fabric where Cairos's hands had gripped him. He continues on as if the past minute hadn't happened, and as if there isn't blood dripping onto his pristine gold floor.

"One last stop before you're shown to your quarters." He pauses for dramatic effect, his eyes sliding to Cairos with something that might be satisfaction, and adds, "The garden."

Cairos's face is wrecked with pain and it makes my chest ache too. Whatever inhumanity could cause a thousand-year-old fae to crumble like this makes me want to destroy the source of it. Makes me want to grab one of those guards' swords and drive it through Valthaeron's heart.

Would it work? Could I do it? Or would I freeze now, knowing what it feels like to take a life?

Valthaeron turns to a set of doors on our left. They're glass, just like the bookshelves, framed in more gold. He pushes them open himself, not waiting for a servant, and cool air rushes in. It smells different out here. Dead. Like rot and old flowers.

Like deep inside the shadowstone mines when the air is stale and wrong.

When we step outside, the garden doesn't look like much of a garden at all.

It looks like a graveyard.

Dead grass is scattered throughout the grounds, brown and brittle, nothing like the lush green lawns outside of the Solmeren houses. Like this place was intentionally left to die. Rosebushes made of glass sit sadly on either side of a crumbling stone path that meanders through the area. The roses themselves are cloudy, like they've been neglected, their delicate glass petals chipped and broken in places. Even the glass trees look dead somehow—their branches drooping, their leaves opaque and dull instead of shimmering like the ones in the forest. The sky above is overcast, with heavy clouds blocking any sunlight.

The whole place feels abandoned. Forgotten.

"It's a pity she's not here to take care of it the way she used to," Valthaeron says, running his hand along one of the glass roses as we pass. It makes a soft, scraping sound that puts me on edge.

She… Bellamie, I wonder? Was this her garden, whoever she is? And the way Valthaeron taunts Cairos about her, it's as if he were the one responsible for her absence.

He doesn't seem the slightest bit nervous that he'll be attacked again by Cairos, not with the guards restraining him. He walks slowly and deliberately, making sure we see every dead thing. Every bit of decay.

It's torture.

I wince as I allow myself to sneak a glance at the deep wound on Cairos's back. The fabric of his shirt has fallen open where the sword tore through, revealing a long gash that still weeps blood. It runs from his right shoulder blade down toward his spine, angry and red at the edges. Blood has already begun to crust along the sides of the wound, dark against his skin.

I've seen wounds like this in the mines. Deep slashes from foremen who went too far with their discipline. Some healed.

Some didn't.

It looks agonizing, but he doesn't show it. It's like he's not even here anymore.

A glass sculpture toward the far end of the garden catches my eye. I've seen it before somewhere, but where? The recognition nags at me, just out of reach, like a word on the tip of my tongue.

It's a bust of a woman with long hair that flows past her shoulders in intricate waves. Her expression is gentle but knowing, like she's keeping secrets behind kind eyes. Her lips curve in a slight smile. The features are delicate but strong with high cheekbones, a graceful neck, and shoulders carved with incredible detail. Whoever made this knew their subject well—loved them, maybe. The glass catches the light, making the features seem almost alive.

And somehow, impossibly, as we move past, the eyes seem to move with us. Following. Watching.

A chill runs down my spine that has nothing to do with the cool air.

Valthaeron slows as we walk past it, as if he wants us to look at it. To really see it. Which I do, because my inability to remember where I've seen this face before is the worst kind of annoyance. It sits in my brain like a splinter, painful and irritating.

It reminds me of someone, but the memory won't come, like trying to remember a dream after waking.

I make a note to think about it later, when my fight-or-flight instincts calm down and I can actually recollect clearly.

We finish the walk through the garden in silence. The only sounds are our footsteps on the stone path and the soft clink of the guards' armor. It doesn't escape me that Cairos looks pained the entire time—not from the slice on his back, but from something deeper. The wound in his heart. He keeps his eyes down, not looking at the glass roses or the dead grass or the trees. Especially not at the sculpture. Like seeing any of it will break something inside him that's already barely holding together.

I know that feeling. Walking past my parents' empty places at our table after they died. Seeing their clothes still sitting in our trunk. The way even small reminders could crack me open if I let them.

I want to reach for his hand, but the guards remain too close and Valthaeron is watching. Always watching.

We enter through another set of doors that deposits us into a hallway with a smaller, circular staircase to our left. It looks like one that would be used by servants only. Never the king. The walls here are plain stone. No gold, no glass, no decoration. Just cold, damp stone that smells faintly of mildew.

"The guards will escort you to your rooms," Valthaeron instructs, his voice echoing slightly in the narrow space. "And if I were you, I wouldn't even consider trying to leave. The guards monitor the hallways well. And outside…" He trails off, pausing a moment before continuing, his eyes finding mine. "Well, you never know what beasts are prowling out there."

We're trapped. He knows we're trapped, and he's toying with us like a cat with a mouse, savoring our fear.

Neither of us responds. What is there to say?

Valthaeron strides away, his footsteps echoing down the hallway until they fade entirely. The moment he's gone, the guards close in tighter. A rough hand grips my upper arm hard enough to bruise, fingers digging into the muscle, and pulls me toward the staircase.

The grip feels like the foremen in the mines. When I dared to slow in my work in order to catch my breath, they'd be there ready to pounce and shake me like a ragdoll until I remembered my senses and sped up.

The hand pulls me away, leaving Cairos behind. I hear his heavy footsteps and risk a glance back to see him surrounded, the blood on his back now visible even in the dim light of the hallway.

Please don't break, I think. *We need you.* I *need you.*

I notice with my last glance before they disappear down the hall that only one guard stays at my side, yet the other five remain in a semicircle around Cairos. It makes me wonder if he's more powerful than I think, and Valthaeron believes it would take five of his trained guards to keep him at bay. Or maybe they're just afraid of him, and what he might do if he breaks.

Upstairs, the hallway stretches across the expanse of the castle with doors spaced evenly along it. Ten doors, maybe more. The corridor is long enough that I can't see the end in the dim light. Boarding rooms, perhaps. Or maybe individual dungeons.

Maybe there's no difference.

Like the housing in Xardon. They called them homes but they were really just places to keep workers between shifts. Places to sleep before going back to the mines. Prisons with beds.

The guard pushes the closest door open, giving me a rough shove into the room that makes me stumble forward several steps.

"Wait—" I start to say, turning back. "Cairos!"

But without a word, he slams the door behind me.

Immediately, I spin around and yank at the doorknob, twisting it hard. It doesn't budge. I pull harder, jerking the handle, fooling myself into thinking I can break free, but it might as well be welded shut.

"Let me out!" I pound on the door with my fist, the sound dull and useless against the thick wood. My hand stings from the impact but I don't care.

Only silence answers my pleas.

When I give up, I press my forehead against the door, breathing hard. They've separated us. Cairos is somewhere down this hall, bleeding and alone, and I'm locked in here like a prisoner.

Finally, I force myself to turn around and look at the room I've been shoved into.

It's the most beautiful prison cell I could ever imagine.

The room is large with a four-poster bed against the far wall. The sheets are cream-colored silk, with pillows piled high. More pillows than one person could possibly need. A wardrobe stands against one wall, carved from dark wood with embellished golden handles. A desk sits beneath a window, and through the glass I can see that dead, forgotten garden. A washbasin on a stand with actual running water, not a bucket that needs to be hauled from a well. A mirror framed in gold. Plush carpet under my feet instead of cold stone or packed dirt.

It's a room for a guest. Not for a prisoner.

But why?

Why not kill me if he has the chance? If he knows from some prophecy that I'll be the end of him, then why let me live?

The rest of my thoughts are with Cairos. With knowing that he's bleeding, locked away in a room just like me.

I spend far too long oscillating between pacing and struggling against the door handle.

When weariness finally creeps in, I pad to the window, watching the dying light and lament the height at which I'm concealed in this castle. Pressing my hand against the glass, cold seeps into my palm. Below, I can just barely make out movement at the edge of the gardens. A shadow, low to the ground, prowling.

Green eyes flash in the darkness.

The shade stalker.

It followed us all the way here from the Tidetreaders settlement? It's impossible.

And yet, it's here. It's watching the castle. Watching my window, maybe. And for some reason, the sight of it is almost comforting, though I can't place exactly why. Maybe because it feels like Cairos. Like this creature with three familiar bands being okay means that Cairos is also okay.

I cross the room and sink down onto the edge of the bed, my legs suddenly weak. The silk sheets are soft under my hands, nothing like the rough blankets at home. Softer than Quinnic's hair when I used to smooth it back from his forehead when he was small.

And I hate them. Hate this room. Hate that I'm here in luxury while Quinnic and Alabris are gods know where. While Cairos is somewhere down the hall, bleeding and alone, reliving whatever trauma this place holds for him. While Valthaeron is probably somewhere laughing at how easily he trapped us.

I wrap my arms around myself and try not to think about how thoroughly I've failed.

How quickly I got caught up in a paper-thin plan, when really I was just walking into a trap that had been set centuries before I was born.

I think of my mother and father. How they'd sit at our broken table and make plans to get out of Xardon. How my father had apologized to me, over and over, for not being able to give us more. For not being able to protect us, and give Quinnic and me a better place to grow up.

I'm sorry, Papa. I tried. I really tried.

But I'm not strong enough.

Not smart enough.

Not enough.

Outside, the shade stalker howls a sound that's almost mournful, like it understands my thoughts.

And despite everything, I close my eyes and let myself pretend, just for a moment, that someone out there is on my side.

18

WALLS

Morning comes too soon, dragging me from sleep like hands pulling me out of deep water. The fitful night did nothing to calm my racing thoughts. If anything, the exhaustion made them worse. Vivid nightmares haunted what little sleep I managed. In them, Quinnic and Alabris worked in the mines, breathing shadowstone dust, withering away from hunger, while I stood frozen, unable to help.

I wake with my heart pounding, the images still vivid behind my eyelids.

I'm alone with these thoughts for only a few moments before a clicking sound comes from the door handle. When the door swings open, a guard fills the doorway. It's one I don't recognize from yesterday, though they all blend together in their identical armor and cold expressions.

"You're to come with me." His tone allows no argument. He stands blocking the doorway, his form large and imposing against the hallway lights beyond. His feet are planted hip-width apart, hands clasped behind his back—a relaxed posture that speaks volumes. I'm not a threat. What kind of danger could a small girl pose to a fae warrior built like a brick wall?

I comply without question, rising from the bed where I'd spent the night curled into a tight ball. Nerves jump in my stomach like trapped insects, but between going to an unknown destination with this guard and staying locked alone in this cold stone room, I'll take the unknown. At least the unknown has the possibility of seeing Cairos, the possibility of moving forward and defeating Valthaeron.

I feel intensely out of place still dressed in my circus uniform from yesterday—the magenta silk that Cairos conjured for me, with its delicate beadwork and gems lining the bodice and skirt. The fabric is wrinkled now from sleeping in it, and there's a small tear in the hem I don't remember getting. The gems catch the torchlight as I move, little sparks of color that seem absurdly cheerful against the gray stone walls and my grim mood. I'm dressed for performance, beauty, and entertainment, not for whatever comes next in Valthaeron's castle.

The guard says nothing else, just turns and expects me to follow. I do, keeping a few paces behind as he leads me down the dim hallway. My bare feet are silent on the cold stone floor, as my shoes were left behind yesterday during the chaos. The chill seeps up through my soles with each step, making me acutely aware of how vulnerable I am here. No shoes, no weapon, no plan. Just a wrinkled circus costume and the fading hope that Cairos is somewhere in this maze of stone, still breathing.

The guard makes varying right and left turns that leave me confused about which way is which, and where exactly we came from. His stop in front of me is abrupt and I nearly walk right into him. He raps twice on the door, then proceeds to unlock it and walk in before anyone responds. More courtesy than I was given, at least.

When I follow him inside, relief floods through my entire body.

It's Cairos. He sits on the edge of the bed, elbows pressed into his knees, his fingers tangled in his loose, messy locks. He lifts his head to see us and recognition flickers in those amber eyes, but they still look hollow, like the windows of a house where no one lives anymore.

The guard takes two brisk steps inside the room and deposits a bundle of supplies on the small table beside the bed —clean linen, a glass jar filled with an incandescent silver, and rolls of bandages. They land next to a small basin of water already situated on the table, the jar rolling to the side and stopping just short of falling onto the floor.

"Lord Valthaeron requires that his… ringmaster be presentable." The guard's voice is flat, rehearsed, like he's repeated these words a hundred times for a hundred different prisoners. His cold gaze cuts to me. "You. Tend to him."

I blink, my exhausted brain struggling to catch up. "Me? I'm not a—"

"Lord Valthaeron has made his wishes clear." Each word is clipped, dismissive. "Make yourself useful. The king has a task for you both, and he expects you to be ready within the hour."

A task. The words send ice through my veins, but also something else. Hope. This is what we came here for. To get close to Valthaeron. To find a way to kill him. To make him taste my blood, maybe, the same blood that killed Grendor when he bit me.

I open my mouth to ask what the task is, but the protest dies on my tongue when I see Cairos's morose expression. The guard won't tell me anything useful anyway, I remind myself.

Cairos's gaze is fixed somewhere past us both, focused on nothing, and seeing everything from six hundred years ago. When he speaks, his voice is rough and empty. "Tell His Majesty I'll be ready."

Cairos showing defeat? He must me in a worse condition than I realized.

The guard dips his head once—a mockery of respect—gives me a final once-over with his eyes that makes my skin crawl, and leaves. The door closes with a heavy, final *thunk* that echoes through the small room.

The sound of the lock clicking into place follows a heartbeat later.

I'm alone with Cairos.

The room is much different than mine. It's smaller and dank, the walls are a dingy gray, and the bed and small table are the only furniture, as if someone forgot to furnish the rest of the space. His window on the far wall is only half the size of mine, but barred as well.

The silence stretches between us, thick and uncomfortable. I can hear my own breathing, too loud in the stillness. Can hear the faint crackle of torches in the hallway beyond the door. Absolutely no sound from him, though. No movement, no breath, like he's carved from the same stone as these walls.

I glance at the supplies the guard left behind. Bandages wound in neat rolls, a glowing silver salve that smells faintly of something metallic, and a basin of warm water that sends up delicate curls of steam that catch the light just beginning to filter through the single narrow window. All of these items look like they're meant for someone who knows what they're doing, which is definitely not me. I have no idea how to heal someone, especially not someone with a sword wound inflicted by a sadistic king's guard.

I turn back to face him, crossing my arms over my chest. The magenta silk of my circus costume feels absurd in this gray, stone room. "So… what's the plan here? Do I just start dabbing at your wound with a clean cloth while you pretend you're fine, or are we going to acknowledge that we probably should've thought this plan through a little more?"

He finally looks at me, his liquid honey eyes focusing for the first time since I entered the room. The corner of his mouth twitches—barely there, a ghost of his usual smirk. "You've got a sharp tongue for someone completely unarmed and locked in a castle full of people who want you dead."

"And you've got quite a gash in your back for someone who's supposed to be strong and immortal." I pick up one of the cloth strips, examining it like I have any clue what I'm looking for. "Funny how that works."

That earns me a low chuckle that's rough and quiet. "Fair point."

He shifts on the bed, and I catch the wince he tries to hide in just a brief tightening around his eyes, a slight catch in his breath. Then his hands move to the hem of his torn, blood-soaked shirt.

"You'll need to…" He gestures vaguely at his torso, then grips the fabric. "Can't bandage over this."

I watch as he pulls the shirt up and over his head in one smooth motion that would look effortless if I didn't see the way his jaw clenches, and his entire body goes rigid for a heartbeat before he forces himself to relax. There's a slight tremor in his hands as he balls up the ruined fabric and tosses it aside.

The angry, red wound on his back is fully visible now, blood dotting up in places where the dried crust has cracked with his movement.

He settles back into position with his legs slightly spread, posture deceptively relaxed despite the obvious pain. The self-assured tilt to his head that says he's perfectly fine and in control.

Except I can see through it all now. There's a sheen of sweat on his forehead that has nothing to do with the temperature, and a pallor beneath his bronze skin, leaving it gray at the edges. He's breathing carefully through his nose, measured and controlled.

He's in agony and pretending he's not.

I pick up the cloth, dip it in the steaming water that must've been placed here recently because it's hot enough to make my fingertips burn, and move closer. "Any idea what task Valthaeron has in mind? This could be our chance."

"Our chance to what? Get you close enough to him?" His voice is tight, controlled. "That's the plan, but he's not stupid. He won't just let you cut yourself and bleed on him."

"Then we make him think it's an accident." I wring excess water from the cloth, droplets pattering back into the basin.

"Maybe." He doesn't sound convinced. "Or maybe he just wants to parade us in front of his court. Show everyone that the cursed ringmaster and the little human girl are under his control."

I press the damp cloth to the dried blood crusted along the edge of his wound. I endeavor to be gentle, but the fabric sticks to the torn flesh, pulling. I expect him to flinch, but he doesn't.

He doesn't make a sound. Just stares somewhere past my shoulder like he's centuries away and I'm nothing but another ghost in a castle full of them.

I work in silence for a while, carefully cleaning away the dried blood, revealing the full extent of the damage. The sword didn't cut deep enough to kill him, but enough to hurt like hell and remind him exactly who has the power here.

My mind keeps circling back to yesterday in the garden, and the way Valthaeron said that name like it was a weapon.

"Who's Bellamie?" I ask, despite my better judgment.

His entire body goes rigid under my hands.

"Someone who died a long time ago," he finally says, voice flat.

I reach for the pot of glowing salve, frustrated by his deflection. "He said her name in the garden like he knew it would hurt you. And it did—I saw your face. You attacked him."

"Drop it, Naevyn."

"No." I scoop a generous amount of the cool salve onto my fingers. "If we're supposed to work together to kill him, I need to understand what I'm dealing with and know why he has this much power over you."

"He has power over me because I've been cursed to serve him for the past six hundred fucking years and a millenia to go if we can't alter the course," Cairos snaps. "That's all you need to know."

"But Bellamie—"

"Was someone I failed." His voice is deadly. "Someone I couldn't protect. And now she's dead and he flaunts what he did at every opportunity. Is that what you wanted to hear?"

The rawness in his tone makes me pause, the salve forgotten in my hand. I take in a shaky breath. "I'm sorry. I didn't mean to—"

"Don't." He cuts me off, and when he speaks again, his voice has shifted. It's lower, edged with that teasing tone I recognize as deflection. "You're much prettier when you're not asking questions I don't want to answer."

"Cairos…"

"You know what other time you're really pretty? When you're putting your hands all over me." The smirk is back in his voice, even though I can't see his face. "If I'd known getting stabbed would lead to this, I'd have pissed off Valthaeron years ago."

"This isn't funny."

"Who says I'm joking?" He glances over his shoulder at me, and despite everything, that devilish glint is back in his eyes.

I want to push, and demand real answers about Bellamie, but I can see the wall he's thrown up, the deflection shield he's using to protect himself.

And pushing someone who's already literally bleeding is not the kindest thing I could do right now.

So I let it go.

For now.

"Fine," I mutter, applying the cream to his wound with perhaps more pressure than necessary. "Be cryptic and hide behind a wall of humor. See if I care."

"Oh, you care." I can hear a hint of laughter in his voice. "You care quite a bit, actually. I can tell by the way you're touching me."

"I'm bandaging a wound."

"Mm. Of course. There's no way you actually enjoy the way your fingers are grazing my skin, or the way we can inhale each other's scent right now."

Fuck. Why is he doing this? The way he calls me out does something to me, and my body responds in the most embarrassing way, with heat pooling down in my core. But I can't let him know that. "You're impossible."

"So you keep saying. And yet you're still here, hands all over me, smelling like…" He pauses, taking in a deep inhale, "Like you can barely handle touching me like this. I'm starting to think you might actually like me, Little Wren."

"I'm starting to think that blood loss has made you delusional."

He laughs, and it's quiet and genuine despite everything. The sound settles warm in my chest, chasing away some of the tension, trying not to think about my body's stupid reaction.

I finish applying the salve in silence, then reach for the clean bandages. My hands shake slightly as I unroll the linen.

"You'll need to sit forward," I tell him. "I have to wrap this around you."

He complies, shifting to the edge of the bed. The movement pulls at his wound and I see the pain flash across his face for just a second before he schools his expression back to something neutral.

I move behind him, close enough that my knees press against his lower back, and reach around his torso with the bandage. This close, I can feel the heat radiating from his skin, smell the salt-copper tang of blood mixed with smoke and cedar and something indefinably *him*.

My arms encircle him, hands meeting at his chest to pass the linen back and forth. His muscles are tense beneath my touch, coiled tight like he's bracing for pain.

"Relax," I murmur. "This won't work if you're wound up like a spring."

"Little hard to relax with your hands all over me, Wren."

Heat creeps up my neck. "Would you prefer I just let you bleed?"

"I'd prefer a lot of things. But I'll settle for whatever you're willing to give me."

I pull the bandage tighter than strictly necessary, just enough to make my point.

His breath catches. "Careful. I might start thinking you like it rough."

My face burns. "I'm trying to save your life and you're—"

"What?" I can hear the smirk in his voice even though I can't see his face. "Appreciating having a beautiful woman's hands on me? Should I apologize for finding a bright spot in an otherwise shit situation?"

"What you should be doing is finding a way to get Valthaeron's teeth on me."

"Now there's a mental image." His tone is one of dark amusement. "Though I'm not sure I like the idea of him putting his mouth anywhere near you. That should be left solely to me."

"That's not what I—" I groan, wrapping the bandage around again, flustered. "You know what I meant."

"Do I? I'm not so sure." He's definitely smirking now. "Because it sounded like you were talking about—"

"Stop." I cut him off, my face so hot now I think I might actually combust. "Just… stop talking while I finish this."

He chuckles, but complies, and I wrap the bandage in silence. Each pass requires me to lean closer, my cheek brushing his shoulder blade while my hands flatten against his chest to get the angle right. I can feel his quick but steady heartbeat under my palms.

When I tie off the bandage, I sit back quickly, putting distance between us before the proximity can make me do something stupid.

"There. Try not to get hurt again before we find out what Valthaeron wants."

He turns to face me, reaching for the ruined shirt. He pulls it on despite the fresh bandages, despite the way the movement makes him go pale. The torn, blood-stained fabric hangs awkwardly over the bandaging, but it's better than nothing.

"Whatever this task is," he says, voice serious now, "we need to play along while we wait for the emerald cycle, and look for an opening, a moment when he's distracted or when you can get close enough to make it look like an accident."

"And if there isn't an opening?"

"Then we wait for the next one." He meets my eyes, and something dark moves in that amber gaze. "We only get one shot at this, Naevyn. If we try and fail, he'll know what we're planning. And then…" He doesn't finish the sentence, but he doesn't need to.

Before I can say anything in response, I hear multiple sets of footsteps in the hallway, approaching.

We both tense, then the lock clicks.

The door swings open to reveal four guards, their expressions cold and professional.

"Lord Valthaeron is ready for you," the lead guard announces, then his eyes move from Cairos and land on me. "Both of you."

Cairos stands slowly, carefully, testing his balance. When he catches me watching, his eyes are determined, and I think I see the tiniest of nods as he gestures for me to walk in front of him.

"Stay close," he says quietly just behind the nape of my neck, just for me. "And be ready for anything."

I nod, continuing to walk as if he had said nothing at all.

Two guards lead, while another two wait for us to pass and take up the rear.

My heart pounds with each step, but I keep my chin up and my expression neutral.

This is what we came here for. To get close to him, and to find a way to end this.

Whatever he asks us to do, we'll find our opening.

We have to.

19

THE FAVOR

The guards lead us through corridors, the ones behind us occasionally prodding Cairos to move faster.

Bastard.

I'd like to see *him* walk at a fast clip with his back torn open.

The lead guard pushes open a set of double doors, and we're ushered into a dining room that makes my breath catch.

It's towering. The ceiling soars overhead, supported by columns that twist like frozen, golden vines. Windows line one entire wall, floor to ceiling, letting in streams of pale morning light that catch on the crystal chandelier hanging in the center of the room. The chandelier is easily twice the size of the ones in the library, with hundreds of glass pieces that throw rainbow fractals across every surface.

And beneath it, a table that's long enough to seat thirty people easily, and I have to wonder if Valthaeron frequently has enough guests to fill it, or if the purpose of the length is solely to make any guests he may have feel very, very, small. Place settings of fine porcelain plates edged in gold, crystal glasses that probably cost more than everything my family ever owned, and silverware that gleams like it's never been touched line both sides.

At the head of the table sits Valthaeron.

He looks less imposing than yesterday, though maybe that's just a symptom of my becoming more used to breathing the same air as him. His salt-and-pepper hair is neatly combed back, his beard trimmed close. He wears a dark green high-collared shirt with intricate embroidery along the shoulders, and gold buttons marching up the left side. Everything about him screams wealth and power and control.

His eyes track us as we enter the room, feeling like a lead weight.

"Ah, there you are." His voice is warm, almost friendly, which is somehow more unsettling than if he'd been openly hostile. "Please, sit. I've had breakfast prepared."

He gestures to the two seats closest to him, one on his right and one on his left. Places of honor, if this were a normal meal with a normal king. But nothing about this is normal.

The guards retreat to positions along the walls, staying close enough to intervene if needed, but far enough away to give the illusion of privacy. One of them closes the double doors with a soft thud that sounds unnervingly final.

Cairos heads toward the seat on Valthaeron's right without hesitation, as if he's trying to convince me to do the same with an act of confidence. I follow, taking the seat on the left, and try not to think about how trapped I feel with Valthaeron between us and the door behind us and guards stationed at both exits.

"I trust you both slept well?" Valthaeron asks, unfolding his napkin with precise movements and spreading it across his lap.

The question is so absurd that I almost laugh. Slept well? In a locked room inside his castle? After he had Cairos slashed across the back for daring to touch him?

Ridiculous.

"Wonderfully," I say, hoping he can't see the clenching of my teeth. "Very restful."

Cairos says nothing, just picks up his napkin and copies Valthaeron's movements like he's done this a thousand times before. Maybe he has. Six hundred years ago, before the curse, when he called this castle home.

The thought makes my stomach turn.

Servants appear from a side door carrying trays laden with food. They move silently, efficiently, placing platters in the center of the table and filling our plates without being asked. Eggs cooked in butter, sausages that smell of smoky herbs, bread still steaming from the oven with honey and jam on the side, fresh fruit cut into perfect pieces, and pastries dusted with sugar. The scent sends my stomach tumbling with hunger, but I don't dare eat yet.

It's more food than I've seen in one place in my entire life. More than my family ate in a month, probably. The kind of breakfast in a world where hunger doesn't exist.

One of the servants fills my glass with something that looks like juice—dark red, probably berry. Then moves to Cairos, then to Valthaeron. Another servant adds garnishes to the plates, little sprigs of herbs that serve no purpose except decoration.

When they're finished, they retreat back through the side door as silently as they came.

Valthaeron picks up his fork and knife, cutting into his eggs that spill warm yellow yolk out onto his plate. "Please, eat. We have much to discuss, and I find conversations go so much better on a full stomach."

He takes a bite, chews, swallows. Perfectly normal.

Except nothing about this is normal.

I stare at the eggs and sausage and bread on my plate and my mind immediately goes to the most obvious place: poison.

This is a trap. It has to be. Why else would he feed us?

He knows. He can tell or sense or smell that I'm human, and he wants to watch me die. This is all a ruse to put us at ease, then he'll make his move, cancelling out the prophecy and sealing himself in the throne for eternity.

My gaze slides to Cairos. Panic rises in me as he's already eating, fork moving from plate to mouth. His face betrays no hesitation or fear. No sign that he thinks this might be our death, served on a porcelain platter.

I watch him chew. Watch him swallow. Wait for him to choke or gasp or show any sign that something's wrong.

Nothing happens.

He takes another bite.

Still nothing.

"You're not eating, Naevyn." Valthaeron's voice yanks my attention back to him. He's watching me, head tilted slightly. "Is the food not to your liking? I can have the kitchen prepare something else if you prefer."

"No, it's..." I search for a plausible excuse. "It's just a lot. I'm not used to eating this much in the morning."

"Ah, yes. Food in the... factions can be a bit more unreliable." The way he pauses before saying factions makes a breath stutter in my throat. I get the sinking feeling that he knows I'm not from here. He cuts another piece of sausage, spears it with his fork. "But you're not in the factions anymore. You're a... guest in my castle. Please, eat. You'll need your strength for the task ahead."

The way he says "guest" makes it clear we both know that's not what I am. Prisoner, maybe. Pawn, definitely. But not guest.

I force myself to pick up my own fork. I move at a snail's pace as I cut into the eggs, and I hope he doesn't notice my fear. The first bite is difficult to swallow from the way my stomach churns, but I manage it.

My eyes stay locked on Cairos, watching for any sign of distress or indication that the food is tainted.

He just keeps eating like this is any other breakfast.

I take another bite. Then another. The food is delicious, objectively, but it sits heavy in my stomach. Every swallow feels like a risk.

Minutes pass. Cairos doesn't choke or cough, or show any signs of poisoning.

Maybe Valthaeron really *did* just want to feed us. Maybe this is his version of hospitality, twisted as it is.

Or maybe the poison is slow-acting, and we won't know until it's too late.

"Tell me, Naevyn," Valthaeron says, placing his fork down with a soft clink that somehow feels threatening. "What do you know about shadowstone?"

The question sideswipes me. My heart gives a kick, but my face stays blank.

"I… what?" I manage.

"Shadowstone," he repeats, gesturing like he's asking me about the time of day. "Surely you've encountered it."

"Well." I swallow. "It's heavy."

Which is the understatement of the century, but still the only true fact I have.

Amusement flickers in his eyes as he watches me squirm. "Yes. Very. But also temperamental. Difficult to coax into form. Unwilling to obey just anyone."

Coax.

Obey.

Temperamental.

We're still talking about a rock, right?

I keep my tone as steady as I can. "I didn't realize."

"Mm." He studies me with unnerving interest. "You will. That's the favor I need from you. You'll be working with it tonight."

I blink. "Working with it? In what way?"

A grin curls at the edges of his mouth, pleased by my confusion. "You and Cairos will forge something for me."

Across the table, Cairos's fork stops mid-air. Suspended. His entire body goes rigid, the way it does when he's seconds away from swearing but is trying to be diplomatic about it.

He didn't know either.

"What is it you want us to make?" Cairos asks, voice too calm.

"A necklace." Valthaeron leans back, fingers steepled. "Elegant. Refined. With a shadowstone centerpiece large enough to hold something significant."

To hold what?

I can't bring myself to ask.

"When do you want it completed?" Cairos asks tightly.

"Tonight," Valthaeron says. "Shadowstone only yields properly under moonlight. I'll have the workshop prepared for you both."

Cairos shuts his eyes for a beat, just long enough to betray irritation, or dread, or both, before he nods. When he opens them again, the mask is already back in place.

Tonight.

We're supposed to forge a shadowstone necklace *tonight*, and then what? Valthaeron will have everything he needs from us and can discard us?.

"I'll need the correct tools," Cairos says.

"Of course," Valthaeron purrs, a wicked smile crossing his face. "I wouldn't set you up for failure." Valthaeron gestures, and one of the guards steps forward. "Take them to the old workshop. The one in the eastern tower. Everything should still be there from… before."

The guard nods and retreats back to his position.

Cairos's jaw tightens. "The eastern tower."

"Just like old times," Valthaeron says, and something cruel flickers in his eyes. "You spent so many hours there, perfecting your craft. Creating such beautiful things. I'm sure it will all come back to you."

The muscle in Cairos's jaw jumps.

This is intentional and Cairos knows it. Another one of Valthaeron's tricks to torture Cairos as much as possible. Probably something involving Bellamie.

"And if we can't complete it in one night?" I ask.

His smile turns cold. "Then you'll work the next night. And the night after that. For as many nights as it takes. Though I would advise against testing my patience. I'm not known for my tolerance of failure." His flare of anger causes tiny drops of spittle to be thrown forth from his mouth, raining down on the remainder of his food.

The threat is clear. Complete this task, or suffer the consequences.

I glance at Cairos and see the tension in every line of his body.

"We'll complete it," he says quietly. "Whatever you need."

"Excellent." Valthaeron sets down his glass and stands. "Then enjoy your breakfast. Build your strength. You'll need it."

He takes one final swig of a liquid slightly darker than ours that might just be wine, then pushes his chair back from the table and moves toward the door. The guards flanking the double doors pull them open, and then he's gone.

We're alone with the guards and the barely touched food and the task that hangs between us like an executioner's blade.

My hands are shaking. I press them flat against my thighs under the table to steady them.

He knows something. Or suspects something. That entire exchange was designed to make me slip, to see if I'd reveal knowledge I shouldn't have.

Cairos sinks back into his chair slowly, like all the strength has drained out of him, shoulders hunched, breathing carefully through his nose.

"Cairos?" I ask, pushing my chair out from the table and making my way around to him. I watch the guards in my peripherals, but they don't move to stop me. "Are you alright?"

He eyes me carefully, not sure if he should divulge, but exhaustion wins out. "The eastern tower is where I used to work. Where I made things… with her. With Bellamie."

Oh.

"He knows that, and he's doing it on purpose?"

"Of course he is. Everything he does is on purpose. Every word, every gesture, every fucking smile. He's had over a thousand years to perfect the art of torture."

What am I supposed to say to comfort a man tortured by the most powerful being in the realm? What *can* I say? Nothing. Absolutely nothing.

So I just rest my hand on his shoulder and squeeze gently.

He doesn't pull away or acknowledge the touch with words. But after a moment, his hand comes up to cover mine, just for a second, before dropping back to the table.

"We should eat," he says finally.

"Is it actually possible to forge a necklace like the one Valthaeron is asking for in one night?"

"I don't know," Cairos says, staring off into space.

That's unhelpful, but I can't press him for any more. He doesn't have anything else to give. So I return to my seat and force myself to eat, though every bite still feels risky.

The silence stretches between us, heavy with everything we can't say. With guards listening, there's no safety in words.

But when I glance up, Cairos is looking at me, *really* looking at me. And in his amber eyes, I see something that looks like gratitude. Like I'm the only thing keeping him from drowning in six hundred years of grief.

The only problem is, I'm not sure if I can even keep my own head above the water.

20

BELLAMIE

Night comes quickly. Well, as quickly as it can when the threat of death causes anxiety to infiltrate even the marrow of my bones.

Still, it comes.

We'd been given instructions to study shadowstone forging in the library until it was time. Under close guard, we were led to a room lined with shelves that stretched at least twenty feet toward vaulted ceilings, golden ladders adorning the sidewalls to allow access to even the highest titles. The space smelled of old parchment and dust, of knowledge preserved across centuries.

Cairos and I grabbed as many books on the subject as we could find, though there weren't many. Cairos took one side of the long reading table while I took the other, both of us flipping through page after page, absorbing as much as we could. I had no experience working with the substance, and while Cairos did, it had been over six hundred years.

According to a slim volume bound in cracked red leather, allowing moonlight to touch shadowstone somehow warmed it from the inside, making it pliable enough to shape. But the moon's power lasted only half an hour, giving us precious little time to work. And once the shadowstone had absorbed moonlight, it was no longer susceptible to it. One chance. That was all we'd get per piece.

I wonder how many pieces of shadowstone we'll be provided for this task.

I guess I'm about to find out.

Guards call for us as the waning sunlight has nearly disappeared, the sky outside the library windows turning deep purple and gold. They lead us once again through the castle's winding corridors, this time up a different flight of narrow stairs, climbing higher and higher until my calves burn. Up into what Valthaeron had referred to as the eastern tower.

When the door is pushed open, I nearly stop breathing.

This is so much more than just a forge. It's a suite. It's… breathtaking.

Whoever had once resided here must have been extremely favored by the king. The space before us opens up in three distinct sections, all part of one large, circular room that takes up the entire top floor of the tower.

To the right sits a bedroom that looks like something from a dream. A four-poster canopy bed dominates the space, draped in sheer golden fabric that cascades in waves down the sides. Windows—so many windows—are spread evenly across the curved walls, offering panoramic views of the castle grounds and settlements below. Where many of the other rooms in the castle have cold, gray stone walls, these have been painted a beautiful, lively cream color that makes the space feel warm despite the night. Crystals hang from a chandelier over the bed, and crystalline sconces are placed evenly between the windows, resulting in beautiful light scattered across the room like stars. The floor has rugs in shades of light pink and purple that were probably dyed with the same berries that made the juice that Valthaeron served to us this morning.

Straight ahead, through an arched doorway, I can see a bathing room. Even now that the sun has set, it feels warm and bright in there, lit by more of those crystal sconces. A large clawfoot soaking tub sits in the center of the room, deep enough to submerge in completely. Glass bottles of brightly colored soaps line a marble countertop to its left, while pink towels are folded neatly on a shelf to the right of the tub, looking soft and plush and absurdly luxurious.

It looks like a place someone loved, and maybe even called home.

To our left is a workshop. The atmosphere changes entirely here, as if we've stepped into a different room altogether. The soft carpeted floors give way to hard stone, practical and heat-resistant. Two large worktables sit in the center of the space, their surfaces scarred and scorched with use and age. Along the back wall stands the forge itself—a circular stone base with a hood above it and a fire pit in the middle, currently dark and cold. Tools line the right wall in neat rows: hammers of every size, a massive sledgehammer, chisels in varying widths, a bellows for stoking flames, tongs for handling hot metal, lenses that are most likely for channeling moonlight, and many other implements I can't even name.

And above it all, a large, circular skylight positioned to catch and magnify the moonlight when it rises.

This is a master craftsman's workspace, designed specifically for delicate, precise work. For creating beauty from dangerous, heavy materials.

When I finally tear my eyes away from the space itself and glance at Cairos, his face has gone pale as death. All the blood has drained from his features, leaving him gray and shallow-looking.

He looks like he's seen a ghost.

The guards deposit four wrapped pieces of shadowstone on one of the worktables, then move back toward the door.

"Get started," one of them gruffs. "Valthaeron expects progress by morning. Do not attempt to leave."

They shut the doors behind them with a heavy thud, leaving us alone in this beautiful, haunting space that clearly means something to Cairos I don't yet understand.

The silence that follows feels suffocating.

"Cairos?" I move toward him slowly, like approaching a wild animal. "Are you all right?"

He carefully schools his features back into an unaffected expression, though his jaw is working. When he speaks, his voice is rough and strained. "Perfectly fine. We should get started."

He's lying. Obviously, painfully lying. But I don't push.

I watch him move to the worktables, his movements stiff and mechanical. He unwraps the first bundle of shadowstone with hands that won't quite stay steady, revealing a chunk of that all too familiar material, roughly the size of my fist.

I turn to the wall next to the forge to find tools, and pick out a few, almost automatically, then carry them over and drop them on the worktable.

Cairos looks at me with an inquisitive expression, then turns back to the shadowstone.

The moonlight is starting to creep over the horizon, just in time.

"So," I say, trying to break the suffocating tension. "Should we start with reviewing what we learned in the library? The technique that—"

"I'm familiar with the technique. There's nothing to review." His voice is clipped, cold as the stone beneath our feet.

Well. Hopefully, his work matches his confidence.

"Right. Of course." I move closer to the table, watching him arrange the tools I found. I move to help him organize the implements, but he cuts me off, signalling with a hand for me to stop what I'm doing.

"Just stay out of my way until I need you." He doesn't even look at me, just keeps adjusting and readjusting the same hammer like it's not in the exact right position already. "This requires concentration, and I can't afford distractions."

The dismissal hits like a slap, and something hot and ugly coils in my chest.

I bite my tongue and force myself to count to five, so I won't tear into him when he's clearly already hurting. I remind myself that maybe I should be patient and understanding and all those other virtuous things.

But fuck that, actually. I've *been* patient. I felt something shift between us in that small stone room this morning, something like his walls finally coming down, but now he's trying to pile them back up again.

"I thought we were supposed to be working together," I accuse.

"We are. You'll assist when I tell you to assist." He finally looks at me, and his amber eyes are stone cold. "Until then, just… don't touch anything."

The hot thing in my chest spreads outward, burning through my veins.

I lean against the worktable and cross my arms, watching him. The moonlight grows stronger, now high enough to spill in through the skylight, bathing the room in silver.

He positions the first focusing lens, angling it with minute adjustments until he's satisfied. Then he places the shadowstone in the center of the worktable, right where the moonlight will hit strongest.

"When I tell you," he says without looking at me, "you'll hold this steady. Don't move it. Don't adjust it. Just keep it exactly where I put it."

Oh, wonderful. Clear, detailed instructions. So helpful. Should I also curtsy and thank him for the privilege of being his assistant?

I swallow the sarcasm. Barely.

The moon rises higher. The light intensifies, focusing through one of the lenses Cairos holds into a brilliant beam that hits the shadowstone dead center. I watch, fascinated, as the surface of the stone seems to soften, like clay warmed up by someone's hands.

"Now, hold it," Cairos instructs.

I step forward and press my hands on either side of the stone, feeling the unnatural warmth radiating from where the moonlight touches. It's strange. Shadowstone is usually dark and cold, but under the moonlight, it feels almost alive.

Cairos picks up a small hammer and chisel. He lines up the chisel with a small divot on the side of the piece of shadowstone, lifting the hammer and preparing to bring it down on the wide end of the chisel. He strikes once, clean and controlled.

The shadowstone cracks.

Not a small crack or a hairline fracture for us to work with. A full split, right down the middle, rendering the piece completely unusable.

"Fuck." The word comes out vicious. He throws the chisel down with enough force that it clatters across the worktable.

I pull my hands back quickly, the warmth from the stone still tingling in my palms. "What happened?"

He runs a hand through his hair, pacing the length of the table, but he comes back quickly to start again.

"I started too soon," he says, reaching for another piece of shadowstone, unwrapping it with movements that are just a fraction too rough. "The moonlight needs to penetrate deeper before it's workable."

"Should we wait longer on this one?"

"Obviously." The word comes out harsh, dismissive, and something in me snaps just a little.

Obviously. Like I'm supposed to just know that.

But I bite my tongue again, and watch as he positions the second piece under the moonlight, his jaw still clenched tight.

Then, we wait. The moonlight does its work, seeping into the stone, softening it from the inside out. This time, Cairos waits longer, maybe a full ten minutes, before gesturing for me to hold it steady again.

I do. I press my hands on either side, feeling that strange warmth building beneath the surface, hotter this time.

He strikes again. Chisel to stone, hammer to chisel, the sound ringing through the tower like a bell.

The stone shatters into a dozen pieces that scatter across the worktable like dark stars, completely and utterly ruined.

"Godsdamn it!" Cairos slams both fists down on the table, making the tools jump. His shoulders are heaving, his hands shaking, and there's something wild in his eyes. Something desperate and furious and barely contained.

I step back, giving him space, and watching him war with himself.

He's breaking. Whatever this place is doing to him, it's tearing him apart from the inside out.

Part of me wants to reach for him and offer comfort. I hear Alabris's voice in my head telling me to be patient and soothe him.

But a louder voice in my head, my own, is pissed.

"Maybe if you explained what you're doing, I could actually help instead of just standing here like a decorative statue."

"You want to be of help?" He rounds on me, and there's heat in his gaze now. Not the heat from this morning, though I'd prefer that tenfold to the volatile look he gives me now. "Then stop asking questions and just do *what* I tell you *when* I tell you to do it."

That's it. The torrent of words I've been locking away behind sealed lips bursts forth.

"You know what? Fuck you. I didn't ask to be brought to this castle or forced to forge shadowstone jewelry for a psychotic king. But I am here, and I'm trying, and you're treating me like I'm the problem."

"You are the problem!" The words explode out of him. "You're—" He cuts himself off, runs both hands through his hair hard enough that there's no way it doesn't hurt. "Just—just hand me another piece of shadowstone."

"No."

His head snaps up. "What?"

"I said no." I plant my feet and cross my arms. "Not until you tell me what the hell is going on. Because this?" I gesture between us. "This isn't about forging a necklace or me being clueless about all of this. This is about something else, and I'm not going to keep playing along while you take whatever it is out on me."

"You don't know what you're talking about."

"Then explain it to me! Because I'm really fucking tired of being kept in the dark. I'm tired of you going hot and cold. I'm tired of feeling like I'm walking on eggshells around you now, when just this morning, you treated me like I matter to you, but now it's like I'm nothing. So which is it?"

His eyes flash. "You don't matter."

The words shatter something inside of me, something that I didn't realize was so close to being broken. All my life, I've fought to matter. To matter enough to my parents that putting food on the table for me was less of a burden. To matter to Quinnic and be a good role model for him. And for some Godsforsaken reason, I've been fighting to matter to Cairos, too.

"Excuse me?" I whisper, sounding more pathetic than I intend.

Cairos doesn't soften, though. "Whatever you think is happening between us, it doesn't matter. It *can't* matter."

"Why not?" I say, regaining a little of my strength back, and I can see his jaw clench. "Because of her? Because of Bellamie?"

"Don't." His eyes go dark as night. "Don't say her name."

"Why not? She's clearly the reason you're acting like this. This was her place, wasn't it? Her rooms. Her workshop." Finally, I understand. This isn't about me. Actually, it has nothing to do with me at all. I take a step closer.

"Stop talking," he commands.

"You worked here with her and created things together. Maybe more than that. And now you're back here, and you can't handle it, so you're taking it out on me."

"Stop."

"No." I'm close to him now, close enough to see the way his chest heaves, and his hands tremble. Close enough to smell cedar and smoke and something underneath that's completely and utterly him. "I'm tired of dancing around this, and pretending I don't see the way you look at me sometimes. The way you looked at me this morning when I was bandaging your wound, and our faces were so close I could feel your breath. It felt like you wanted—"

"Stop!" The word tears out of him, raw and desperate.

"Why? Why can't I—"

"Because you're exactly like her!"

The confession explodes into the space between us, and suddenly *he's* the one who can't stop talking.

"Everything about you. The way you put everyone else first, even when it costs you." His nostrils flare as I stand here, stunned. "You worked yourself to the bone so your brother wouldn't have to. Took in your friend when she had nowhere else to go, even though it meant more weight on your shoulders." He pauses, his amber eyes searching mine. "You see people suffering and you can't walk away, even when you should. Even when it would be easier."

His chest is heaving, eyes bright with something that might be tears.

"Bellamie was like that," he says, quieter now but no less devastated. "She was light and fire and fearlessness. She believed in justice and mercy and the inherent goodness of people, even when they gave her no reason to. She looked at Valthaeron's cruelty and said 'This ends.' She looked at the different factions serving the king against their wills in different ways and said 'You deserve freedom.'" Cairos looks down at his own palms. "She looked at me and saw something worth saving. And then she died because of it. Because she was brave and good and believed she could change him, and because I wasn't strong enough, fast enough, or smart enough to stop it. I just stood there and watched him kill her and take her soul, and there was nothing I could do."

"Cairos—" I reach for him, but he jerks away.

"So don't." His voice is raw. "Don't touch me. Don't look at me like that. Don't—" He laughs, bitter and broken. "Don't be *kind* to me. Because I don't deserve it and I can't… I can't do this again. I can't care about someone and watch them die. I can't stand here in her tower, in her workspace, surrounded by her things, and feel—"

He cuts himself off, closing his eyes and taking a shuddering breath.

"Feel what?" I ask, my own voice unsteady.

When he opens his eyes again, the look he gives me is anguished. Guilty. Like he's confessing something unforgivable.

"Feel things for you that I have no right to feel. When you remind me exactly of her and being near you is like being haunted by her ghost. When I look at you, I see everything I loved about her and everything I failed to protect."

The words hang in the air between us, devastating and complicated.

I don't know what to say. How to process the fact that when he looks at me, he sees a dead woman, and whatever I thought was building between us might just be him projecting six hundred years of grief and guilt onto the first person who reminded him of what he lost.

The thought makes me feel physically sick. Hollow. Like I'm not even real, just a shadow of someone else.

"So that's it? I'm just… a replacement?"

"No." He shakes his head violently. "You're not—that's not—" He makes a frustrated sound. "I see you, Naevyn. You're not her. I know that. But you remind me of everything I loved about her, everything I lost, and I—" He presses the heels of his hands against his eyes. "Out there, back in the factions with you, it was easier to ignore just how much you're like her. I could pretend I'd never known someone like you, and I was drawn to you against my better judgment. But here… here, I can't stand it. I can't stand being here with you, feeling things I swore I'd never let myself feel again. Because I know how it ends. I've lived through it once already."

The chasm of silence that stretches between us is deep and resounding as I search for words to say, and Cairos does the same.

Finally, he speaks. "The moonlight won't last forever. We should get back to work, Bells."

The name slips out like it's been dancing on the tip of his tongue all this time.

Then his eyes snap to mine, horror dawning across his features. "Naevyn. I meant—fuck. I'm sorry."

But the damage is done.

21

MINE

I turn away before he can see my face crumple.

Don't cry. Don't you dare fucking cry in front of him.

But my throat is tight, and my eyes burn, and I'm suddenly furious. At him, at myself, at Valthaeron, and at this entire fucked situation.

"Naevyn." His voice sounds close behind me.

"Don't, please. Just don't."

"I need to explain."

"You already did." I wrap my arms around myself, staring at the darkened forge across the room. Anywhere to keep myself from turning around and looking at him. "I'm exactly like her. I get it. When you look at me, you see a dead woman. Message received."

"That's not what I meant." Frustration bleeds into his tone. "You're twisting it."

"Actually, I'm not." I whirl to face him. "It sounded pretty clear to me. Everything about me reminds you of her. I'm just a replacement. Someone convenient for you to project your feelings onto."

"No." He takes a step toward me, and I take a step back. The motion stops him cold. "Naevyn, that's not what this is."

"Then what is it? Explain it to me. Make it make sense. Because right now all I'm hearing is that I'm not actually me to you."

I pray to the Gods that he can't detect the hurt in my voice, the way I feel on the verge of tears.

"You're you, I know that. You're… fuck, I'm doing this wrong. I'm making it worse."

"Yeah. You are," I say flatly.

"Let me…" He reaches for me and I sidestep, putting the corner of the worktable between us.

"Don't touch me right now." My voice quiets. "I can't think when you touch me."

And that's the problem, isn't it? One brush of his fingers and my brain seizes up. One look from those amber eyes and I forget why I should be guarded. One moment of his attention and I'm ready to do something monumentally stupid like believe he actually sees me.

But he doesn't. He sees her.

"Naevyn." There's something raw in the way he says my name. "Please. Just give me a moment."

"Fine." I cross my arms, holding myself together through sheer force of will. "Explain."

He circles the worktable slowly, opening up the space between us, and I shift to add distance. Some twisted dance neither of us know the right steps to.

"Yes, you remind me of Bellamie," he starts, and I flinch. "Your fire. Your stubbornness. Your kindness. All of that feels familiar."

"Great. Wonderful."

"Will you let me finish?" His voice drops lower, and there's an edge of command in it that makes my spine straighten involuntarily. "Yes, you remind me of her. But that's not why I'm standing here losing my fucking mind."

I blink. "What?"

"I'm not bothered because you remind me of her." He stops circling, plants his hands flat on the edge of the worktable next to me, and turns to look at me with eyes that burn. "I'm bothered because I want you so badly I can barely breathe. Because every time you look at me, I forget how to think. When you touch me, even just to bandage a wound, I have to remind myself not to pull you closer and never let go. Something about you draws me in so fucking much, I think I'll die if I don't have you."

My mouth goes dry.

He wants me. Not her. Me.

"I spent hundreds of years telling myself I'd never feel this again, because Bellamie was my one chance and I'd lost it. That I was destined to be alone for the rest of my immortal life because I'd already used up my miracle." He pauses, taking a deep breath through his nostrils. "And then you walked into my life. And suddenly I can't stop thinking about you, wanting you. Can't stop feeling like my soul recognizes yours even though that should be impossible."

"Cairos…"

"Fae call it *cirance*," he says quietly. "Soul recognition. When you look at someone and just know they're meant to be yours. That some fundamental part of you has found its other half."

My heart hammers against my ribs.

Soulmates. He's talking about soulmates. Destiny. Some cosmic bullshit that should sound ridiculous, but it doesn't. Not when he's looking at me like that.

"I thought Bellamie was my *cirance*," he continues. "My one recognition. And when she died, I thought that was it. That I'd spend eternity alone."

"But?" I breathe.

"But then I met you." His eyes lock on mine, and the intensity in them makes me want to both run and stay in equal measure. "And I felt it again. Stronger than before. More consuming. And yes, you remind me of her. But that's not why I'm terrified. I'm terrified because what I feel for you has nothing to do with her and everything to do with you."

Oh.

Oh fuck.

"You're your own fire," he says, voice dropping lower. "Your own fury. And I want you. Not because you remind me of someone else. Not because you fill a hole she left. But because you're you. You're devastating, and I want you so much it physically hurts."

The confession hangs thick in the air between us.

I don't know what to say or how to process the fact that underneath the arrogance and sarcasm, he's been hiding all of this.

"I don't know if I believe in fate. Or soulmates, or any of that," I admit.

"Neither do I." He moves then, leaving only inches between us. He's so close that I have to tilt my chin upward just to see his face properly. "But I know that when I look at you, something in me recognizes something in you. And I'm tired of fighting it."

"Cairos," I start, but don't know how to finish.

His hands come up to frame my face, his thumb tracing along my jaw, sending lightning bolts racing through my body. Then his mouth crashes down onto mine.

Oh. My. Gods.

His lips are hot like fire, claiming mine with a hunger that makes my knees weak. This isn't gentle or tentative, but centuries of loneliness pouring out through his mouth and his hands, and the desperate way he pulls my body against his.

I should push him away. He just confessed more real things to me in the last ten minutes than he has in the previous weeks I've known him, and it's more than I'll be able to process in a lifetime. I should tell him we need to talk more, to figure out what's real and what's not, and establish some kind of boundary before we cross lines we can't uncross.

But I don't.

I kiss him back just as desperately, my hands balling up the fabric of his shirt, and suddenly I understand what he meant about recognition. Because something in me *does* recognize this. Recognizes *him*. Like my body knows his body, even though we've never done this before. Like we've kissed a thousand times in a thousand lifetimes, and this is just remembering.

That's insane. That's completely fucking insane, and I need to stop thinking and just feel because holy gods he tastes like…

His tongue traces my bottom lip, and I open for him without thinking. The kiss deepens, turns molten, and I make a sound that's embarrassingly close to a whimper.

He makes a sound, too, but his is between a grunt and a growl. One of his hands slips up into my hair, and the other grips my waist, pulling me closer, closer, until there's no space at all.

His canines scrape against my lip. Not hard enough to draw blood, but enough to remind me that he's fae, that he's other, and that there's danger in this. The feeling of his teeth on me kickstarts a warmth between my legs.

"Fuck," he breathes against my mouth. He breaks the kiss just long enough to drag his nose along my jaw, inhaling deeply. "You smell ready, and it's just for me. It makes me want to…"

He cuts himself off, but his grip on my waist tightens.

Want to what? Finish the sentence. Gods, please finish the sentence.

But he just kisses me again instead. His teeth graze my lip again, making me gasp, and he swallows the sound like he's starving for it.

My hands find their way under his shirt, mapping the scarred planes of his chest and abdomen. His body is all smooth, lean muscle, and touching him like this, skin to skin, nothing between us but heat and desire, makes something in my brain seize entirely.

This is happening. This is actually happening. I'm kissing Cairos in Bellamie's tower, and he's kissing me back. I should stop this, should think about what it means, but…

"Don't think," he murmurs against my lips, like he can read my mind. "Just feel. Please. I need you just to feel."

So I do.

I stop thinking about Bellamie and soulmates and whether this is real or not. Stop thinking about Valthaeron and prophecies and the fact that we're supposed to be forging a necklace. Stop thinking entirely.

And just feel.

I register the way his mouth moves over mine, every shift of his lips sending sharp little quakes through me. His hands drag over my body like he's trying to memorize every curve, every place I might break for him.

My own hands won't stay still, either. They're skimming his chest, his shoulders, the warm line of his neck, threading into his hair because I need him closer than close.

And when I bite his bottom lip the way he bit mine, he lets out a low, desperate growl that sparks straight down my spine.

"Naevyn. Gods, you're…"

He doesn't finish. Just kisses me deeper, harder, until I'm backed against the worktable and he's pressed against me, and I can feel every hard line of him.

This man wants me. This thousand-year-old fae who's been through hell over and over again is here with me, acting like I'm his salvation.

The realization hits somewhere between one kiss and the next, and it's devastating and empowering and terrifying all at once.

That's when his mouth leaves mine to trail down my jaw, my neck, and when his teeth graze the sensitive spot just below my ear I actually moan. The sound seems to snap something in him because his grip tightens and he pulls me impossibly closer and—

"I want to take you to that bed." His voice is rough, wrecked. "Want to strip every piece of fabric off of your body. Want to taste every inch of your skin until you forget anyone that existed before me. I want all of you. Your body, your soul, your every thought. I want to mark you so every other fae knows you're mine."

Holy fuck. Holy fuck holy fuck holy…

My brain has completely abandoned me. Every rational thought has been replaced by pure sensation and want, and the desperate need for him to make good on every word he just said.

"Then why don't you?" The words come out breathy.

He pulls back just enough to look at me, and his eyes are molten. Pupils blown wide, nearly swallowing the amber. "Because once I start, I won't be able to stop. And you need to be sure. You need to know what you're getting into."

"I'm sure." Am I? I don't know, but my body is sure, and right now that feels like enough.

"You're not." His thumb traces my swollen bottom lip, and the gentle touch is somehow more intimate than the kiss. "You're caught up in the moment. In the emotion and the adrenaline. But tomorrow…"

"Tomorrow doesn't exist." I catch his wrist, hold his hand against my face as our eyes stay locked on one another's, smoldering and intense. "There's only tonight. Only right now. And right now I want…" I swallow hard. "I want you."

He closes his eyes like the words cause him pain. "You don't know what you're asking for."

"Then tell me. Explain it to me."

When he opens his eyes again, there's something feral in them. Something barely contained. "Fae don't love like humans. When we bond, when we *truly* bond with someone, it's consuming. Possessive. I would want all of you. Your body, your soul, your every thought. I would want to mark you so every other fae knows you're mine. I would want things you're not ready to give."

Mark me? What does that even mean? And why does the idea of belonging to him make heat pool between my thighs instead of making me run?

"Maybe I'm ready," I whisper.

Cairos takes a deep breath in through his nostrils as if he's warring with himself.

"You're not," he says finally. He steps back, putting distance between us, and I immediately miss the heat of him. "And I'm not going to take advantage of you in a moment of vulnerability. Not like this."

His hand traces my cheek, grounding me back in reality.

"You're right." I wrap my arms around myself, suddenly cold. "This is too much. Too fast."

"It is," Cairos says, but he doesn't sound happy about the admission. "We should sleep now."

He's right. I know he's right.

But knowing doesn't make it any easier to fight this pull between us.

22

TRAPPED

No invitation to breakfast comes from Valthaeron this morning. Instead, a tray is brought up to my room containing eggs and sausage, biscuits, green grapes, and an orange sliced to look like a swan. More of that crimson berry juice accompanies it, and my mouth waters uncontrollably at the scent of all this food.

I stare at the elaborate spread and hope that Cairos received rations just like this. Or better. He deserves better with all that he's been through. With everything Valthaeron has put him through.

My heart leaps at the thought of him, and I wonder if he's thinking of me, too.

I shake off the thought and begin to eat, the artfully-prepared food nearly melting in my mouth. Savoring it would be ideal, but an anxiety rises in me about being separated from Cairos that makes me eat significantly faster than usual. Every bite holds a bitterness from the longing I feel.

When I finish, I dress quickly in the deep purple tunic that's been left for me in the wardrobe. The fabric is soft and luxurious, and I try not to think about what it means that Valthaeron is clothing me like a doll.

I knock on the door to let the guards know I've finished eating, hoping—desperately hoping—that they'll reunite me with Cairos. Leaving him last night as the guards escorted us to our separate rooms felt like losing the only beacon of light in a dark and desolate place, and the hours since have only made that ache worse.

Unfortunately for me, the two guards stationed outside my door lead me down the stairs and out to the garden instead.

"King Valthaeron requests that you work here today," one gruffs.

"He what? Work here how?" I ask, but my questions fall upon deaf ears as the guards station themselves near the door to the castle, dismissing me with their silence.

I cast around at the garden that's long since been dead. The rose bushes look like glass tumbleweeds that might fly away if the wind blows too hard, and the climbing plants resemble twisted, skeletal vines trying to claw their way up and over the garden walls. Dead leaves crunch beneath my feet, and the flowerbeds are nothing but dirt and desiccated stems.

The only good thing about being here today is the sun. It hits warm against my skin, a feeling I hadn't realized how much I missed. The golden light bathes the garden and gives it a hint of the life that it's missing, painting everything in shades of orange and gold that make the death seem beautiful, in a way.

How am I supposed to "work on it"? Valthaeron *is* aware that I'm not fae, right? That I don't have magic and I can't just wave my hands and bring dead things back to life.

I know these thoughts are unhelpful, but I can't help but have them as I stumble down the vine-ridden path. The garden feels like a test I'm destined to fail. Like another one of Valthaeron's games, designed to humiliate me or prove some point I don't understand yet.

I consider beginning to pull the dead plants, but something about that feels wrong, somehow. Disrespectful, maybe. Like disturbing a graveyard. Instead, I kneel down in the dirt—uncaring about the purple tunic that's probably going to be stained with dirt—and gently pull the vines away from what might have once been a fountain, careful not to let the fragile glass break. The stone is cracked and dry, but underneath the decay, I can see hints of careful craftsmanship. Someone loved this place once, and tended to it with care.

Knowing that it was Bellamie's garden makes a sort of reverence rise in my chest. I feel unworthy being here, trying to fix what she so carefully created.

The thought comes unbidden, and I push it away as quickly as it arrives. I don't want to think about her. Don't want to imagine her here, walking these paths, touching these roses when they were still alive.

I focus on the vines instead, carefully untangling them from the fountain's base. It's slow work, methodical, and my fingers ache within minutes. But at least it's something. At least I'm doing *something* besides sitting in that tower room thinking about the way Cairos's lips felt against mine.

What feels like hours pass as I make my way along the path, clearing it as the sun rises higher in the sky. When my fingertips begin to feel numb, I rise from my knees and brush off as much dirt as I can. The bench across from the familiar statue looks like a reprieve, and I gratefully take a seat. I close my eyes for a moment, letting the sun warm my eyelids from the outside in, turning my vision red. When I open my eyes, the world holds shades of purple and blue that weren't there before. I focus my gaze on the statue in front of me and swear I see her eyes move.

I swipe at my eyes with the back of my hands, squinting them closed, then opening them again. That had to be an illusion.

When I look at her again, there's no more movement. Still, the statue looks sentient somehow, like there's life behind the eyes. More than that, even. Intelligence. Awareness. Like someone trapped inside is looking back at me.

"Hello?" I whisper, casting a glance behind me at the guards still stationed by the door. They're not paying attention, talking quietly to each other.

Nothing. Of course it's just my mind playing tricks on me. Maybe I've been out here in the hot sun for too long, or maybe my brain is just dizzy with too many thoughts of Cairos. Either way, I'm probably going crazy.

But those eyes. Gods, those eyes. The pupils look black, and they actually seem to be *watching* me.

"Is anyone in there?" I whisper again, leaning closer, knowing full well that if anyone catches me asking questions to a statue, I'll probably be locked back in my tower.

"Mmfph," mumbles the statue.

I jump back so quickly I nearly fall over, my heart slamming against my ribs. My hands fly to my mouth to muffle the scream threatening to escape.

Holy gods. Someone's in there.

Someone is *actually* in there.

My breath comes in short, panicked gasps. This isn't possible. This *can't* be possible. Statues don't talk. Glass doesn't make noise. But I heard it. I definitely heard it.

"Are you—" I have to stop, swallow hard, and try again. "Are you hurt?"

"Mmfph," the statue answers, and this time I can see the way the lips don't move, but the sound definitely comes from inside. From whoever she is.

My hands are shaking so badly I have to press them down into my thighs. Clearly, I'm not going to get any answers like this. I lean in closer, studying her face, and somehow her glass eyes look pleading and desperate. Like she's screaming for help but can't make the words come out.

Like she's been screaming for a very, very long time.

"Oh gods," I breathe, the horror of it crashing over me. "Who are you?"

The eyes seem to focus on me more intently. Or maybe I'm imagining it. Maybe I've actually lost my mind, and I'm hallucinating conversations with garden statuary.

But the sound was real. I *know* it was real.

I study her face, trying to place it. She's beautiful with delicate features, high cheekbones, and a serene expression that must have been in place before whatever turned her to glass. But I don't recognize her. Don't know who she is or why she's here or how long she's been trapped like this.

"I'm going to help you," I say, and I'm surprised by how steady my voice comes out despite the terror coursing through me. "I promise. I don't know how yet, but I promise."

My mind races. What do I do? How do I help someone who's been turned to glass? Is she even alive in there? Can she feel? Can she think? Has she been aware this entire time, trapped in her own body, unable to move or speak or—

I'm going to be sick.

I have to tell Cairos. I have to get him to help me. Maybe he can use his magic to communicate with her. Maybe he knows what this is and how to break it. Maybe he even knows who she is.

Because I don't.

"I have to keep working," I whisper to the statue. "So the guards don't get suspicious. But I'm going to help you. I'm going to get Cairos, and we're going to figure out how to free you. Just—just hold on. Okay?"

"Mmf," comes the muffled response, and I choose to believe it's agreement.

I force myself to stand, to pick up another handful of vines. I go through the motions of clearing the garden, but my hands are shaking so badly I can barely grip anything.

Before I move away to the next section, I face her one more time, and before I can stop myself, I press my hands on either of her shoulders. "I promise," I whisper again.

Warmth floods through my palms.

Not just warmth, though. *Heat.* Like touching sunlight concentrated into liquid form. It rushes up my arms, through my chest, filling me with something that feels familiar and foreign all at once. Like recognizing a song I've never heard before. Like coming home to a place I've never been.

Magic.

This is magic.

I gasp and pull my hands back like I've touched something electric, stumbling backward. The sensation lingers in my palms, tingling and alive and utterly impossible.

"What the—" I stare at my hands, then at the statue, then back at my hands. "What was that?"

The statue's eyes seem brighter now. More alive. Like whatever just passed between us woke something up.

My heart is racing. My whole body is trembling. I don't understand what just happened, but I know it was important.

I look back at the guards again. Still not paying attention.

I press my hands to the glass one more time, and the warmth floods through me again. Stronger this time, like she's trying to tell me something.

"I hear you," I whisper. "I don't understand it yet, but I hear you. And I'm going to help you. I'm going to find out who you are and how to free you."

And I swear the glass beneath my palms grows warmer, like she's saying *thank you.*

I pull away, my hands still tingling with residual magic, and force myself back to clearing vines. My mind is spinning with possibilities and questions and the overwhelming weight of what I've just discovered.

There's someone trapped in this garden.

Someone Valthaeron locked away in a prison hidden in plain sight.

And somehow, I need to free her.

"Time's up," a voice commands from behind me. A shriek escapes my lips as I scramble to attention, hoping with everything I have that I wasn't caught talking to a statue.

The guard lets out a grunt, then turns and walks down the path. I follow after him, fighting the urge to look back, just one more time.

As we enter back into the castle, I work to convince myself that everything is fine. Completely fine. My brother is back in Xardon, I've witnessed the mass murder of fellow humans at the hands of a man I suddenly find myself falling for, and I'm supposed to create an artifact for an evil king. Oh, and there's a person stuck in a statue in the garden, and I'm the only one who knows she's there.

Everything is…

Fine.

Fine. That's what Cairos is as he crosses the hallway in front of us wearing only a towel.

My feet stop moving. My brain stops working.

Water drips from his black locks, the wet strands curling outward in a messy way that should be illegal. Droplets trace paths down his very bare, very defined chest, following the contours of muscle that I definitely wasn't staring at before but am absolutely staring at now.

His abdomen is a study in controlled power. Muscle carved into definition that speaks of unimaginable strength. Those mesmerizing tattoos across his left shoulder and abdomen, disappearing beneath his towel. And there, just below his ribs on the left side, is that scar. A long, wicked thing that looks like it should have killed him. The pale line cuts across his skin, a reminder of violence survived, and somehow it only makes him more devastatingly attractive.

My mouth goes dry.

He catches my eye just before disappearing behind the wall, but not before I see the way his lips curve into that insufferable smirk that says he knows exactly what he's doing to me. The one that makes me want to simultaneously punch him and pull him closer.

"Move along," one of the guards grunts, and I realize I've been standing frozen in the middle of the hallway like an idiot.

Right. Moving. That's something people do.

I force my feet to work, my cheeks burning hot enough to rival Xardon. Of course he'd walk past wearing nothing but a towel. Of course he'd catch me staring. Of course he'd look like that, all wet and gleaming and built by someone who clearly had opinions about what the perfect male form should be.

And of course my traitorous body would react like I've never seen an attractive man before. Though, the reality is I've never seen anyone who looks like him. Never seen shoulders that broad or a waist that tapered or—

Stop. Stop thinking about his body. There are more important things to think about. Like the woman in the garden, and how I need to tell Cairos about her without the guards overhearing.

But my mind keeps circling back to water droplets and muscle definition and that scar that I suddenly want to trace with my fingers.

I am absolutely losing my mind.

The guards lead me up the stairs toward the tower, and I really try to focus on anything other than the image of Cairos in a towel that's now permanently burned into my brain.

I'm thirsty. That's the problem. I've been out in the garden all day in the hot sun, and now I'm dehydrated and clearly not thinking straight. That's why my heart is racing. That's why my skin feels too hot. That's why I can't stop thinking about the way water droplets traced down his chest, following that line of muscle down to where the towel hung low on his hips…

"Water," I croak out to the guards. "Can I have water?"

One of them looks at me with barely concealed annoyance, but he nods. "It will be brought to your room."

My room. Not the tower. Not with Cairos.

Which is probably for the best, considering I apparently can't be trusted to form coherent thoughts in his presence when he's fully clothed, let alone when he's dripping wet and half-naked.

But I need to talk to him.

Tonight. I'll tell him tonight when I can actually speak in complete sentences and not just stare at him.

The guards deposit me in my room and close the door with that familiar heavy thunk. I sink onto the bed, my purple tunic stiff with dried sweat and dirt, my hands still aching from pulling vines all day.

And I try very, very hard not to think about Cairos in that towel.

I fail spectacularly.

23

THE BOND

That night brings circular thoughts and an anxiety that threatens to tear me to pieces. I wait to be called to the forge with Cairos, but no one ever comes. After the previous days, I don't expect a break from toiling, but maybe that's what Valthaeron wants—to keep us on edge, not knowing what to expect. I lie there tossing and turning, restless, for as long as I can stand.

I roll out of bed more quickly than I intend, adrenaline shooting through my entire body and jolting me upright. My feet hit the cold floor, a reminder of where I am. I wrap my arms around myself, giving my arms a rub to keep out the chill. Outside, clouds cover the sky, making the already-darkened landscape look black as pitch.

Suddenly, the door swings open behind me. My breath hitches as I whirl around. The room is too dark to see, but a low voice cuts through the silence.

"You've been waiting for me."

"Cairos," I say quickly, tightening the silken robe I've been wearing. "No, I couldn't sleep."

"Why couldn't you sleep?" He asks, closing the door behind him with a quiet click, then taking heavy steps into the room.

"I—I just—" I stutter out. Shit. What can I even tell him? That thoughts of him in just a towel had me in too much of a tizzy? That I'm problem-solving how to save a woman trapped in a garden statue, but I can't even recollect that properly because he's here in my room now after dark?

In the dim light of the moon that manages to sneak out around the clouds, I think I can make out a tiny smirk upturning his lips. He isn't going to let me out of this one. He's just going to stand there waiting, eyes dancing while I scramble for an answer.

I take a moment to gather my thoughts because I refuse to let him see me squirm. Deep breath in, breathe out.

"I was thinking about something. The garden," I answer finally.

The smirk disappears, replaced by straight lips and lowered brows.

"What about the garden?" Cairos shifts his weight from one foot to another.

"There's a statue there… who is that?" I ask.

His entire body goes rigid. The playful energy that filled the room just seconds ago evaporates, replaced by something cold as ice.

"The statue," he repeats slowly, his voice carefully controlled. "You mean the glass one near the path?"

"Yes. There's someone inside it. Someone alive."

He blinks. Then, to my absolute fury, he laughs. "You think there's someone alive inside a glass statue?"

"I know how it sounds—"

"It sounds like you've been out in the sun too long. Heat stroke can do funny things to the mind, Little Wren."

"I'm not imagining it." My cheeks burn, but I refuse to back down. "I heard her. She tried to speak to me, but all that came out were muffled sounds."

"Muffled sounds… from a statue."

"Yes."

"A glass statue."

"Stop saying it like that. I know what I heard, Cairos. And when I touched her, I felt something. It was like she was trying to reach me through warmth. I… I think it was magic."

His expression becomes more guarded. "You touched the statue."

"Yes."

"And you felt… magic." He's interested now. "What kind of magic?"

"I don't know. It was warm, and it felt like recognition." I struggle to find the right words. "Like she was trying to tell me something important."

He's quiet for too long, then he shakes his head, and I want to hit him. "That statue has been there for over six hundred years. It's glass. Nothing more."

"Then who is it? Who was she?" I demand, crossing my arms for emphasis.

I see his jaw working before he answers. "Her name was Orlia. She was… someone important. Someone Valthaeron killed a long time ago."

"But what if he didn't kill her?" I press. "What if he turned her to glass instead? Trapped her inside as some kind of punishment?"

"That's not possible." But there's doubt in his voice now. "Curses don't work that way. You can't trap a living consciousness inside glass."

"How do you know?" I challenge. "Have you tried?"

I'm baiting him now, and I know it. He doesn't rise to it, though.

"It isn't possible."

"Why?"

"Because I would have known." His voice rises slightly, losing some of that cocky control. "I would have sensed it. Felt it. I've been in that garden countless times since that statue was erected and never once have I—" He cuts himself off, running a hand through his hair in frustration.

"Never once what?"

"Nothing." He turns away from me. "You're imagining things. The heat, the stress, and being in this castle is getting to you."

"I'm not crazy."

"I didn't say you were crazy." He spins back around, and now there's a desperate edge to his voice. "I'm saying you're mistaken. That statue is just glass. It has to be just glass."

Understanding crashes over me. "You don't want it to be real."

"Of course I don't want it to be real." His voice cracks slightly. "Because if you're right, if she's been trapped in there all this time, aware and suffering, then I've failed her all this time." He stops, his breathing harsh.

"Who was she to you?"

His silence is deafening, and I'm about to repeat the question when, finally, he speaks. "She was Bellamie's mother."

The words land heavy in my chest. "Oh."

"So you see why I can't—why I *won't*—entertain this idea that she's somehow alive in there. Because if she is, if she's been conscious this entire time, then what I've failed to do is inconscionable."

"Cairos—"

"You're wrong." He says it with finality.

"Then come with me tomorrow." I close the distance between us. "Come to the garden with me and see for yourself. Touch the statue. Feel what I felt."

"And when I feel nothing? When it's just cold glass?"

"Then I'll accept that I was wrong." I look up at him. "But if I'm not, we can't just leave her."

Conflict is clear in every line of his face, even in this darkened room. "I'm not saying I believe you, but if you're right—and that's a big if—then she'd be freed when Valthaeron dies anyway. Every spell, every curse bound to him would unravel."

"So we save her by killing him."

"Precisely," Cairos confirms.

There's a quiet that's comfortable now, with the question of how to save Orlia tabled.

"You know, for someone who's supposed to be confident, you sound awfully afraid of being wrong," I say, breaking the silence.

The corner of his mouth twitches despite himself. "I'm not afraid of being wrong. I'm afraid of you being right."

"That's the same thing."

"It absolutely isn't." But he's almost smiling now, some of the tension bleeding out of his shoulders. His gaze drops to my mouth, then drags back up. Slow. Deliberate. "I wouldn't want you getting cocky."

"Hard not to when you're here in my room, in the middle of the night, breaking at least a dozen rules."

His smirk returns, slow and dangerous and absolutely devastating. "Are you suggesting I had ulterior motives?"

"I'm suggesting you couldn't stay away, even though it's in your best interest."

His hand comes up to cup my jaw, thumb brushing across my cheekbone with agonizing slowness. "I've never been very good at doing what I should."

My breath catches. The room suddenly feels warmer. "Cairos—"

"You're still thinking about it, aren't you?" His voice drops lower, intimate, wrapping around me like smoke. "About seeing me in that towel earlier. About how close I was to being naked. About what might have happened if I'd dropped it."

Fuck.

"You're absurd."

"You're avoiding the question." His thumb traces my lower lip now, and I feel the touch like a live wire straight between my thighs. "Your pulse is racing. Your pupils are dilated. And you're looking at me like you want to either kill me or kiss me, and I'm hoping very much that it's the latter."

"We were talking about the statue," I manage weakly.

"We were. Now we're talking about this." He leans in closer, his breath warm against my lips. Close enough to kiss but not quite touching. The bastard. "About the way you've been watching me, and frankly, the way I've been watching you. About all the reasons we shouldn't do this, and yet, how little either of us seems to care."

I should pull away, but I'm not. I can't. My body has other plans entirely.

His forehead drops to rest against mine, and I feel the contact like lightning, his hot breath against my cheek. "Tell me to leave, Naevyn. Tell me you don't want this and I'll walk out that door right now."

I should.

But I can't.

Instead, I fist my hands in his shirt and pull him down to meet me.

"Don't leave," I whisper against his mouth in the most pitiful way. "Stay."

His response is immediate and devastating. His hand slides into my hair, pulling it and angling my head back as he claims my mouth in a kiss that's hungry and ruinous.

"Gods," he groans against my lips, his other hand gripping my hip hard enough to bruise. "Do you have any idea how long I've wanted this?"

"Show me," I breathe back.

And he does.

His mouth moves to my neck, teeth grazing my pulse point, and I gasp, arching into him. His body is solid heat against mine. The hand in my hair tightens, just enough to make me whimper, and I feel his smile against my throat.

"Sensitive there?" His voice is pure sin. "Good to know."

"Shut up and kiss me."

"So demanding," he laughs. But he does, his mouth crashing back onto mine with bruising intensity. His tongue sweeps past my lips, claiming, conquering, and I give as good as I get, my nails digging into his shoulders through his shirt.

His hands skim down my sides, tracing the curve of my waist, the dip of my hip. He palms the edge of my robe, teasing it open with a touch that's far too gentle for the fire I see burning behind his eyes.

"Lift your arms," he commands against my throat.

I do.

He slides the silk up and over with excruciating care, knuckles brushing the undersides of my breasts, the dip of my ribs, and gods, it's more intimate than being stripped in one motion. He drinks in every inch as it's revealed, slow and deliberate, like each patch of bare skin is a secret he's being trusted to keep.

The robe slips from my wrists and pools noiselessly onto the floor.

He steps back a half-pace to take me in as best as he can in the dim light. His gaze is reverent. Ravenous. One corner of his mouth lifts like he's been waiting to see me like this forever.

"Fuck," he murmurs. "You are… everything."

My cheeks flush, but I don't look away. I won't. Not when he's looking at me like I'm everything he's ever dreamed of.

Then I reach for him.

My fingers find the hem of his shirt and I slide it up, slow and deliberate, tracing each plane of muscle revealed beneath. I press a kiss to his sternum, then another along the ridges of his abdomen as I lift the fabric. He shudders.

"Off," I command.

He obliges.

The shirt drops somewhere behind him, forgotten.

He walks me backward until my legs hit the bed, and then we're falling, his weight pressing me into the mattress in the best possible way. I can feel every inch of him. His chest as it presses into my now-bare breasts, the muscles in his arms bracketing my head, and oh gods, the thick length of him pressing against my thigh through his pants.

"Cairos," I gasp when his mouth moves lower, trailing fire down my throat to my collarbone.

"Say it again." His teeth find the side of my neck, tugging. "I want to hear my name in your mouth when I make you fall apart."

Fuck. I'm in so much trouble.

But I don't care. Can't care. Not when his hands are exploring my skin and every nerve ending in my body is screaming for more.

He continues trailing bites and kisses down my neck, slowly—agonizingly slow—as I wait for him to go lower.

"Cairos," I breathe, and his answering groan vibrates through me.

"That's it, Little Wren." His hands grip my breasts, kneading them. "Let me hear you."

His palms are smooth, oh-so-perfect as they mold over my breasts, as if they belong there. He navigates them expertly, like he already knows their shape, their weight, and expects the way my breath catches when his thumbs graze over the peaks.

"You're so soft," he murmurs, like he's talking to himself more than to me. "And so fucking responsive."

He rolls one nipple between his fingers, slow and deliberate, watching my face like he's studying the way I come undone. My back arches instinctively, offering more, chasing the next touch, the next rush of sensation.

I hate how easily he reads me. Hate it, and want more of it.

"Sensitive," he says again. His mouth follows the path of his hands, replacing fingertips with lips and tongue, until he draws one aching peak into his mouth and sucks.

I gasp, the sound high and sharp and entirely involuntary. He groans like that reaction was his reward, his hips grinding his rock-hard bulge unconsciously against my thigh as if he's already barely holding on.

His tongue flicks, teases, then soothes the bite of cool air with another slow pull into his mouth. My hands find his broad shoulders, and I dig my nails in because it's all too much and not enough at once.

"Cairos," I whisper, and he hums against my skin, the vibration sending a fresh pulse of heat between my thighs.

He switches to the other breast, dragging his lips across my chest like he's savoring the taste of me. His hand slides lower, tracing the curve of my waist, settling at the front of my hip like a promise of what's to come.

"You make the prettiest sounds," he says, lifting his head just enough to speak against my skin. "And I haven't even gotten to the best part yet."

"Then stop teasing," I manage, despite the pleasure sending me out of my mind.

The smug bastard grins against my skin and closes his lips around my nipple again, sucking harder this time, sharp teeth scraping just enough to make me cry out and clamp my thighs together in response.

He doesn't rush.

He takes his time playing with me, tugging and biting and pressing soft kisses across the swell of each breast, like he's worshipping them until I'm squirming beneath him, hips rocking up for any kind of friction against my swollen clit, my breath a fractured mess.

"Are you begging yet?" he asks, and the gleam in his eyes is pure trouble.

"No," I lie.

His chuckle is low and wicked. "You will be."

Then his hand slips lower, and I break. I can't control my impulses as I trail my fingertips down to the waistband of his trousers, unfastening them with more urgency now. My knuckles brush the hard length of him and my brain stutters again.

Still huge. Still terrifying.

Cairos watches my face like it's his favorite thing.

"Impressed?" he says with a cocky edge.

"Just wondering how this is going to work."

He laughs, and it's low and hot and completely wicked.

"You'll be fine," he says. "Eventually."

Cairos stands and unbuttons his own pants, his arm muscles rippling as he works at the buttons. I take this moment to catch my breath, unable to tear my eyes away from his body. He unclothes himself slow enough to make me forget how breathing works. His eyes lock on mine as he glances up through his lashes, watching me for any sign of a reaction.

And when he's finally bare?

Oh gods.

My mouth goes dry. My brain breaks clean in half.

He's huge.

Not just big. Not even "I hope I survive this" big, but "I might need to pray to all of the Gods that I get through this" huge.

I try not to stare, but fail miserably.

Cairos notices. Of course he notices.

"That face… is that awe or terror?"

"Mild, maybe moderate terror."

He grins wider, unrepentant. "I'd say 'I'll be gentle,'" he murmurs, leaning back down over me and placing a muscular fist on either side of my head, "but we'd both know I'm lying."

I try to laugh, but it comes out breathless. Because now he's hovering over me, his body radiating heat, every inch of him pure tension and promise. His cock rests heavily against my thigh, and my breath stutters at the weight of it.

And then he kisses me again, hot and consuming, like he's starving and I'm his last meal. Like he's trying to distract me from the monstrosity that he plans to plunge deep inside me. His hands roam with possessive certainty, cupping, sliding, teasing. One hand stays beside my head while the other grips my hip, anchoring me beneath him.

I whimper shamelessly now.

He kisses me again, hard and deep and dizzying, all teasing gone. His other hand slides between my thighs and finds me slick and ready. He hums against my mouth, clearly pleased with himself, then moves lower.

"You're soaked," he murmurs. "You've been aching for this as long as I have, haven't you?"

"Shut up," I manage, panting.

He bites my bottom lip and chuckles. "Make me."

Gods help me, I try. But everything else blurs.

He lines himself up at my entrance and doesn't pause for long. "Eyes on me, love," he says, voice low and firm. "I want to watch you take me."

And then he pushes in.

The stretch is impossible. My body fights it, then yields, trembling around the intrusion. I claw at his back, gasp, arch. He moves slowly, inch by excruciating inch, until I feel filled past reason. So deep I can barely breathe.

He's not even all the way in yet.

"Gods, Cairos," I gasp.

His voice is wrecked, tight with restraint. "You feel… so fucking perfect."

I moan as he sinks deeper. Too much. Too good. I've never felt like this before—never so utterly possessed, so utterly his.

And then something shifts.

Not physically, but deeper. A thrum beneath my skin, a tug in my chest. Like thunder beginning to rumble. It's slow and quiet at first, then stronger and stronger.

I blink.

The air thickens and warms. My vision swims.

Cairos stills inside me, eyes widening.

He feels it too.

When I look down at our bodies, there's a golden thread pulsing faintly between our chests. It wraps around something inside me. Buries into something in him.

"What…" I gasp. "What is that?"

His gaze is fixed on me. "That's us."

He pulls back slightly, and my body protests the loss. So does his, apparently, because he groans like he's torn in half.

"It's soul-bonding," he murmurs, voice rough with awe. I stare at him, heart slamming against my ribs. "I warned you that when fae bond, we bond entirely. A part of me is now shared with you, and you with me."

"Soul-bonding?" I repeat.

Cairos cups my face, eyes searching mine with an intensity that steals my breath. "It means our souls recognize each other. That they've... chosen each other."

I can't speak. A human girl like me, touched by a magical fae bond? I can't even comprehend it.

"You're mine," Cairos murmurs, his thumb stroking my cheek in a gentle way that makes my eyes sting.

And then he moves again, pressing inside me until I see stars.

There's no more slow build. No more teasing.

He fucks me like he's staking a claim in the core of me, nothing but primal, violent need in his movements.

Each thrust is deep, ruthless, devastating. I arch beneath him, whimpering and crying out, unable to do anything but hold on. My legs wrap around his waist instinctively, locking him closer, pulling him deeper as if I were confident I could survive any more of his length.

And the bond, Gods, the bond, it pulses brighter with every collision of our bodies. A hot, glowing thread that feels stitched into my heart, anchoring me to him. Our breathing is in sync, our bodies too. I can't tell where I end and he begins anymore.

He fucks me, carnal, like I belong to him. Like I've *always* belonged to him. Like this moment has lived in his bones since time began, and he's only now finally getting to claim it.

And he *is* claiming it—claiming me.

My fingers claw at his back, and I feel the muscles bunch and flex beneath my palms. I can hear his ragged breathing. I can feel the way his control is fraying with every thrust. How hard he's fighting not to lose himself entirely inside me.

He hits something deep, and I shatter.

My cry is sharp and uncontrollable. My thighs squeeze tighter around him, and my back bows off the bed as pleasure slams through me, white-hot and searing.

Cairos groans in response, but he doesn't stop.

He keeps fucking me through it, chasing his own edge, chasing mine again, pounding into me with that terrifying, delicious rhythm that makes me feel like I'm going to break and be reborn in the same moment.

And then he kisses me hard, lips and teeth and tongue all exploring, the sensation driving me wild.

Because I need him too. Every part of me. My body. My soul. This bond. It's all reaching for him, drawing him in, pulling us closer.

He thrusts again, harder and deeper, and I scream.

The bond flares.

The golden strands grow brighter. A burst of gold light flashes behind my eyes that blinds me to everything but him.

Cairos. My tormentor. My salvation. My… mate? Gods, is that what this is? A feeling so strong and eternal and binding. I don't want this to end. Not ever.

Then he flips us without warning, pulling me on top of him. My thighs straddle his hips, and I nearly sob at the shift in angle. The new depth. The way he fills me from below, hitting my cervix with every upward thrust.

"Ride me," he commands, low and rough.

"I—gods—I can't—"

He grips my hips, helping me move. "Yes, you can," he purrs. "Take it, Naevyn. You were made to take me."

Fuuuck.

I do. I rise and fall over him, shaky at first, then bolder. His hands roam, squeezing my ass and guiding my rhythm. I relax forward, leaning over him, my fingers splaying out over his chest, feeling the way his heart pounds strong and steady like a drum.

He reaches between us and finds my clit, drawing circles over it with his thumb. My whole body coils. My vision narrows to him—his cock driving into me, his fingers teasing, the look of pure, unadulterated pleasure on his face as he watches me fall apart again.

And gods, I do.

My climax hits like thunder, fast, violent, and consuming. I clench around him, scream his name, and the bond flares bright gold between us.

He follows a second later, roaring like an animal, spilling inside me as his body locks, every muscle drawn taut. I collapse onto his chest, panting and trembling.

We lie there, entwined, slick with sweat and dazed, trying to catch our breath.

Cairos brushes a strand of hair off of my face with a gentleness that definitely wasn't there a minute ago. "You alright?"

"Barely," I say breathlessly.

"Do you regret it?"

I lift my head, tilting up to face him and meet his gaze, his eyes burning into me. "No."

He smirks and runs a hand through my hair as I rest my head back on his chest, listening to the thrumming of his heartbeat as it slows. "That's my girl."

The bond hums between us, quiet now, but present.

I trace idle patterns across his chest, following the ridges of old scars, the dips between muscles. His breathing evens out beneath my ear, deep and steady, and I feel myself beginning to drift with it.

"You should go," I murmur, though I make no move to let him leave.

His arms tighten around me. "Not a chance."

"They'll notice you're gone."

"Let them." His voice is rough with exhaustion, but there's steel underneath. "I'm not leaving you tonight."

I want to protest and remind him of the risk he'd be taking, but the words won't come. Because right now, I don't feel fear about the morning. I feel safe. Whole. His.

Sleep takes us both, tangled together in my bed in the dark, and for the first time in longer than I can remember, I don't dream of running.

24

PROPHECY

I gasp as I awaken, Cairos slipping out from underneath me.

"No," I moan out in protest, blinking at the early morning light streaming through the window.

I see Cairos smile through my blurry eyes. "This won't be the last time we touch, Little Wren. I promise."

Now it's my turn to smile, even if just a little. "I thought you said you wouldn't be afraid if they were upset," I argue.

"I'm not afraid. I have obligations." Cairos stands, pulling on his pants one leg at a time and then fastens the button, much to my dismay. At least his bare chest is still on display for me to drool over, which I unabashedly do.

"Obligations such as…?" I sit up, holding the sheet so it covers me while I reach out to run my finger along the scar that trails down his abdomen and disappears beneath the hem of his pants.

"The circus." Cairos bends down to snatch his shirt off the bed and pull it over his head as I let my hand drop.

"What do you mean?" I ask, suddenly far more alert than I was just a moment ago.

"Valthaeron met with me yesterday and called for another circus, and I have to go. Today."

Sheer panic bubbles up in my stomach. My lungs empty themselves of oxygen as I suddenly struggle to breathe.

"You can't."

Cairos pauses, his shirt half-tucked into his pants. "Naevyn —"

"No." I'm on my feet now, sheet clutched to my chest, heart hammering. "You can't go back there. You can't just… after last night…"

"Last night doesn't change my obligation." He speaks carefully, like he's afraid I'll spook.

"Your obligation?" The word comes out sharp and bitter. "To murder people?"

His teeth clench as his jaw tightens. "What else am I supposed to do?"

"Refuse! Say no! Literally anything except killing—"

"And then what?" He rounds on me, and there's something desperate in his eyes now. "Valthaeron kills me for disobedience? Or better yet, he comes after *you* to teach me a lesson?"

I think on that for a long moment, our eyes still locked on one another. When I speak again, my voice is small. "So you're just going to keep killing for him? What about the plan? If it works, he'll be gone soon anyway." My voice breaks. "We're talking about families, Cairos. Children. People who did nothing wrong."

"You think I don't know that?" He's not yelling, but there's an edge to his voice that cuts deeper than shouting.

"Then stop! Just—stop."

"I can't." He reaches for me, but I step back. The hurt that flashes across his face almost breaks me. "Naevyn, please. I don't have a choice."

"There's always a choice." Tears burn hot behind my eyes. "You're just too much of a coward to make it."

He stares at me, and I watch something in him shut down and close off. All of the closeness and vulnerability from last night is gone in an instant.

"Fine." His voice goes flat. Empty. "I'm a coward. But I'm a living coward, and you'll be safe because of it."

He shoves his feet into his boots and strides toward the door, pulling it open.

"Cairos, wait!" I call after him, desperate, but he doesn't turn around.

"I'll be back in three days."

The door closes behind him with a quiet click that sounds like a death knell.

For a moment, I just stand there, frozen. Then the panic hits like a wave. It's cold and suffocating and wrong. My chest tightens until I can't breathe, and suddenly I'm stumbling toward the washbasin, still clutching the sheet to my body.

I make it just in time.

My stomach heaves, once, twice, until there's nothing left but bile and the bitter taste of betrayal. I sink to my knees on the cold floor, one hand braced against the bathtub, the other holding the sheet up for modesty, though I'm not sure why anymore.

He's really gone. He's really going to do it.

I close my eyes and let the tears come, hot and angry and heartbroken, while the memory of his hands on my skin feels like a lie I told myself in the dark. A loud, ugly sob escapes my lips, and I do nothing to stop it.

The nausea eventually subsides, leaving me hollow and shaking. I press my forehead against the cool porcelain, trying to steady my breathing, but my reprieve is short-lived.

A sharp knock at my door makes me jump.

A guard's voice yells, muffled through the wood. "Lord Valthaeron requests your presence at breakfast. Immediately."

My blood runs cold. Of course he does. Of course he'd want to see me right after sending Cairos off.

"I'll be out in a minute," I manage, surprised my voice sounds almost steady despite my scrambling to my feet.

I stumble over to the wardrobe, dressing quickly in the first item of clothing I touch, which happens to be a burgundy dress.

I can hear the guard's steps outside the door, but I take one last moment to look in the mirror. The girl staring back at me looks to be in shambles, with red-rimmed eyes, pale skin, and hair a disaster. I look like someone who just had her heart broken. Like someone who just watched the man she slept with, a man whom she thought turned over a new leaf, retreat back to his old ways.

The walk to the dining hall feels like walking to my own execution. Each step echoes too loudly. The boots of the guards that escort me smash down onto the stone, marching in a rhythm that makes me feel sick. My stomach is still churning, empty and acidic, and the thought of food makes me want to retch again.

The doors to the dining hall stand open. Valthaeron sits at the head of the table, already eating, looking perfectly at ease in the morning light streaming through the wall of windows that overlook the Solmeren faction below. He glances up when I enter, and something like amusement flickers across his face.

"Ah, Naevyn. Come, sit. You look unwell." His feigned ignorance makes an anger rise in my chest, and I have to physically bite my tongue to keep from cursing at him.

I force myself to cross the room, to pull out the chair to his right. The smell of eggs and some kind of meat makes my stomach roll again.

"I'm fine," I lie through gritted teeth.

Valthaeron takes a slow sip of wine, which I find to be a questionable breakfast choice, and watches me over the rim of his glass with those spooky eyes. "Rough night?"

My throat tightens. Does he know? Of course he knows.

"I slept fine."

"Mm." He sets down his glass, his eyes scrutinizing. "How curious. I could have sworn I heard movement in the halls last night. Footsteps passing my chamber." He pauses, cutting into his food with deliberate precision. "But perhaps I was mistaken. I really should remind the guards to lock everyone's doors. Such a careless habit."

The words land like a punch to the gut. He knew. He *wanted* Cairos to come to me.

"Why?" The question escapes before I can stop it.

"Why what, girl?" He doesn't look up from his plate, but I can see the satisfaction in the set of his shoulders.

"Why send Cairos to the circus? Why now?"

"Because he has a job to do. A duty to perform. Surely you understand that." He meets my gaze. His mouth curves downward, his eyebrows draw together, but the sympathy doesn't reach his eyes. "I know you're upset. You care for him. Perhaps you even imagine yourself in *love* with him. Young hearts are so impulsive."

"He's going to murder people," I say flatly.

"He's going to collect souls, yes. As he always has. As he always will." Valthaeron leans back in his chair.

I fight the urge to scream at him, and call him any number of vile words I picked up in the mines.

"The sky is clear today," he continues, finally glancing toward the high windows. "Which means the conditions will be ideal tonight."

A small warning bell goes off in my chest. I keep still.

"For what?" The question is pointless, but I ask it anyway.

"The forging, of course. You'll attempt it at moonrise."

The room gives a little sway. I steady myself with the edge of the table because I refuse to sway with it.

"Tonight? But Cairos—"

"Yes." He pushes a piece of egg to the side of his plate but doesn't eat it. "You've already lost a night. I don't recommend losing another."

My throat tightens. I haven’t breathed properly since Cairos left, but somehow inhaling feels even more difficult now.

“I don't know how to do it by myself,” I say.

“Circumstances have changed.” His eyes settle on me, completely unfazed by the panic beginning its slow rise under my skin. “You’ll adjust.”

I push my plate an inch farther away. I couldn’t eat even if he ordered me to.

“I don’t think I can do it alone,” I admit before I can catch the words and shove them back down.

He studies me for a beat too long, an ounce of annoyance flashing in his eyes. “You don’t have the luxury of not doing so.”

He rises smoothly. Breakfast is over, apparently, even though mine never began.

“Come,” he says, already walking toward the door. “There’s something I want you to see before tonight. Some… motivation, perhaps.”

My stomach twists with dread, but I stand anyway as he moves past my place. What choice do I have?

He leads me through corridors I haven’t seen before, deeper into the estate. We descend stone stairs that spiral down, down, until the air grows cold and damp. Torches flicker along the walls, casting dancing shadows on the stone.

Finally, we reach a heavy, wooden door. Valthaeron produces a key and unlocks it, pushing it open to reveal a small chamber. The walls are lined with shelves, and on those shelves are books and scrolls. Not like the main library before, though. These are tomes that are hidden away from plain sight.

“My private collection,” Valthaeron says, confirming my thoughts. “Very few are permitted here.”

Maybe I should be honored, but all I can feel is existential dread.

He moves to a particular shelf and pulls down a scroll, yellowed with age. He unrolls it carefully on a stone podium in the center of the room.

"You've heard pieces of the prophecy. Fragments whispered by frightened fae who only know part of the story. But this is the complete version. Every word. Every detail. Read it."

My heartbeat stutters as I step closer. What if this is a trap? Valthaeron's way of getting me alone so he can kill me?

I glance back at him, and he gives a reassuring nod, not moving from his position.

I force myself to get closer to the parchment. The words are written in an old dialect that I can somehow decipher. Magic, maybe? It reads:

When darkness feeds on mortal breath,
And reaper's hands deal only death,
A forge-born child with fire's might
Shall craft the jewel that ends the night.

The mortal with the touch of fae,
Born of flame and mortal pain,
A warrior shaped by mortal death,
Yet breathing still despite its claim.

She'll forge the key that breaks the chain,
The end of death, or death's new reign,
Bound to the Emerald Cycle's turn,
When all that dies may rise or burn.

The necklace wrought by her own hand
Will tip the scales where kingdoms stand.
Alone, she'll face the ancient king,
With power forged from suffering.

Her crimson touch shall fell the old,
A thousand years undone, grown cold,
The right hand of the tyrant's throne,
Will crumble into dust and bone

.

In her veins flows bane or cure,
Only she can make it pure.

My breath catches. "The mortal with the touch of fae…"

"Yes. Interesting, isn't it? One might wonder what that means. One might even suspect it requires a certain… intimacy with the fae."

The room spins. He planned all of this. Last night was orchestrated. It wasn't…

Wait.

Does Cairos know? Is he in on all of this?

No. I can't think of that now, can't wonder. I'll lose my focus if I do.

"You see now," Valthaeron continues, moving to stand beside me and placing his hands on my shoulders, "why I've been so patient? Why I allowed Cairos his little infatuation? You needed to be marked by him, in every sense of the word. The prophecy demanded it." He pauses, giving my shoulders a nauseating squeeze before dropping his hands. "But now that requirement has been fulfilled, and Cairos is nothing but a liability. A distraction keeping you from what you must do."

"And what must I do?" My voice sounds hollow, distant.

"Forge the necklace." He taps the prophecy with one long finger. "You see these lines? 'The necklace wrought by her own hand will tip the scales where kingdoms stand.' That necklace is the key to everything. To ending the cycle of death that plagues this realm."

"By killing you?"

He laughs, one that's edged with a threat. "Is that what you think? That I'm the villain in this story?" He shakes his head. "Prophecies are double-edged swords, Naevyn. They can be interpreted a hundred different ways. Yes, you might face me. You might even try to end me. But look at this line: 'The end of death, or death's new reign.' Do you understand what that means?"

I stare at the words, trying to parse them.

"It means the necklace you forge could end my reign… or it could strengthen it beyond measure in ways that mean the collection of souls may no longer be a necessity. It could free this world from death. And here's the beautiful part: I don't know which it will be. Not yet. Not until you forge it and we discover what you're truly capable of."

"Why would you risk that?"

"Because it isn't a risk at all. The magic you possess, the fire in your blood… only you can create what's required. And if the prophecy proves true in the way I suspect, if that necklace grants the power I believe it will… you'll stand beside me, Naevyn. Not as a captive, or a tool, but as someone who shares that power. Immortality. Dominion. Everything you could possibly want."

"I don't want that."

The smile he gives in response is knowing. "Right now you're angry and heartbroken, thinking only of Cairos and his betrayal. But when you've forged something of true power, when you feel what it's like to hold that kind of strength in your hands… We'll see what you want then."

He gestures back to the prophecy. "As for the risk? There's very little. Tell me, Naevyn, are you thinking clearly right now? Or is your mind clouded with thoughts of Cairos? With anger over what he's doing at the circus?"

My jaw clenches.

"Exactly. And if you can't forge this necklace alone, if you let your feelings for him interfere, more souls will die. Not by my hand, but by yours. By your failure." He leans closer. "So I suggest you put aside your childish heartbreak and focus on what matters."

"And if I forge it? If I succeed?"

"Then we'll discover together what the prophecy truly means. Perhaps you'll be strong enough to try to kill me, though I suspect you'll realize that ruling beside me is far preferable to watching everyone you've ever cared about die." His voice is laced with poison. "I warn you, girl, don't think about trying anything clever. Don't imagine you and your little friends can plot some heroic rebellion. I've seen prophecies twisted, seen mortals try to outsmart fate. It never ends well. And if I suspect for even a moment that you're planning something foolish, I'll simply have to reconsider Cairos's role in all of this. Perhaps not having him as a distraction at all could be very… motivating for you."

The threat hangs in the air long after he's finished speaking, wrapping around my throat like a noose. *Reconsider Cairos's role.* The words are careful, but their meaning is crystal clear. If I step out of line or try anything at all, Valthaeron will kill Cairos. And the worst part, the part that makes my chest feel like it's caving in, is that I believe him. After everything Cairos has done, after he walked out this morning to slaughter innocent people, I should hate him. I should want him gone. But the thought of Valthaeron ending him, of never seeing those amber eyes again, never hearing his voice… it breaks something inside me that I didn't even know was still whole. I'm trapped. Completely, utterly trapped. If I fail to forge the necklace, people will continue to die. If I succeed but refuse to use it against Valthaeron, everyone I love dies anyway. And if I try to fight back, to be clever, to find some way out of this nightmare… Cairos dies. The man I hate for what he's doing right now. The man I can't stop loving despite it all.

Valthaeron straightens, his expression returning to that mask of calm control.

"The forge is prepared. You have tonight to prove you can do this alone. You'll go to the forge tonight when the moon rises, and create the pendant. You are to sleep in Bellamie's room tonight, adjacent to the forge, and I will personally retrieve the pendant in the morning. And Naevyn?" He pauses at the doorway. "That line about your blood, 'bane or cure'… I'd think very carefully about what that means before you make any rash decisions."

Then he's gone, leaving me alone with the prophecy and a hundred questions I can't answer.

He needs the necklace. Whether it will destroy him or empower him, he needs it. And he's betting that I'm too weak to use it against him.

Or maybe he's betting that I'll succeed, and the necklace will serve his purposes after all.

I read the prophecy one more time, my eyes lingering on those final lines: *In her veins flows bane or cure, only she can make it pure.*

My blood. My choice.

I know what I have to do.

I have a necklace to forge.

And a king to kill.

25

ALONE

The hours crawl by, feeling like torture.

I sit sequestered in my room, staring at nothing in particular, trying to recite the words of the prophecy in my head over and over until they all blur together. *The mortal with the touch of fae.* I can still smell him on my skin, cedar and cinnamon and something darker. I should wash it off. Should scrub every trace of last night from my body until there's nothing left but my own scent, just in case.

But I don't. Losing that would feel like losing him, and no matter how much anger, how much betrayal I feel toward him right now, I can't bring myself to do that.

The sun tracks across my floor, counting down the hours of daylight at an intolerably slow pace. I watch it move and measure time by the shadows it casts. Somewhere out there, Cairos is at the circus. Somewhere out there, humans will die within the next twenty-four hours.

I try not to think about it. Try not to imagine Quinnic deciding to go, dragging Alabris along for a night of entertainment. Try not to picture their faces in the crowd when Cairos—

My stomach turns upside down.

The chances that the circus would happen in Xardon again are slim to none. Still, I can't help worrying and wondering.

I force myself to eat the food a servant brings at midday, choking down dry bread and a piece of fruit. I need my strength. To be ready. The servant eyes me with poorly concealed curiosity, and I wonder what rumors are spreading through the estate. Does anyone know I slept with Cairos? Can they smell it on me? Does anyone know he left this morning to murder people?

Does anyone care?

The afternoon drags into evening. I try to rest, but sleep won't come. Every time I close my eyes, I see Valthaeron's face and the threat of losing everyone I love if I don't succumb to his wishes.

Perhaps you'll realize that ruling beside me is far preferable to watching everyone you've ever cared about die.

The offer should disgust me and make me want to fight harder, to resist with everything I have. But there's a small part of me that whispers: what if he's right? What if trying to fight him only gets everyone killed? What if the smart thing, and the *safe* thing, is to forge the necklace and give him exactly what he wants?

I shake the thought away violently. That's what he wants me to think. That's how he wins. I just hope bravery shows up when I need it most to defy him.

Dusk falls finally, my room turning shades of purple and grey. I light a candle and watch the flame dance, thinking about fire and forging and the power that's supposed to live in my blood. Even when Grendor died, I didn't feel like I had any kind of power. In fact, I felt powerless. Powerless to get away, seconds away from my own death if my blood hadn't been a poison to him.

But tonight, I need to feel powerful. I have to.

The moon rises, and it streams into my room so brightly, I almost believe it's the sun. But when I walk over to the window, I see it. The full moon. Maybe it will help me in the forge. Gods, I hope it will.

Time to find out if I can do this.

I take a deep breath and exit my room. Valthaeron seems to have given up on keeping guards stationed outside. Or maybe I underestimated how dangerous he believes Cairos is, and my mortal presence here isn't a threat at all. My hands shake as I make my way through the dimly lit corridors toward the forge.

The castle is quieter at night, but not silent. I hear distant voices, footsteps on floors above, and the creaking and shuttering of doors. Every sound makes my heart jump, but I can’t place why. I’m doing exactly as I was told. At least, that's what I tell myself to push away the thoughts swirling in my anxious mind. It isn't what I’m going to do right now that’s made me so jumpy. It's what I plan to do after.

I push the heavy door open, closing it quietly behind me. It feels wrong being in Bellamie’s forge by myself. No Bellamie, no Cairos. Just a human trying to do the impossible.

I turn away from the bedroom and toward the forge area, making my way to the place where Cairos usually stands. I pick up the first piece of shadowstone and hold it up to the light. It’s beautiful in its way, black as a starless sky but shot through with veins of silver that seem to move when I tilt it. The stone is cool to the touch, almost cold. There are only two pieces left that Valthaeron provided, and I can’t be sure he’d give me any more if this fails, or if he’d just write me off as not being the girl from the prophecy.

I take in a deep breath. Two chances, that’s it. I can do this. The necklace needs to be more than just decorative. It needs to hold magic, channel my power, and “be the key that breaks the chain”, whatever that means.

The large window is set into the ceiling at the perfect angle to catch the moonlight, and beneath it sits the workbench with the massive lens mounted on an adjustable arm. I’ve watched Cairos use it before, standing beside him as he focuses the moonlight down onto the shadowstone until it becomes workable.

Alone she'll face the ancient king.

Alone. No Cairos to guide me and tell me when the stone is ready, or catch me if I falter. Just me and the moon and the stone.

The tools are still arranged from when Cairos used them, and I hope that I can remember which tools I use for what.

I pick up the first piece of shadowstone and place it on the workbench directly beneath the window. Moonlight falls across it, making the silver veins shimmer. Even after all my time here, the beauty of it still catches my breath.

I adjust the lens arm, positioning it between the moon and the shadowstone just as I saw Cairos do. The effect is immediate. The concentrated moonlight focuses into a beam, and where it hits the stone, the surface begins to warm. I wait minutes, as Cairos had instructed, until the stone grows even hotter.

Finally, I can see heat radiating from it. It isn't an aggressive heat like the sun in Xardon, but rather something cooler and more ethereal, like standing too close to winter itself.

This is it. This has to be it.

I grab the smallest chisel with shaking hands and press it against the glowing stone. The tip catches on the surface, and for a moment I think it's working. Maybe I just need to be gentler than Cairos was, so as not to crack the stone. I tap lightly with a small hammer, trying to shape the stone into the circular pendant form I need.

The chisel skitters across the surface, leaving barely a scratch.

I try again, pressing harder just the tiniest amount, and angling differently. Same result. The shadowstone remains stubbornly solid, refusing to yield.

Cairos hit the stone harder, but each time, his shattered. I can't let that happen. Maybe I need more light. More intensity.

I adjust the lens, bringing it closer, and focusing the beam even tighter. The stone begins to glow with heat until the whole piece seems to be made of captured moonlight. It has to be malleable enough now.

I try the chisel again. Then a file. Then my hands, trying to simply work the stone like clay.

Nothing. It's as hard and unyielding as ever, just brighter.

Frustration builds in my chest, hot and choking. I've done everything right. I've followed every step I learned, used the tools the way I was taught. The moonlight is focused, the stone is glowing, but it won't cooperate and become what I need it to be.

I pick up the chisel again and hit it harder, my anger focusing through the tools.

Finally something happens. Just… not what I need.

It shatters into sharp fragments.

"No." The word comes out broken. "No, no, no."

I stare at the fractured stone, my vision blurring with tears. I have one piece of shadowstone left. One chance.

I let the tears burn my eyes, but not for long. The moon is perfectly positioned and I can't ruin this chance. I swipe at the tears with the back of my sleeve, sniffling as I do, then get on with it.

The last piece of shadowstone feels heavy when I lift it. It's slightly larger than the first, darker, with fewer silver veins running through it. My last chance to prove I can do this. My last chance before people continue to die because I failed.

The weight of it makes me want to scream.

I set the stone on the workbench and just stare at it for a long moment, trying to think. There has to be something I'm missing. Some element I haven't considered. I think again about the prophecy because it's where my last shred of hope lies. The only clue I have.

In her veins flows bane or cure, only she can make it pure.

My blood. The prophecy specifically mentions *my blood.*

My blood was poison to Grendor. My blood is apparently somehow important to this entire thing. What if that's the missing ingredient? What if shadowstone needs to be… bonded to me somehow before it can be forged properly?

It's insane and desperate. But I'm out of options.

Then I glance at the tools again and the small knife I saw earlier catches my eye. Maybe *that's* why there's a knife here in the first place. Maybe *that's* how Bellamie was able to forge things.

I pick up the small knife that's laid on the table with the other tools and turn it over in my hands. The blade definitely looks sharp enough for what I need. My left hand trembles as I position the knife against my right palm.

This is crazy. This could be wrong. This could ruin everything. This could—

I slice before I can talk myself out of it.

The pain is immediate and bright, blood welling up in a clean line across my palm. I gasp, nearly drop the knife, but force myself to hold steady. Dark red blood pools in my cupped hand, and I angle it over the shadowstone.

One drop.

Two.

Three.

The blood hits the black stone and for a heartbeat, nothing happens.

Then the shadowstone erupts with light.

Not the silvery glow from the moon before, but something else entirely. Golden light, bright as a sunrise, pulses from deep within the stone. The blood doesn't pool on the surface. Instead, it sinks in, absorbed, like the stone is drinking it.

The light flares once more, blindingly bright, then fades. When my vision clears, the shadowstone looks… different. The black is deeper now, richer, and the silver veins have taken on a faint golden tint. And it's warm. Actually warm, even without the moonlight.

My heart pounds so hard I can feel it in my throat. This is it. *This* is what was missing.

I wrap my bleeding hand hastily in a strip of cloth torn from my dress and position the blood-touched stone back under the window. My fingers quiver as I adjust the lens, focusing the moonlight down onto the stone once more.

The reaction is immediate and completely different from before.

Where the first stone had simply glowed under the moonlight, this one seems to come alive. The golden veins pulse and writhe beneath the surface like they're alive. The stone breathes, expanding and contracting subtly with each heartbeat. *My* heartbeat, I realize. It's synchronized to me.

And it's getting warm. Hot, even. The kind of heat that radiates from shadowstone when it's properly prepared, and ready to be worked.

I reach for the chisel out of habit, but something stops me. Some instinct that says tools aren't what I need. Not for this.

I unwrap my bleeding hand and reach for the stone directly.

The moment my skin makes contact, I feel the stone yielding beneath my fingers, malleable like clay warmed in the sun, or wax on a lit candle. My blood has awakened something in it, and the moonlight is sustaining it, keeping it in this perfect state of pliability.

I work quickly, shaping it with my hands and fingers and will. The stone responds to my touch, yielding where I push, smoothing where I stroke. I can feel my power flowing into it, a fire in my chest to save Cairos from his carnage and all those people from death. It burns through my veins, hot and fierce and alive, and where my blood-slicked fingers touch the shadowstone, it shapes exactly as I need it to.

The pendant takes the form of a teardrop shape under my hands. It's smooth and perfect, with a hole at the top for a chain. The surface is flawless, reflecting the moonlight like dark water. And in the center, so faint I almost miss it, is a pattern of whirls and spirals that look almost like flames.

I did it.

I actually did it.

The pendant is still warm as I thread it onto a simple silver chain I find among the supplies. It hangs heavy around my neck, heavier than such a small object should be. I can feel it against my skin, pulsing in time with my heartbeat.

The necklace wrought by her own hand.

I clean up my workspace with trembling hands, putting away tools. I don't need to clean up, but I *do* need time to collect myself. To plan what I need to do. Valthaeron instructed me to stay here, but I can't. He'd be foolish to come by himself in the morning and while Valthaeron is a lot of things, I wouldn't think him a fool. No fool can last over a thousand years in power.

No, I'll need the element of surprise. I'll need to go tonight, when he's not expecting me.

My cut palm throbs with each movement as I finish putting the tools back on the wall, but I barely notice. All I can think about is what comes next.

Alone she'll face the ancient king.

I have to find Valthaeron. Have to… what? Kill him? Try to? The prophecy says I'll face him, but it doesn't say I'll win.

Perhaps you'll realize that ruling beside me is far preferable to watching everyone you've ever cared about die.

The offer echoes in my mind as I exit the forge. Partnership, power, and safety for everyone I love. All I have to do is give him the necklace, let him use it however he intends, and stop fighting.

It would be so easy.

The thought makes me sick.

I slip back into the dimly lit corridors, moving as quietly as I can. The pendant feels like it's burning against my chest, a constant reminder of what I've created, and what I'm about to do.

I need to find his room. And then what? Hold it out and wish him dead? The plan is half-formed at best, fueled more by adrenaline and desperation than any real strategy.

Valthaeron said he heard Cairos's footsteps last night. That he heard him pass by his chamber. Which means Valthaeron's room must be somewhere between mine and Cairos's.

I retrace the path I imagine Cairos took, moving through halls I've walked a dozen times during my captivity here. The estate is a maze of hallways and doors, but I've memorized the route between my room and the main areas well enough.

Halfway down a particularly long corridor, I freeze. Voices. Two guards turning the corner ahead, their armor clinking softly with each step.

I dive into a shallow alcove, pressing myself against the wall, and holding my breath. The pendant feels impossibly obvious, like it's glowing, announcing my presence. But the guards walk past without pausing, discussing castle security in bored tones.

I wait until their footsteps fade completely before I move again.

The second near-miss comes when I'm passing through a gallery area lined with portraits. A servant emerges from a side door without warning, carrying an armful of linens. I barely manage to slip behind a statue before she sees me, my heart hammering so loud I'm certain she'll hear it.

She hums to herself as she passes, oblivious, and I sag against the cold marble in relief once she's gone.

This is insane. I'm going to get caught. I'm going to get myself and everyone else killed.

But I keep moving.

Finally, I find it. A door that's different from all the others. Where most are plain wood, this one is carved with intricate patterns. And set into the wood at regular intervals are pieces of shadowstone, polished to a mirror shine.

This has to be his room. It's too ornate to be anyone else's.

My heart stutters as I reach for the handle. It's not locked. Why would it be? Who in this estate would dare enter Valthaeron's private chambers uninvited?

The door swings open silently, and I slip inside.

The room takes my breath away immediately.

It's easily three times the size of my own quarters. The ceiling arches high overhead, painted with constellations that seem to glow in the candlelight. Every surface drips with wealth. The carpets are thick, tapestries weaved out of golden thread, and furniture carved from wood so dark it's almost black.

But it's the shadowstone that dominates. Chunks of it are embedded in the walls like windows, glowing softly. A chandelier made entirely of the stuff hangs from the ceiling, each piece cut and polished to perfection. Even the bed frame incorporates shadowstone, the posts topped with spheres of it. It's beautiful, terrifying, and exactly what I'd expect from an ancient king who feeds on souls.

And it's empty.

The bed is made, undisturbed. No sign that anyone has been here recently.

Where is he?

I stand in the center of the room, pendant heavy against my chest, and try to think. It's well past midnight now. Where would Valthaeron be at this hour?

I peek back out the door and check that the coast is clear. As soon as it is, I pad out into the hallway, trying to make the door close as noiselessly as possible.

Then I hear it. Faint, but unmistakable. A voice drifting up from somewhere below.

His voice.

I follow the sound back out into the corridor, down the main stairs. The voice grows louder with each step, echoing off stone walls. He's not alone. I can hear other voices, too, though I can't make out words yet.

The sound leads me to a pair of double doors I've been through before.

The dining hall.

What is he doing in the dining hall in the middle of the night?

I press myself against the wall beside the doors, trying to hear, to gather information before I do something stupid. My pulse pounds in my ears. The pendant feels like it's vibrating against my skin.

This is it. This is the moment I walk in there and face him.

But what if I fail? What if the necklace doesn't work, and I walk in there and he just kills me?

Or worse, what if he doesn't, and instead makes me watch while he kills everyone I love?

I think of the prophecy: *Alone she'll face the ancient king, with power forged from suffering.*

I've suffered. Gods, I've suffered. When my parents died. The last few years without them, raising up Quinnic. Watching everyone die at the circus. Facing the possibility of my own death with Grendor. This morning, watching Cairos leave, the hours I've spent today trapped between impossible choices. If suffering is what powers this magic, I should have enough to level this entire castle.

I reach up and touch the pendant. It's vibrating with the power I poured into it. My power. My blood. My choice.

In her veins flows bane or cure, only she can make it pure.

I take a deep breath. Then another. My legs feel like water, and I'm not sure they'll hold me when I try to move.

You can do this. You *have* to do this.

Another breath.

My hand finds the doors. Push them open.

Just walk in. Don't think. Don't hesitate. Just move.

One step. Two. The pendant burns against my chest, and I don't know if it's real heat or just my imagination.

I can see him now through the widening gap. Valthaeron sits at the head of the long table, golden candlelight casting shadows across his face. I can't make out the others in the room, but it's definitely Valthaeron at the head of the table.

This is insane. This is suicide.

But ten million souls.

I picture their faces. Strangers I'll never meet, families I'll never know. Children who deserve a chance to grow up. People who shouldn't die because I was too afraid to act.

The end of death, or death's new reign.

My choice. My responsibility.

I step fully into the doorway, and Valthaeron's eyes lock on mine across the room. He doesn't look surprised, or even angry. He just smiles, slow and knowing, like I'm right on schedule.

"Ah, Naevyn," he says, his voice carrying easily through the hall. "I was wondering when you'd arrive. Come in. We've been waiting for you."

26

BROKEN

Every instinct I have is screaming at me to run, but I won't listen. I plant my feet firmly into the ground, refusing to give up now.

Valthaeron sits at the head of the table with a goblet of wine in his hand, looking for all the world like we're about to have a pleasant conversation. But he's not alone. Three figures sit with him, spread out along the length of the table. Two men and a woman, all of them looking equal in his power.

Fae. All of them.

"Don't be shy," Valthaeron continues, taking a leisurely sip of wine. "You've forged the necklace, haven't you? I can feel it from here. Quite impressive work, actually. Even better than I expected."

The woman at the table leans forward, her silver hair cascading over one shoulder. Her eyes are the color of ice, and when she smiles, her teeth are all too sharp. "So this is the prophesied? She looks rather… fragile."

"Looks can be deceiving, Pryor." Valthaeron sets down his goblet with deliberate care. "Show them, Naevyn. Show them what you've created."

My hand moves to the pendant before I can stop it, fingers closing around the warm metal. The moment I touch it, absolute power surges through me, leaving me feeling hot and wild and fierce. It rushes up my arm, spreads through my chest, fills every corner of my body with liquid fire.

This is it. This is what the prophecy meant. This is the power I need.

"Beautiful," Valthaeron murmurs, and I can't help but to squirm under the scrutiny.

One of the men laughs, a bellowing, raspy sound that echoes off the glass wall. "She's terrified. Look at her—she can barely stand."

"Give her a moment, Barthaine. It's not every day a mortal decides to kill a king." Valthaeron stands, beginning to move around the table toward me, each step measured and unhurried. "That is what you've decided, isn't it? You've come here to fulfill the prophecy? To end my reign?"

"Yes." The word finally breaks free, small and defiant.

"How wonderfully predictable," he says, clasping his hands together. He's closer now, having slowly paced around the table. I can see the ancient cruelty in his eyes. "Did you really think I'd tell you about the prophecy if I believed you could actually succeed? Did you think I'd give you the tools you needed, the time you needed, if there was any chance you'd use them against me and *win*?" Valthaeron lets out a laugh wrought with malice, and the other fae join in.

My cheeks flare red. My fingers tighten around the pendant. The power surges stronger, begging to be released.

"You're a test, Naevyn. A curiosity. I wanted to see if you could forge the necklace alone, if you had any real strength without Cairos holding your hand." He stops a few feet away, studying me. "And you did! You actually succeeded. I'm *genuinely* impressed. But now comes the disappointing part where you realize that forging a pretty trinket and actually having the strength to use it are two very different things."

"You're wrong." My voice shakes, but I force the words out anyway. "The prophecy—"

"The prophecy is a children's story." Valthaeron's smile vanishes. "And you're about to learn a very painful lesson about the difference between destiny and delusion."

He moves.

One moment he's standing in front of me, the next his hand is around my throat, lifting me off my feet. The pendant burns against my chest, power screaming through me, but I don't know how to direct it or how to make it do anything.

"Disappointing," Valthaeron spits in my face. Then he throws me sideways.

I crash into the table hard enough to splinter the wood, goblets and plates flying in every direction as I tumble to the ground. Wine sprays across my face, mixing with blood from where something sharp caught my cheek. The pendant tangles in my hair, the chain digging into my neck. A wounded cry pummels its way out of me.

I try to get up, but my body won't cooperate. Everything hurts. Everything is spinning.

"Perhaps we should end this quickly," Pryor says, sounding bored.

"No." Valthaeron's voice cuts through the ringing in my ears. "It's not every day that we have a mortal here to play with. I want to see if she has any fight in her. If there's anything worth salvaging."

Footsteps approach. I roll onto my back, gasping for air, and see him standing over me. He's not breathing hard, and he hasn't even drawn a weapon.

The pendant. I need to use the pendant.

I grab it with both hands and pull it forward, willing the magic to manifest—to protect me. The stone grows scorching hot again, and golden light flares between my fingers. For one brilliant moment, I think it's working.

Then Valthaeron's boot connects with my ribs.

The impact drives all the air from my lungs and sends me skidding across the floor. My head slams against the wall hard enough to make me see stars. The pendant's light flickers and dies.

"Come now," Valthaeron says, stalking toward me. "Is that really all you have? All that fire, all that rage and heartbreak over Cairos, and *this* is the best you can manage?"

I press one hand to the cold floor, trying to sit myself up. I barely make it halfway to a sitting position before my arm gives out.

"Pathetic." He bends down and grabs a fistful of my hair and hauls me upright, forcing me to look at him. "I gave you everything. Knowledge, time, opportunity. I even made sure you had the proper motivation. And this is how you repay me? With this feeble, half-hearted attempt?"

Blood runs into my eyes from a cut on my forehead. I can't see straight. Pain sears the edges of my vision, threatening to blind me.

But I can still feel the pendant humming against my chest.

In her veins flows bane or cure.

My blood. That's what activated the shadowstone.

I reach for the pendant with one shaking hand while Valthaeron monologues about disappointment and wasted potential. My fingers find the sharp edge where I'd filed it smooth, and find a spot that's still slightly rough.

I press down hard.

The stone digs in and reopens the hand I'd sliced earlier. Blood wells up, hot and bright, and drips onto the pendant's surface.

The reaction is instantaneous.

White-hot light bursts forth from the necklace. The power from the pendant courses through my veins, through every screaming nerve in my battered body.

Valthaeron jerks back with a snarl, releasing my hair like it's hurt him. I nearly collapse to my knees, but when I catch my balance, my legs hold.

I can see my veins glowing through my skin, lit from within by whatever power I've unleashed. It's too much. Too hot. Too everything. But I don't let go of the pendant.

"Now that's more interesting," Valthaeron says, and for the first time, he actually sounds surprised.

I don't give him a chance to say more. I thrust my bleeding hand toward him, and the power follows in the form of a plume of fire.

It catches him square in the chest, sending him stumbling backward. The other fae scatter, chairs clattering as they abandon the table. Pryor hisses something in a language I don't understand.

The fire keeps coming, pouring out of me in a torrent. I'm not directing it, and I definitely can't control it, but it doesn't matter. It knows what I want, and who I need dead.

Valthaeron raises one hand, and the flames simply… stop. They freeze midair, suspended between us like a golden curtain. He smiles pleasantly, like that was easy for him.

"Better," he says. "But not enough."

He closes his fist, and the flames reverse course.

The backlash hits me, driving me to the ground, where I lie, useless. The pendant's light flickers and dims. My vision swims, darkening at the edges.

"You see?" Valthaeron's voice seems to come from very far away. "This is why you fail. You have all this power granted by the prophecy, but no discipline. No control. You're like a child, playing with a magic you don't understand."

Through the haze of pain, I see him draw his sword. It's beautiful in a terrible way. The blade is black—shadowstone, I recognize—and seems to consume the light surrounding it, the edge so sharp it looks like it could sever the throats of the Gods themselves.

"I really did hope you'd be more interesting," he says, raising the blade. "But I suppose even disappointments have their uses. Your blood will strengthen the necklace significantly, I imagine."

He plunges it downward toward me.

I try to roll away, but my body won't respond. The sword descends in a perfect arc, and at the last second, some survival instinct makes me twist.

But not enough.

The blade pierces into my left shoulder with a sound like tearing fabric, except the fabric is my flesh. For a split second, there's no pain—just pressure, just the sensation of something foreign punching through muscle and sinew and scraping against bone.

Then the agony hits.

It's all-consuming and then some, like someone has shoved a poker fresh from the forge into my shoulder and is twisting it deeper. I can't stop my scream as the sword grinds against my shoulder blade. The metal is so cold it burns, colder than ice, colder than death itself.

Valthaeron pulls the blade free with a wet, sucking sound that's somehow worse than the initial strike. I feel every serration, every inch of metal sliding back through destroyed tissue. Blood follows the sword out in a hot rush, soaking through my shirt in seconds, spreading across my chest in a warm, sticky flood.

I writhe and scream as the pain radiates outward in waves down my arm to my fingertips, up my neck to my jaw, and across my chest until every breath feels like inhaling shards of glass. Blood pools beneath me, so much blood, darker than the wine that had spilled earlier, spreading across the stone floor.

My vision tunnels. I can feel my heart hammering, pumping more blood out through the wound with each desperate beat. My fingers twitch uselessly, and when I try to press my right hand against the injury, my palm comes away red and dripping.

The wound is deep. I can feel the wrongness of torn muscle and severed things that should be connected. Blood runs down my torso, drips off my sides, and pools in the hollow of my collarbone. It's warm at first, then goes cold, and that terrifies me more than anything.

I'm going to bleed out right here on this floor. I'm going to die watching my own blood spread across stone, while Valthaeron stands over me looking disgusted at my mortality.

"Pity," he says, studying the blood on his blade. "You almost had potential."

He raises the sword again, angling it toward my throat this time. The killing blow.

My left arm won't move. My right is slick with blood. The blood loss has made a weakness come over me that makes me abandon all of my fight. The pendant's light has guttered out completely. I have nothing left. No strength, no power, no hope.

I close my eyes, waiting for death to come.

The sound comes first, and it's like the world tearing apart. The crash of breaking glass, so loud it makes my ears ring, even with my hearing muffled by adrenaline and blood loss. I feel glass shards rain down over me, slicing my skin. Screams from somewhere distant. Then a roar that makes even my bones vibrate, that I feel in my chest cavity, that drowns out even my own ragged breathing.

I want to stay here, swimming in my subconsciousness, but I force myself to open my eyes again.

There's a shade stalker.

It's monumental. Larger than any living thing should be, and definitely larger than I remember from the forest. Black as midnight with three glowing bands around the top of its paw, and eyes that burn green with toxicity.

The creature crashes through the wall of windows in an explosion of glass and moonlight, shards raining down like deadly snow. It lands beside me and Valthaeron, massive paws hitting the stone with enough force to crack it, and the snarl that rips from its throat is the most terrifying sound I've ever heard.

Pryor screams. One of the men tries to run, but the shade stalker's massive paw catches him mid-stride. Claws the size of daggers punch through his chest, and when the creature throws him, he hits the far wall with a wet crunch and doesn't get back up.

The other male fae draws twin blades and rushes the creature with inhuman speed. He's fast, deadly, and precise.

The shade stalker is faster.

It twists impossibly, avoiding both blades, and its jaws close around the fae's sword arm. Bone snaps like dry wood. The fae howls, trying to stab with his remaining blade, but the creature shakes him like a dog with a rabbit in its maw. Blood sprays across the walls, the floor, me.

When the shade stalker releases him, the fae doesn't move, or even whimper.

Pryor begins chanting, her hands wreathed in ice-blue light. Frost spreads across the floor toward the creature, creeping up its legs, trying to immobilize it. The shade stalker snarls and leaps, moving so fast it's just a blur of black fur and green light.

Its claws find her throat before she can finish whatever spell she was trying to cast.

The whole thing takes maybe fifteen seconds. Three ancient, powerful fae, reduced to broken bodies and spreading pools of blood in the time it takes to draw breath.

And now those burning green eyes lock onto Valthaeron.

The king stands perfectly still, sword still raised, his expression unreadable. He doesn't look afraid.

"I'd wondered where you'd gotten to," Valthaeron murmurs.

The shade stalker crouches, muscles bunching, preparing to spring. A low growl rumbles from deep in its chest, building and building until it's all I can hear.

Then it launches itself at Valthaeron with terrifying speed.

Valthaeron moves to meet it, sword flashing. The blade catches moonlight as it arcs toward the creature's throat.

But the shade stalker dodges midair, leaving Valthaeron's sword to cut only empty space, and then massive paws slam into his chest with the force of a battering ram.

The impact sends him flying.

He crashes into the far wall hard enough to crack stone, his sword clattering from his grip. For a moment, he just hangs there, suspended in a crater of shattered masonry, then slides to the floor in a heap.

The shade stalker lands in a crouch, breathing hard, those green eyes fixed on the fallen king. Waiting to see if he'll get up.

Valthaeron growls. His hand scrabbles for his sword, fingers closing around the hilt.

The creature tenses, preparing to strike again.

A groan bubbles up my throat and gurgles out of my mouth.

The shade stalker stops and goes completely still.

Those burning eyes turn toward me.

The pool of blood I'm lying in feels more like an ocean now. My vision is swimming, the pendant's chain tangled around my fingers. I can barely hold my head up. Every part of me hurts in ways I didn't know were possible.

The shade stalker moves toward me, and some distant part of my brain screams at me to run, but I can't. I couldn't even roll away if I wanted to. If this creature, the one who's been watching me since the forest, has a desire to kill me, then that wish will be fulfilled.

The creature's massive head lowers until we're eye to eye. Up close, I can see the intelligence behind that burning green gaze. See something that looks almost like… concern?

Its jaws open, revealing teeth the size of daggers, and I wait for death.

Instead, it gently, carefully closes its mouth around my waist.

The world tilts, and I feel like I could vomit as the creature lifts me like I weigh nothing. For one disorienting moment, I'm dangling from its jaws, pain searing through my entire body, then it tosses its head, and I land on its back, sprawling across fur that's surprisingly warm.

My fingers find purchase in the thick onyx coat, and I barely manage to hold on before the creature bolts.

It runs for the shattered windows, glass crunching under its paws. Behind us, I hear Valthaeron shouting something along with the scrape of steel on stone as he retrieves his sword.

Then we're through the window and out into the night.

The estate falls away behind us as the shade stalker runs. It moves like liquid shadow, impossibly fast, leaping obstacles I can't even see. Cool night air rushes past, carrying the scent of flowers and spices.

My face and belly are pressed against the creature's warm fur, too exhausted and hurt to ride any other way. Still, I'm grateful because I'm alive. Somehow, impossibly, I'm alive.

Then I remember the pendant. I remember hearing something skitter across the blood-slicked floor.

My hand fumbles to check, and my heart sinks. The pendant is gone. The chain remains, but where the shadowstone should hang, there's nothing. Just broken links where it tore free during the chaos.

Shit. Valthaeron is going to find it. The one thing I needed, the one weapon the prophecy promised, and I lost it.

Darkness creeps in at the edges of my vision again. I'm losing too much blood, getting weaker by the second. The shade stalker's rhythmic gait becomes a lullaby, and I find my grip on its fur loosening.

Stay awake, I tell myself. *Have to stay awake. Have to...*

But the darkness is patient, and I'm so tired.

The last thing I see before consciousness slips away is those three glowing bands around the creature's front leg, pulsing in time with its breathing.

Three bands.

Three...

The thought dissolves before I can finish it, and the world goes black.

27

DARKNESS

I come to at the slight jostling created by the shade stalker as it runs along. Agony courses through my body in different places, my left shoulder being the most agonizing of the pain points.

Why am I in so much pain?

I wonder for only a moment before it all comes pummeling back to me. Valthaeron. His shadowstone sword. The fight in the dining room. Then…

The shade stalker coming to my rescue.

My eyes don't want to open, too afraid of the gore I might find on my own body. The sounds around me tell me where I am, though. A faint twinkling sound comes from all around me.

The forest. I'm in the glass forest. The shade stalker runs with purpose, as if it knows exactly where to go.

I certainly don't, but for some reason, I trust this creature to bring me to safety.

My fingers are still tangled in its thick fur, though I don't remember consciously holding on. Each stride sends fresh waves of pain radiating from my shoulder, and I can feel blood —still warm and flowing—soaking into the creature's dark coat. My left arm hangs useless, dead weight that swings with each movement, and every bounce makes me want to scream.

I can't waste the energy, though, and I *definitely* can't risk being spotted by fae that wouldn't take so kindly to me.

The glass trees blur past in streaks of moonlight and shadow. Their chiming grows louder, then softer, then louder again as we weave through the forest. Or maybe that's just my consciousness flickering, struggling to maintain its grip on reality.

I let my eyes fall closed again. It's easier that way. Easier to just feel the rhythm of the creature's gait, the warmth of its body beneath me, the cool night air rushing past.

Time becomes meaningless. If seconds or minutes or hours pass, I can't tell. I drift in and out, surfacing occasionally to register pain or movement or the persistent twinkling of glass, then sinking back down into merciful darkness.

At some point, I realize I'm shivering. Not from cold, but from blood loss. My body is trying to compensate, trying to keep my core warm even as my extremities go numb. My teeth want to chatter, but I clench my jaw against it, which only makes my head throb worse.

The necklace. I lost the necklace.

The thought surfaces through the fog of pain, sharp and devastating. All that work, all that suffering, and I lost it. Valthaeron has it now. Has the one thing the prophecy said I needed to face him.

I failed. Failed completely. When Cairos finds out that I made exactly what Valthaeron needed and then left it with him? Maybe he's right. Maybe I am just a worthless human.

Tears leak from the corners of my closed eyes, mixing with the blood and sweat on my face. I'm so tired. So tired of failing and hurting and being powerless despite all the fire that's supposed to burn in my veins.

The shade stalker runs tirelessly, breathing steady, its massive muscles bunching and releasing beneath me in perfect rhythm.

I surface again to the sensation of slowing. The creature's gait changes from a run to a lope, then to something more careful. The glass chiming fades, replaced by the chirp of night insects, and the distant howling of what I hope is only a wolf and not some less friendly shade stalkers.

We've left the glass forest.

I force my eyes open, blinking against the darkness. The shade stalker walks through a clearing now, only the random tree around for him to dodge. The open air makes me feel scared and vulnerable. My fingers tighten in his fur as if that alone will save me from any nearby threats.

My shoulder screams with each movement. I can feel the wound pulling, a wet, hot, viscous liquid continuing to seep down my arm. How much blood can a person lose before they just… stop? I feel like I should know the answer to that. Like maybe I learned it once, somewhere, but the knowledge slips away like water through my fingers.

The creature stops suddenly, and goes completely still. It tenses up, waiting for whatever threat might be around us.

But there's nothing. Just silence and darkness and the rapid beating of my own heart.

Then I see it.

Between two massive oak trees, the atmosphere is… off. It ripples like the heat shimmering off sun-baked stone back in Xardon, except it's nighttime and cool. The distortion is subtle, easy to miss if you're not looking directly at it, but once I see it, I can't look away.

What *is* it?

The shade stalker takes a step toward it, then another. I want to protest and ask why it's heading toward that questionable space, but my voice won't work. My throat is too dry and tight with pain and fear.

We reach the rippling air, and the creature doesn't hesitate. It walks forward through the rippling, and the world… changes.

Time hangs suspended.

That's the only way I can describe it. One moment we're moving, the next everything slows to an impossible crawl. The shade stalker's stride becomes languid and dreamlike. Each footfall takes an eternity to complete. My hair, which had been whipping in the wind of our passage, now drifts around my face in slow motion, each strand floating independently like I'm underwater.

The sensation is deeply strange. My stomach lurches, and if I had anything left in it, I'd be sick. The air feels thick, resistant, like we're pushing through something solid. Sound distorts, too. The shade stalker's breathing becomes a deep, drawn-out rumble that vibrates under my chest. My own heartbeat slows to a sluggish thrum… thrum… thrum…

Colors bleed and blur at the edges of my vision. The darkness of the forest behind us stretches and pulls, while ahead, light begins to seep in.

The pressure builds in my skull until I'm certain my head will split open. My injured shoulder burns with a cold fire that spreads through my entire left side. I try to scream, but the sound comes out low and distorted.

Then, just as suddenly as it started, it stops.

We burst through the other side of the portal and time snaps back to normal. The shade stalker stumbles slightly, catching itself, and the sudden return to regular motion makes my stomach heave. I taste bile and blood.

But we're somewhere else now. Somewhere completely different.

The forest is gone. We're on the outskirts of a village. I can see buildings in the distance, lights in windows, the glow of street lamps. And closer, much closer, rising up against the night sky like a towering, colorful beast…

The circus tent.

My heart, which had been struggling along, suddenly kicks into overdrive. The circus. We're at the circus. Which means…

Cairos.

The shade stalker moves with renewed urgency, skirting the edge of the village, staying in the shadows. It knows exactly where it needs to take me.

We circle around the back of the tent, past glass wagons and equipment and sleeping animals in cages. The creature moves silently despite its size, large paws padding quietly on the dirt-covered ground. He slips between obstacles effortlessly. No one sees us. No one raises an alarm.

Then I see him.

Cairos stands near the back entrance to the tent, talking to another fae I've never met—one of the performers, judging by the elaborate costume. His back is to us, but I'd know the set of his shoulders anywhere, the way he holds himself, the dark, tousled fall of his hair.

The shade stalker walks right up behind him and stops.

The other fae sees us first. His eyes go wide, his mouth falling open, and he takes several rapid steps backward. Whatever he was saying dies on his lips.

Cairos notices his reaction, turns to see what's spooked him, and freezes.

For one terrible, seemingly endless moment, he just stares. His eyes travel from the massive creature to me sprawled across its back, taking in my blood-soaked clothes, my useless arm, the pallor of my skin in the lamplight.

Then his face transforms.

The mask he wears shatters completely. What's left is raw and panicked and furious all at once.

"Naevyn," he pleads. My name comes out strangled, like he's choking on the words. He's moving before he finishes saying it, closing the distance between us in three long strides.

His hands reach for me, but he stops just short of touching, like he's afraid I'll break. "What—how—"

The shade stalker lowers itself carefully, going down on its haunches to make it easier for Cairos to reach me. He takes the invitation, hands finally making contact, and the moment his fingers brush my uninjured side, something in me just… releases.

I've been holding on so tight, forcing myself to stay conscious, to keep breathing, to survive. But now he's here, and I don't have to be strong anymore.

"Hey, no, stay with me." His voice cuts through the fog trying to pull me under. "Naevyn, look at me. Keep your eyes open."

I try. I really do try. But everything hurts so much, and I'm so tired.

Cairos's hands move to my shoulders, carefully maneuvering me off the shade stalker's back. The moment he touches my left shoulder, I scream because I can't help it. The sound that comes out is broken and pitiful, and I hate it. I hate being this weak.

"I'm so sorry. I'm so, so sorry." He's got me cradled against his chest now, one arm under my knees, the other supporting my back. The pressure on my wounded shoulder makes spots dance across my vision. "I've got you. I've got you."

He takes two steps toward the tent, then stops. Turns back to look at the shade stalker, and some sort of understanding passes between them.

He carries me into the tent through the back entrance. The other fae has vanished. Maybe he went to get help, or maybe he just fled from the massive predator that appeared out of nowhere.

The interior of the tent is dimly lit, the show clearly over for the night. Cairos navigates through the backstage area, heading for what looks like a private area curtained off from the rest.

He lays me down on something soft, though I can't tell for sure what it is. Can't focus on anything except the agony radiating from my shoulder and the way Cairos's hands hover over me like he doesn't know where to start.

His hands move to my shirt, and I realize he's trying to see the wound. The fabric is soaked through, stuck to my skin with drying blood. When he tries to peel it back, fresh blood wells up and I make another sound I'm not proud of. He improvises and tears open the neckline of my dress.

When my bare skin is revealed, Cairos's nostrils flare and his jaw works, barely containing his rage. Then, when he speaks, his voice is deadly. "Who *fucking* touched you?"

I try to answer, but all that comes out is a weak sound that might be a word or might be a whimper.

"Fuck," he snarls when he looks closer at the oozing wound. "This is bad. This is really bad."

He strips off his own shirt in one fluid motion and presses it against my shoulder, applying pressure that makes me arch off the cot. White-hot pain explodes behind my eyes, and for a moment I can't see, can't breathe, can't do anything but exist in a world made entirely of agony.

"I know, I know, but I have to stop the bleeding." His free hand cups my face, thumb stroking my cheek. "Stay with me, Little Wren. Just stay with me."

The endearment cuts through the pain, sharp and bittersweet. Little wren. He called me that again this morning, right before he left to murder people. Right before everything fell apart.

I manage to focus on his face. His eyes are wild, pupils blown wide, and there's something inhuman in them now that almost reminds me of the shade stalker's burning green gaze.

"Val…" I try to force out the name, but my tongue feels too thick, too heavy. "Valth…"

Understanding dawns in his expression, followed immediately by a rage so pure and absolute it's terrifying to witness.

"Valthaeron." He doesn't phrase it as a question. "Valthaeron did this to you."

I manage the smallest nod.

The sound that comes out of him isn't human. It's the same snarl I heard from the shade stalker, guttural and deadly and full of promise. His hands shake where they press against my wound, and I realize dimly that he's fighting for control, fighting against the urge to leave me here and go tear Valthaeron apart with his bare hands.

"I'm going to kill him." The words are barely intelligible, spoken through clenched teeth. "I'm going to fucking kill him."

"Tried… tried to… necklace…" My head feels fuzzy, my words coming out slurred and confused.

"Shh," Cairos says, brushing back the hair that's stuck by blood to my forehead. We'll talk about it later. Right now we need to—"

"Cairos?" A new voice, female, coming from beyond the curtain. "Cairos, what's going on? Brennan said he saw—"

Selenia pulls back the curtain and stops dead. She takes in the scene of me bleeding all over the cot, Cairos shirtless and covered in my blood, the makeshift dressing he's pressing to my shoulder, and her expression shifts from one of curiosity to alarm.

"Get Hessa," Cairos snaps without looking at her. "Now. And tell her to bring everything. *Everything*."

Surprisingly, Selenia doesn't have any cutting remarks about how stupid of a human I am. Instead, she spins around, darting back into the tent.

Cairos looks back down at me, and some of the rage has been replaced by something worse. Fear. Real, genuine fear.

"You're going to be okay," he says, and I can't tell if he's attempting to convince himself or me. "You're going to be fine. Hessa's a healer. She'll fix this. You just have to hold on a little longer."

I want to tell him I'm trying. To tell him about the prophecy, about forging the necklace alone, and losing it to Valthaeron. Even though I'm furious with him for what he did at the circus tonight, I'm so desperately glad to see him.

But the darkness at the edges of my vision is growing, spreading inward like an ink spill. My body has given everything it has. There's nothing left.

"Naevyn. Naevyn, no, stay awake. Look at me." His hand is on my face again, patting my cheek, trying to keep me present. "Don't you dare. Don't you fucking dare leave me."

I try. Really, honestly try.

But the darkness is patient, and I'm so, so tired.

The last thing I see before everything goes black is Cairos's face above me, twisted with anguish, his lips moving in words I can no longer hear.

Then sweet nothing.

28

RECOGNITION

Darkness.

Then not-darkness, but something close. Grey fog that feels thick enough to drown in. I float in it, untethered, suspended between waking and oblivion.

Voices drift past sometimes. Familiar ones. Cairos, tight with worry. Fenric, measured and steady. Hessa, sweet and soothing. They blend together, words stripped of meaning, until they fade back into the fog.

Time doesn't exist here. There's no day or night. No sense of hours passing. Just the fog and the floating and occasionally, distantly, pain.

But the pain is growing. Sharpening. Pulling me toward consciousness like a rope that tethers me between here and there. I desperately want to stay here, disconnected from the pain, but resistance is useless.

My shoulder throbs with a bone-deep ache. My mouth tastes like death. My tongue is heavy and thick, stuck to the roof of my mouth. Every part of me feels stiff.

I need water. The thought surfaces through the fog, insistent and desperate. I need water or I'm going to die of thirst right here in this bed.

Bed?

The word catches, snagging on something. I'm in a bed. Not the cot from the circus tent, a real bed.

I try to open my eyes.

It takes three attempts. The first two times, my eyelids flutter but won't quite lift, too heavy with exhaustion. But the third time, they crack open just enough to let in light.

Too much light. I squeeze them shut again, a small sound of protest escaping my throat.

"Naevyn?"

The voice is close. Very close. Male. Familiar.

I force my eyes open again, blinking against the brightness. Shapes slowly resolve into something recognizable. A ceiling, dark wood with golden trim. There's a window with long, flowy curtains filtering afternoon sunlight. And leaning over me, close enough that I can feel his breath on my face, is Cairos.

I jerk back instinctively, and the movement sends a spike of pain through my shoulder that makes me gasp. My body hated the movement, the use of my muscles.

"Easy, easy," Cairos says, placing one hand on my uninjured shoulder. "You're okay. You're safe."

I stare at him, trying to make sense of what I'm seeing. He looks like shit. Dark circles shadow his eyes, his hair is a mess like it hasn't been tamed in days, and I think he's still wearing the same costume from the circus. It's a simple white shirt, with flowy sleeves rolled to his elbows, and there's something in his hands. White cloth. Bandages.

"Where—" My voice comes out as a croak, barely audible. I try again. "Where am I?"

"My room. In Daersbane." He sets the bandages aside on a small table beside the bed. "You've been unconscious for two days."

Two days. The words don't quite register at first, but when they do, it takes everything I have to resist sitting up in a panic.

I've lost two days. Valthaeron could have done anything in the last two days, now that he has the pendant.

"Shit. Valthaeron—"

"We'll talk about Valthaeron soon. For now, you need to stay still and drink some water." Cairos reaches for a glass on the bedside table, sliding one arm behind my shoulders to help me sit up slightly. "Come on. Slowly."

The movement makes my head spin, and for a horrible moment, I think I'm going to be sick. But then cool water touches my lips, and nothing else matters except drinking.

I gulp it down greedily, too fast, and Cairos pulls the glass back.

"Slower," he says. "You'll make yourself sick."

I want to grab the fucking glass and drain it, but my hands won't cooperate. They lie useless at my sides, too weak to even lift. So I let him tip the glass back to my lips, let him control the pace, hating every second of this helplessness.

When the glass is finally empty, he sets it aside and carefully lowers me back down. I take stock of my surroundings properly now that my vision has cleared.

The bed is a four-poster mahogany structure draped with black silk sheets that feel cool and expensive against my skin. The duvet is the same rich black, and I'm tucked deep underneath it. The posts are carved with intricate designs, and where they meet the canopy frame, there are touches of gold that catch the light.

The room itself matches the bed's elegance. Dark wood furniture with those same gold accents, a wardrobe against one wall, a desk covered in papers near the window. Everything is tasteful, masculine, and expensive. This is Cairos's private space, and I'm in his bed.

The realization makes something flutter in my chest that I don't want to examine too closely.

"Why am I here?" I ask slowly.

"Because I wanted you where I could keep an eye on you. After what happened, I wasn't letting you out of my sight."

"Controlling much?"

The words come out sharper than I intend, but instead of getting defensive, Cairos's expression softens. Almost smiles. Like my snark is somehow reassuring.

"You have no idea," he says quietly. Then, seeming to shake himself, he picks up the bandages again. "Hessa asked me to change your dressings. She's meeting with another faction today, so she can't be here, which means I have the pleasure."

I notice now that my shirt—not my shirt, actually, but a soft cotton one that's way too big and definitely Cairos's—is unbuttoned at the top, revealing my shoulder and the edge of a bandage wrapped around my upper arm and across my chest.

"You've been changing my bandages?" The thought of him tending to me while I was unconscious feels intimate in a way that makes my skin warm.

"No. Before, it was Hessa. And she's apparently much more skilled than I because she managed to let you sleep. Meanwhile, you wake up the first time I so much as sit on the bed."

"Maybe I was just more excited to see you," I retort, berating myself for being so forward. Cairos doesn't fault me, though, just smiles and shakes his head, turning his attention back to the bandage.

He shifts closer to get a better angle. "Can I…?" He gestures to the bandage, and I realize he's asking permission.

It surprises me. This is Cairos, who rarely asks for anything, who takes what he wants with arrogant confidence. But here he is, waiting for my consent to touch me.

"Yes," I say quietly.

He starts unwrapping the bandage around my shoulder, his movements careful and practiced. His fingers are warm where they brush my skin, and I try not to think about how close he is, how I can smell the forest and musk and something uniquely him.

"How does it feel?" he asks, focused on his work.

"Like someone stabbed me with a sword made of shadowstone and I almost died."

Cairos lets out a huff of amusement. "So… not great."

"Not great," I agree.

He works in silence for a moment, unwinding the old bandage. When he finally pulls it away, cool air hits the wound, and I hiss slightly.

"Sorry." He examines my shoulder, and I can't see his expression, but his touch remains gentle. "It's healing well. Hessa said there'd be a scar, but the muscle damage is mostly repaired."

"Lucky me."

"You're alive. That's all that matters," Cairos says, voice low.

I don't know what to say to that, so I say nothing. I watch as he applies some kind of sweet-smelling, herbal healing ointment, then begins wrapping fresh bandages.

"There's, um." He clears his throat. "You have other wounds. From the glass. On your abdomen."

Oh. Right. The shards of glass that cut me when the shade stalker tore through the window.

"Hessa's been treating those too, but she asked me to put on fresh bandages. I can wait for her, though, if you'd rather—"

"Just do it." I'm too tired to be modest, and honestly, after everything we've been through, this seems ridiculous to be awkward about.

He lifts the fabric slowly, carefully, pushing it up. His fingers brush the bare underside of my breast as he adjusts the shirt, and despite the pain and exhaustion, my body reacts.

I gasp, the sound escaping before I can stop it.

Cairos freezes. "Did I hurt you?"

“No.” The word comes out faster and breathier than I intend, heat rising in my cheeks. “No, I’m fine. Keep going.”

He does, but I can feel the tension radiating from him now, the careful way he’s trying not to touch anywhere he doesn’t have to. The bandage wrapped around my middle is stained with small spots of blood.

He begins unwrapping it, and to reach the bandage where it wraps around my back, he has to lean close. So close I can feel the heat of him. I could count his eyelashes if I wanted to. Each time he needs to lift my back slightly to pass the bandage underneath, his arm slides around me, cradling me against his chest for just a moment before lowering me back down.

It’s intimate. Too intimate. And I’m acutely aware of how vulnerable I am right now.

The last of the bandage comes away, and Cairos goes completely still.

The silence stretches, thick and strange. I can hear him breathing and feel the tension in his body where he’s leaning over me.

“Cairos? What’s wrong?” My voice sounds small when I ask.

“No.” The word is barely a whisper. “No, no, no. What is this?”

His rough, calloused fingers brush across my left rib cage. Over the birthmark that’s been there my entire life. An irregular mark, slim and maybe the length of my thumb, that I’ve never thought twice about.

“It’s just a birthmark,” I tell him.

Cairos continues studying it, running his finger back and forth over the length of the mark. His face has gone pale.

“What’s wrong with you?” I prompt. “You’re scaring me. You look like you’ve seen a ghost.”

“This is not a birthmark.” His voice is strange, strained, like he’s forcing the words out.

"What are you talking about? I've had this all my life. It's definitely a birthmark. You're acting crazy."

"I mean it's not a birthmark." He speaks with clenched teeth, his voice dropping to a low, deep growl that makes the hair on my arms stand up. "It's a fucking scar."

I recoil from his fingers, from the intensity in his voice, and I'm reprimanded by another shooting pain originating at my shoulder. Maybe he really *has* lost it. "What do you mean?"

"What do you mean, 'what do I mean?'" He's not quite shouting, but his voice is rising, rough with emotion. "I said it's a scar. You weren't—" He breaks off, and confusion floods through me as I try to make sense of what he's trying to say.

"I don't understand! I don't—"

"I know it's a scar because I watched you receive it!" He does shout now, pain marring his voice. "I watched the dagger pierce through your skin. I watched his dagger drive into Bellamie's side—into *your* side—as you got *so* close to dethroning him." His voice cracks, and his eyes are desperate, pleading now. "You're Bellamie."

The words don't make sense. They're sounds without meaning, syllables strung together in an order that my brain refuses to process.

"What are you talking about?" My heart is hammering now, panic rising like bile in my throat. "That doesn't make any sense."

"It makes perfect sense." He's staring at me now, really looking at me, and there's something wild and desperate in his eyes. "All this time. All the times you reminded me of her, I should've known. Should've seen it."

"Seen what? Cairos, you're not making any sense. I'm not—I can't be—" The words stick in my throat.

"Look at it." Cairos's finger traces the mark again, and I flinch. "Really look at it, and tell me that's a birthmark. Tell me that doesn't perfectly match the shape of a dagger."

I can't see it, not really. My neck won't crane at the right angle. But I've seen it a thousand times in mirrors, never thinking twice about it.

Except, now that he's mentioned it… the shape is wrong for a birthmark, isn't it? Too straight on one edge. Too deliberate.

"No." I shake my head, ignoring the way it makes my vision swim. "No, that's impossible. I'm just a human."

"You have the same facial structure. The same blue eyes. Damn near the same voice." Cairos is leaning over me now, both hands braced on either side of my head, caging me in. "I thought it was just a resemblance. Chance, really. But this… this scar. I was there when she got it. I held her while she bled. There's no way, no *possible* way you could have the exact same scar in the exact same place unless—"

"Unless I'm her." The words fall from my lips.

He nods. I watch his throat work as he swallows.

"But I'm not." Even as I say it, the protest sounds weak. "I'm Naevyn. I'm from the human realm. I grew up in Xardon. I have memories. A life."

"Both things can be true. You lived this life *and* the last. Valthaeron killed Bellamie with a shadowstone dagger."

"So?" I ask, not grasping what he's trying to say.

"Shadowstone is a substance that can hold souls indefinitely. They can also be released. Valthaeron must've learned how to release a soul to live again." Cairos stares at the scar while he speaks, pain crossing his features like he's reliving Bellamie's—my—death all over again.

"So he… *chose* to bring me back? Why would he do that?" My mind spins trying to conceive why Valthaeron would kill Bellamie, then bring her back.

"The prophecy. Vitalia."

"Vitalia?" I repeat.

"In fae, it means *life given again*. To fulfil the prophecy. It was something that used to happen commonly, a gift of rebirth given by the Goddess Aurelius to souls with unfinished business.

"What happened?" I ask.

"Draven, the god of death, felt cheated and began taking souls that weren't yet ready to pass. The only thing Aurelius could do was step back and allow things to happen naturally. Since then, it's been forbidden. Even if one discovers *how* to reincarnate a soul, the ramifications of doing so should be... monumental."

"But... nothing happened. If this is true," I pause, taking in a wheezing breath, "then Valthaeron should be toast. But he's not."

"Exactly. The Gods of our world would never allow this. Unless..." Cairos's jaw works while he thinks.

"Unless what?" I ask.

"Unless one of two things: the Gods themselves fear Valthaeron, or he formed a pact with them." Cairos drums his fingers against his knee.

"I'm not sure which of those is worse," I whisper.

Thoughts of Valthaeron forming some sort of pact with the Gods makes me feel delirious. How the fuck would we defeat a king backed by literal Gods. Not only that, but I have no idea who I even am anymore. Or *what* I even am.

"Hey." Cairos strokes my cheek with the back of his fingers, breaking me out of my spiral. "Breathe. Just breathe."

"How can I breathe when everything I thought I knew is a lie? That my life isn't even real."

"You *are* real. Listen to me. You are real. Naevyn is real. Whatever you were before, whoever Bellamie was, that doesn't change who you are now."

I want to believe him, but doubt is spreading through my mind like poison.

"I need something from you," Cairos says suddenly.

"What is it?" I ask.

He takes a breath. "When Bellamie died, I thought I'd never feel anything again. For six hundred years, I didn't. I just… existed. Collected souls. Tried to push down the guilt that I felt every damn day. But I was hollow."

His right hand is still on my face, thumb now brushing away tears I didn't realize were rolling down.

"Then you showed up."

The way he says it makes my breath hitch.

"This stubborn, reckless human who should have died in that tent but didn't. Who bit back when I threatened you. Who saw me as more than just the monster I believed myself to be." He pauses. "And I felt something I hadn't felt in centuries."

"What?" I whisper.

"Recognition." The word settles heavy between us. "That first moment I saw you when you tried to run. When you demanded I ask your name, my soul knew. I didn't understand it then. I tried to tell myself it was just grief and the memory of old wounds, but that was just a lie. It was more, and deep down, I knew it was more."

I remember that moment. Remember the inexplicable pull toward him, even when every logical part of me screamed to run away.

"At first, yes. You reminded me of Bellamie. And I hated it. My anger toward you flared every time that you made me feel things I'd buried."

Each word feels like a confession. Like he's stripping himself bare.

"But?" I prompt, needing to hear the rest even though I'm terrified.

"But then you kept surprising me. You killed a millenium-old ringmaster. You stood up to me when anyone else would have cowered. You faced Valthaeron, ready to die if it meant freeing us."

I squeeze my eyes shut, forcing the blurry tears to fall so I can see Cairos again.

"And somewhere along the way, I stopped being reminded of Bellamie and started seeing you. Just you."

My heart is hammering so hard I'm sure he can hear it.

"When I'm with you, when I *look at* you, it's not her face I see. It's yours. When you're furious with me and your eyes flash. When you're half-dead from blood loss and still trying to argue." He swallows hard. "That's not Bellamie. That's Naevyn. That's the woman I—"

He stops like the next words are the hardest he's ever had to say.

I'm holding my breath, suspended, terrified, and hopeful all at once.

"The woman I love."

The words crash over me, sending a fresh wave of tears rolling down my cheeks.

He loves me.

"Bellamie was my soulmate." The admission makes my heart clench, but he keeps going. "We found each other, loved each other, lost each other. And I thought that was it. That I'd had my one chance."

Oh gods. Tears are streaming down my face now, endless.

"But you…" His voice cracks. "*You* are my soulmate, now. The same soul I loved before, yes, but also someone entirely new. Someone I'm discovering all over again. And I understand now. I was always going to find you in this lifetime and the next. In every lifetime."

The words steal the air from my lungs.

"The universe, the gods, whatever it was, they brought you back to me. Maybe Valthaeron thought he was pulling strings, but in the end, he was the pawn. Because you and I?" His eyes scan my face like he wants to take in all of me at once. "We were always going to find each other again. Now that I know what you are, now that I understand we're bound together, the thought of losing you again…"

He closes his eyes briefly, like the thought causes physical pain.

"I need to protect you. Not because you're weak—Gods know you're one of the strongest fucking people I've ever met—but because you're mine and I won't survive losing you a second time."

I can barely breathe. Definitely can't speak. No one has ever looked at me like this.

"What we've become is real." His voice drops to barely a whisper. "And I don't love you because you're Bellamie reborn. I love you because you're Naevyn. You're everything."

The words nearly knock me out. Everything. I'm everything to him.

This man who's lived a thousand years, who's probably seen empires rise and fall, is looking at me like I'm the only thing that matters to him.

I swallow. Breathe in, breathe out. Try to compose myself the tiniest bit so that I can speak.

"I think…" My voice shakes as I sniffle and try to compose myself enough to speak properly. I take a breath. "No. I *know*. I love you too."

His eyes widen slightly, like maybe he thought I'd reject him. Something about the way he drinks in my words makes me want to keep going.

"Even though you're arrogant and controlling and you just turned my world upside down," I continue. "Even though you make me so angry sometimes, I want to scream. Even though I don't know who I really am now." I meet his eyes. "I love you. And that scares me."

"Why?"

"Because loving you means I have something to lose. And I've lost too much already. I've already got my family back in Xardon to lose and the thought of that tears me up inside. Add you to that, and…." The admission feels like tearing open an old wound. "What if Valthaeron wins? What if I die again? What if—"

"We won't lose each other." His voice is fierce. Almost feral. "Whatever comes next, we face it together."

"Even if Valthaeron orchestrated us together, all of it?"

"Especially then. Because he thought he was creating a weapon that would be his salvation. Instead, he gave me back my soulmate. He gave me you. And that's going to be his downfall."

For a moment, we just stare at each other. Then his mouth is on mine, sweet and slow. He's gentle with me now, drinking me in as his lips move against mine in mesmerising ways. I kiss him back as fervently as I can manage, ignoring the pain in my shoulder. Ignoring everything except the way he tastes.

The kiss deepens, and I can feel the pull between us that transcends just this moment. It's vast and ancient and ours.

When we finally break apart, we're both breathing hard.

"That was…" I start, dazed.

"Not nearly enough." His forehead presses against mine. "But we have a war to plan and a bastard of a king to destroy."

He's right. We've lost too much time already with me being unconscious. Still… I can't bring myself to pull away. And apparently, neither can Cairos. We stay like that, just breathing each other in. Time seems to stop around us.

It's crazy, but I can almost feel our breathing happening together, our heartbeats synchronizing until I can't tell where I end and Cairos begins. And it feels so, so right.

Then, he pulls away. Painfully, he pulls away.

"We need to tell the others about Bellamie, and what this means."

"I know," I answer.

"Valthaeron orchestrated all of this, and we're going to make him pay," he says, straightening. "But first, you need to get dressed. Can you stand?"

"With your help."

"Always." He slides one arm behind my back, the other under my knees, and lifts me from the bed. "Come on, Little Wren. We have a war to fight."

As he carries me toward the wardrobe, I catch my reflection. Dark auburn hair a matted, tangled mess. Blue eyes red from crying. A face that apparently belongs to someone else.

But when I look at it, all I see is me.

Naevyn.

The woman Cairos loves. His soulmate.

And whoever Bellamie was, whatever Valthaeron intended for his latest circus, I'm going to write my own ending.

With Cairos by my side.

In this lifetime and every one after.

29

STRATEGY

Cairos catches everyone up while I practice standing and walking again. Thankfully, the pain isn't what I thought it would be. Hessa returned and performed one more healing session on me before our meeting here, which took away a substantial amount of pain.

Now we're all standing in the practice hall under the glass dome, and the tension is suffocating.

"So let me get this straight," Jexen says, his accent sharp. "Not only is she human, but she's also somehow the dead fae we all knew? And we're just supposed to accept that?"

His teeth are sharpening, canines elongating into points.

"Yes," Cairos says flatly.

"Or what?" Jexen takes a step forward. "You'll make us?"

Both twins hiss simultaneously, and I resist the urge to step back.

"Enough." Hessa's voice cuts through the rising tension. She stands between them, hands raised and eyes pleading. "Fighting each other accomplishes nothing. We need to focus."

"Focus on what?" Selenia sneers from her perch on the trapeze bar. "On the fact that Valthaeron played us all like fools?"

“On how we’re going to stop him,” Fenric says calmly, moving to stand beside me. There’s something protective in the gesture, almost paternal.

Selenia’s laugh is bitter. “Stop him how? With what? The necklace is gone. Valthaeron has it, and we have nothing.”

I wince at the words. This is my fault. He would never have the piece he needs if it weren’t for me.

“We have her,” Cairos says, standing up for me. “Her blood works with shadowstone.”

“Her blood.” Kyreth’s lip curls. “The blood of a human.”

“The blood of a *fae soul* in a human body, Kyreth,” Cairos corrects, meeting his glare. “The blood of a powerful fae, which, I should remind you, is poison to creatures like you.”

Jexen hisses at the threat, and Cairos moves. One second he’s beside me, the next he’s between me and the twins, his entire body coiled.

“Careful,” he says, voice dropping. “That’s the second time you’ve threatened her. There won’t be a third.”

“Boys,” Hessa sighs. “Can we please act like adults for five minutes?”

“She’s not one of us,” Kyreth insists. “She doesn’t belong here.”

“And yet here I am, like it or not,” I mutter.

Fenric’s hand lands on my uninjured shoulder. “Whether you believe her doesn’t change the facts. Valthaeron’s been manipulating all of us for centuries. He sent Bellamie’s soul to be reborn, knowing she’d find her way back.”

“For what?” Selenia demands. “To forge a necklace? Any good Solmeren blacksmith could’ve done that.”

“The necklace wasn’t the point,” I say. “*I* was. My blood is what’s valuable to him, and now he has it in the shadowstone.”

“Valuable how?” Jexen asks.

“My blood activates shadowstone in ways normal fae blood doesn’t. It’s poison to fae, but it also…” I pause, thinking through what Valthaeron said. “He needed it to amplify his power. According to the prophecy he showed me, shadowstone infused with my blood magnifies magic, making it more potent. That's why he orchestrated my rebirth, why he needed me specifically to forge the necklace. He's been planning this for centuries."

"Planning what?" Selenia demands.

"I… don't know, exactly." I admit. "A ritual, maybe. Something that requires shadowstone bonded with both fae and mortal essence. My blood gives him access to both Bellamie's fae soul and my human body combined in the stone. The only sure guess I can make is that he needs it for something that will make him more powerful."

"Which is why we can't let him keep it," Cairos finishes.

"But knowing that my blood is also poison to fae, I've been thinking…what if I can use that? Use my blood to trap Valthaeron instead of killing him?"

"Trap him?" Kyreth's eyebrows shoot up. "Not kill him?"

The room goes quiet.

Cairos's jaw tightens beside me.

Words stumble out of me, my cheeks feeling warm with the eyes of all of these people on me. "He's an immortal fae who's been collecting souls for centuries. Souls that he probably uses to enhance his power. Trying to kill him would be fruitless. *Was* fruitless when I tried. But trapping him…"

"Trapping him might just work," Fenric finishes, stepping forward. "Shadowstone is excellent at containing things. Souls, magic, power. If your blood makes it toxic to fae, but also amplifies its properties…"

"Then shadowstone infused with her blood could be a prison," Hessa says slowly. "One strong enough to hold even Valthaeron."

"But he already has the necklace," Selena points out. "The one she made with her blood. What's stopping him from using it for his ritual?"

"Nothing. Which is why we need to forge another one. A trap he won't see coming," I say, looking from face to face to see if I can read their expressions. Hessa looks excited. Cairos and Fenric determined. Selenia and Kyreth annoyed. And Jexen looks… irate.

Jexen's teeth are sharpening as he steps forward. "And how exactly do you plan to get close enough to use it?" His voice comes out sharp, almost a hiss. "You think he'll just let you waltz up and trap him in a pretty necklace? No. We kill him."

An argument ensues, half the troupe insisting on death while the others push for a prison. The back and forth is dizzying.

"Wait," Jexen says loudly, his voice cutting through the conversation. "If we kill Valthaeron, the curse breaks. Which means we all lose our dragon forms."

He goes still after saying it. Then his jaw clenches, and when he speaks again, his voice is rigid. "And that's a problem."

"A problem?" Selena's eyebrows rise. "Being free of a curse is a problem?"

"Yes." Jexen's hands curl into fists at his sides. "Have any of you thought about what happens after we kill the king? The Solmeren are going to rise up. They've been waiting centuries for an opening like this. The moment Valthaeron falls, they'll make their move."

Kyreth goes quiet, understanding dawning on his face.

"Without our dragon forms, how do we fight them?" Jexen continues, his voice rising. "How do we escape the castle when it's overrun? How do we protect the factions from the chaos that's coming?" He looks around at all of us. "We've been dragons for six hundred years. That's our only advantage. Our only way to survive what comes next."

"He's right," Hessa says softly, her expression pained. "The Solmeren won't just let us walk away. They'll want blood for what the king has done. And without our dragon forms…"

"We're just fae," Jexen finishes. "Easy targets."

I take a step forward, my mind racing. "So, it's settled. We trap him instead of killing him. We just need shadowstone."

"Even if that could work," Kyreth says carefully, "Valthaeron controls the shadowstone supply. There's none unattended in all the Herethia."

"Then we find some," I say firmly. "Or we make him vulnerable long enough to use what he's already wearing."

Jexen looks at me, and for the first time, there's something like respect in his eyes. "You're serious about this."

"I'm serious about all of us surviving," I say. "Including keeping your dragon forms for when the Solmeren come knocking. I worked the mines in Xardon for years. I know where the shadowstone is, how to get it, and how to move it without anyone noticing," I volunteer.

"You want to go back?" Cairos's voice is dangerously quiet. "To the human realm?"

"I want to get what we need. And if I'm being honest, I want to get my family out before Valthaeron can use them against me." I look around the room.

"We only have two days until the emerald cycle," Cairos warns gravely. "It's now or never."

Fenric nods slowly. "That is the word of the prophecy."

"So tomorrow, I go back to Xardon. Just for one day. I'll work the mines like I always did, keep my head down, and gather shadowstone in my pockets. Then Cairos opens a portal, and we bring Quinnic and Alabris back before anyone realizes what's happening."

"*That's* your plan?" Selena's voice drips with disdain. "Hope no one recognizes the girl who disappeared?"

"I wasn't gone that long. And I was just another miner. It's not like anyone paid attention to me."

"The guards are hires of the king. If they recognize you—" Kyreth starts.

"They won't."

"But if they do?"

"Then we run." I shrug. "Cairos opens a portal, we grab Quinnic and Alabris, and we get out. Simple."

"This is not simple," Jexen says, but still, I can hear the shift in his tone. He's considering it.

"It's the best plan we have," Fenric says. "And we need to move fast. If Valthaeron completes what he must with that necklace…"

He doesn't need to finish. We all know what happens if an already-powerful immortal king gains access to amplified magic.

"Fine," Kyreth says finally, pointing at me. "But if this goes wrong, I'm blaming you."

"Fair enough."

Cairos pulls me aside as the others start discussing logistics. His hand on my elbow is firm, guiding me away from the group.

"This is a terrible plan," he says once we're out of earshot.

"You have a better one?"

"Several. None of which involve you potentially walking into a trap."

I pull my arm free. "I'm the only one who knows the mines well enough to get in and out without raising suspicion."

"You disappeared from Xardon weeks ago. The guards will notice if you suddenly show up again."

"Maybe, maybe not. Either way, we need the shadowstone, and this is the best way I can think of to get it."

Cairos huffs. He's quiet for a moment, jaw working. "I'm staying with you."

"Okay."

"And if the guards recognize you, we leave immediately. No heroics, no looking for anyone. We portal out."

I glare at him for a moment, but he hits me with the same straight face right back.

"Fine."

His eyes narrow slightly, like he's surprised I'm not arguing. "That was too easy."

"Because I'm not stupid enough to think I can fight my way out of the mines if things go bad." I meet his gaze. "But I *am* going back. With or without your approval."

Cairos grunts in agreement, and I know that's the best I can hope to get from him surrounding a potential suicide mission.

I just hope I'm not miserably wrong about this.

30

REUNITED

The portal Cairos creates dumps us out in an alley three blocks from my house.

I stumble as my feet hit solid ground, Cairos steadying me with a hand on my upper arm. The familiar smell of Xardon hits me immediately—red dust, sweat, and desperation. Home. Or what used to be home.

"You good?" Cairos asks, scanning the alley.

"Yeah." I adjust the rough miner's clothes Cairos conjured for me based on my description. It looks exactly like the same threadbare shirt and pants I wore for years. It feels wrong now, though, like putting on a costume of who I used to be. "Let's go."

We stick to the back paths, avoiding the main thoroughfares. It's mid-morning, so most people are already toiling away at the mines, or wherever else they scrape together a living. The sun is already brutal, heat radiating off the terra-cotta buildings in waves that make the air shimmer.

Cairos stays close, his presence both comforting and conspicuous. Even in plain clothes, he doesn't look like he belongs here. He's too tall, too broad, and too well fed. And he moves with a confidence that everyone in Xardon has had beaten out of us in one way or another.

We walk for a few minutes, and I keep my head down to evade notice. I occasionally peek up through my lashes and find people staring unabashedly at Cairos, but he either doesn't notice or doesn't care, so I do the same.

"That one," I say finally, pointing to the sandy hovel I called home for years. "The one with the cracked stucco."

We approach cautiously. The patchy grass looks even more yellowed than I remember, the building even more worn. Has it only been weeks? Gods, it feels like years.

I push open the door and find it unlocked.

"Quinnic? Alabris?" My voice echoes in the empty space.

Nothing.

The house is too quiet. Too still. The hearth is cold, with no tea brewing. No sounds of movement from the back room.

"They're not here," I say, panic starting to claw up my throat as I walk around, frantic.

Cairos moves through the space efficiently, checking the back room, and looking for signs of a struggle. "No blood. No signs of a fight. No sign of Valthaeron."

That should be comforting, but it's not. I notice things as I look around. The soup pot is gone from the hearth. Alabris's teacups are missing. The storage trunk is open, half-empty.

"They've been selling things," I realize, my voice hollow. "To survive."

"Naevyn." Cairos is at the door, and something in his tone makes my stomach drop.

I join him. He's looking at the neighbor's house, where an older woman is sweeping her stoop. She glances over, does a double-take when she sees me.

"Naevyn?" She sounds shocked. "Is that really you?"

"Where are they?" I ask, not bothering with pleasantries. "Where are Quinnic and Alabris?"

Her expression shifts to something like pity. "Oh, honey. You don't know?"

"Don't know what?" I demand.

"The boy… he's been working the mines. Took your place after you disappeared. The guards have been rough on him. *Real rough*." She shakes her head. "And the girl with no fingers, she's been trying to sell what little you had left. Last I saw her, she was headed toward the docks. Desperate for food, poor thing."

Oh gods. The docks. The second most dangerous place in this entire shithole of a district.

"He's at the mines right now?" I ask.

"Should be. Unless…" She hesitates. "Unless they finally sent him down below. He's been causing trouble, that one."

Oh gods. Quinnic, you stupid kid.

"Thank you," I manage, already moving, though not sure where to go first. Save Alabris from the docks? Or Quinnic from the mines?

Alabris is an adult—she can handle herself. But Quinnic?

Cairos keeps pace beside me as we head toward the mines. "Down below in the mines is where they send people as punishment. It's dangerous down there. Cave-ins. Accidents. And the men…" I don't finish.

We're running now, not caring who sees. The mine comes into view, and I scan the workers in the sorting area desperately.

There. Red hair, medium build, but already thinner than last time I saw him. Moving too slowly with a bucket that's clearly too heavy.

"Quinnic!" I don't care that I'm shouting, or that heads are turning.

He looks up, and the expression on his face cycles through disbelief, relief, and then fury so fast I can barely track it.

He drops the bucket. Shadowstone spills across the ground, and a guard immediately starts toward him, shouting.

"You've got to be kidding me," the guard snarls. "That's the second—"

He stops when he sees me. Recognition flashes across his face.

"You," he says, and his hand goes to the club at his belt. "The girl who disappeared. Where the hell have you been?"

"Family emergency," I say quickly. "But I'm back now."

"Family emergency." He spits on the ground near my feet. "And you think you can just waltz back in here? After leaving this little shit to take your place?" He gestures at Quinnic, who's now backing away slowly.

Cairos steps forward, and something in the way he moves makes the guard hesitate.

"The girl's back," Cairos says, his voice flat and cold. "So the boy can go."

"Who the hell are you?" the guard asks, rounding on Cairos.

Cairos doesn't answer. Just stares down at the guard with eyes that have gone dark, and I can see the moment the guard decides this isn't worth it.

Except other guards are noticing now and starting to move toward us. This is going bad fast.

"Naevyn." Quinnic's voice is raw. "Where were you?"

"I'll explain everything, but we need to go. Now."

His blue eyes are hard. Hurt. "You left us. You just left without saying anything."

"I didn't have a choice. Please, we have to go. Now!"

"There's always a choice!" His voice cracks, and gods, he sounds so young. "I've been working here for weeks, Nae. Do you know what they did to me when I couldn't carry the buckets fast enough?"

I didn't, but I can see the bruises on his arms now, the way he's favoring his left side, the split lip that's only partially healed.

“I’m sorry,” I say, and I mean it. “I’m so sorry. But we need to find Alabris and leave. Right now.”

“Leave? Leave where?” He’s backing away from me now, and I realize with growing horror that he doesn’t trust me. “Are you going to disappear again? Leave me to deal with this?”

“Naevyn,” Cairos warns. More guards are coming. At least six now, moving to surround us.

“I’m not leaving without you,” I tell Quinnic. “Or Alabris. But I need you to trust me.”

“Why should I?”

“Because I’m your sister, and I came back for you.” I step closer, lowering my voice. “And because I can explain everything, but not here. Not now.”

One of the guards steps forward. “Nobody’s going anywhere.” He turns to me. “You’re coming with me to explain your absence to the boss. Boy, back to work. And you—” He points at Cairos. “You’re trespassing on private property.”

Cairos doesn’t even blink. His voice is deadly. “Touch her and see what happens.”

The guard’s hand is already reaching for my arm. He makes contact, starts to pull, and then Cairos moves.

One second the guard is standing, the next he’s on the ground, clutching his wrist, which is bent at an angle that makes my stomach turn.

The other guards react immediately, rushing forward.

I swoop down and snatch a single piece of shadowstone off the ground, stuffing it into my bodice. The weight of it nearly holds me down, but we need this.

Cairos is a blur of controlled violence, moving with his inhuman speed and strength. A sword swings toward his head. He catches the guard's arm mid-swing, rips the sword out of the guard’s hands, tossing him off-balance, and uses it to sweep the legs out from under another.

“We need to get to the docks!” I scream.

More guards are coming. I can hear shouting and see workers stopping to watch. This is about to get very, very bad.

"Go," Cairos says, dropping the last guard. "I'll catch up."

"What? No—"

"Go!" His voice leaves no room for argument. "Get to the docks. Find Alabris. I'll take care of this and meet you there."

Before I can protest, he shifts.

The man standing before us quickly turns into a substantial onyx dragon, scales gleaming in the sunlight, wings spreading wide enough to cast shadows over half the sorting area.

"Holy shit!" Quinnic exclaims.

Screams erupt from the workers. Guards stumble backward, some dropping their weapons and running.

"Run!" I grab Quinnic's arm and pull him away from the chaos. Behind us, I hear Cairos roar, the sounds of more panic and shouting erupting from around him as he gives us the distraction we need.

We sprint through the streets, Quinnic stumbling beside me, still in shock.

"That was—did you—was that a—"

"Dragon? Yes. He's with me. Keep running."

We sprint through the streets, the sounds of the frightened bystanders fading the further we run. My side burns. My lungs burn. But I use the pain to push me to run harder.

Finally, the docks come into view, and I scan desperately for Alabris. The smell of salt water, the sounds of ships being loaded, and drunk men shouting obscenities grow closer.

"There!" Quinnic points.

Alabris is near the end of the dock, arguing with a man twice her size. She's holding what looks like our last blanket, trying to trade it for coin, but the man is laughing at her.

"Alabris!" I shout.

She turns, sees me, and her face crumples. "Naevyn?"

The man she's bargaining with notices us approaching and sneers. "Friends of yours?"

"We're leaving," I say when I make it to the end of the dock, reaching for Alabris. "Right now."

"Leaving?" Alabris looks between us, confused and scared. "Naevyn, what's happening? Where were you?"

"I'll explain everything, I promise. But we have to—"

A roar echoes across the city. Cairos, still in dragon form, soars above the buildings, heading toward us.

The man Alabris was bargaining with takes one look at the sky and jolts sideways, losing his balance on the edge of the dock, and landing with a harsh splash in the ocean.

Normally, that would send me into a fit of laughter, but not today.

"Is that…?" Alabris's voice is barely a whisper, her eyes glued to the skies.

"Just trust me," I beg. "Please."

Cairos soars toward us, and I can feel Alabris's desire to flee coiled up like a spring ready to let loose, but I hold her in place. Cairos lands on the dock with enough force to crack the wood. Several support beams groan under his weight.

Quinnic is backing away, while Alabris is frozen in place, staring.

"Get on," I say, moving toward Cairos. "Both of you."

"Are you insane?" Quinnic's voice goes up an octave. "That's a—"

"Dragon. I know. And we don't have time for this. Get on or stay here. Your choice," I plead.

Quinnic looks at me like I've lost my mind. Then he looks at Alabris, who's still clutching that ratty blanket, and something in his face hardens.

"Come on," he says to her, voice shaking but determined. He helps her toward Cairos, and together they scramble up. I follow, making my way up his lowered wing.

The three of us settle on Cairos's back, me in front, Alabris in the middle, Quinnic behind, all of us holding on for dear life.

Guards round the corner onto the docks, then see us and start shouting. One of them raises a crossbow.

Cairos doesn't wait. He launches skyward just as the arrow whistles past where we stood just a moment ago. Alabris's grip on me is so tight I can barely breathe, and I pray that Quinnic's grasp is just as strong to keep him from falling.

We're climbing fast, the city falling away below us. I can see the mines, the docks, all of Xardon spread out like a map. From up here, it looks beautiful, but I know that's only because I can't see the dirty streets, the violence that goes on below.

Then Cairos does some kind of aerial maneuver that makes reality itself seem to tear, and suddenly we're flying through a rippling portal in midair.

The sensation is just as disorienting as before. Time stretches, colors blur, my stomach lurches. Alabris is making small, terrified sounds.

Then we burst through the other side, and we're somewhere else entirely.

The glass forest spreads out below us, trees chiming in the wind. In the distance, I can see the glass village.

Cairos descends, landing gently in a clearing. The three of us slide off his back, shaky and disoriented. Quinnic immediately bends over, hands on his knees, and expels the contents of his stomach onto the ground. Alabris, usually the caretaker who would hurry to aid Quinnic in a situation like this, just stands there, staring at everything with wide eyes, still clutching the blanket.

"Are you okay?" I ask Quinnic, rubbing his back with one hand.

He moves to stand upright again, still looking rather green. "Never better," he answers.

Cairos shifts back to human form, and Quinnic lets out a frightened yelp.

"You're going to have to get used to that," I tell him.

"Get used to it?" He scoffs, and I can see the anger coming back now that the immediate terror has faded. "Nae, what the hell is going on? Where are we? What was that thing—" He points at Cairos. "—and why does he look like a person now?"

"I can explain."

"You keep saying that, but you haven't explained anything!" His voice cracks. "You disappeared for weeks. We thought you were dead! Or worse. And now you show up with some… some dragon man and tell us to trust you?"

"I'm sorry." The words feel inadequate. "I'm so sorry. I didn't want to leave. I didn't have a choice." I pull Quinnic into a fierce hug for the first time in ages. At first, he tries to push me away, but his fight doesn't last. Before long, he's sinking into me, letting out all of the tension and fear and anger that's been suffocating him.

When I finally let him go, he looks a fraction more sympathetic.

"Quinnic, listen to me. The king—Valthaeron—he's not human. He's fae, and he's been using us. He's been using the shadowstone for his personal gain and is planning to do something terrible. I was abducted at the circus, and I couldn't come back because if I did, he would have come after me, and that might've put you in harm's way, too."

Quinnic stares at me. "You've lost your mind."

"I wish I had." I gesture to Cairos. "But you just rode on a dragon, and flew through a portal. So maybe consider for a moment that I'm telling the truth."

He opens his mouth. Closes it. Opens it again. Then his eyes narrow, focusing on Cairos. "Wait. I know you."

My head snaps toward him. "What?"

"I know you," Quinnic repeats, pointing at Cairos. "You showed up at the mines one day."

My stomach drops. I turn to Cairos, whose expression has gone carefully blank. "You did what?"

Cairos doesn't respond, his jaw tight.

"He was at the mines, watching me," Quinnic continues, studying Cairos like he's trying to place a half-remembered dream. "He was there for a day, and I thought he was a new worker, then he just… left."

"And me," Alabris adds quietly. "You came to the house, and said you were looking for someone…" She trails off, her eyes wide. "But you weren't. You were checking on us."

Confusion floods through me, and I round on Cairos. "When?"

"Does it matter?" His voice is flat, dismissive.

"Yes, it matters!" I step closer. "When did you go to Xardon?"

His jaw works. For a moment, I think he won't answer. Then, quietly: "While you were training at the Tidetreaders' settlement. On the silks."

"That's where you went and you didn't even tell me?"

"You were occupied." He says it like it's nothing, like sneaking off to check on my family, and never uttering a word about it is perfectly normal behavior.

"That's not—" I stop, take a breath. "Why?"

"Because you wanted to know they were safe." He says it simply, like it's the most obvious thing in the world. "And I knew Hessa wouldn't have been able to get away from funeral duties soon enough."

My chest tightens. "Cairos…"

"It's not a big deal," he cuts me off, and there's a defensive edge to his voice now.

"You had a black eye when you came back," I say, everything coming back to me. "I remember thinking it was weird, but… What happened?"

"Nothing," Cairos says flatly.

"Obviously, it wasn't nothing," I snap. "What happened?"

His nostrils flare. "I was detained by guards. It was never supposed to take that long."

"Detained." The word feels heavy in my mouth. "They hurt you."

"I'm fine."

Something protective flares in me that I never realized was there. He's fine now, yes, but the knowledge that the king's guards detained him and harmed him only fuels our mission more.

Quinnic clears his throat awkwardly. "So.... fae. Like what I was talking about with the immortal beings."

"Yes," I say, grateful for the subject change even as my mind spins.

"So I was right." He laughs now. "I was actually right, and you told me I was crazy."

I roll my eyes. Of course Quinnic would be focused on proving me wrong. "Fine. I admit you weren't crazy. I was just…" I trail off. "I was wrong."

Alabris finally speaks up again, her voice small. "Are we safe here?"

"Safer than Xardon, but nowhere is truly safe while Valthaeron is alive," I respond gravely.

"Then what's the plan?" Quinnic asks, sobering.

"We trap him," I say simply.

"We?" Alabris looks at Cairos, really looks at him. "Who are you, anyway?"

Cairos has been silent since the black eye revelation, and now when he speaks, his voice is even colder than before. As if putting up walls.

"Cairos," he says flatly. "And your sister is under my protection, which means you are too."

Quinnic bristles at his tone. "We can handle—"

"You can't," Cairos interrupts, voice hard. "Unless you want to go back to those mines and face those guards. I'm sure they'd be thrilled to see you."

"Cairos," I berate him, but my voice is softer than I intend.

Quinnic's jaw twitches, but he doesn't argue.

"You're a dragon," Alabris says quietly.

"Yes."

"And you… help her?"

"I keep her alive," Cairos says. "Among other things."

The way he says it makes me flush, and Quinnic definitely notices.

"Oh gods," Quinnic mutters. "You're sleeping with the dragon."

"That's really not relevant right now."

"My sister is sleeping with a dragon," he says again, louder.

"Dragon-shifter," I correct hopelessly. "But can we please focus on the part where we're about to take down a king?"

Quinnic looks at me for a long moment. Then, despite everything, he laughs. It's a little hysterical, but it's the best I'm going to get.

"Fine," he says.

As we start walking through the glass forest, Cairos and I taking the lead, I hear Quinnic mutter behind me, "This is insane. This is absolutely insane."

"Welcome to my life," I say over my shoulder. "And get ready to join me."

31

CLAIMED

Cairos delivers us to an empty glass house on the edge of the village, before heading back to strategize with Fenric. It's far enough from the main practice hall that we won't be bothered, but close enough that I can see the glow of its lights in the distance.

The house is small, just one room really, but there's a large window that catches the moonlight perfectly. I gathered glass leaves from the forest on the way over and tucked them into my pockets. Their curved surfaces should work as magnifiers, focusing the light down onto the shadowstone.

Quinnic and Alabris follow me in, both of them still wide-eyed and skittish. Everything here is too clean and elegant compared to the dusty hovel we called home. I remember the absolute shock and awe that I felt when I first arrived here, too.

"You can sit," I tell them, gesturing to the cushioned bench against one wall. "This is going to take a while."

Alabris settles onto the bench, but Quinnic stays standing. He doesn't trust me anymore. That thought makes my heart ache. My most important job since losing my parents was taking care of Quinnic, and I failed.

“So,” he says. “You’re going to forge something. With magic?”

“With moonlight and my blood, technically.” I lay out the shadowstone I grabbed from the mines on the floor beneath the window. One piece. One chance to get this right. “Magic is… complicated.”

“Everything about this is complicated,” he mutters.

The piece gleams in the low light, that internal luminescence catching and holding. I position the it directly under the window.

“I still can’t believe we’re here,” Alabris says softly. “That this place is real. That you’re… whatever you are now.”

“I’m still me.” I pull out the glass leaves, examining each one. “Just me with a really fucked up backstory.”

Alabris snorts in response.

“Tell me about him. The dragon,” Quinnic says.

“Cairos.”

“Yeah. Him.” Quinnic’s jaw tightens. “Are you two… I mean…”

“We’re together,” I say simply.

“Together.” He laughs, sharp and bitter. “My sister’s fucking a dragon, and now they’re a happy couple. Great. That’s just great.”

“Quinnic!” I berate.

“What? You want me to be happy about it?” He asks, throwing his hands up in the air.

I position the knife against my palm. “You don’t have to be happy about it.”

“No shit.”

I cut before he can say more. Blood wells up, and I let it drip onto the shadowstone. Golden light erupts from within, the stone drinking in my blood like it’s been waiting for it.

“Holy shit,” Quinnic breathes, anger momentarily forgotten.

I hold the glass leaf above the stone, angling it until the moonlight focuses into a concentrated beam. The shadowstone starts to soften and become malleable.

"How did you learn to do this?" Alabris asks, leaning forward.

"Trial and error. The threat of being discarded if I don't." I start shaping the stone with my hands. "The usual."

"That's not usual," Quinnic mutters.

"It is now," I say without looking up.

I work in silence for a while. I feel Quinnic watching me, his earlier anger cooling into something more like exhaustion.

"What was it like?" Alabris asks quietly. "When you were gone. Where did you go?"

So I tell them. The circus, Grendor, Fenric. The fae, the curse, the prophecy. Shade stalkers. Forging the first necklace. Fighting Valthaeron.

"I still can't believe I was right," Quinnic says when I mention the soul collecting. "At the docks. When I said there were immortal beings using us. I was right."

"You were drunk."

"Drunk but right." There's a hint of his old grin now. "Told you something crazy was going on."

I almost laugh. "Yeah, you did."

"And the dragon, Cairos, he saved you?"

"It was Fenric, actually. But Cairos had my back, too. He's the reason I'm still here."

Quinnic is quiet for a moment. Then asks, "You love him?"

The question catches me off guard. I look up, meeting his eyes.

"Yes."

"Even though he's a dragon who kills people?"

The word "kills" hits harder than I expect. I think about the souls I saw in the circus tent, and the hundreds or maybe thousands of them over the centuries. All those lives drained away. All that blood on Cairos's hands, whether he chose it or not.

"Killed. Past tense. And he didn't have a choice." I turn back to the shadowstone, focusing on the pendant so I don't have to look at Quinnic. The truth is more complicated than that. He did kill people. The curse forced him, but he still did the work. His dragon still drained those souls. I've seen what it looks like—the wisps of light flowing from body to mouth, the way people go limp and empty. I watched it happen to Blaine. To hundreds of others.

And I love him anyway.

I don't know what that says about me. That I'm either practical enough or dumb enough to separate the man from the monster. Maybe that I'm damaged enough not to care. Or maybe I just understand that sometimes survival means doing terrible things, and years of slavery, committing unspeakable acts, doesn't make you evil, just trapped.

"Yeah," I say finally. "Even though."

He snorts. "You always pick the complicated ones."

"There are no simple ones here, Quinnic."

"Right" He watches me work for another minute. "You know, for what it's worth, Nae… I'm glad you're not dead."

"Thanks," I snort. "I'm glad you're not dead either."

"Yeah, well. Close call on that one."

I thread the pendant onto the chain. It pulses warm against my palm, alive with magic. Rougher than the first one from the lack of tools here, but it's mine.

"It's beautiful," Alabris says softly.

I hold it up to the light. "It's a weapon, but yeah. I guess it is."

Footsteps outside. All three of us tense, but I recognize the gait.

Cairos.

He fills the doorway, donning his usual black shirt now, hair slightly disheveled. The shirt fits him well. Too well, actually, showing off the breadth of his shoulders and the way his body tapers down to his waist. His eyes find mine immediately, dark and intense, making my skin prickle. Then his gaze flicks to the pendant, and the moment breaks.

"You finished it."

"Just now."

His gaze moves to Quinnic and Alabris. Neither of them quite meets his eyes.

"How are they settling in?" he asks me, not them.

"Fine," Quinnic answers anyway, voice tight.

Cairos's mouth quirks, just slightly.

"Hessa is just outside. She has rooms prepared, and a hot meal," he says. "You should rest. Tomorrow will be…"

"A shitshow?" I supply.

"I was going to say 'difficult'."

"We should go," Alabris says quickly, standing. She grabs Quinnic's arm. "Let them… talk."

"We don't have to—" Quinnic starts, but Alabris is already ushering him toward the door.

"Yes, we do," she says firmly.

Quinnic shoots me a look as they leave. Then they're gone, and it's just me and Cairos.

The air feels heavier suddenly. Charged.

"Your brother doesn't like me," Cairos says.

"Can you blame him?"

"No." He stops in front of me, close enough that I have to tilt my head back. "But I don't particularly care what he thinks."

"He's my brother."

"And you're mine." The possessiveness in his voice sends heat curling low in my stomach. "That's all that matters."

I should probably argue and tell him that I'm *not* his, and I don't belong to anyone. I should also remind him that he should care about Quinnic's opinion of him.

But the words won't come.

“Let me see it,” he says, nodding to the pendant.

I hold it up. He takes it carefully, studying the way the light catches in the golden threads.

“You did this alone once, but you won’t have to tomorrow.”

“But the prophecy says—”

“Fuck the prophecy.” His hand comes up to cup my face. “I don’t care what some ancient words say. I’m not letting you face him alone again.”

“Cairos…”

“No.” His voice drops, rough and fierce. “I’ve lost you once. I’m not doing it again. Prophecy or no prophecy, I’m going to be there.”

The intensity in his eyes steals my breath. “We might die tomorrow.”

“I know.”

“Both of us. We could both die.”

“I know,” he says again, stepping closer, his voice dropping low. “Is that what you’re afraid of?”

“Partly.” I set the pendant down on the windowsill. “Mostly, I’m afraid that I’ll fail, and I’ll get everyone killed. That—”

He kisses me.

It’s not gentle or sweet. It’s claiming and full of everything we’re both feeling. Full of the fear, the need, and the wonder about whether tomorrow might be our last day breathing.

I kiss him back just as fiercely, hands roaming his back, pulling him closer. He makes a sound low in his throat and backs me against the wall, the cool glass pressing into my spine. The pressure of his body against me causes a spike of pain from my recovering shoulder, but I don’t care about anything right now besides the feeling of him.

“We could die tomorrow,” I say again when we break apart, both of us breathing hard.

“Then let’s not waste tonight.” His hands are everywhere all at once—on my waist, sliding under my shirt, fingers tracing the curve of my ribs. My breath comes in sharp, jagged inhales, not knowing where his hands will land next. Heat floods through my body, making it nearly impossible to think clearly.

Still, I manage to eke out a question. "Here? In this glass house where anyone could—"

"I don't care." His mouth finds my neck, his slightly sharpened teeth scraping against the sensitive skin there, sending chills down my arms. "Here. Now. Anywhere. I don't care where we are as long as I get to have you one more time before we walk into that nightmare."

One more time. Like it might be the last.

The thought should scare me. Instead, it only serves to make me need him more. I press closer until there's no space between us.

"Okay," I breathe. "Okay, yes."

He pulls back just enough to look at me, and what I see in his eyes makes my knees weak. Raw hunger mixed with something deeper, something that looks like devotion and possession all tangled together.

"I'm going to make you forget," he says, voice dropping to something dark and promising. "About everything except the way my cock feels inside you."

The threat makes a wet heat pool between my legs. His lips land on mine again before I can formulate a response, and thinking becomes impossible.

His fingers tug gently in my hair to angle my head back before moving to my waist, digging in hard enough to leave marks. He slides one hand up under my shirt, palm hot against my skin. I arch into his touch, and a needy sound escapes me.

"That's it," he murmurs against my lips, then trails his mouth down to my jaw. "Let me hear you. Let everyone hear you. Let them know who you belong to."

The possessiveness should probably annoy me, but my brain is too fogged with want to form a coherent protest.

He pulls my shirt off in one smooth motion, tossing it aside without looking. Then his mouth is on my neck, sucking hard enough that I know there'll be a mark tomorrow.

His lips are moving lower, to my collarbone, then the hollow of my throat, and I can't seem to form thoughts anymore. I suddenly feel unsteady on my feet, like my body has spent all of its energy preparing for him.

"Cairos—"

"I've got you." His hands grip my thighs, lifting me slightly. "I've always got you."

I fumble with his shirt, desperate and clumsy. My fingers won't cooperate, shaking too much to work the buttons. He helps me, shrugging it off impatiently, and then his chest is pressed to mine.

The feel of skin on skin makes me forget why I was worried about the glass walls. Makes me forget everything except heat and muscle and the way his heart pounds against my ribcage.

"Do you have any idea what you do to me?" he growls.

I can barely breathe, let alone answer. "Tell me."

"You make me forget I'm cursed. Forget I'm a monster." His hands are working at the hem of my pants, and I'm too far gone to help, just standing there letting him undress me like I've lost all function. "You make me feel human, like I'm something more than death and darkness."

The pants come off, and suddenly the reality of being naked crashes back into focus. The cool glass at my back. The moonlight streaming through semi-transparent walls. The complete and total exposure.

"Cairos, anyone could see us," I gasp out.

"I don't care who sees," he says, teeth grazing my neck. "Let them see exactly who's fucking you. Who you're begging for."

Gods, he's going to ruin me, and I don't even care.

Cairos steps back, just for a moment, and his eyes rake over me from head to toe. The hunger in his gaze is almost frightening in its intensity.

I want to cover myself. To tell him this is insane and we should at least close the curtains.

Wait. Do these glass walls even have curtains? I can't remember. Can't think.

"Beautiful. So fucking beautiful. And all mine."

Then he's on me again, and words become impossible. His mouth finds my breast first, and the sensation makes my knees weak. He's not gentle about it. His teeth grazing, tongue circling, sucking hard. His hand cups the other breast, thumb brushing over my nipple in a way that makes me gasp.

"Perfect," he murmurs against my skin. "Every part of you."

He kisses his way down my body with deliberate slowness. Too slow. Agonizingly slow. My brain is seizing up, caught between embarrassment at our location and desperation for him to move faster.

He pauses at the mark on my rib cage, the one that proves I'm Bellamie reincarnate. He presses his lips there, soft and reverent, before continuing.

"Mine," he growls against my skin, the tenderness disappearing as his teeth graze the sensitive flesh. "Mine to protect. Mine to love. Mine to fuck until you can't remember your own name."

His hand slides between my thighs, and I gasp at the contact.

Oh gods. *Oh gods.*

"Please," I manage, hips bucking against his hand before I can stop myself.

When did I lose control of my own body? When did I become someone who begs?

"Please, what?" His fingers move, circling but not quite touching where I need him most. "Tell me what you want. Say it."

Bastard. He's going to make me beg for it. Luckily for him, any semblance of humility I once had has fallen away like dust in the wind.

"You. I want you. Now."

Mercifully, he complies. His fingers slide inside me, and my knees nearly buckle. He works me with precision that suggests he knows exactly what he's doing, and I hate that I'm so desperate for it that I'm making sounds I've never made before.

"That's it," he murmurs, watching my face. "Let go."

The orgasm builds fast, pleasure coiling tight. I'm close, so close, right there—

He stops.

My eyes snap open, and if I could form coherent words, I'd curse him out. "What the—"

"I want to be inside you when you come." He stands, working at his own pants with one hand while the other stays on my hip. "I want to feel you fall apart around me."

Then he's bare, and my breath hitches in my throat. I felt him before, yes, but last time all I caught were glimpses of him in the moonlight. But here, in this torch-lit house, I can see every inch of his length, hard and thick and flushed with want.

Gods. The size of him makes my stomach flip with a mix of nerves and anticipation.

Then he lifts me like I weigh nothing, my back pressed against the glass wall, my legs wrapping around his waist automatically. I can feel him, hard and hot, pressing exactly where I need him, and suddenly the glass walls don't matter anymore. Nothing matters except this.

"Last chance," he says, but there's no real question in it. His eyes are wild, pupils blown. "Tell me to stop and I will."

Stop? How am I supposed to think about stopping when I can barely think at all?

"Don't stop." My nails dig into his shoulders. "Don't you dare stop."

He drops me onto him in one smooth thrust, and the sensation steals what's left of my coherent thought. There's a stretch, a burn that makes me bite against his shoulder to keep from crying out. It's too much and not enough all at once.

For a moment, neither of us moves. I'm trying to adjust, to let my body accommodate the size of him.

"Fuuuuck," he breathes slow against my neck.

Then he starts to move, and I'm lost. He holds me up as he pulls out, thrusting again and again. It's rough and desperate, and I can't process anything except the sensation. My back slides against the glass with each thrust. Cool surface. Hot body. The contrast makes everything sharper, more intense.

Somewhere in the back of my mind, I'm aware that we're completely visible. That anyone could walk by, and I should care about that.

But I don't. Not when he's moving like this. When every thrust hits something deep inside me that makes stars explode behind my eyelids.

"Look at me," he demands.

I do, and the intensity in his eyes nearly undoes me.

"When you stand before him tomorrow," Cairos growls, voice shredded at the edges, "and that bastard king thinks he has you cornered—"

A particularly deep thrust punches the breath from my lungs. I gasp, clutching his back, *drowning* in him.

"When you feel afraid, I want you to remember this." Another brutal snap of his hips. "Remember me, *buried inside you*. Remember every inch."

Gods.

"Remember what I'm capable of." He pulls almost all the way out, then slams back in, dragging a moan from my throat.

"Remember you're mine," he snarls, his mouth hot at my ear, "because when we burn his whole fucking world down—*it's me* you'll stand beside."

The words send heat spiraling through me. Mine. His. The possessiveness only strengthens the way I'm clenching around him, making sounds I didn't know I could make.

"I belong to myself," I manage weakly, but there's no conviction in it. Just desperate need.

"No," he says, and he stills completely. "Not right now, you don't."

The loss of movement makes me whimper.

"Cairos…" I say, pleading.

I can feel him pulsing inside me, right where I need him, but not moving. Not giving me anything. "Tell me who you belong to," he commands.

"That's not—I don't—" I can't form full sentences. Can't think past the aching need.

"Say it," he repeats, voice dropping to something dark and commanding. "Or I stop right here."

He wouldn't. He couldn't. We're both too far gone for him to do that.

But he's not moving. Just holding me there, buried inside me, doing nothing while I shake and struggle to breathe.

"You're an asshole," I gasp out.

"I know." There's satisfaction in his voice. Smug, arrogant satisfaction. "Now say it."

"I…" My pride wars with my desperate need for about half a second before need wins. "Fine. Yours. I'm yours."

"All of you?" He reaches between us, thumb brushing against my clit once, the lightest touch, and I nearly sob. "Say it properly."

"All of me." The words come out broken, pleading. "Every part of me is yours. Happy?"

"Not quite." He starts moving again, but slowly. Too slowly. Torturing me with it. "Say 'I belong to you.'"

"That's the same thing."

His thumb presses harder, circling once before stopping again. "Say it."

I'm going to kill him. After this is over, after I can think straight again, I'm going to actually kill him.

"I belong to you," I gasp out, hating how true it feels even as I say it. "Fully to you."

"Good girl," he purrs in my ear, breath hot against the side of my neck.

The praise sends an unexpected shock of heat through me. My body clenches around him involuntarily, and he groans.

"You like that," he says, and it's not a question. His hand slides between us properly now, finding my clit, circling with the pressure I've been desperate for. "You like being mine."

I do. Gods help me, I do.

"Yes." His pace increases, and I'm clinging to him, with no coherent thoughts left.

His thumb presses harder, and I'm right there, right on the edge, so close—

"When all this is over," he grumbles, "when that king is dead, and his kingdom is ashes, I'm going to take you to my bed and spend days reminding you exactly what you fought for."

The orgasm hits me like lightning. I cry out his name, too loud. Anyone nearby definitely heard that, but I don't care. My body clenches around him, waves of pleasure rolling through me so intense I forget where I am, forget every single thing I've ever known except this feeling.

He follows seconds later, my name on his lips, and I feel him pulse inside me as he cums.

We stay like that, both shaking, hearts pounding. His arms are the only thing holding me up. My legs are useless, trembling, unable to support my own weight.

Slowly, reality filters back in. The glass walls. The moonlight. The fact that we just—that anyone could have—

Oh gods.

He lowers me gently, and my feet find the floor but my knees are weak. He doesn't let go or step back. His hand comes up to cup my face, and the tenderness after everything we just did makes my chest tight.

"I love you," he says. Simple. Direct. "Whatever happens tomorrow, I need you to know that."

My throat is tight. When did this happen? When did I become someone who gets to have all this?

"I know." I cover his hand with mine, turning to press a kiss to his palm. "I love you too."

And I do. Even if I can barely think straight. Even if my brain is still foggy and my legs are still shaking, I love him.

Tomorrow we might die. But tonight, we had this.

We dress slowly, neither of us quite ready to let go of this moment. He helps me with my shirt, fingers lingering on my skin. I trace the scar running down his abdomen, memorizing the pattern of it. When I'm finally clothed again, he pulls me close, pressing his forehead to mine, and we just breathe together.

"We're going to survive this," he says, and there's steel in his voice now. Certainty.

"How do you know?"

"Because I refuse to lose you again." His arms tighten around me, almost crushing in their intensity. "The universe can fuck off if it thinks I'm letting you go. I'll fight the gods if I have to. I'll tear apart the fabric of reality itself. Whatever it takes."

Despite everything, I smile.

"The universe better watch out then."

"Damn right."

32

THE RECKONING

I wake tangled in Cairos, his arm heavy across my waist, and his breath steady against my neck in that luxurious bed of his. For just a moment, I let myself pretend this is normal. That we're just two people who fell asleep together after a night we'll never forget.

But I know that isn't the truth. Far from it, actually.

Today, we trap the king, or die trying.

"You're awake," Cairos murmurs against my shoulder.

"Hard to sleep when you're contemplating murder."

"Does it still count if he's an immortal villain who's been forcing innocents to drain souls for centuries?"

"Pretty sure it still counts." I turn in his arms to face him. In the early morning light filtering through the glass walls, he looks almost human. But the canines protruding too low when he speaks, the point of his ears, and his too-perfect face say otherwise.

I trace a finger along his jawline, feeling the slight stubble there. "How did you all end up in the circus anyway? You used to live in the castle. What happened?"

His expression shutters. "Long story."

"We have time."

"We don't, actually." He shifts like he's going to pull away, but I tighten my grip.

"Cairos."

He seems to mull it over, and I think he's going to deflect again. Then he lets out a deep breath. "We were castle staff. I was captain of the guard. Hessa was a housemaid, Selenia was Bellamie's personal attendant, Kyreth and Jexen managed the grounds and stables, Fenric was a battle strategist, and Grendor was Valthaeron's right-hand man. All of us got close to someone we shouldn't have."

"Bellamie," I say quietly.

"Valthaeron thought she was dangerous, and to him, she was. She was his daughter."

"What?" I shoot up straight in bed, twisting my body to face him. "His *daughter*? I'm his daughter?" My voice rises to almost a shriek.

"Shh, Little Wren. Not really. Bellamie was a bastard child, her father unknown. The queen, Orlia, insisted until her death that Bellamie was his, but it was long known that Valthaeron was sterile. He'd been through twelve wives at that point, each of them unable to produce a child. Then Orlia, when clearly at odds with him and heading toward banishment like the rest, became pregnant, he knew. All along, he knew Bellamie wasn't his."

I inhale slowly, trying to digest the information.

"Valthaeron wouldn't risk further embarrassment, though," Cairos continues. "It was his chance to prove that he *could* father a child. Bellamie was raised as a princess—*you* were raised as a princess—but it's like you knew something wasn't right. You loathed him. You shared that with me often."

"When did we meet?" I ask suddenly, realizing Cairos has an entire history of my past life that I don't have access to.

He looks down at his palms before answering, as if they have the answer. "We were just children. My family was

Solmeren and deemed worthy enough to mingle with you, a decision Valthaeron surely came to regret."

I smile despite myself. "Surely," I agree.

"To make a four-hundred-year-long story short, you grew more and more restless, angry at Valthaeron for bringing humans to the castle. Before the curse, he harvested their souls right there in his throne room. You plotted his death, plotted to murder him. But Valthaeron caught wind first. What we didn't know was that Grendor truly did agree with Valthaeron's plans. He pretended to be one of us, but really, we were whispering our plans right into the ear of Valthaeron himself."

Cairos has a faraway look in his eye now, like he's no longer here with me, but back in that castle with Bellamie and the rest of them.

"What happened?" I prompt gently.

"Valthaeron retaliated." Cairos shakes his head slowly, brows furrowed like he's feeling the pain in this very moment. "Orlia disappeared. We were told that she had an accident when she was out horseback riding, but I never believed that. And neither did you. You confronted him the next night." Cairos hesitates, closing his eyes and taking in a deep breath. I place one hand on top of his, which he squeezes. His voice is low, barely perceptible when he speaks again. "That was the night he killed you."

"I'm so sorry," I say. It sounds odd, really, apologizing for how my own death hurt someone else, but everything about this situation is odd. "Can you tell me what happened that night?" I ask, hoping that I'm not pushing him too hard.

He squeezes his eyes closed for just a moment before speaking.

"Bellamie told us she was going to kill him. She believed in shadowstone's magical properties. Valthaeron had enlisted her to forge armor and weapons for him, so she was very familiar with the mineral."

"Thats why her room is attached to the forge," I muse.

Cairos nods, then continues. "When melted and forged by fire, shadowstone can create incredibly strong weapons, which is what she was trained to do. Bellamie loved to read, though, and she came across an ancient tome that mentioned the use of blood in working with shadowstone to enhance its power. She believed a concentrated blow with her blood and Valthaeron's own fortified weapon could end him. She snuck into the throne room with the rest of us and stole his sword, but Grendor had already warned Valthaeron." Cairos sits up, leaning back against the headboard, and looking down into his open palms. "It was a trap. He had already swapped out his sword for a fake, and when we turned to leave, he was there. He didn't say anything, just… stabbed her in the ribs. I remember the scent of her blood filling the air. I remember catching her, dropping to my knees, and applying pressure to the wound. Anything to keep her alive. But she was gone the second his weapon pierced her skin. The shadowstone was too strong."

A single tear falls from his eye now, rolling down his cheek. A man as powerful as this, brought to tears by Valthaeron. A surprising, unexpected rage blooms in my chest at the thought of it all.

"I'm going to end him," I declare. "This time, he'll be the one dying."

Cairos blows air out of his nose. "That's how I know Bellamie's still in there. That's exactly what she would say."

"I'm honored to have a part of her in me," I say.

"Maybe that's why the shadowstone didn't affect you as badly as it should have when you were stabbed by Valthaeron. You've built up an immunity in your past life." Cairos presses his palms to his eyes, wiping away the wetness. "When I saw you injured that night, bleeding out on the back of that beast…" He stops, his throat bobbing. "I thought you were gone. Again. And I—"

His voice cracks, just slightly, and he has to pause to gather himself.

"I felt like I was dying too," he says finally, the words rough and low. "Like if you went, I'd follow. Not because of duty or some curse, but because I couldn't do that again." He shakes his head. "Six hundred years I've existed without her. Without *you.* And the moment I found you again, the thought of losing you became unbearable."

His hands drop from his face, and he looks at me with raw honesty that makes my chest ache.

"I've survived centuries of this curse. Endured things that should have broken me. But watching you bleed, knowing I might lose you before we even had a chance…" He reaches out, fingers gentle as they trace the scar on my ribs. "That almost destroyed me in a way centuries of slavery never could."

I cover his hand with mine, holding it against my heart. "I'm still here."

"I know." His thumb brushes my skin. "And I'm going to make damn sure you stay that way."

"About the curse… when did that happen?" I ask.

"It was the same night. When I finally realized she wasn't coming back, I went into a rage. All I saw was red. I destroyed every valuable thing in that room. Killed the other guards that surrounded Valthaeron. All except Grendor. He surprised me. Wielding the shadowstone sword, he tore me open when I went to kill the king himself. That's what caused this scar." Cairos gestures to the long scar tracing down his abdomen that I've noticed a dozen times. "They left me bleeding out on the floor of the throne room while Valthaeron carried out his curse. Said if we wanted to act like clowns, we could be them, cursing us to harvest souls until the day we die. The punishment if we miss even one cycle? Death."

"That's why you couldn't miss the last cycle," I whisper. "You'll die if you don't."

"I'm not proud of it. Of putting my life above the humans."

"It's an impossible choice," I reassure him. I pause, frowning. "But why dragons? Of all the things he could've cursed you to become, why that specifically?"

Cairos's expression darkens. "Because it was the cruelest thing he could think of. Dragons are symbols of power in our culture. Creatures of stories that were passed down through generations. They're known as protectors, guardians, and creatures of legend that the fae revere. We were supposed to be Bellamie's protectors." His jaw clenches. "He turned us into the very thing we failed to be. Made us powerful, yes, but enslaved. Gave us strength we can't use to save ourselves. It was mockery disguised as power."

"That's sick."

"That's Valthaeron." He runs a hand through his hair. "And the circus was just another layer of humiliation. He wanted us to be loved and feared simultaneously, knowing we were neither heroes nor monsters by choice."

I think about the crowd at the circus and the way they gasped and applauded. The way children pointed in wonder at the dragons swooping overhead, never knowing those same dragons were about to drain the lives of everyone in the tent.

"He turned your greatest strength into your prison," I say quietly.

"Exactly." Cairos looks at me, and there are centuries of pain in his eyes. "Every time we transform, every time someone looks at us in awe, it's a reminder that we failed her. That all this power means nothing when you're still a slave." His brows pinch together, distraught, before composing himself again. "Speaking of power, we should get ready. We don't want to miss our chance."

"Cairos." I catch his hand again. "Wait. You mentioned Orlia… Is that Bellamie's mother?"

"Yes," Cairos confirms. "That statue in the garden—that's her."

A gasp I can't stop escapes my lips. Bellamie's mother has been trapped in that statue for centuries.

"We have to save her," I start, pushing my way out of the bed. Cairos catches my arm.

"Not now. After."

I pause, but I know he's right. Valthaeron would never let us back into his castle, not after what I did. And she's been trapped there hundreds of years already. What's a few days more?

"Okay," I agree, slumping back and taking Cairos's hand in mine. "Thank you for telling me all of this."

He looks down at our joined hands, something conflicted crossing his face. "You deserved to know. You're—" He stops himself. "It's your story too."

"We're going to finish what she started," I say.

His hand tightens on mine. "We will."

We dress in silence, both of us moving with the efficiency of people preparing for war. I slip the pendant over my head, tucking it under my shirt. It pulses warm against my skin, a constant reminder of what needs to be done.

When we emerge from the glass house, the village is already awake. Fenric is waiting outside with Hessa, both of them looking grim.

"The others are gathering at the practice hall," Fenric says. "Jexen and Kyreth are scouting the perimeter of Valthaeron's castle. Hessa didn't have a lot of luck on her travels, but the Aelthren faction holds a mighty grudge. They will engage the Solmeren to allow our passage to the castle."

I want to ask what sort of grudge he's referring to, but there's no time. The most important thing today is that we have a plan. "Where are Quinnic and Alabris?" I ask.

"In my house. Safe." Fenric's expression softens slightly. "Your brother wanted to come with you. I had to explain in very certain terms why that was a terrible idea."

"I can only imagine how that conversation went," I laugh, then sober. "I need to see them before we go."

Cairos nods. "I'll meet you at the practice hall."

I find them in the sitting room of Fenric's house, both looking like they barely slept.

"You're going," Quinnic says when he sees me. Not a question.

"Yeah."

"And we're supposed to just sit here and wait?"

"That's the idea."

"That's bullshit." He stands, and I can see the fear beneath the anger. "You left us once already. What if you don't come back?"

The words hit harder than I expect. "Then Fenric will take care of you. He's already agreed."

"I don't want Fenric." Quinnic's voice cracks. "I want my sister."

I cross the room and pull him into a hug. He resists for half a second, then his arms wrap around me so tight I can barely breathe.

"I'm coming back," I say against his hair. "I promise."

"You can't promise that."

"Watch me."

When I pull back, Alabris is standing beside us, her eyes red.

"Be careful," she says quietly. "Please."

"Always." I squeeze her shoulder gently. "And if something does happen—"

"Don't," Quinnic interrupts. "Don't say it like that. Not when you just got done promising you'll come back."

I look at both of them, my family, and force myself to smile.

"I'm coming back," I say again. "And when I do, we're going to figure out what the hell comes next. Together."

Alabris nods, wiping at her eyes. Quinnic just stares at me, trying his best to look tough, but he doesn't fool me.

"I love you both," I say. "Don't forget that."

Then I leave before I lose my nerve.

~

The practice hall is packed. All of the performers are there, plus a handful of fae I don't recognize—some of the Aelthren, I assume. Everyone's armed, looking ready to kill.

Cairos is at the center, discussing strategy with the twins. When he sees me, he breaks away.

"Your brother?"

"Pissed. But he'll stay put."

"Good." He takes my hand, lacing his fingers through mine. "Are you ready?"

"Not even a little bit."

His mouth quirks. "That's my girl."

Fenric claps his hands, drawing everyone's attention. "Listen up. We move in twenty minutes. Cairos and Naevyn will approach from the main entrance. They'll make it obvious and draw attention while the rest of us split up and enter through the side passages and windows. We've scouted three entry points on the east wing, two on the west."

"The Solmeren?" Selenia asks from her perch on a trapeze bar.

"The Aelthren will engage them outside the castle walls. That should buy us time." Fenric's expression darkens. "But not much. Once Valthaeron realizes what's happening, he'll call them all back. We need to move fast."

The Solmeren. The name of that faction carries so much more weight knowing that that's where Cairos came from. Does he have family there? People he knows who could die in this conflict as well? When I look at him, I try to discern any hint of emotion in his face, but there's none to be found. His features are like stone.

"What's the plan once we're inside?" Jexen asks.

"Chaos," Cairos says. "We cause as much chaos as possible. Keep Valthaeron distracted while Naevyn gets close enough to use the pendant."

"How do we know the girl will be able to succeed this time? Did she not already attempt to use the pendant against him?" Jexen asks.

"I have a name," I counter, unable to hold in my disdain at being called "the girl."

"Yes, and the events of tonight will decide if that's relevant," Jexen retorts.

Anger simmers in my veins, threatening to boil over, but I grit my teeth instead. The last thing we need right now is discord between us before we go on the most dangerous mission of our lives.

"Last time, Naevyn went on guesses alone. She attempted to use the pendant to kill him with an outward blast," Cairos explains. "This time, we're going on knowledge. As we're all aware, absorbing a soul is like taking a deep inhale, which is what Naevyn will be performing this time around."

The other performers nod with understanding.

"And if he tries to kill her first?" Kyreth's voice is skeptical.

"Then I kill him." Cairos's tone leaves no room for argument.

Hessa steps forward, her expression determined. "We can use our aerial skills to our advantage. The throne room has high ceilings and multiple levels. We can attack from above to keep him off balance."

"How do you know he'll be in the throne room?" I ask.

"Because Valthaeron loves theatrics," Fenric says solemnly. "And he'll relish in reminding us of the last time." He pulls out a rough drawn map of the castle, spreading it across the floor.

"Here's the layout we drew up from memory last night. The throne room is here, at the center of the castle. It has multiple entrances, but Valthaeron will have guards at each one."

"Not for long," Kyreth says, cracking his knuckles.

The next fifteen minutes involve planning entry points and the ensuing offensive. When we're done, Cairos pulls me aside.

"Stay close to me," he says, voice low. "No matter what happens."

"I thought the plan was for me to get close to Valthaeron."

"The plan is for you to stay alive. Everything else is secondary."

I open my mouth to argue that I don't need his protection, but the look in his eyes is silencing.

Fenric calls out the time. "Everyone, get in position."

The group disperses, moving toward the practice hall doors. Hessa gives me a quick hug before we leave, whispering "be brave" against my ear. The twins exchange a look with Cairos, something unspoken passing between them.

We file out into the clearing beyond the village, where there's enough open space for the transformations. The air is crisp, carrying the scent of grass and morning dew that would be peaceful if we weren't about to fly into battle.

"Time to shift," Fenric announces.

The transformations never get less breathtaking. One by one, the performers change. Bones crack and reshape, skin gives way to scales, and their bodies expand into massive forms. Within moments, six dragons stand where six fae once were.

Cairos shifts last. His transformation is slower and more controlled, beginning at his head and continuing down to his toes, until every inch of him is decidedly dragon. The colossal black creature with amber eyes turns to me, lowering his wing in a familiar gesture.

I climb on more easily this time than last, finding handholds in the ridges along his spine that I remember from before. The scales are warm under my hands, the muscle beneath solid and reassuring.

The Aelthren are mounting the other dragons.

When everyone is settled, Cairos launches skyward.

The rush is just as intense as last time, with wind tearing at my hair and clothes, the ground dropping away, my stomach lurching with the sudden ascent. But I'm ready for it now, leaning into the movement instead of fighting it. My heart kicks into action as I take in the altitude. Below, the village becomes a collection of tiny buildings, then specks, then nothing as we climb higher. The other dragons flank us, wings beating in synchronized rhythm.

The castle appears on the horizon, surrounded by the white stone homes of the Solmeren territories just below. From up here, I can see the layout clearly. The Solmeren settlements form a ring around the castle like a protective barrier. Or a siege wall, depending on your perspective.

Cairos banks right, and I lean with him, trusting the motion. He's diving now, the other dragons following. We're dropping fast, aimed at the Solmeren territories below.

At the last possible moment, Jexen, Kyreth, and Hessa pull up, flying low over the Solmeren homes. Dozens of Aelthren leap from their backs mid-flight, hitting the ground in rolls and coming up fighting. I catch glimpses of chaos erupting below—surprised Solmeren guards, weapons being drawn, and shouts of alarm.

Fenric and Selena circle wide, heading for the east and west sides of the castle, respectively. They approach with stealth while attention is focused on the Aelthren's assault.

But Cairos doesn't slow. He flies straight for the castle's main entrance, bold and obvious, with me gripping his scales tight. This is the plan, I remind myself. As much as I wish I could be lying low like the rest of the troupe, this is the plan.

Cairos lands hard in the courtyard before the main doors, and I slide off his back with more grace than last time. The moment my feet hit stone, he's transforming back. The dragon shrinks, and scales become skin, until Cairos stands beside me in his fae form.

Around us, guards are running toward the commotion at their borders, but a few remain stationed at the castle entrance. They see us and freeze.

"That's right," Cairos says, voice carrying across the courtyard. "We're here. You might want to tell your king."

One guard turns and runs inside. The others draw their weapons, advancing slowly. Fenric and Selenia arrive just in time, dropping the last four Aelthren who engage the guards at the door, before flying up and around to their positions on the sides of the castle.

Cairos and I walk forward together, past the battling fae, toward whatever end this brings.

And behind those doors, I can feel the pull of destiny and prophecy about to come to a head.

Here we are.

33

THE COST

Cairos waves a hand, and black fog swirls forward, making the doors swing open before us. The entrance yawns wide, dark, and uninviting.

Cairos strolls in like he owns the place, and I match his stride, refusing to look as terrified as I feel.

The castle halls are quieter than when I was here before. Valthaeron probably called the guards into the throne room with him, leaving the corridors eerily empty. Our footsteps echo off the marble floors, and I can't help but remember the last time I walked these halls as Valthaeron's guest, playing his game.

Not anymore.

We navigate deeper, following Fenric's map. The pendant pulses against my chest under the fabric of my tunic, warm and insistent. It knows we're getting closer. Twice, we hear shouts in the distance along with crashes and the sound of fighting. Some of the others must have made their way inside. Good. The plan's working.

Finally, we reach doors so immense they make everything else look small. Gold traces patterns across dark wood. Even the damn doors are a power display.

“The throne room,” Cairos says.

“You think he knows we’re here?”

“Oh, he knows.” His hand finds mine, squeezes once, then he shoves the doors open.

The throne room is easily as big as the circus tent, maybe bigger. Ceilings stretch up into shadow, supported by black marble columns shot through with gold veins. Tapestries hang from the walls showing centuries of Valthaeron’s rule in brutal, graphic detail. And high above, near the peak of the ceiling, I spot four circular windows letting in streams of dusty light.

That’s where they’ll come from. The troupe. The thought of Valthaeron being blindsided by attacks from above makes the tiniest of smiles cross my lips.

The guards stationed along both side walls don’t escape my notice, either. I count at least ten, but I catch other movement in the shadows. We’re outnumbered.

My eyes shift to the two thrones sitting on a raised platform of black stone at the center of the room. Both are carved from shadowstone, but one’s larger and more ornate. The king’s throne. The other sits empty beside it—smaller but still beautiful. Dust covers the seat, and cobwebs stretch between the armrests.

Bellamie’s mother sat there once. *My* mother. The queen who figured out what her husband was and died for it.

I won’t let you down, I vow silently.

Valthaeron killed her to be the sole ruler for six hundred years, centuries of living he didn’t deserve.

And speaking of the bastard himself—he’s sitting in his throne, dressed up in his finest shadowstone armor from head to toe. He acts like he’s unafraid, but his preparations reveal his true feelings. He watches us with mild amusement, like we’re entertainment that showed up right on schedule.

“Naevyn,” he says, my name echoing off all that shadowstone. “I was wondering when you’d come.”

"Surprise," I say, stepping forward. Cairos moves with me, half a step behind, ready for anything.

Valthaeron's eyes flick to Cairos, then back to me. "And you brought Cairos here again, to where everything started. How… sentimental."

"We're here to end this," I say, keeping my voice steady.

"End this?" He laughs, the sound bouncing around the room. "My dear girl, this is no end."

He stands, and power ripples through the air. He feels even stronger than just days ago.

"You think you can stop me with that little trinket around your neck?" He gestures at the pendant. "How quaint."

"My blood killed Grendor," I say.

"Grendor was weak." Valthaeron spits. He descends the steps, moving tantalizingly slow. Each footstep echoes. "I, however, am something else entirely."

He raises one hand, and suddenly the room fills with streams of darkness. It's coming from him, from the pendant I forged that now rests at his sternum, radiating outward in waves that make even the marrow of my bones ache.

"Do you know what this is?" he asks, and I notice for the first time that his teeth are sharp, ready for battle. Spittle rains from his mouth as he makes his speech. "This is the culmination of all of my planning coming to fruition. Everything I've done was in preparation for this moment specifically."

"What moment?" Cairos demands.

"The moment I transcend." Valthaeron's smile is the stuff of nightmares. "Your curse, it was never about sustaining my life. It was about accumulating enough power to perform the ritual. The ritual that will make me truly immortal. One of the Gods."

Shit. "That's why you needed the pendant."

"The prophecy states that the pendant created by a human fae amplifies magical energy." He grasps the pendant, holding it out, "And now, with the souls of millions fueling this ritual, with the shadowstone powering it… I will become something this world has never seen."

The darkness becomes almost blinding, somehow.

"Now," Cairos commands.

And all hell breaks loose.

Cairos shifts mid-leap, his body transforming in a blur of motion. One second, he's human, the next he's a massive onyx dragon, wings spread wide, filling nearly half the throne room. He releases a roar that shakes the pillars, then dives at Valthaeron.

The king doesn't even flinch. He raises one hand, and a barrier of darkness materializes. Cairos slams into it, the impact sending shockwaves through the room.

Guards storm into the center of the room from the shadows, and I barely dodge their advance.

Then the others appear.

Hessa crashes through one of the circular windows in the tower of the throne room, raining glass down upon us. She drops from the ceiling on a silken rope, spinning down with grace before launching herself at one of Valthaeron's guards. The twins come through the east entrance in dragon form, breathing fire that scorches the marble floor. Selenia vaults through another window and lands in a crouch, then springs forward with lethal precision.

It's chaos. Beautiful, deadly chaos.

I run toward Valthaeron, the pendant clutched in my fist, but he's too fast. He moves like water, flowing around attacks, deflecting magic with casual waves of his hand. The darkness keeps pulsing, and I can feel it pulling at something deep inside me.

"Naevyn, left!" Cairos shouts.

I dodge just as a guard swings a blade at my head. Fenric appears from nowhere, tackling the guard and sending them both crashing into a column.

I keep moving, trying to get close to Valthaeron, but there are too many guards, too much chaos. A blast of magic explodes near my feet, and I stumble backward.

"Where did the prophecy even come from?" I shout over the din, still trying to close the distance, and hoping that speaking will distract him just long enough that he lets his guard down.

Valthaeron turns his attention solely to me.

"You really don't remember, do you?" He deflects an attack from Jexen without even looking. "I suppose that's a mercy."

"What are you talking about?"

He moves then, faster than I can track. One moment he's across the room, the next he's right in front of me, hand raised, power gathering at his fingertips.

"The prophecy," he says softly, almost gently, "came from your mother."

Time stops.

My mother. Bellamie's mother.

The statue in the garden. The woman with the kind face, the gentle smile. The one whose features looked so much like mine.

An ache spreads through my chest, sharp and sudden and devastating.

"No," I breathe.

"Yes." Valthaeron's hand is still raised, power crackling around his fingers. "She was a seer. She saw the future and what you would become. Saw that you could be the one to end my reign." His smile is terrible. "So I killed her for it. And then I killed you."

I knew he killed her. Heard every sickening detail from Cairos this morning, but the words on Valthaeron's lips send a white-hot, blinding rage flooding through me. "You bastard—"

He strikes.

The blast of dark power hits me square in the chest, and I go flying. I slam into a column hard enough that stars explode behind my eyes. Pain radiates through my entire body.

"Naevyn!" Cairos's roar is deafening.

Through blurred vision, I see him charge Valthaeron. They collide in a tangle of scales and magic, Cairos's magic deflecting off of the king's armor. Valthaeron laughs in response.

I force myself up, every muscle screaming in protest. I reach up and touch the pendant. It's still around my neck, still pulsing and ready as if it can sense the battle going on around us.

I just need to get close enough to use it.

But every time I try inhaling, breathing in to capture him, nothing happens. The shadowstone protecting him is impenetrable.

Around me, the throne room has become a war zone. Bodies of guards litter the marble floor. Fenric is fighting three at once, his movements precise and brutal. Jexen tears through guards in his dragon form, emerald scales splattered with blood.

A scream cuts through the chaos. I turn to see Hessa hit the ground hard, her left arm bent at an unnatural angle. She tries to get up, can't, and a guard moves in for the kill.

Selenia drops from above on red silk, wrapping it around the guard's neck and yanking him backward before he can strike. She's bleeding from a gash across her forehead, red streaming down into her eyes.

"Hessa, get out!" I shout, and she crawls toward the edge of the room, cradling her broken arm.

Jexen swoops overhead in dragon form, silver scales gleaming. He dives at the king, claws extended, going for his face.

Valthaeron doesn't even look, he just raises the pendant.

A spear of pure shadow materializes, shooting out from it.

It punches right through Jexen's chest.

The dragon's scream is almost human. He crashes to the floor twenty feet from me, the impact shaking the entire room. The transformation happens involuntarily—scales giving way to skin, dragon shrinking back to fae. He lies there gasping, blood pooling beneath him, the shadow spear still protruding from his chest.

"No!" Kyreth roars, abandoning his fight to reach his brother.

I watch in horror as Kyreth transforms mid-air, landing in fae form and sliding to his knees beside Jexen. He's trying to stop the bleeding, pressing his hands against the wound, but there's too much blood. Too much.

"Stay with me!" Kyreth yells. "Don't you fucking dare—"

Valthaeron laughs, and the sound makes my skin crawl.

"One down," he says casually, like he just swatted a fly. "How many more?"

Rage floods through me again, hot and overwhelming. But rage won't help. I need to think. I need—

My eyes catch on the aerial silk hanging loose from one of the high windows, and an idea hits me.

Valthaeron is focused on the twins now, watching Jexen cradling his dying brother with that same amused expression. His back is partially turned to me, with Cairos's huge form blocking his peripherals. The other troupe members are scattered, some fighting and some trying to come back from injuries.

I run for the silk.

My hands find the fabric, and I start climbing, using the technique I practiced so many times in the forest. Hand over hand, coiling the silk around my wrist as I go. My shoulders burn from earlier impacts, my ribs ache, but I push through it. Below me, I can hear Jexen screaming at Kyreth to stay awake, Fenric shouting orders, the clash of steel on the guard's shadowstone swords.

The higher I climb, the better angle I'll have.

Valthaeron raises his hand again, another shadow spear forming. He's aiming for Jexen this time. Going to kill both twins together.

"No, you don't," Selenia snarls.

She drops from another window, wrapped in red silk, spinning like a top. She unwraps mid-air, the fabric whipping out to catch Valthaeron's arms just as he's about to throw the spear. For half a second, he's restrained, distracted, the spear dissolving.

Perfect.

I'm high enough now. Maybe twenty feet up, directly above him. I wrap the silk around my waist twice, testing the hold. My hands are shaking as I pull the pendant from my neck.

Below me, Valthaeron is fighting Selenia and Cairos at once, his barrier weakening. They're trying to hold him, putting everything they have into it, but he's too strong, and he knows it. Lucky for us, what he *doesn't* know is that killing him isn't the point. Trapping him is.

I push off the wall and swing down in a wide arc, silk uncoiling as I drop. Gravity and momentum carry me straight toward him. He's breaking free, reaching for Selenia to snap her neck—

I slam into him from above.

My legs wrap around his shoulders, one hand fisting in his hair to keep balance. The pendant presses against the unprotected back of his neck, right where spine meets skull.

"Surprise," I gasp.

He roars, a sound that's not remotely human. The darkness around him flares, burning against my skin. He twists violently, trying to throw me off, his power pushing at me in waves that make my ears ring.

His hand reaches back, closes around my wrist—the one holding the pendant. His grip is like iron, crushing, and I feel my bones grinding together.

“Did you really think it would be that easy?” He yanks my arm forward, scratching into it with his nails hard enough to draw blood. The action nearly dislocates my shoulder. He turns to look at me. Up close, his eyes are completely black, no whites visible. Not human. Not even close. “I’ve been alive for millennia. I’ve survived wars, plagues, and rebellions. What makes you think one little girl with a magic necklace could stop me?”

A drop of blood from my arm plinks down onto his shadowstone armor, and some of the darkness around him peters out with a hiss.

Of course. My blood has always been the key. Shadowstone drinks it up, it's thirsty for it.

“Because I’m not just one little girl.” I tighten my legs around his shoulders, refusing to let go even as my wrist feels like it’s breaking. “I’m everyone you’ve ever hurt. I’m every soul you’ve stolen. I’m the daughter you murdered for telling the truth.”

His expression shifts. The memory sends him off-kilter for just long enough.

I twist my body weight backward and use the momentum, and slam my forehead into the back of his skull as hard as I can.

Pain explodes through my head. Stars burst behind my eyes for the second time. But his grip loosens, just like I need.

I wrench my hand free and slice my own arm with the jagged edges of my poorly-shaped pendant. Blood pours down onto his armor with a deafening hiss, and the shadowstone melts off of him.

“No. No!” Valthaeron thunders, but it's too late.

I press the pendant against his neck. My blood from earlier is still coating the stone, still active. The shadowstone pulses hot, hungry, and ready.

I remember what Cairos told me. Not a push outward. A pull inward. Create the void first. Make the stone want to consume.

I breathe in.

It's not air, it's something else. Something cold and dark and ancient. It feels like inhaling death itself, like breathing in centuries of stolen souls all at once. The feeling makes me want to heave, but I fight against it.

The pendant burns against my palms, searing my skin, but instead of letting go, I squeeze harder.

The shadowstone opens, a void appearing in the center of the pendant. It's hungry. Starving, even.

Valthaeron realizes what's happening. He yells, thrashing, power exploding outward in waves that throw everyone in the room backward. But I'm locked onto him, legs and arms wrapped tight, pendant pressed to his skin.

I keep breathing in. Deeper. Pulling harder.

The darkness around him flickers out completely, and his struggles become weaker.

"No," he gasps, his voice raspy. "No, you can't—this isn't —"

I breathe in deeper. The void in the pendant grows, pulling, consuming. His soul is fighting it, trying to resist, but the shadowstone is stronger. The hunger is stronger.

Valthaeron's scream becomes something inhuman, agonized. The wispy light is being sucked into the pendant now, streaming from his eyes, his mouth, his chest. Centuries of stolen souls, all that accumulated power, all being drawn into the shadowstone.

My vision is starting to blur. Black spots dance at the edges. A chill permeates my bones as every ounce of energy is being used to restrain his soul. The cold is overwhelming, freezing me from the inside out. But I still don't stop. Can't stop.

One more breath. One more pull.

The last of him streams into the pendant, and Valthaeron goes limp beneath me.

I fall.

Cairos catches me, his arms strong and steady. The pendant slips from my burned hands, dangling from its chain around my neck. It's glowing now, pulsing angrily with Valthaeron's soul.

"You did it," Cairos is saying, but his voice sounds distant, like he's speaking to me underwater. "Naevyn, you did it."

Around us, the throne room is silent except for harsh breathing and quiet moans from the injured. Valthaeron's body lies crumpled on the floor, empty. Just a husk now.

Then I hear a wet, rattling breath from across the room.

Jexen.

I stumble out of Cairos's arms and run clumsily to where the twins are. Jexen is still there holding his brother, covered in blood. Jexen's eyes are open but unfocused, the shadow spear still protruding from his chest.

"Did she…" Jexen's voice is barely a whisper, and a wet gurgling sound accompanies his voice. "Did she get him?"

"She got him, it's over. The curse is breaking—can't you feel it?"

And I *can* feel it. Something in the air is changing, unraveling, like invisible threads being cut one by one.

Jexen's eyes find mine. He tries to smile. "Good. That's… that's good."

"You're going to be okay," I say, even though we both know it's a lie. "The curse is broken. You're free now."

"Free," he repeats, like he's testing the word. His hand reaches out, shaking, and I take it. His skin is cold. "Naevyn."

It's the first time he's said my name. First time he's ever acknowledged that I have a name.

"I'm here," I say.

"Thank you." His eyes are starting to glaze. "For ending it. For giving us… freedom…"

His hand goes slack in mine.

Kyreth makes a sound that's part sob, part roar. He pulls his brother close, rocking, and the rest of us just stand there, watching a man mourn his twin.

The curse might be broken. Valthaeron might be trapped.

But the cost was still too fucking high.

34

SURVIVORS

Three days after the battle, we burn Jexen's body on a pyre with the Aelthren faction. They insisted on handling the cremation because fire is sacred to them, and they wanted to honor one of the warriors who helped free the realm. They built a pyre out of a material they called cinderstone, harvested from the region where they settle. They stacked wood in precise patterns that supposedly help the soul find its way to whatever comes next. I don't know if I believe that, but watching the flames rise into the evening sky, I hope they're right.

Kyreth stands closest to the fire, face blank, and eyes dry. He hasn't cried since Jexen died in the throne room. He hasn't spoken much either. Just helped build the pyre mechanically, like if he focused on the task, then he wouldn't have to feel anything.

The rest of us stand in a semicircle around the flames. Hessa's arm is in a sling, the bone set but still healing. Selenia has a bandage wrapped around her head, covering the gash that took twelve stitches. Fenric's knuckles are split and swollen. Hessa has done her best to heal us, but her magic is weak. We all look like hell, but we're alive.

Jexen isn't.

"He would've hated this," Kyreth says suddenly, kicking one of the stones that's rolled out from the fire. "All the ceremony. The solemnity. He would've wanted us drunk and telling stories about him."

"There are quite a few of those," Fenric says quietly. There's a quiet pause before he speaks again. "Remember when he tried to juggle fire in that tavern in the Emberwilde territories? Nearly burned the whole place down."

A smattering of chuckles rises from the fae around the fire. One of the Aelthren walks to a nearby house and emerges with two bottles of amber-colored liquid. Spirits. He takes a swig and passes the bottles around.

"Or when he convinced that Stoneborn merchant he could turn gold into shadowstone," Selenia says, then takes a swig. "Poor bastard paid him actual gold to demonstrate."

Selenia passes the bottle to me next. I take a long, hot drink, savoring its burn on the way down. Rum. Gods, I haven't had rum since we were back in Xardon, before all of this.

"He didn't give a fuck about me. Not much of a story, but it's all I have to tell," I say.

Kyreth does laugh now. Really laughs until tears are streaming down his face, and I can't tell if they're from humor or sadness.

"He was terrible," Kyreth says through sobs. "The absolute worst."

We stand there as the fire burns, sharing stories, drinking, and laughing through tears. It's not the solemn funeral I expected. It's messy and painful, but somehow exactly right.

When the flames finally die down to embers, Kyreth steps forward and places something on the ashes—a silver scale, preserved somehow from one of Jexen's transformations.

"Eight hundred years," he says to the remains. "Eight hundred years you were stuck with me. Now you're finally free, you stubborn ass. Don't fuck it up in whatever comes next."

Then he turns and walks away, shoulders heaving almost imperceptibly.

Cairos's arm wraps around my shoulder and squeezes. We've barely had a moment alone since the battle—there's been too much going on for that.

"Come on," he says quietly. "Let's get out of here."

We end up in a small structure near a lake, one that the Aelthren said we could stay in until everything dies down. Going back to the glass village wasn't safe, not with the giant target painted on our backs by the Solmeren. We couldn't stay at the castle for the same reason. Picking up Quinnic and Alabris and going into hiding under the protection of an alliant faction seemed like the only way.

The space is lit only by a single torch on the wall. It's a simple house, with just a bed and a hearth, but somehow that makes it feel even more like home to me. It's peaceful.

I sink onto the floor, back against the wall, exhausted in ways that go deeper than physical tiredness. My whole body aches. My ribs are bruised from slamming into that column, my muscles are scorched by Valthaeron's power, and I have a headache that won't quit from headbutting him. Everything hurts.

Cairos sits down beside me, our shoulders touching. For a long moment, neither of us speaks. We just sit in the quiet, breathing and relishing in being alive.

"How's the arm?" he asks finally, nodding at the bandage wrapped around my forearm.

"It hurts, but I'll live." I flex my fingers, testing the movement. The wounds are healing, leaving marks that'll probably scar. "How are you?"

It's a loaded question. How's he handling Jexen's death? The curse still being active? The fact that we trapped an immortal king but didn't actually solve anything permanently?

And on top of all of that, Orlia's soul may still be stuck in that statue Cairos snatched on the way out of the castle.

"Tired," he says. "Angry. Relieved. All of it at once."

I look at him more closely. He looks different, somehow. Less hollow. More present.

"Your wrist," I say, noticing. "One of the bands is gone."

He lifts his arm, studying the two tattooed bands that circle his wrist.

"What happened to it?" I ask.

He's quiet for a moment as I reach out, fingers tracing the remaining bands. "They appeared the night I was cursed. Just manifested on my wrist. I never understood what they meant, but I figured it was part of the curse, some visible reminder of what Valthaeron did to us."

"But one disappeared now."

"When we fought back," he corrects, and there's something sharp in his voice. Something that wasn't there before. "When I chose to use my power against him instead of for him."

I shift to face him fully. "What do you think they mean? The bands?"

"I've had hundreds of years to think about it." He touches the first band. "I think this one is me. My actual self. The core of who I am beneath everything else."

"And the second?"

"The dragon, or the curse, maybe." He flexes his hand. "It's still there because Valthaeron isn't dead, just trapped. So I'm still cursed, still able to shift. This band represents that part of me. It's forced on me, but mine now nonetheless."

"And the third band that's gone?"

His expression shifts, something like wonder crossing his face. "The shade stalker. The piece of me that died with Bellamie. It was my grief and rage made manifest, walking around separately for six hundred years." He's quiet for a moment. "As we were leaving the castle after the battle, I saw it. He was watching from the shadows like he always does. But this time he didn't stay separate. He walked toward me and just… rejoined. Dissolved into shadow and flowed back into me like it had never left. And when it did, the band disappeared."

My chest tightens. "Because you're whole again."

"Because you came back. You're her, but you're also you. And having you here, alive and safe, healed something I didn't think could be healed. That broken piece rejoined the rest of me." He looks at the two remaining bands. "I'm still cursed. I'm still a dragon. But the part of me that split off in grief is home now. I'm complete."

"How does it feel?"

"Overwhelming." He laughs, but there's no humor in it. "I can feel everything now. Real anger at Valthaeron, at what was done to all of us. Fear that I'll lose you again. Joy that you're here at all." He looks at me, and there's something raw in his eyes. "For so long, the curse kept my feelings dulled. Now it's all so intense I feel like I could drown."

"That sounds… overwhelming."

"It is," Cairos says, looking at me and brushing a stray hair behind my ear. "But it's also good to feel again, even if it hurts."

I take his hand, the one with the two remaining bands. "You're not alone in this. We'll figure it out together."

"I know." His voice drops lower. "That's the other thing that's different. Before, I felt care for you. Love, even. But it was different. Dulled, even though I didn't realize it at the time. Now it's vibrant and real. Now, when I look at you, I feel so much it's almost painful."

My throat tightens. "Cairos…"

"I'm not good at this," he says bluntly. "But I need you to know I can feel now. Really feel. And what I feel is that I love you."

I kiss him before the weight of everything else can intrude. His arms wrap around me, pulling me close, and for a moment, there's nothing but this. When we break apart, I rest my forehead against his.

"I love you too," I say. "Both versions of me love you."

He pulls me closer, and we sit like that for a while. Just breathing. Just being. But eventually, reality creeps back in.

"We need to talk about what comes next," I say reluctantly.

"I know."

I pull the necklace out from under my shirt, looking at the pendant. It's warm against my palm, pulsing faintly with trapped light. Sometimes I swear I can feel Valthaeron in there, pressing against the shadowstone, testing for weaknesses.

"The Stoneborn examined this yesterday," Cairos says, watching the pendant pulse. "They estimate we have months, a year at most, before he breaks free."

"So we need a permanent solution."

"We need allies first." His voice goes back to that commander's tone. "The Solmeren are fortifying, preparing for war. They outnumber us significantly. We need the other factions unified and willing to fight."

"They're afraid to go against Valthaeron," I say.

"Some of them. Others see this as their chance to finally change up the status quo." He touches my face gently. "Harmond's working on sending messages. He's given word that the Tidetreaders will back us. The Aelthren respect what you did. The others will follow and we'll win out over Valthaeron."

"How do you sound so sure?" I ask, watching the way his hair falls down over his eyes when he looks down at his palms as if searching for answers.

"We actually… we have a plan. We've spoken with the Aelthren, and they have an elder who remembers before Valthaeron's reign. When the dragons kept the peace."

Sitting up straighter, I ask, "Dragons? Like, real dragons?"

"As real as the air I breathe. Another fae faction that held the role of peacekeepers."

“I thought you said dragons were just a tale?”

“Not according to the elder.”

I blink. “So… if they aren't here anymore, what happened to them?”

“Valthaeron claimed he killed them all when he took power. Wiped them out so nothing could threaten his rule.” His expression is conflicted. “But the Aelthren suggest maybe he didn’t. Maybe some survived and went into hiding.”

I see where this is going. “You want to find them.”

“I think we need to. If they’re real, and if they’re as powerful as the legends say, they could help us against Valthaeron when he breaks free, against the Solmeren, and against anyone else who might try to seize power. The realm needs something strong enough to maintain peace but wise enough not to abuse that power.”

“That’s a big if. They might all be dead.”

“It’s worth investigating.” He touches the two bands on his wrist. “And I think finding them might help me understand this.”

I tuck the necklace back under my shirt. “So the plan is: unite the factions, prepare for war with the Solmeren, find ancient dragons who may or may not exist, and permanently destroy an immortal king’s soul before he breaks free?”

“When you put it that way, it almost sounds impossible.”

“It *is* impossible.”

“Good thing we’ve already done several impossible things this week,” Cairos says, attempting to reassure me.

I lean back against the wall, closing my eyes. My shoulders are so tense they’re practically up by my ears, and the headache is getting worse. I’m exhausted, and we just traded one terrible situation for five more.

“You know,” Cairos says, voice dropping lower, “I have a tool that’s excellent for stress relief.”

I open one eye to look at him. He's watching me with an expression that's all suggestion and dark promise, one hand gesturing toward said tool.

Despite everything, I almost laugh. "I'm glad you're feeling like yourself again."

"What? I'm offering assistance." But there's a hint of a smile on his face, the first real one I've seen since the battle.

"You're being inappropriate."

"Helpful." He pulls me against his side, arm around my shoulders. "But I can wait until you're not half-dead from exhaustion."

"You're so generous."

"I've been told."

This time, I do laugh, and some of the tension bleeds out. We sit there in comfortable silence for a while, and despite all the impossible problems ahead, I feel something like peace.

That evening, Cairos and I stand in the courtyard watching stars appear. The necklace pulses warm against my chest—a reminder that our victory is temporary.

"You think we can actually do this?" I ask. "Build something better?"

"I think we have to try." He wraps his arms around me from behind. "The alternative is going back to how things were."

"It's going to be hard. The Solmeren won't give up. Valthaeron will break free. The factions barely trust each other, and we don't even know if these dragons exist."

"All true." He presses a kiss to my temple. "But weeks ago, you were carrying buckets in a mine. Now you're helping reshape a realm. Things change."

I turn in his arms to face him. "Promise me something."

"Anything."

"Promise me that *we* won't change."

"Promise," he agrees, nudging my head up to face him. Then he presses his lips to mine, and for a moment, everything ahead disappears. There's only this, only us. Alive, free, and facing an uncertain future together.

Tonight, we rest.

Tomorrow, we fight again.

If you enjoyed this book, it would mean the world to me if you would leave a review on the site where you purchased, and also, share with your friends!

Review Links

Amazon: https://www.amazon.com/stores/Eliza-Benner/author/B0DRNP4931?ref=ap_rdr&shoppingPortalEnabled=true&ccs_id=df3cc8db-e51e-4205-9391-62055b1a7a60

Goodreads: https://www.goodreads.com/author/show/53882033.Eliza_Benner

I love to engage with my readers, so please drop by and say hello!

I can be found on Facebook as “Eliza Benner – Author”, Instagram as “elizabennerwrites”, or TikTok as “Eliza Benner Author”!

SIGN UP FOR MY NEWSLETTER HERE TO GET UPDATES ON THIS SERIES AND MY OTHERS: https://www.elizabenner.com/

•❋————✧❋✦❋✧————❋•

BOOKS BY ELIZA BENNER

CIRCUS OF SOULS SERIES:
BOOK ONE: VITALIA
BOOK TWO: Coming soon!

WINGS OF SHADE AND STARLIGHT SERIES:
BOOK ONE: THE STRATOS
BOOK TWO: THE OUTLANDS
BOOK THREE: THE DRACONIS
BOOK FOUR Coming Soon!

ABOUT THE AUTHOR

Eliza Benner is a romantic fantasy author who finds inspiration in both quiet moments and grand adventures. When she isn't engrossed in writing her next novel, she can be found planning impromptu trips, devouring books, or spending time with her husband and five children on their hobby farm in Minnesota.

Made in the USA
Coppell, TX
25 February 2026

72772532R00226